THE FROZEN STEPPE

CHRONICLES OF THE SECOND SUN: BOOK TWO

JAY OLSEN-THRIFT

BALACH YOR
KHERIZHAN
THE IMALAR WOODS
MOONVSWYN
NA ROC OF NORTH
PROMITES
ELIMERE
ELIMAINE
EILHAISON
N
DAARIA

CONTENTS

1. Prologue ... 1

2. Chapter I: Seth ... 9

3. Chapter II: Munne ... 16

4. Chapter III: Ray ... 40

5. Chapter IV: Ray ... 55

6. Chapter V: Munne ... 62

7. Chapter VI: Seth ... 76

8. Chapter VII: Munne ... 89

9. Chapter VIII: Ray ... 98

10. Chapter IX: Seth ... 111

11. Chapter X: Munne ... 128

12. Chapter XI: Seth ... 141

13. Chapter XII: Ray ... 157

14. Chapter XIII: Seth ... 171

15. Chapter XIV: Munne ... 188

16. Chapter XV: Ray ... 199

17. Chapter XVI: Munne ... 215

18. Chapter XVII: Seth ... 229

19. Chapter XVIII: Ray	244
20. Chapter XIX: Munne	260
21. Chapter XX: Seth	272
22. Chapter XXI: Ray	285
23. Chapter XXII: Seth	304
24. Chapter XXIII: Munne	318
25. Chapter XXIV: Seth	328
26. Chapter XXV: Ray	339
27. Chapter XXVI: Munne	355
28. Chapter XXVII: Seth	362
29. Chapter XXVIII: Munne	374
30. Chapter XXIX: Ray	392
31. Chapter XXX: Seth	407
32. Chapter XXXI: Munne	416
33. Epilogue	429
34. List of Characters	433
35. Appendix	437
36. Acknowledgements	443
37. About the Author	444

PROLOGUE

The Wall: Day 24, Month 11, Year 13,239

Standing on top of the Wall, Na'roc of North stretched as far as the eye could see. It was always winter in those desolate lands. Snow fell every day, some days worse than others. Two months ago, snowstorms drifted towards the Wall, plunging the lands south of the border into an early winter. Looking northward there was nothing except the snow. East and west were not much of a sight either. The Wall was built between two mountain peaks referred to as the Twins, a perfect fortification in a natural pass leading south to the lands of Promthus. At least the lands south of the Wall had more color. Trees and mountains covered the landscape, indicating the border between Promthus and the Imalar Woods. Not too far to the south was a windmill and small farm that provided provisions to the men stationed at the Wall.

Addam had been stationed at the Wall for almost three years. Being that far north was miserable, but it beat being anywhere south of the Hourglass Lakes. He had cousins and a brother who were on the front lines near Merrioff and the border with Moonyswyn. The last he'd heard from his family, the fighting was fierce. That letter had arrived over three months ago, though, so he didn't know if his cousins and brother were still alive. Letters only arrived at the Wall during the warmer months unless it was an urgent message from the king. The best he could hope for was an early thaw and a speedy courier.

"About time to head downstairs," Addam's fellow soldier, Stuart, said hopefully, raising his voice over the wind. "My fingers and toes are about damn frozen. Will do me good to get a bowl of soup."

Addam grunted and nodded in agreement. The two had been standing atop the Wall for nearly four hours, the standard shift during winter. They were in the sixth guard tower, closer to the eastern Twin. Torches and a small pit fire burned around them, but the wind seeped through their armor and clothing regardless.

Stuart had been at the Wall a couple of years longer than Addam and was one of his closest mates. The two had bonded over their status as third sons, both being sent north to preserve their bloodlines. They had trained with Prince Robyn before his disappearance. Both were due trips south in the next few months to visit family and warm their bones. Stuart had a wife in Trent. Last he heard from her she was with child. By the time he left the Wall, he would get to meet his son or daughter. Addam's family was on the other side of the lakes in Ferilin. He had no woman waiting for him at home, which suited him just fine. He was of the mind to let his older brothers get married and have children, leaving him to forge his own path. Although so far that path had led him north, to a place where he could never quite shake the chill from his bones or feel the whole of his fingertips.

It'll be good to get down for a few hours, Addam thought as they made their way to the stairs leading to the outpost below. As they descended, their two replacements were climbing up the stairs. They nodded to each other in passing, nothing to report or announce.

Below the Wall were a few small outposts, each providing lodging, meals, and an armory for the guard towers above. Addam and Stuart's outpost covered the sixth, seventh, and eighth guard towers on the Wall. The journey to the outpost took roughly twenty minutes, but it got their blood flowing. By the time they entered the mead hall they were ready to shed their cloaks and outer coats. The scent of meat and stew filled the air. Addam was practically salivating. Provisions were not as ample in the colder months, so their daily meals were cut from three to two and they only ate meat twice per week. Tonight was one of those lucky nights.

A great fire pit filled the center of the mead hall, tended to by the apprentices of the outpost. Tables lined both sides of the fire pit, several men already feasting upon their suppers. Opposite the entrance was some semblance of a kitchen. The stew cauldron was positioned over the edge of the fire pit. There was a small alcove of hutches, countertops, and a large stone oven behind it. Addam and Stuart made their way to the cauldron, greeting some of the men at the tables.

"Regis! Been some time. Good to see you!" Addam called out to a grisly older man hunched over his bowl of stew. The man nodded and waved his spoon in acknowledgement.

Another man, Lesnet, cackled. "Addam 'n Stuart must've run down those stairs. Barth just left."

"Didn't want to miss out on supper!" Stuart laughed.

One of the apprentices was ladling stew into two bowls for the men. Stuart mumbled his thanks and left to join the other men in one of the empty seats.

Addam hovered by the apprentice for a moment, eating a spoonful of stew. "Mark, is it?"

The apprentice looked up from the cauldron and nodded. "Yes, sir."

"You serve the Seventh, right?"

"Yes, sir."

"Good men over there," Addam grunted. He shoveled another spoonful of broth into his mouth, enjoying the tender carrots. "How long you been up here?"

Mark stirred the stew idly. "Nearly six months, sir."

"And did the boys at the Seventh train you to call everyone 'sir'?" Addam grinned, nudging the boy with his elbow. He couldn't have been any older than seventeen, eighteen at the most. Mark had a long mess of brown hair on his head, and he stood taller than Addam. He was dressed in thick woolen clothes, but it was obvious the boy lacked muscle.

Mark's cheeks flushed. "No, my mam made the impression. She always told me to be respectful."

"Good lesson." Addam nodded. "Which city you from?"

"Ferilin."

"A fellow mate! Ferilin's my home as well. Blue Breeze Farm is my family's." Addam's father and uncle ran the farm together, growing greens and sheep for Ferilin.

"Mam always enjoyed getting wool from your family," Mark said. "When we could afford it."

Addam understood. Several families sent their boys and men to the Wall to earn coin, though the more lucrative offer was to join the war down south. "Do you have any others?" he asked.

"Nah, just three sisters."

Addam nodded. The boy was here for a modest but steady supply of coin, and his family wanted him to return with all his limbs still attached.

From behind Addam came grumbles and a couple of men clearing their throats. Mark realized there was a line and began serving more bowls of stew.

Addam took his leave, calling over his shoulder, "We should catch up some time!"

"Yeah," Mark agreed.

Addam took a seat near Stuart and a handful of other men, setting down the bowl of stew before removing his snow-dusted cloak and draping it across the back of his chair, flakes falling to the floor.

A man named Rhonold pointed at the cloak with his spoon. "Nasty out there, eh?"

Addam nodded, and Stuart let out an agreeing guffaw.

"Gonna be hard getting up for the dawn shift," Stuart mumbled, shoveling food into his mouth.

Rhonold and Lesnet laughed. They washed their stew down with mugs of ale. Addam and Stuart hadn't gotten their drinks yet—both men had wanted to fill their bellies first.

"Watch beats training," Rhonold retorted. "I'll be gettin' up to whip the new bloods into shape."

"It'll get the blood flowing at least," Addam said.

Rhonold conceded with a scowl, draining his mug. He stood and stalked off to fill it again.

"What would you lads do to kill time 'til your shift?" Lesnet asked, scooting over to take Rhonold's spot. "Four hours to kill."

"Sleep, shit, or maybe visit the armory," Stuart rattled off. "They always got blades needin' sharpening."

Lesnet grimaced. "Where's that bloke with the cards? Maybe he'll come by for supper soon."

"Hestin, I think's his name," Addam answered.

"Good lad," Stuart grunted.

Each of the three men ate, drank, and sat in silence for a few moments. Rhonold returned with three mugs, nudging Lesnet with his knee. Lesnet grumbled but made no other protest and slid back to his original seat to allow Rhonold to sit down. The man set one mug in front of himself, giving the other two to Addam and Stuart. The other two men raised a toast to Rhonold, all four clinking mugs before drinking deep.

"Thanks, mate," Addam said, forcing down a swig of the ale.

The four men continued idle chatter for almost an hour, long after their bowls were empty. Rhonold and Stuart took turns getting up to fetch more ale, but Addam only nursed the one drink. He wasn't too fond of the taste anymore, after he had nearly drowned himself in it in the months after Prince Robyn's disappearance two years ago. However, there was little else to drink around the outpost, and it warmed his belly and cheeks. He was sure other men at the outpost drank for the same reason, although they never talked about it. Nothing much to talk about a man who goes missing in Na'roc of North, even if it's the crown prince.

Lesnet rose and was about to say something else when the doors to the mead hall were thrown open, the cold air sobering the men inside. A royal herald entered, panting heavily. He wore a hauberk bearing the royal sigil—a crown sitting atop an hourglass-shaped lake—along with a light cloak, hood drawn. As he entered, he yanked the hood off, revealing a young, tired face. He must have been in his early twenties at the latest.

The sight of the herald sent a chill down Addam's spine, the warmth from the ale vanishing. A couple of the men nearest the entrance leapt to their feet and rushed to assist the messenger, calling to others for food and drink. They helped the man to a seat near the fire pit. Addam, Stuart, and the others all stood and moved closer.

"What's a herald doing here in winter?" Stuart whispered. Someone from the crowd hushed him.

"Where's Captain Bronhyld?" the herald called out.

More murmurs spread throughout the room. One of the men handed the herald a mug of water, and he drained it while waiting for an answer. Addam listened to the chatter around him.

"Where's the captain?"

"Took to bed early, didn't he?"

"Isn't Bronhyld on watch tonight?"

"Boy! Go to the captain's cabin!" one voice roared over the others. Addam saw Mark set his ladle down and hurry off into the night, not even grabbing a cloak to cover himself.

The herald was given a bowl of stew by Regis. The herald thanked him profusely and devoured it. In between bites the two talked, although Addam couldn't hear their words over the din. He tried shuffling his way closer to the herald, but the crowd was thick. All the men were trying to get closer to hear the messenger's words.

After several moments, Captain Bronhyld arrived with Mark trailing behind him. Bronhyld was a tall man with a head of black hair and a full beard. Streaks of white and wrinkles around his eyes revealed his older age. He had served at the Wall for nearly twenty years, hailing from a noble house back in Auora. The captain was wrapped in a thick cloak lined with fur, covering his evening clothes underneath. It was obvious that the apprentice had disturbed the man while he was in bed. No signs of sleep could be found on his face, though. He was wide awake and alert.

"What news?" Bronhyld asked. At the sound of his voice, all the men in the mead hall hushed, their attentions shifting to their captain.

The messenger hastily set his spoon down and rose to his feet, bowing. "Captain Bronhyld, sir."

"What news from Auora?" the captain asked again, standing in front of the herald.

"Sir." The herald plucked a scroll from a bag on his hip, passing it to the older man. "Urgent news from the king. I fear I may already be too late in its delivery."

Bronhyld frowned and broke the seal on the scroll, unraveling it to read its message. Addam struggled to read the expression on the captain's face. It wasn't until he raised his eyes from the parchment that Addam and every other man in the mead hall realized how dire the news was.

"Watches will be doubled immediately. The scouting towers must be manned again," Captain Bronhyld told his men. He shifted his attention back to the herald. "How many days ago was this letter penned? How long have you ridden?"

"Five days. Messengers were sent to all cities and villages."

"Have you delivered this news to any of the other captains here?"

"No, sir. Your post was closest on my journey."

"You've done an honorable service. Rest here tonight and travel back to Auora in the morning," Bronhyld said softly to the herald. He looked back at the gathered assembly, searching for someone. "Nowan, you're to take this message to the other outposts and share the news with Captains Mirrin and Weiss. Tell them the scouting towers must be manned. Report their responses to me. Go, swiftly."

The summoned man, Nowan, appeared before the captain and was handed the scroll. He left the mead hall with haste.

"Captain, what's happened?" one of the other men dared ask.

"Princess Niamnh has been kidnapped," Captain Bronhyld said, his voice grim.

A heavy silence fell over the room. None spoke, but Addam, and surely the other men, wanted answers. *Who would kidnap the princess? Are the Provira behind this? Has the war reached the island of Auora?*

"We're to watch for anyone traveling with a young woman with dark skin and pale hair. Double the watches. Regis, coordinate with the seventh and eighth to man the Eastern Twin. I want that beacon lit by sunrise." Captain Bronhyld issued the orders with a calm, resolute voice.

Addam latched onto that calmness, trying to steady himself amidst his thoughts, as the others no doubt were doing as well. Though this situation was different, memories of a similar winter evening resurfaced in his mind. Two years ago, Bronhyld had been the one to declare Prince Robyn lost, along with the other four men who had traveled with him beyond the Wall.

The princess has been kidnapped.

Addam's chest tightened and he raised a hand to clutch at his hauberk. Murmurs broke out among the men. Beside him, Addam heard Stuart and Lesnet talking in hushed tones. Several men left the mead hall, some to spread word to those on the wall, others to dress themselves and man the wall themselves.

"Sir, how likely is it that she'd end up here?" one man asked. "Not questioning your orders, sir, just trying to make sense of it."

Others seemed to agree, although not eagerly. All were thinking of blaming the Provira for this offense.

"Aye, I know you're all thinking. South would make sense," Bronhyld said to the crowd. "But we're loyal men to Promthus and to King Nelle. If there's a chance his daughter is being taken north, we'll find her."

The crowd rumbled in agreement. They cared for their king and for their prince who had disappeared nearly two years ago beyond the Wall. The bitterness and sorrow were still fresh for some of the men garrisoned at the Wall, Addam included. Though their time together was short, Prince Robyn had been a stalwart companion to Addam during their training. The prince chose to go north on a hunting expedition. Addam had asked to join, of course, but Captain Mirrin wouldn't allow it since he was still in training. A week after the prince left, Addam was sent to the seventh outpost to complete his training under Captain Bronhyld. Word of Prince Robyn's disappearance was not sent to the east and west outposts until two months later. Addam had convinced himself that if Mirrin had let him go with the prince, that he would have brought him back safely. It was a foolish notion, but he had missed his friend dearly. He still did.

"He seeks to atone for Prince Robyn," Addam heard Stuart whisper. Addam and Lesnet turned their attention to him, and they both nodded solemnly. "Justice for the princess, if no justice for the prince."

The crowd thinned out as more men left to bolster their ranks. Addam finished the remainder of his ale then gathered up his cloak.

Stuart is right, Addam thought as he left the mead hall. *Justice for the princess, if no justice for you, my prince.* He returned to the Wall and began to climb.

CHAPTER 1: SETH

Stone had never felt colder nor more comforting to Seth. It drained the warmth, the life, from his skin, and he welcomed it. Laying in his room, he burrowed deep into the nest of blankets until he felt the chilled stone slab underneath him. When he forced himself out of that nest to relieve himself, he found himself craving the cold, eager to touch it once more. Anything to get rid of the grief that raged within his heart, burning so hot that he lost all other feelings.

The suns rose and fell outside, their light occasionally pouring into his room on bright days. If he listened close enough, he could hear the kytling on those days. Where he once found hope in the little bird's song, it now felt like he was being taunted by the outside world. More often the days were wet and dark with storms. The thunder kept him company, its constant rumbling soothing him back into a slumber. It was preferable to the silence of his room, which had the tendency to make his mind race and search for something to cling to. In those blurred days, the only thoughts his mind turned to was his mother's death scream and his father's face covered in her blood.

Seth had lost count of the days he spent locked away in his chambers since his mother's murder. His mind played cruel tricks making him watch the light fade from his mother's gray eyes over and over. His father's eyes, black as his heart. Over and over.

The stewards tried getting him to eat, but he would barely touch the platters they brought him. Nothing piqued his interest, nothing looked appealing. He would drink water, and on occasion some passionflower tea. Eventually the platters became more extravagant as they tried persuading him to eat. Charred boar, sweet pastries, and baked vegetables. Dishes that were often only served for elaborate celebrations, or when they had a particularly bountiful harvest season, which hadn't occurred in several years. Seth knew his father and the Asaszi were digging deep into their reserves, spending precious coin on trying to get him to eat. While all the dishes smelled enticing, he did little more than take small nibbles from them before turning his back and facing the window instead.

Let them waste it all on me. Let us starve together. Better to die now than by Father's hand later.

When the stewards brought his meals, if they were an Asaszi, they would talk to him about the goings-on within the pyramid.

"The recent work of Lord Kharisss isss *mossst* impressssive," the Asaszi hissed in delight. "After he rid himssself of that dissstraction, it wasss like the cloudsss had parted. Hisss most recent experiment wasss a resssounding sssuccesss."

They only saw Mother as a distraction, Seth thought bitterly. *Not for the person she is. Was.*

A large knot filled his throat. Even if he wanted to yell at the Asaszi, he couldn't. He sat through their incessant rambling about his father and tried to distract himself with sounds from the rainforest outside his window to little avail.

Seth noticed one particular steward had begun sitting with him after delivering his meals. At least, he thought it was the same steward. It certainly was not an Asaszi steward. This one covered their face and hands, so it had to be one of the Provira. One of the fools who had devoted themselves to Amias's cause. They were all so eager to fall on their swords for the pointless war with the Elviri and Proma, his sister included. The thought made Seth's skin crawl, and he avoided looking at the steward whenever they were in the room. He didn't want to be reminded of his sister's folly, nor all the lives being needlessly thrown away because of his father's desire for...

For what? Have the Provira always been so stupid and foolish that the Elviri and Proma chose to throw us out with their chamber pots? What reason did the other races have for discarding us like that?

Seth imagined his father and the other elder Provira must have said or done something so terribly offensive that exile was the only option. Perhaps his father had looked one of the chieftains of Lithalyon in the eye, or perhaps the *Se'vi* himself, and viciously mocked or ridiculed them. But even if he'd done that, why would they have punished the entirety of the Provira race? Lisanthir never mentioned the Provira, despite—

Seth's heart seized painfully in his chest, so much that he immediately shut down all of his thoughts and rolled onto his side, curling in on himself and clutching at his skin to try to relieve the pain. His thoughts instead turned to the books he had found in the Great Library of Lithalyon.

What did Father do with them? He probably destroyed them. Or maybe he found Grandmother's writing about him and the Tserys, *and that's why he killed Mother.*

If Amias could, he would destroy everything in Lithalyon. Seth remembered his father discussing some plans with Osza and Astohi the night before his mother's murder, something about meeting an Elviri envoy near the border. The Asaszi king had also mentioned mustering their forces to greet the Elviri.

Are they planning to invade Lithalyon? While I've been locked away in my room, like some useless— He silenced his thoughts. His chest ached, and his stomach twisted into several knots. He felt like he was going to be ill. Underneath his self-deprecating thoughts was another more ominous one. *Did Octavia go with Astohi to Lithalyon?*

Twice per day the veiled steward brought him his meals. At first the steward would place his platter of food on the nightstand and then stand by the door, waiting. They never spoke, which was customary for a Provira steward. The Asaszi stewards almost always had words for him, always about Amias, which he didn't want to hear. But the Provira stewards were sworn to silence, at least when in the presence of Seth and his family.

The first few times the steward lingered by the door, Seth forced himself to take a couple of bites of his meal. It seemed to please the steward, who would then exit the room but leave the platter behind. Seth would then roll back over in bed and not touch the food again. The steward must have picked up on that because they began staying longer, moving closer to the bed, and waiting until Seth ate more than just one bite or two.

But he wouldn't give them the satisfaction.

Amias must still want me for some purpose, he thought bitterly. *Why else would the Provira loom over me with their silent judgment?*

When Seth was a child, Amias encouraged him to sit in on all of his experiments and learn what he could, and like a fool blinded by love, he always did. He thought that if Amias saw him there, he would love him a little more and be proud of his son. Even if the experiments frightened him and gave him all kinds of night terrors. Even if the sight of charred spellsingers and maimed soldiers lingered behind his eyelids when he tried to hide from it all. After his legs were paralyzed in the cloud, Amias still encouraged him to come, but it was all wrong. His tone no longer felt encouraging and loving, it became hard and cold. A silent threat: *participate or suffer.* And so, Seth continued to go, continued to suffer anyway, because his personal suffering was still less than any suffering Amias could dole out himself.

But with how quickly he killed Mother, what use can I be? I'm just a stain on his name, a disgraceful result of one of his experiments. If any of us can still serve a purpose, it's Octavia, his perfect little pyredan *daughter who would gladly mutilate and kill herself for—*

His stomach lurched so violently that he had barely any time to throw himself to the edge of his bed before he vomited up what little contents swirled inside his stomach. The steward was by his side in an instant, pulling a handkerchief from their robes to wipe at his mouth and clean up the puddle of filth. Seth's throat burned and he desperately needed water, but he didn't want the steward to help him. He pushed at their hands until they withdrew from his bedside, returning to their post at the door.

When it was apparent they wouldn't be leaving until Seth did *something*, he reached for the cup of water on his nightstand and took a few gulps of the cool liquid. Swallowing, he felt and tasted the remnants of his vomit and grimaced, disgusted with himself.

The steward eventually left the room, leaving the tray of dinner untouched on the nightstand.

On another day, while ignoring the steward and the steaming plate of vegetables and grains on the nightstand, Seth caught a whiff of his body odor and wrinkled his nose. He hadn't bathed since before his mother's death. He knew that he should take care of his body, but he had no desire to do so. The stewards hadn't forced him into his wheelchair and dragged him off to be made clean, or get a change of scenery, so he was content to stay in the nest he had made with his blankets and silks, or perch in his wheelchair by the window. There was no one outside of his chamber that he cared to see.

Except Octavia and Lisanthir. His stomach threatened to spill its contents again, but he swallowed it back down with a wince.

Moments after his mother's murder, Amias had ordered the stewards to take Seth back to his chambers. There was no opportunity to speak to Octavia or to even look upon her face in the aftermath of their father's madness. That had been the last time he had seen his sister. He didn't want to dwell on what happened with Lisanthir either.

I should never have left Lithalyon.

Memories of the great Elviri city paraded around his mind, taunting him with visions of a life he could never have. A life he caught fleeting glimpses of when he had escaped from Yiradia, running on legs magically restored to him by a potion concocted by the Asaszi. He had been a different person in Lithalyon, free to explore the city, walk on his own two feet, read books in the great libraries, and befriend other Elviri who shared his interests. More visions appeared of the cobbled streets, golden leaves from the mighty tree Aelrindel floating down and covering rooftops and gardens alike, the glow of the setting suns covering the city in the early evening, the wind dancing through Lisanthir's black hair...

He cursed silently and pulled a blanket over his head, listening for something, *anything*, to distract him from the pain in his chest. One of his thighs twitched, pulling his attention down to his legs. His dead, useless legs. Curling in on himself, he kneaded the muscle and fat on his left leg. His hand ghosted over his knee and down to his shin, and all he felt was his fingers pressing into emptiness. He felt the bones underneath his fingers, the sharp edges of his knee, the loose skin. Weak. Dead. Broken.

It had all been a lie. A cruel taste of what I—the Provira—could have had had we been born in a more forgiving world. Had Father not ruined it for the rest of us.

The steward sighed and straightened their posture. With bitter resentment, Seth forced himself to focus on the steward's noises as they brushed off their robes, opened the door, and walked out. He cursed his father. He cursed Osza and Astohi. He cursed himself.

The next evening, the steward brought with them another tray of food and drink, the scent of passionflower tea mingled with roasted fish filling the room. It wasn't often they prepared fish in the pyramid. The scent reminded him of the smoked fish he had eaten with Lisanthir at the one tavern back in Lithalyon. The Four Adavas.

Would it still be standing after Astohi and Father march on the city?

Seth's stomach growled, the scents enticing him forward. He forced himself into a sitting position. The steward set the tray on his lap and then stood by the edge of the bed. In addition to the fish were several stewed vegetables and roots, prepared with peppers and spices found in eastern Moonyswyn. The kind of flavors he preferred. There was also a small bowl of sweet porridge topped with crushed lytsi nuts and tart khobo fruit.

Seth breathed in the scents of the food and closed his eyes. He was hungry today. After so many days of avoiding food, he found he could avoid it no further. He raised the cup of tea to his lips and inhaled slowly, savoring the floral scent. The cup was near blistering, but he was happy to feel it, to feel *anything* beyond the gnawing sadness within. He held the cup until his fingers screamed in pain. He set it back down without taking a sip.

As Seth picked up his fork, the steward shifted on their feet, drawing Seth's attention. He watched them for a moment, a knot beginning to form in his throat, but his hunger devoured the knot and filled his mind. He was too hungry to think about anything else. He no longer cared if the steward wanted him to eat, or if they were going to hover over him until he ate.

Seth took a bite of the fish and closed his eyes, allowing the spices to mingle on his tongue and set a small fire in the back of his throat. He enjoyed the heat that came with spicy food, today more than ever before. The tea and porridge would soothe his throat and complete the meal.

Despite his hunger, Seth took his time eating the various dishes. The steward stood and watched until he was done, then removed the tray and disappeared back into the pyramid.

Sleep came easier that night now that he had a sated stomach.

CHAPTER 11: MUNNE

Munne had been to the island city of Auora several times throughout her two hundred and fifty years, but it had never been so... turbulent. The bridges to the eastern and western shores of the Hourglass Lakes were under lockdown. No one could enter or leave the island without passing through multiple checkpoints both on the mainland and on the island itself. Her traveling party had been stopped on the western shore despite having Rhorek Gondamire, knight-general of the Proma army, in their midst.

If the Warlord of the Elviri and a knight-general from Auora cannot freely travel to Auora, what will become of the caravan I'm supposed to meet inside the city? Munne's stomach churned unhappily. She hadn't seen the caravan at any of the western checkpoints, nor anywhere else on her journey from Elimere to Ferilin. *It's not like there are many roads leading from home to here, but perhaps they beat us somehow and they're now waiting for me within Auora.* The thought brought her little comfort.

She felt compelled to let go of her horse's reins and touch her forearms where Ely, the shapeshifter from her dreams, had left an imprint on her skin the night before. Touching the red marks would sooth her worries, but she didn't want to draw attention to herself, so she endured her discomfort. Ely had left his mark so that the nightmares that had been plaguing her mind for weeks would be kept at bay.

"Because it's important that you travel to Kherizhan," he had said to her the night before in her dreams. *"Because we need each other if we're going to stop the* Ardashi'ik *Ardulphyx from returning to Daaria."* Munne's blood chilled, even under the warmth of the two suns. Ely's magic—whatever it was—would keep her safe for the time being, but she needed to find the caravan leader soon. He knew the way to Kherizhan and would ensure she'd get there safely.

But with the disappearance of the Proma princess, how quickly will I be able to set out for Kherizhan? She already had to wait for the other two members of her triple, Araloth and Mayrien, to arrive, but how much longer would she have to wait beyond that?

Despite Auora being under lockdown, several boats were out on the water. Munne thought it curious, given the dire circumstances of the princess's disappearance. As she and her seven companions journeyed across the western bridge toward the city, she realized that most of the boats on the water belonged to the king's men, not fishermen. Soldiers stood on watch, some with eyeglasses raised to their faces. No doubt they were keeping an eye out for any boats that were either approaching or leaving the city docks, ready to rush out and meet them. Interrogate them.

The city itself was unruly and loud. As Munne and the group passed through the main gates of the city, several soldiers were ordered to escort the party to the castle. Normally Munne and her Barauder companions would have traveled to the Sky District at the top of the island—without an escort—where there were lodgings for ambassadors of other lands. She tried to consider what reasons the Proma would have for taking the Elviri Warlord and a trio of Barauder ambassadors directly to the castle, with an escort no less, but she couldn't produce a satisfactory answer. Not until they began climbing up the main road through the city called the Golden Path.

She heard panicked screams and barking orders from further into the city. Soldiers lined the Path, weapons at the ready, looking out to the surrounding neighborhoods. Munne's escorts were uneasy, often glancing side to side. It seemed that conflict had arisen on the streets, appearing more like a war zone than a city. Auora was no longer safe.

Her thoughts drifted to the caravan leader, the memory of his scarred face with his mismatching eyes sent a small shiver down her spine. She had told him they'd meet at the Pike and Pint, but the tavern would no doubt be shut down amidst all this chaos.

Did the caravan make it to Auora before the princess was kidnapped? Are they dead in the streets? Munne urged her horse forward, riding alongside Rhorek. "Something's happened to this city beyond the disappearance of your princess," she hissed.

Rhorek grunted in agreement. "Aye, but I don't know the extent of it. Mayor Ervaitt told me that some of the street rats had turned on each other the same night that the princess..." He trailed off, either too upset to repeat it, or reluctant to reveal more information.

Munne could read in between his words, at least a little bit. She knew Auora had its problems with gangs and violence. She wondered if their uprising had anything to do with the princess. Perhaps she'd get the chance to ask once they were within the castle walls. "Am I to assume we'll be staying in the castle?" she asked Rhorek a little louder. Out of the corner of her eye, she saw Lagazi, eldest of the Barauder, and her two kin perk up, taking interest in the conversation.

Rhorek took a moment to gather his thoughts. "Yes, it's my understanding that the lodgings of the Daarian Council have been relocated to the castle for the time being."

"That's a kind and generous thing the king has done," Munne responded.

Rhorek spoke so only Munne could hear his words. "Aye, the castle should be safe enough."

She frowned but said nothing. The only other time she could recall the Proma city being pitched into this level of chaos was a little over one hundred years ago, at the end of her lifepath rotations. The Provira had worn out their welcome in Promthus and were subsequently banished from the land. Munne didn't see the chaos with her own eyes, but she had overheard the reports—and later read those reports—from the Elviri ambassadors who were staying on the island during those years. The Provira had lashed out at their hosts, lighting fires in the streets as the guard swept through the city and forcefully evicted the mixed-bloods. That had happened after Huntaran, Munne's father, exiled the Provira from all Elviri provinces. The Proma hadn't heeded the warning from the Elviri, and Auora had paid the price.

The journey up the Golden Path was mercifully uneventful. Whatever disorder reigned in the lower districts hadn't made its way onto the main causeway. She wondered if she looked over the edge of the Path, how many bodies she would see in the streets below. If she'd catch a glimpse of the caravan leader's mismatching eyes. As they climbed higher, the screams faded. The landing to the Crafting District was heavily barricaded and manned by a mixture of soldiers and knights. From the surrounding area, Munne could hear soldiers calling to each other.

"Halt!"

The traveling party obeyed the command. Rhorek stepped to the front of the party and spoke with a calm voice. "We're bound for the castle with ambassadors from Elimere and the Black Lakes. What news of the higher districts?" he asked.

One of the knights behind the barricade saluted him. "Sir! The Crafting District is in disarray. We've been escorting residents up to the Market District. There are a few inns and churches there that are being used as refuges. The Sky District has seen its share of rats as well, but I haven't heard news from the men up there since yesterday morning." The knight ordered his men to step aside, and the party continued their ascent. Looking behind, Munne saw tendrils of smoke coming from the lower districts.

At the entrance to the Market District stood another barricade. The road joined the district at this level, so they were no longer separated from the city. Ambushes could come from any direction between there and the bridge to the castle. The guards surely knew that because they spared another four men to escort the party to the castle.

Munne gathered Alathyl's reins in her left hand and rested her right hand next to the hilt of her sword. She kept her eyes on the rooftops. The streets in the Market District were much calmer than those in the districts below. They passed through one of the larger marketplaces, which had been completely deserted. Some stalls had been ransacked and left for someone else to pick up the pieces. Other stalls had been emptied in advance, leaving nothing but a wooden shell of a stand.

It's not right to see a city's market abandoned like this, Munne thought.

They turned away from the Golden Path, and the castle bridge came into sight. A few of the soldiers let out sighs of relief, but Munne stayed on guard until they were on the bridge crossing over to the smaller island. Once they were within the walls of the castle, their escorts returned to the city.

As the party dismounted from their horses, a few stable hands emerged to tend to the horses. A steward, escorted by a knight, approached them. His dark hair was hidden beneath a foppish hat, and he wore dark blue embroidered robes to match. Dark circles clung to his eyes.

"It's good to see you again, Knight-General Gondamire," the steward said, a smile of relief plastered on his face. He turned to Munne and the Barauder and bowed. "And welcome, ambassadors, to Castle Auora." Munne nodded politely in his direction. The Barauder offered similar gestures. "I'm to escort you to your chambers. Please, follow me."

The steward took off without another word, leaving Munne and the Barauder to follow at a brisk pace. She offered a parting nod to Rhorek and his men as they left the stables. She tried to keep up with how many turns and flights of stairs they climbed, but it proved too tedious. Castle Auora was a maze, and it was nothing short of a miracle that the royal family, advisors, and staff could navigate through its halls without getting lost. Several other men and women passed by the traveling party, their heads bowed and focused on the task at hand. No one offered any greetings to Munne or the others, which she found odd.

Either the Proma are ruder than I remember, or the revolts and the princess's disappearance have shaken them.

When the steward stopped in front of a large wooden door, Munne wasn't sure how far above the entry hall they were or what direction they were facing. She hoped there was at least one window within the chambers so that she could look out at the lakes. She dared to hope a little more that if there was a window, it would look west to the Telatorr Mountains, and she could catch a glimpse of home.

"This wing of the castle is where the ambassadors of the Daarian Council are temporarily residing. We've made every effort to recreate the rooms from the embassy in the Sky District," the steward explained as he opened the door and gestured for them to enter.

The three Barauder passed the threshold first, murmuring quietly to one another. Beyond their hulking figures Munne could see a large room with fireplaces and numerous comfortable chairs and lounges. Though the architecture was vastly different, the common room felt warm and inviting, much like the one in the Sky District.

"Are there any other ambassadors here currently?" Munne asked the steward.

"Eldo Talltree from the Imalar Woods arrived a few days ago. I believe he's making arrangements to leave the city within the week."

She was thankful that the Imalarii found no trouble on the road, but she was also reminded of the task her father had set her on—serve as a guard to the Imalarii and stay away from the frontlines of the war with the Provira. No doubt Eldo would wish to discuss their plans to travel to the Imalar Woods once he learned of her presence. She almost wished she had tried her luck with getting to the Sky District, rather than stay in such close proximity to the result of her father overruling her authority.

Munne found herself speaking without thinking. "Is there anything I can do to assist the king with the troubles in his city?" The tips of her pointed ears burned. *Am I truly so desperate to get away from my father's orders that I would thrust myself into the problems that plague Auora? But I can't just leave the Proma without offering some kind of aid. As Warlord, I have to do something.*

The steward didn't respond immediately, and she found herself hanging onto the silence. She didn't know if she wanted him to give her an answer or not, which frustrated her.

"Lady Vere'cha, join us for tea," Lagazi, eldest of the three Barauder ambassadors from the Black Lakes, called from deeper within the chambers.

"I'll pass along your question to the king's advisors." The steward bowed and left Munne to the Barauder and her thoughts.

Lagazi, S'raak, and Druuk had settled down around a table near one of the fireplaces. They had found a kettle and a set of clay cups from one of the cabinets. Druuk was heating the water above the fire while S'raak pulled a pouch of herbs and plants from her satchel. She carefully selected a mixture of flowers and leaves from the assortment and split them between four of the cups. The three Barauder were clearly out of place in the castle just as they had been on horseback.

Fish out of water. Munne was equal parts amused and mortified by her own thoughts. She pinched the tip of her right ear to keep herself from chuckling.

The description wasn't entirely inaccurate, though, given the Barauder had a set of gills on their necks and had emerged from the Black Lakes as children.

Beyond their unique physicality, their clothing was rather simple compared to the rich decorum surrounding them, spun from plant fibers and wool. The Barauder did not covet gemstones and fine silks like the other races in Daaria.

Lagazi, the eldest of the three, leaned back comfortably in her chair and merely observed the others' activities. As Munne approached, she gestured to the seat across from herself. "Allow your mind to rest for a few moments."

"Thank you, Lagazi." Munne took a seat and waited to be served a cup.

S'raak finished dividing up the herbs, Druuk poured the hot water over them, and soon the four of them were sitting together in silence as the tea steeped. The Barauder were not a people of many words, which Munne appreciated in that moment. She leaned forward to breathe in the scent of her tea. It smelled of the earth with faint whiffs of something sweet and reminiscent of the sea.

Lagazi smiled and spoke. "Irocht flo'ir, among other plants. It grows in abundance on the shores of Itorh. S'raak and the other priestesses of Itorh harvest it at the end of each summer so that we may send our travelers away with a piece of home." S'raak said nothing, but Munne could see the gleam of pride in her dark eyes.

Another comfortable silence fell over the table.

"It's a shame to see Auora in this state," Druuk murmured after a few moments, staring at his cup.

"The Proma do not appreciate what they have," S'raak said with disdain, her lip curling upward in a snarl.

"They build too high, so they have lost touch with their lakes," Lagazi responded. The other two Barauder nodded silently.

"But why the chaos?" Munne asked. "Were the people so enamored with their princess that they're rioting in the streets over her disappearance?" She shook her head and leaned forward in her seat. "Something else is at play in the background."

Lagazi reached for her cup of tea, cradling it with both hands and taking a sip. The other two Barauder picked up their own cups and took a sip. Munne did the same, blowing on the water first to cool it down before drinking. She had visited the Black Lakes only twice in her life, both times over a hundred years ago, long before any of her companions had emerged from their lakes.

Tasting the tea reminded her of their land, the soft earth they built their villages on, the pungent scent of salt, fish, and flowers lingering in the air. After the war with the Provira was settled, she would need to visit there again and renew her experiences of their strange lands.

"It's noble that you would assist the Proma with their dilemmas, but have you not already sworn your sword to another conflict?" Lagazi asked from over the rim of her cup.

The tips of Munne's pointed ears flushed. She took another sip of her tea. She knew the Barauder spoke of her commitment to the Imalarii, but her thoughts went to the caravan leader and their promised journey to Kher-izhan.

"I do not mean to bring shame to you, Lady Vere'cha. I merely offer you a chance to reflect on your choices. Enjoy your tea and allow yourself rest before you throw yourself into conflict." The Barauder ambassador offered her a small grin, the corners of her dark lips curling upward around her lower fangs.

Munne nursed her cup of tea over the next hour, and the Barauder kept her company in her silence.

Munne's mind felt sharper after her respite with the three Barauder. She felt that she could approach Eldo and discuss their travel plans with relative calmness. Afterward she would try to find Rhorek and discuss what was happening within the city.

The Imalarii was enjoying a midday meal in his chambers. His door was open, so Munne stepped inside the threshold and announced her presence. "Good day, it's Lady Munne Vere'cha."

"Lady Vere'cha! Please come in and join me," Eldo said, and so she accepted. He sat at a small table covered in roasted vegetables, freshly baked bread, and a fillet of smoked fish. Next to the table was a small stool he had used to climb into his chair. Only one plate had been prepared at the table, but a second chair sat opposite him, so that was where she took her seat. He had recently bathed, his brown curls hanging limp against his head. His brown eyes were warm as he spoke. "I'm glad you made it safely to the city. I arrived three days ago, and things have become absolutely dreadful. The first night there were attacks all throughout the city, and the city guard had to escort me to the castle. Have you heard any news of what's going on out there?"

"The only thing that they have shared with me is that Princess Niamnh is missing," Munne answered.

Eldo's jaw dropped. "Oh dear, what a horrible thing!"

Munne nodded, her expression grim. "I've requested an audience with King Nelle to discuss how the Elviri can be of assistance."

Eldo set his utensils down and wiped his mouth with his handkerchief. He met Munne's gaze, and she felt like the Imalarii was picking her apart, her words and intentions unraveling before him. At last, he nodded. "And what of the Imalar Woods?"

Munne pursed her lips and breathed in through her nose. "The other members of my triple should arrive in Auora within the week if the mountain passes are kind. After I have spoken to the king and met with my triple, I will decide how best to allocate our resources for our allies."

Eldo nodded again. He couldn't argue against her offering to help the Proma. There was still so much mystery surrounding the city and their princess. Munne and Eldo both would be fools to ignore the possibility that the Provira were somehow involved.

"Thank you for bringing this to my attention. I'll remain in Auora until your triple has arrived."

Munne bowed her head and got to her feet. She had the sudden desire to bathe and to seclude herself away from everyone else. Rhorek could wait.

Shortly after Munne bathed, the steward from earlier in the day reappeared, moving with haste. His cheeks were flushed with exertion. She and the Barauder gathered in the common room to hear his announcement. "Esteemed guests. Lady Vere'cha, I've received word that the king and his advisors are willing to meet with you at midday tomorrow."

"Excellent news," Munne responded. "Where will I be meeting them?"

"I'll be escorting you to their meeting chambers in the morning," the steward said. He bowed. "Your evening meal will be delivered in a few hours. Please, enjoy, and I'll return tomorrow."

He left as quickly as he arrived. Munne exchanged a look with Lagazi, eyebrow arched.

"Skittish one," Lagazi muttered.

"Because of their missing princess, no doubt," Munne replied. She decided to wait to speak to Rhorek until after her meeting with the king's counsel. That would give them both the opportunity to learn more about what's happened in Auora over the past few weeks.

As they waited for dinner to be delivered, there was little else to do besides sitting or pacing about in the common room. The Barauder continued to enjoy their tea and meditation. Two members of the castle staff brought trays of fruits, pastries, and cold water not too long after the steward made his appearance. Both women moved at a near-frantic pace while flitting about the chambers, ensuring everything was clean and presentable. Munne was tempted to interrogate one of them, but they moved so quickly she didn't have the chance to do so. With a frown, she picked up a pear and walked in circles around the common room.

"Lady Vere'cha, would you like a book to read?" Lagazi asked, a hint of amusement in her tone.

Munne glanced over at the Barauder and saw a grin plastered on her murky blue face. "I... could do with the entertainment," Munne sighed.

Lagazi stood and went to her room. She returned a few moments later, clutching a leather-bound journal to her chest. She handed it to Munne and said, "This is a collection of tales about the Lake Mothers. Perhaps this will hold your interest for the time being."

Munne accepted the book and bowed her head. "Thank you, Lagazi. I can't recall having read something like this before. I'm sure it'll be a delight."

Much more delightful than Malion's journal had been. Her lip twitched, trying to curve into a grimace, but she controlled herself. The journal of her ancestor had proven to be an insightful and horrifying account of the last few months of his life before killed himself and his wife. All because of the *Ardashi'ik*, who now tormented her own mind.

An image of the Black Lakes had been carved onto the cover of Lagazi's book—a cluster of three large lakes connected to the ocean by thin rivers. The leather was rigid and uneven underneath her fingertips. The pattern was reminiscent of the scales of a snake but unlike any she had seen before.

"Where did this leather come from?" she asked Lagazi.

"It's the skin of a *taoroch*. They are great beasts that share the Lakes with us. We covet the annual hunt, and we find use for all parts of its body, from its long snout to its sharp claws and spindly tail," Lagazi explained, running a finger over the leather. Her movement was slow, reverent. Secured around her wrist was a bracelet made from the same leather as the book. "To fell a *taoroch* is a blessing from Our Father. To brandish its leather, a sign of love from the Mothers."

"The leather is marvelous," Munne said, nodding to both the book and the bracelet.

Lagazi nodded, accepting the compliment, and then returned to the table with her tea. Munne crossed over to one of the lounges and got comfortable, placing the remains of her pear on a nearby table. Munne was familiar enough with the Barauder to know that they believed that each of the three lakes in Balach Yor represented one of their goddesses, and that the sea to the east was their creator, The Father. She spent the next couple of hours reading through Lagazi's book, enthralled by the stories contained within. She read of the boldness of Y'lah, warrior mother; the cleverness of Itorh, sage mother; the kindness of Sirh'ah, healing mother.

As she flipped through the pages, servants carried in platters of food and set them on one of the larger tables. The scents of freshly baked bread and roasted fish filled the air. Her stomach growled and she opted to pause her reading in favor of enjoying a hot meal. Eldo and the three Barauder joined her at the table and soon they were eating and chatting merrily.

When Munne retired to her bedchamber, she found herself dreading what was to come. Ely's handprints still burned on her skin, so her dreams should be free from the nightmarish tunnels and winged beast, but that didn't quell the panic building within. As she squirmed underneath her blankets, she rubbed her hands against her forearms.

You said you'd return tonight, Ely. I hope it's you I see and not the Ardashi'ik.

Munne opened her eyes and found herself in the dreamscape forest clearing from the previous night when she had been in Ferilin. She was beginning to acclimate to her surroundings, as strange as they were with their dark, formless shapes. No moon or stars cast any light on the clearing, yet she could see without issue. She looked around for her dream visitor, feeling relief when she saw him approaching.

Ely.

He came to her in the same form as last night—flaming red hair, dark brown horns, pale green eyes, and even paler skin. From neck to toe he was covered in black robes.

"Good evening, Munne." Ely's raspy voice sent a small shiver down her spine. "I hope your travels fared well today?"

"We reached Auora with no trouble, but something's wrong with the city," Munne answered. "The princess has disappeared, and the city has fallen into anarchy." She was startled by how easily she offered that information up.

"Worry not. I harbor no ill will towards the Proma." Ely waved a dismissive hand. She noticed he was wearing black gloves again as well. "Although it *is* troubling to hear, since they're your allies."

"I've offered to help them, if I can."

Ely locked eyes with her and remained silent for an uncomfortable amount of time. She tightened her jaw and held his gaze, though she had to tilt her chin up to do so.

He opened his mouth to speak, but Munne said, "I'm still the Warlord of the Elviri, and one day I will be *Se'vi*. I'm sworn to protect my people and allies. As much as I wish I could run to Kherizhan, I must do what I can to aid those around me."

The corner of Ely's lips curled upward into an uneven grin. "Protector and guardian, indeed. The Proma do not realize their luck in having you for an ally."

Her stomach curled pleasantly in on itself, which caught her off-guard. "You're not... disappointed that I'm staying in the city?"

Ely looked past her at the surrounding forest, taking a few steps towards the edge of the clearing. "I would urge you to find others to take your place in Auora, as I'm sure you will. I believe I can hold the darkness at bay for a while yet."

Munne looked at the darkness beyond Ely. The pleasant warmth in her stomach turned ice cold. Although her nightmares of the caves and the screaming were far away, they were still within reach. They echoed in the far recesses of her mind. She had no desire to return to that place.

"Think no more of it tonight, Munne," Ely murmured, drawing her back to the clearing and to him.

"Tell me something about where you're from," she said suddenly, looking at his face and focusing on the way his horns curled around his head and the loose strands of fiery hair falling across them.

He looked away into the distance and then met her gaze again. His pale green eyes glowed with warmth. "There were so many waterfalls. You could fall asleep to their low rumbling every night."

Munne smiled and her thoughts immediately went to Elimere and the two waterfalls that flanked her father's manor. In the summer months, she would leave her doors open so the quiet roar would lull her to sleep. She wondered if Ely lived in a valley flanked by waterfalls, like her, or if he lived at the base of a tall cliff with a river tumbling down from high above. Off in the distance, she could hear a low rumble reminiscent of a waterfall.

"Is there anything else you'd like to discuss tonight?" Ely asked quietly. "Or shall I leave you to rest in preparation for your meeting with the king tomorrow?"

Munne stood and listened to the distant waterfall for a few moments before murmuring, "I think I'd like to rest."

When Munne awoke the next morning, she found herself cradling her arms and savoring the warmth Ely's imprints brought her. They had faded to a dull pink, but still held considerable power and comfort.

"You are a curious creature," she said quietly, a faint smile on her lips. "Ely." His name felt pleasant to say.

Once again, he had given her a peaceful night's sleep, free from the nightmares that had been plaguing her for months. She was appreciative of his…

Magic?

He must be an agent of the gods, if he can touch my mind this way, Munne mused as she climbed out of bed. But even the gods' powers were limited, and he had said he wasn't one of them. *So, what kind of magic is this…?*

The only clothes she had brought from Elimere were riding clothes, which were not appropriate for an audience with the king. In hindsight it had been foolish of her to not pack at least one set of dress robes, considering her elevated station. Chastising herself, she changed into her nicest coat and trousers, pulled on her boots, and exited to the common room.

The steward appeared moments later and bowed to her. "Lady Vere'cha, are you ready to meet with the council?"

She set the book down with care then stood. "Yes. Lead on." The steward bowed again and left the chamber, Munne following.

She tried keeping track of their journey through the castle, but she quickly abandoned the effort. After many twists, turns, and stairs, the steward opened a large pair of wooden doors, revealing the king's council room. It was lavishly decorated with suits of armor, painted shields, and antique weapons. In the middle of the room was a large circular wooden table with several chairs surrounding it. Most of the seats were already occupied by older Proma who Munne vaguely recalled from previous visits. She recognized Rhorek and he gave her a brief welcoming smile. One chair was much larger than the rest with a tall back covered in plush scarlet cushions. It clearly belonged to King Nelle, who had not yet arrived.

"Lady Munne Vere'cha of Elimere," the steward announced as she entered the room.

Munne bowed before the gathered council, then took a seat in one of the plain chairs opposite from the king's chair. "Thank you for seeing me on such short notice, my lords."

"Welcome, Lady Vere'cha," Rhorek said on behalf of the table. "I believe you are familiar with most of the men here."

He introduced each man, giving their name and rank: Aman Fernis, representative of Ferilin; Gunthor Ingwen, representative of Trent; Willem Tomtully the Younger, representative of Merrioff; Nathen Munhart, captain of the city guard; Brien Mauntell, military advisor; and Lords Luca Nathfer and Rees Delsaran, representatives of the Welkin Coalition, an organization made up of representatives from the noble and wealthy households in the Sky District.

"We are absent a few members due to complications in the city. It was safer for them to remain at home," Captain Munhart said, referring to the other empty chairs. The captain was a middle-aged man who looked like he had seen enough fighting and killing to last three Proma lifetimes. His armor was dented and discolored in spots, his helmet resting on the table in front of him. Streaks of gray ran through his dark brown hair and beard.

The streets must have been in a more dire situation than they had appeared yesterday, judging by the captain's appearance. Between the dark circles under his eyes and the rough stubble on his face, it seemed that he hadn't found any time to sleep in the past few days.

Munne looked around the room at the decorations. There were no windows in the room. A large fireplace filled the back wall behind the king's chair, a small fire crackling within. Hanging above the mantel was a display of two longswords and a wooden shield. Painted on its surface was the sigil of the royal family—a gold crown resting atop an hourglass-shaped lake.

A few moments later the doors opened, revealing King Nelle and his three Sworn Swords. One of the Sworn Swords remained outside, shutting the doors behind the others. Munne and the other men rose as the king crossed the room and took a seat. They returned to their seats, leaving the two Sworn Swords standing beside their king.

"Thank you all for attending today," King Nelle said, his voice soft and weary. He was a fair man with blue eyes and blond hair that touched his shoulders. Munne had last visited the king only two years prior, and in that short time he seemed to have aged twenty years. Dark circles hung below his eyes and wrinkles covered his skin. His beard was a blend of blond, white, and gray. "We'll continue our discussions about the state of the city. Lady Vere'cha, it's my understanding that you've offered aid from your people?"

Munne nodded and replied, "Yes, Your Majesty."

King Nelle let out a small sigh of relief. "That's reassuring news. Captain Munhart, what do our men need the most?"

"Supplies are much needed with so many expeditions sent out and certain areas of the docks compromised," the captain said slowly. "Extra men could prove beneficial as well to aid those in the streets."

"Pardon the question, but what expeditions?" Munne asked.

Captain Munhart looked at King Nelle, who let out another small sigh, notably distraught.

The king composed himself and spoke. "My daughter Niamnh went missing three nights ago. She was kidnapped from her bedroom and all we know is that the fiends escaped onto the lake. The same night, the city erupted into chaos, and now the damned street rats and thugs are trying to kill each other."

"We sent nearly a third of our men out of the city to find Princess Niamnh," Brien Mauntell interjected. He hadn't aged as gracefully as his companions. Though his hair was black as a raven, his beard was more white than black. Wrinkles covered his face and neck. Munne recalled that he had been a lieutenant in the Proma army several years ago. "The remainder are split between guarding the castle and patrolling the city."

"At first the fighting was contained to the lower tiers, but they're getting into the higher tiers and terrorizing the citizens," Captain Munhart continued. "They're attacking guards when we come to the aid of the people."

Munne leaned forward in her seat, resting her elbows on the table. "I can send word to the outpost at Ferilin and request a portion of the troops come to the city to assist with guarding the streets. I'd like to join your men to assess how many more I'll need to summon from Elimaine."

"Thank you, Lady Vere'cha. We're fortunate you arrived when you did," said Lord Rees Delsaran. He was a short, round man with a nasally voice. He wore luxurious clothes befitting his station, gold leaves decorating the chest of his purple tunic.

The other men around the table nodded and murmured their agreement.

Captain Munhart began to speak. "I can arrange for you to join one of the patrols stationed at the bridge tomorrow—"

"Captain, with all due respect, it would be more beneficial for us both if you send me into the city proper," Munne interjected. *And this way I can search for both the caravan leader and any signs of the Provira. I'm certain the mixed-bloods have something to do with Princess Niamnh's disappearance.*

The captain locked eyes with her and was silent for several moments. He was the first to look away, turning to his king who nodded.

"In that case, Lady Vere'cha," Captain Munhart's voice was tense. "I'll make arrangements for you to join the early morning patrol tomorrow."

Munne bowed, saying nothing. The next morning couldn't come soon enough.

"Captain, give us your status report from this morning," King Nelle said.

"Yes, Your Majesty. We've evacuated most of the residents in the Crafting District and brought them to the Market District. Fires have broken out in some of the craft halls, and we're working to put them out as quickly as we can, but we need more men in that district."

"Can't we spare some men from the lower districts?" Lord Delsaran asked.

"There aren't enough men to get the lower districts under control," Captain Munhart snapped. "It's chaos down there. If the same rats lighting fires in the Crafting District start lighting them down at the docks, it'll spell danger for us all."

Rhorek raised his voice. "Have we sealed off the tunnels?"

Tunnels? It's a miracle there's even enough earth to build upon. Where do these tunnels go?

"All the ones we know of, sir," Captain Munhart responded.

"And what of the Sky District, Captain?" Lord Delsaran demanded. "People are afraid to leave their homes. Is the city guard going to clear the rats from our homes and businesses?"

"Lord Delsaran, I have sent as many men as I can spare to the Sky District. From the reports I have heard, the citizens are resisting leaving their homes." The captain sounded exasperated.

"If we abandon our homes, who's to stop the street rats from stealing our belongings?"

"If you don't abandon your homes, you could get killed!" Captain Munhart roared. "Surely your neighbors wouldn't want to risk their lives, especially when we still don't know *why* the gangs have been causing this chaos?"

"Lord Delsaran, Captain Munhart." Lord Luca Nathfer raised his hands to stop the conversation. He was an older man with silver hair and brown eyes. He wore fine red and silver regalia, his family sigil of an owl emblazoned on his chest. "Bickering won't solve our problems. Lord Delsaran and I can write to the other lords and ladies and urge them to seek shelter elsewhere. Perhaps the church in the Sky District? Do we know if that has been secured yet?"

Captain Munhart shook his head. "One of the gangs has taken up residence there. We've been keeping an eye on them, but we don't have the manpower to drive them out."

"Have we been able to secure *anything* in the Sky District?" Lord Nathfer asked.

"My men have set up a post near the Rose Theater. Reports say that it should be empty. I can tell the men to secure the theater, and we can escort citizens there for the time being."

Lord Nathfer turned to Lord Delsaran. "If we're able to gather our neighbors together, we could then move somewhere else, like one of the inns in the Market District."

Lord Delsaran grimaced, and the sight flooded Munne's mind with anger, her stomach twisting sharply. *The selfishness of the Proma never fails to disappoint,* she thought with contempt.

"If we're able to evacuate the Sky District and bring everyone to a central location, it would allow me and my men the chance to send larger patrols out into the city," Captain Munhart said.

All eyes focused on Lord Delsaran, and it made Munne's skin crawl. It frustrated her that the wellbeing of Auora and its guards were in the hands of a man who looked like he had never even picked up a sword. And yet the man sat on the royal council and had King Nelle's ear.

"I can see the benefit of that," Lord Delsaran said, his nasally voice grating in Munne's ears.

"The various household guards could also work together to defend the inn," Lord Nathfer suggested.

Lord Delsaran's sour expression sweetened. "That could work, yes…" He trailed off, drumming his fingers together.

"Lords Delsaran and Nathfer, draft your letters and Captain Munhart will ensure they are delivered to the residents of the Sky District," King Nelle ordered. "You two are dismissed."

The two lords rose to their feet, Nathfer towering over Delsaran. They bowed to their king and then left the council room.

Once the doors were closed behind them, King Nelle continued. "Lord Fernis, please work with Lady Vere'cha to compose a letter to the Elviri outpost outside of Ferilin. Captain Munhart will ensure you have an escort ready to depart the city within the hour."

"Yes, Your Majesty," Lord Aman Fernis said, rising to his feet.

Munne stood as well, bowing towards King Nelle and taking her leave with the Ferilin representative. Fernis took the lead as they departed the council room and made for a nearby study. He stood a little shorter than Munne, and from behind she could see a bald patch forming on the back of his head amidst his black hair. She had met Fernis a few times prior when she visited Auora. They often exchanged correspondence, especially concerning the Elviri outpost just outside of Ferilin.

"It's good to see you again, Lady Vere'cha," Fernis said quietly as they entered one of the studies not too far away.

"Thank you, Lord Fernis. I hope all has been well, aside from recent events," she replied.

The study was a small room, meant for letter-writing and paper-drafting after council meetings. Inside were two tables, two chairs, a bookcase containing important documents, and a beautiful tapestry of the city-island. Lord Fernis gestured for Munne to sit behind one of the desks, and he pulled the second chair around to the opposite side.

"I met with Commander Ethelmar a few days ago when we passed through Ferilin," Munne said. "He shouldn't be surprised to hear from me. Has word been sent to the cities about the princess's disappearance or the chaos in the streets?"

Lord Fernis nodded. "The King had us send word the morning after the princess's disappearance, so the guards would know to look out for her."

"I wonder if Mayor Ervaitt has already met with my kin about this, then," Munne mumbled to herself. Then she said to Lord Fernis, "How do you normally communicate with Mayor Ervaitt? Do you leave the city to deliver each message?"

"No, my lady. We usually send messenger birds. This time, however, I'll be traveling there myself, as I'm... hoping to stay in Ferilin until the city is safe again."

Munne frowned. "You wouldn't stay in the castle?"

Lord Fernis looked away from her and fidgeted in his chair. "I-I have family back in Ferilin, so I would rest easier being with them rather than here."

She thought of her parents and nodded. "After I patrol the city tomorrow, I'll need to send another letter to Elimere."

"I'll send word to the rookery before I depart. Any of the stewards should be able to escort you there when you are ready."

Munne thanked him and began her letter to Ethelmar.

Munne awoke early the next morning, reluctant to drop her hands from her arms where Ely's handprints lingered on her skin. She allowed herself a few moments in bed before throwing the blankets back and preparing for the day.

The steward waited for her in the common room along with a new person, this one carrying armor. The steward bowed. "Good morning, Lady Vere'cha. Captain Munhart requested that we bring you more appropriate attire for the morning patrol," he said.

Munne took the armor—a chainmail shirt, a faded green hauberk, and an iron helmet—and thanked the two. She returned to her room and changed into the shirt and hauberk. They fit well enough, although the shirt was a little too large. She set the helmet down then pulled her hair back and tied it into a low ponytail. She grabbed her sword belt from a nearby bench and fastened it around her waist, then picked up her two blades, inspecting each before sheathing them.

Sunslight flickered against the pale golden hilt of her arming sword and its guard before being absorbed in the round pommel. The blacksmiths of old had crafted the hilt and pommel in the likeness of the symbol of the Eldest Days, the pommel the singular sun and the hilt wrapped in its fiery rays. The blade had passed down from Warlord to Warlord, a prized heirloom of their station. Cesa had bestowed the blade upon her when she swore her vows of office before her father and the other Elviri rulers. She took comfort in the weight of her arming sword as she slid it into its sheath on her left hip, eyes lingering over the runes stitched into the fine leather.

The second sword was a short sword, its blade just shy of the full length of her arm. There was no guard atop its leather hilt, its pommel flat and undecorated. Though not as beautiful as the arming sword, the short sword carried great sentimentality; it had been forged by Araloth's father when their triple first formed as a token of appreciation, each member receiving a matching blade. The short sword's sheath was plain and unadorned as it rested against her right hip. The blade slid in with no resistance.

With her blades secured in their sheaths, Munne picked up the helmet and tucked it underneath one arm, exiting to the common room.

"I'm ready," she said, and the stewards escorted her out.

The journey through the castle went quickly, and in the main foyer they were greeted by five guards in armor that matched hers.

"Lady Vere'cha," one of the guards greeted her, bowing.

Munne returned the bow. "Good morning. Where will we be patrolling?"

"Captain said we'll be helping put out fires in the Crafting District and looking for any citizens still needing an escort up to the Market District."

She pursed her lips and nodded. *Not exactly what I wanted, but this will do. Whatever it takes to get me into the city.*

They set off across the bridge to the main island, and she donned her helmet. A cool breeze from the lake whisked past them. She glanced at the lakes and marveled at their beauty. Very few ships were on the water, giving the lakes a sense of calmness. Birds flew overhead, shadows against the blue sky.

Looking ahead, the main island towered over the bridge. The Sky District was truly an impressive sight to see from a distance. Steeples and towers rose up into the sky, rivaling those of the castle. From further down the island, smoke rose over the rooftops, its acrid scent filling her nose. Munne frowned, concerned about the structural integrity of the homes and buildings smoldering in the lower districts. It was good that they'd be extinguishing the fires, but what they really needed to do was find the people responsible for setting the fires and lock them up. Maybe they would get lucky and find some while on patrol.

On the other side of the bridge were a few small handcarts filled with barrels of water. A group of guards surrounded one cart, two men lifting the handles and dragging it away while the other four men drew their swords and flanked the cart on all sides.

"You two, grab the handles. Lady Vere'cha, the rest of you, surround it and let's move out!" the leader of their group called out.

Munne and the guards fell into line. She took up the rear, drawing the longer of her two swords as they descended into the Crafting District. Her heart was beating with a calm cadence in her chest, her gaze shifting from one rooftop to the next. *Will any of the gangs try attacking this fire control brigade? They must've tried it before, if I'm serving as an escort.*

The streets were quieter today than the day before. While she was relieved not to hear people crying out for help, the silence was just as unnerving. Places like that were supposed to be boisterous and full of life. There was no sign of her caravan leader, nor anyone else in this part of the city.

The group turned off the main road, following a plume of smoke that rose above the rooftops. All around Munne was the scent of charred wood, wool, and other crafting materials.

How many people's livelihoods have been destroyed in these fires? And for what? Munne thought bitterly. The revolts made no sense to her. *Only the Provira could cause such mindless destruction as this.*

The cart stopped in front of a two-story workshop. Dark smoke billowed out of the windows and crept high into the sky. Nothing on the outside of the building had caught fire, which meant it was contained in the building's interior for the time being.

As the two guards set the cart down, the one at the front of the pack started barking orders. "You three, grab buckets and start putting out what you can. Norwolke, Lady Vere'cha, stay on guard. Sergeant said there's been sightings of street rats around here. Protect the cart."

Munne turned and unsheathed her short sword, her grip on both hilts flexing and tightening. Her heartbeat accelerated a little as the thrill of a potential fight coursed through her veins. *Let anyone try to stop us. We'll get this fire under control and move onto the next place.*

Norwolke stood to her left with a shield in one hand and a sword in the other. Munne watched the streets for any signs of life. Shop signs swung with the lake breeze. She heard the fires hissing and crackling behind her as the guards tossed bucket after bucket on the building. She tuned out their shouts, instead listening for any other signs of life on the streets.

Then came a faint whistling.

A javelin soared through the air and would have struck her chest if she hadn't heard the hiss of it cutting through the wind. She sidestepped the projectile quickly, scanning her surroundings for its wielder. There was a flash of movement up ahead, and Munne nearly missed a person pulling their head back from around a corner. The soles of their boots slapped on the stone as they ran away from the burning building.

She sheathed her swords and took off after them. "Someone's out there!" she shouted over her shoulder.

"Guard the cart, Norwolke!" the lead guard ordered as he took off after Munne, but she was already turning the corner.

The person—a woman—held another javelin in one hand as she tore down the side road. She was rather nimble despite wearing a heavy tan robe that fell to her ankles. Munne sprinted after her and quickly closed the space between them. They twisted around corners and wound their way further into the Crafting District. She could hear the guard's armor clanking in the distance.

When Munne was sure she had closed the distance between her and the woman, she lunged and tackled her to the ground. The javelin flew out of the woman's hand and landed several feet away. She had a few other sheathed daggers on her body. Munne felt their pommels and sheaths dig into her hauberk. The woman's head bounced off the stone road, and she let out a painful shriek.

"Why were you attacking the guard?" Munne asked as she adjusted herself on top of the woman, pinning her legs down and pulling her wrists back.

"Fuck the guard!" the woman spat. She thrashed underneath Munne but couldn't shake her weight.

"Lady Vere'cha!" The guard had finally caught up with her. She heard him sheath his sword and stand next to her.

"This woman threw a javelin at us."

The guard picked up the other javelin and looked it over before looking at the woman. "One of the Disciples, is it?"

"Not anymore," the woman replied, spitting a wad of blood onto the road. "It's the *Suneaters* now."

Munne arched an eyebrow, maintaining her grip on the woman's arms. She waited for the guard to respond, opting to follow his lead.

"Some little new upstart, eh?" the guard asked, kneeling beside Munne.

"Not little. It's a *revolution*," the woman retorted.

"I wonder if this has to do with the princess," Munne muttered.

"Princess?" the woman spat again. "Fuck the princess. We want *Naro*."

Munne rolled her eyes, then noticed the guard had frozen in place. She took stock of the woman on the ground, then gave the guard her full attention as she asked, "Who's Naro?"

CHAPTER III: RAY

A heavy gust of wind nearly knocked Ray off of her feet as she climbed out of the boat. The northern shores of the Hourglass Lakes were frigid, much colder than Auora was. She had never traveled off of the island before. It was a strange new world for her, so open and expansive.

She wished Ajak was there to see it with her. Her heart ached at the thought of him.

She wasn't quite sure how long it had been since their grand escape from Castle Auora. They had entered the castle just before sunset, spiked Princess Niamnh's dinner with an elixir Naro had given them, and had the scuffle with the kitchen woman and knight a few hours later. They escaped with the drugged princess soon after. They had been so close to leaving the island when—

A knot formed in her throat. The memory of Ajak's body falling from the well opening replayed in her head all night. So had the memory of Wendelgar's death. The boatman who hadn't even stepped foot inside the castle. Ray hadn't even known the man, she had no idea if he was an honest sailor or another rogue like herself. She had laid next to his cooling corpse for a few hours, and she didn't even know the man's full name. She hadn't dared lift her head up to see who had shot Wendelgar. Their boat had been far enough away from the docks that she hadn't heard anyone speak or move after he crumpled forward with an arrow protruding from his chest. In his dying moments he had gasped and gargled on his own blood. And she had done nothing. She had been terrified of being discovered and killed. Eventually his sputtering ended, and the boat was silent. Even the princess had stopped her unintelligible mumbling. They had floated on the lake for what felt like hours.

It should've been me and Ajak in that boat.

"Where are we?"

Ray looked down to see Princess Niamnh pushing Wendelgar's corpse off of her and pulling herself into a sitting position. Her hands were shaking as she gripped the side of the boat. Dark blood stained the skirt of the maid's dress she was wearing. The apron Ray had used to cover the princess's hair had fallen from her head, revealing wet silvery-white locks that clung to her face. Her movements were sluggish, but she was regaining her faculties.

"North," Ray replied softly.

Princess Niamnh looked at her surroundings, then up at Ray, her face twisted in confusion. "Who are you?"

Ray opened her mouth to respond but immediately stopped herself when a wave of dread crashed over her and she felt her eyes begin to water. *Who am I? A scared girl hiding beneath a costume.*

She looked up to the sky to distract herself. It was still dark out, but the first tendrils of light began to caress the sky from the two suns in the east. A nearly full moon hung low in the sky to the west, giving her enough light to gather her bearings.

The princess interrupted her thoughts once more. "W-who is this man? Is he... *dead?*"

Ray glanced down at Princess Niamnh again, a wave of guilt and nausea passing over her. She'd been so focused on getting out of the boat that she hadn't considered when the princess would wake up, or how she'd react to seeing a corpse beside her. Ray prepared to jump into the boat, to slap her hand over the princess's mouth to stop her from screaming, but she just... *sat there*. Staring.

"H-he was the boat man," Ray said lamely, too distracted by the other girl's odd behavior to say much else. She watched as Princess Niamnh continued to stare, shivering and swaying with the cold lake breeze.

After a moment, the princess snapped out of her stupor. "Well, if you won't give me your name, can you at least give me something warmer to wear?" The princess was still in the kitchen woman's clothes, and she was shivering violently.

Ray's own hands and face were cold. They needed warmer clothes. *Didn't Naro tell us there'd be a supply stash nearby?* She parted her lips and took a deep breath. Naro was depending on her to complete this mission. She had to take the princess north. *He said we'll be saving the city.* Ray reached out to grab the princess's hand. "My name's Ray Finnegan. Now come on; we need to move."

"Where are you taking me?" the princess asked, yanking her hand away.

Ray quickly weighed her choices before answering. She couldn't come up with a lie quick enough, so she settled for the truth. "Na'roc of North, to get that Doshara out of you."

A look of fear crossed the princess's face as she tried rising to her feet. She must've still been under the effect of the drug Ray and Ajak had given her to keep the Doshara from emerging and killing them during the kidnapping. The princess stumbled and fell backwards into the shallow lake water, the sound deafening.

Ray jumped across the boat and reached her hands under the princess's armpits, dragging her to the shore. The princess kicked and flailed weakly against Ray's grip, but she maintained her hold. Water soaked into Ray's clothes, chilling her to the bone.

"Come on, stop struggling," Ray muttered through gritted teeth. "You're just getting us wet, and we need to *move.*"

The princess slowed her thrashing and allowed Ray to stand her up on her feet. She swayed from side to side as she tried to reorient herself. "You shouldn't know about him," Niamnh said.

Him?

Once the princess felt stable, Ray took her hands off of her. The princess took one step back and looked up at Ray. They were about the same height now that Ray realized it.

"Don't you want to get rid of that demonic *thing*?" Surely the princess hated sharing her body and mind with a bloodthirsty spirit. *She should be thankful, glad even, for me taking her to Na'roc of North—*

The princess was the first to avert her eyes, her shoulders shivering.

"There should be supplies around here somewhere." Ray turned and began inspecting their surroundings. They had landed on a small strip of land that was clear of rocks and debris. The forest began not too far from where they were standing. The trees were sharp, pointed, and plentiful. She had only seen forests like those from a distance.

Fishing a now-soaked map from her shirt, she peeled it open and tried to read it by moonlight. The map belonged to Wendelgar. Ray found it on his person when she'd finally dared uncurl from the bottom of the boat and look around. On one side of the parchment was a map of the lakes with a dotted path leading to a spot on the northern shore, and on the reverse side were written instructions on how to find the supply cache.

Although she had never left Auora before, Naro had taught her how to read maps. She had quite a few fond memories of staying up late with him in his room, poring over maps of Daaria.

After landing, head northwest into the forest. Forty paces inside the tree line will be a stone marker with an arrow painted on it.

Wendelgar also had a compass on him, which she had used to guide the boat north. She pulled that out from her clothes and held it up, searching for "northwest".

She beckoned to the princess. "There're supplies not too far from here. We'll change and keep moving."

The princess was looking down at the boat again. At Wendelgar's corpse. Another lump formed in Ray's throat. They should do something about the body.

What would Ajak and Naro do?

Ray grimaced and stepped back into the boat to rifle through Wendelgar's belongings one last time. Besides the map and compass, he didn't have much else on him. His clothing was still relatively dry, despite the bloodstains. It was drier than what the two girls were wearing, anyway. There was a small coin purse tucked away in his shirt, and a small knife in his boot. She pocketed the knife and gave him one more look over. If she could get the arrow out of his back, she could take his coat. She tried pulling the arrow from his back, but she struggled with it and only ended up tearing at his skin and clothes. Rather than waste more time and damage his body further, she decided to focus on getting rid of any evidence that they had landed here.

"Help me push this boat back into the water," Ray called over her shoulder, although she doubted the princess would come to assist. She braced herself against the boat and pushed. Ray wondered if she would have the strength to finish the job on her own.

To her surprise, the princess abided and stood on the other side of the boat. She wasn't using the best form, and her movements were still heavy and sluggish, but she was genuinely trying to help. Soon the boat was floating back into the lake. Ray sent up a silent prayer to the Protector for Wendelgar as she waded back to shore.

"...Protector guide his path," the princess murmured under her breath.

Ray cast a curious glance over her shoulder as she heard the words. The two made eye contact and Ray quickly averted her gaze.

After landing, head northwest into the forest.

"Come on, we need to go northwest." Ray whipped out the compass and began walking in the specified direction.

The princess followed behind, and when Ray cast a few glances over her shoulder, she noticed the girl had her arms wrapped around herself to try to control her shivering. They needed to change clothes soon. Even with the oncoming dawn, the land was very cold. Their destination would be even colder.

As they climbed the rocks up to the tree line, sunslight began to stretch across the sky in earnest. The darkness of the forest beckoned to them. The king's men would soon be scouring every corner of Promthus looking for the princess. They needed to be deep in the woods and heading north as soon as possible. Ray looked back at the girl behind her again. How much trouble would the princess cause during their journey? Would she try to stall, giving her knights time to catch up to them?

Or is she simply biding her time until the Doshara can resurface inside her and attack me? Protector above, I hope Naro's elixir keeps that thing locked up for as long as possible.

They passed the first few trees and entered the forest proper. Pushing her grim thoughts aside, Ray began counting her footsteps, changing the length of her stride to better match Naro's or Ajak's.

"What are you doing?" the princess asked.

Ray had reached thirteen paces. She paused and tossed an answer back over her shoulder. "Counting, if you don't mind, Your Highness." Ray waited a moment to give the princess time to respond, and when she didn't, she resumed her count at fourteen.

Forty paces into the woods was nothing special. The instructions mentioned a stone marker with an arrow painted on it. She strained her eyes searching the forest floor for the stone.

"Come stand right here," Ray said, beckoning to the princess.

The princess obliged and stood next to Ray without question. Ray's eyes narrowed, and she threw a curious look Niamnh's way, but let it slide. She couldn't afford to distract herself with the princess's puzzling behavior; she had to find the supply cache.

"I'll be right back." Ray turned around and went back to the beach, holding the instructions up in the air.

She tried to decipher the writing with the fading moonlight, but it only made her eyes hurt. She would need to light a torch if she wanted to see better. It took her a few moments to find a suitable stick and rock, but soon she was disappearing back into the woods, surrounded by warm firelight. If anyone had been on the lake, they may have caught a brief glimpse of flames as she disappeared behind some trees, but by the time they would have landed, she hoped to be long gone.

The princess was still standing in place when Ray returned, which twisted Ray's stomach for a reason that didn't make much sense to her. "You didn't try running away?"

The princess shrugged, the light of the torch casting a shadow over her face. She looked tired, her words bitter. "Where would I go? Even though you slayed my Sworn Sword and captured me, you're my only hope of survival out here."

Ray frowned, her lips parting, but no words came to her. *Ajak didn't kill the knight. He wouldn't have. But it* is *true, we did kidnap her. I'm now responsible for the safety of us both. But how safe am I with the Doshara inhabiting the princess's body?* Her eyes darted back to the forest floor, desperate to think of anything else. She hunted for the marked stone and found it only a few paces away from where she and the princess were standing. It had a dark arrow painted on it, the color worn down and faded with time. The arrow pointed to her right. She looked back at her instructions.

Though the arrow points east, go north instead. Walk thirty paces, then turn west and walk thirty more.

Ray tucked the instructions into her shirt and fished out the compass again to confirm her directions. The torchlight flickered across its surface. Its heat was a welcome improvement in the cold forest, though it did make her realize just how heavy and uncomfortable her soaked clothes were. Her feet squished around in her boots, much to her chagrin.

She oriented herself and began counting the thirty paces north. Princess Niamnh fell in step behind her, like a living shadow. Slivers of sunslight began to creep into the forest as they traversed further inland. The trees grew denser, and she had to squeeze through a few particularly narrow gaps in order to progress. Soon she was turning west and counting another thirty steps, which put her directly at the base of a rather large grove of trees.

Circle to the fourth tree on the right and reach for a large branch. Climb up past three more large branches, and the safehouse ladder will be nailed into the bark.

Doubt wriggled into her mind as she circled the cluster. She wondered if the ladder would truly be on the fourth tree to the right, or if she would have to climb a few trees before finding it. Naro wasn't the kind to write puzzling instructions or riddles, so she had to hope his words were true.

"I'm going to climb up and find a way into this safehouse. Hold this torch up high so I can see where I'm going," Ray said to the princess with false confidence. She handed the torch to her, then tucked the map away into her shirt. Ray reached up and grabbed hold of a rather large branch, and hoisted herself up into the tree.

If she ignored her surroundings, it was vaguely reminiscent of the tunnel that went from the Gutters to the Crafting District back in Auora. Not nearly as tall, though, which was a blessing. She was careful about which branches she took hold of and put her weight on. Eventually she did find the "ladder" Naro described in his instructions, though it wasn't much of a real ladder. Planks of wood had been nailed into the tree trunk, leading farther up into the foliage and branches. Her thoughts shifted to a series of questions about how feasible it had been to build a safehouse in the trees.

After twenty or thirty planks, her hand painfully slapped against the bottom of a wooden landing. She cursed under her breath and shook her hand to try to get rid of the pain. "Found it," she called down to the princess on the ground.

"How am I supposed to find it?" the princess responded.

Ray cursed again. She would have to go back down and talk the princess through the climb. *I should check it out first anyway because what if it's in shambles? Or have some wild animals turned it into their nest?* They would also have to put out the torch. Before she went back down, perhaps she could find a small torch or lamp that she could light inside of the safehouse.

She instinctively reached for one of her knives, but none were at her sides. She panicked for a moment thinking herself unarmed but then recalled she had slipped Wendelgar's knife into her boot.

"Let me check it out first, then I'll come back down and show you up," Ray finally answered.

Knowing about the landing this time, she was careful to grab onto the edge and pull herself up. She got to her feet as quickly as possible, pulling the knife from her boot. By the Protector's mercy, she could just barely make out the frame of the safehouse in the light of the rising suns. She was standing on a small ledge with a door frame in front of her. There was no traditional door standing there. Instead, there was a rather large, tattered cloth hanging from the threshold. She held the knife steady and pushed her way through the curtain. The inside was just as dark as the outside, but she didn't hear any growling or other animalistic sounds.

She relaxed a little and started to look around the room. The floors seemed solid and complete. There were four walls, and the only opening that she could see was through the tattered cloth. Her legs bumped against several objects as she made her way around the space. There was enough room for what she assumed were four small beds and a few crates and barrels. Everything appeared good enough for Ray at first glance. There were no lamps or candles lying around on any of the surfaces in the shelter. She assumed there were some in the various containers, but she couldn't see well enough to dig through those. She needed to find some way to get light, but that would have to come after helping the princess up.

She took her time returning to the forest floor, carefully climbing back down the tree. Princess Niamnh looked so small and frail in the torchlight, her white hair clinging to her dark cheeks. The kitchen maid's dress was so large on her that she looked like a small child playing dress-up. Ray beckoned the princess over and reached out for the torch, which the princess handed to her.

"Look up. Grab this tree branch and then climb up four more branches. You should see or feel some planks nailed to the tree. Climb up that, and you'll hit the underside of a ledge," Ray instructed. Alarm flashed across the princess's face. "What, can't climb?" Ray guffawed. *Who doesn't know how to climb?*

The princess frowned and turned toward the tree, jumping to grab at the sturdy branch. Ray was impressed by her boldness but realized almost immediately that she would need help. She dropped the torch to the ground and ran over to help the princess up. Once she was in the tree, Ray turned her attention back to the torch, which had caught some of the surrounding brush on fire. She stamped on the torch and the small surrounding flames before they could spread any further.

Ray couldn't just leave the extinguished torch on the ground. It would give away the safehouse's location. The burned foliage would also be a clue, but there was little she could do about it beyond ripping up other grass and throwing it on top. Too much effort for something that could so easily backfire. She settled for picking up the torch and finding another way to get rid of it. Sliding the still warm torch into her belt, she quickly followed the princess up the tree.

The second climb was easy enough, even with having to call out instructions and words of confidence to the princess. Soon they entered the safehouse as the suns poked through the foliage in earnest.

Maybe I don't need the torch after all.

There were indeed four beds and a plethora of crates and barrels in the safehouse. "There should be clothes in one of these containers. Help me look," Ray said as she pulled the extinguished torch from her belt and set it down on one of the crates. She opened the crate to her right, kicking up a thin layer of dust—much less dust than she expected. *How recently was this stuff put here?* Inside were traveling supplies like bedrolls and cooking utensils. She continued her search, finding more gear like snowshoes and weapons.

"I think these... we could use these?" the princess mumbled.

Ray turned around and looked inside the crate the princess was kneeling in front of. Sure enough there were fur coats, thick cloaks, and an abundance of winter clothing. The first shirt she pulled out was too large for her, but it would have been a perfect fit for Ajak or Naro.

A knot formed in her throat, and she had to choke down a sob. Weariness had put her off-guard. She needed to rest. "Y-Yeah, there should be something in there that'll fit." Ray's voice was barely above a whisper.

Mercifully, the princess didn't question or acknowledge her moment of weakness. The other girl continued digging through the clothes then looked back up at Ray. "All of these supplies... These are all here because of your plan to kidnap me?"

Ray nodded before she could stop herself.

"I see," the princess murmured. She sifted through the clothes, and eventually gathered a shirt, pair of pants, and underclothes. She stood then hesitated. Before Ray could speak, she turned her head back toward her. "Please don't look."

Ray wasn't sure how to respond. *Of course not, Your Highness.* Or maybe, *why would I do that?* None of her responses seemed adequate, though, so she just kept staring into the crate of clothing in front of her.

Once the princess finished changing and settled down on one of the beds, it was Ray's turn to feel some degree of shame and awkwardness as she undressed and redressed, something she hadn't felt since before she joined the Walkers. The new clothes felt nice on her skin, and she appreciated how *dry* they were. She returned to the crate with the bedrolls. Ray handed one to the princess before rolling out a second one on a bed. They would pack them up and take them after they slept.

"We'll get some sleep and then be on our way later in the day." The princess didn't respond as she crawled into her bedroll. Ray frowned. "You're not going to run away while I sleep, are you?"

"No," came the immediate reply. Another silent moment passed before Princess Niamnh added, "Not tonight, at least."

Ray was oddly comforted by those words. The princess had to be speaking at least a lick of truth because surely the thought of escape had crossed her mind. But after being drugged, nearly falling into the freezing lakes, and disappearing into a mysterious forest, tonight would not be the night to try to escape. Ray could understand; she would be thinking the same thing if their roles were reversed.

As Ray settled back into her bedroll, she realized she held one of the larger shirts in her hand. She imagined that it would have gone to Ajak had he been there. She didn't fight the tears that welled up in her eyes. She just held the shirt up to her face to muffle her quiet sobs until she fell asleep.

When Ray awoke later in the day, the first thing she saw was Princess Niamnh sitting up and staring at her hands. Wind rustled through the branches outside the treehouse. Ray looked around the room and picked out small details in the sunslight. Each of the four beds stood at different heights and were carved from different types of wood with nothing but simple mattresses on them. A couple of longbows leaned against one stack of crates. Large bundles of rope were coiled and resting atop a barrel.

As soon as Ray got out of bed, she knew she would need to start sifting through the crates and barrels to prepare their travel packs. She didn't know how long they had slept, but a gnawing fear crept into her mind—had they slept too long? Had it been a mistake to rest even for a short while? With the war going on to the south, surely the king's men would prioritize searching the southern shores of the Hourglass Lakes. They wouldn't turn their attention north any time soon. Ray had time to get the princess to Na'roc of North before then. But who knew about their escape? Who shot Wendelgar?

"I still can't feel him," the princess said softly.

If it weren't for the adrenaline coursing through her veins and heightening her senses, Ray would have missed her words entirely. "The Doshara?"

The princess nodded. She glanced over at Ray, and then slid her hands back into her bedroll, looking away almost immediately.

Is she ashamed of something? Brushing aside her confusion, Ray worked her way out of the bedroll and to her feet. "We need to get moving. We'll pack up what we need and then move along." They would have to be considerate of how much they packed. They still had to climb back down the tree. She rolled up her bedroll and then returned to the first crate from earlier with four large backpacks inside.

Meant for her, the princess, Ajak, and Naro.

She focused on how sturdy the leather felt between her fingers as she pulled out two of the four backpacks. Half of the cooking utensils followed. She felt the cold, hard iron pots as she pulled each one from the crate. She nearly got a splinter from the rough wooden handles of the spoons and knives.

Another crate contained the smaller items like waterskins, tinderboxes, a couple of rolled-up parchments, and a peculiar compass box. Ray recognized it as Naro's. She had seen him fiddling with both the box and compass in his office on numerous occasions over the years. She lifted it from the crate, her fingers caressing the top and opening it with the utmost care. The box itself was carved out of a special kind of tree that grew near the Black Lakes. He had told her the name before, but the memory had faded away. The wood was an ashen gray color. He had never painted the outside of the box. *To honor the wood itself*, he had said once. The inside was full of color, small cracks running through the paint indicating the age of the trinket. The compass lay atop a mural of the night sky. On the opposite side was a bright singular sun painted with golds, oranges, and reds. A ring of white glyphs circled the sun, and she idly wondered what language it was written in. It didn't look like any writing she had seen before.

How long has this box belonged to Naro? Did it have a history before him?

The compass itself was made from brass and hung from a matching chain. Its cover was actually a sunsdial, making it a means of telling time as well as direction. Ray plucked the compass from its box to get a closer look at its face.

An off-white color caught her eye. A piece of parchment was tucked underneath the compass. Ray lifted the compass slightly and plucked the parchment free, returning the compass to its rightful place inside of the box. She set the box on the floor before turning her attention to the parchment. It had been folded several times into a small square. Inside was Naro's neat handwriting.

There has been a change of plans, as you are already aware. Travel east for two days. On the third day you should cross the River Thuala. Another four days after that, the forest will thin, and you will be in Na'roc of North.

If you can see the Wall, turn north and travel until it is out of sight. Only then should you turn east again. Travel east until you find their villages, or they find you.

Ray read the last sentence again twice.

Or they find you.

Echoes of her mother's warnings and bedtime stories filled her head. *If the cold don't get ya, they will.*

Naro and her mother were referring to the Enthai, fierce creatures covered in thick fur with claws for fingers and teeth as sharp as the sharpest knife. Creatures infamous for hunting down any Proma who entered their lands, slaying men and women alike. It was whispered in the streets of Auora that Prince Robyn was slain by the Enthai when he traveled beyond the Wall two years ago. Ray had even heard a tale or two about how the Enthai would even eat small children who wandered beyond the Wall. And now she was willingly and intentionally entering their lands, seeking their help.

Or they find you.

Another more recent and pleasant memory wriggled its way to the front of her mind. Naro had promised that as long as she bore the mark of the Walkers, the Enthai wouldn't kill her. All of the clothes in the safehouse had the blue handprint and lidless eye painted on them. She clung to the hope that the mark would ensure her safety. She had to.

"What can I do to help?" The princess's voice cut through Ray's foggy memories, bringing her back to the treehouse.

Without turning, Ray gave the command over her shoulder, "Make sure your bedroll is rolled up and tied tight. Then finish putting on your gear. There are coats in this other crate."

The princess didn't respond, but Ray heard her shuffling around. She shrugged away the remaining fog in her head and went about sorting through the supply crates and filling their backpacks.

Although she didn't speak much, the princess was actually quite helpful with the packing. Ray was surprised that she didn't have to order the princess about or prod her into moving. It was certainly helpful since they needed to depart as soon as they were able, but in the back of Ray's mind, a tiny bit of doubt burrowed into her thoughts.

She must be working with the Doshara to plot a way to get rid of me.

Naro had ensured the treehouse was loaded with everything they could possibly need, including longbows for hunting and a few knives. Soon there was only one unopened crate remaining. Ray opened it, and the only thing inside was a large satchel with a piece of parchment on top. More instructions from Naro, no doubt. She pulled the parchment out and once again felt herself slipping into a comfortable fog of memories as she stared at his handwriting, but the contents of the letter sent a shiver down her spine.

Ingredients for the princess's elixir. Handcuffs for when you make camp. Do not take any chances. She must be brought to the Enthai.

Past the parchment were a few smaller cloth pouches in the satchel. Ray was certain they were the same ingredients she saw Naro mixing when he made the sleeper elixir back in Auora.

How long are these elixirs supposed to last? Has the Doshara already reemerged? How will I know? Will I have any warning?

"What's that?" Princess Niamnh asked.

Ray resisted the urge to jump out of her skin, instead managing to calmly remove the satchel from the crate and sling it over her shoulder. She tucked the parchment into the satchel as she stood, knowing she would need to burn it so the princess couldn't read it. She would also need to prepare another elixir the next time they made camp. Perhaps she could play it off as tea.

"Just some stuff from the city. Silly things the boss didn't want to travel without." She hesitated for a moment before blurting out, "Y'know, teas and soaps. Fancy things."

"That sounds pleasant," the princess murmured. Something akin to hope or happiness flickered across her face.

Ray thanked the Protector. "Yeah, well, um it's time we head out. Long journey ahead of us."

She looked around the safehouse one last time, ensuring they had gone through every crate and barrel. The princess had found the crates with traveling rations, rope, and other supplies. It seemed like they had been through everything. She looked at the princess and felt a crushing wave of nausea and fear. Although the princess was now dressed in thick sturdy traveling clothes, she was still royalty, a prim and proper princess. Ray had to escort her across northern Promthus and into Na'roc of North. It wasn't going to be a pleasant escort, more akin to transporting a prisoner. And who was the true prisoner—Princess Niamnh or the Doshara inside of her?

Ray stepped out onto the ledge overlooking the forest, eager to get started on their journey. It would be a pain to try to climb down with all of the supplies. Ray decided to use the rope to lower it all down, which didn't take too long because they only used the rope for the heavy and awkwardly shaped things. Soon they climbed back down the tree, the daylight making it easier to see the planks nailed to the trunk. The princess was quiet, just like the day before, but at least she kept up with Ray as best as she could. Once they were at the bottom of the tree, they picked up the backpacks.

They each carried a heavy backpack, bedroll, and an assortment of smaller pouches and satchels. Ray patted her sides for the two knives she strapped on before picking the hunting bow up off the ground. She had a quiver of maybe twenty arrows, so it would be imperative that she retrieve every arrow she shot. She felt another wave of fear rising up and reached for Naro's compass and opened it, focusing intently on the needle.

She repeated his words in her head, *"Travel east for two days."*

Following the needle, she began walking east.

CHAPTER IV: RAY

The first day's journey went better than expected but not nearly as good as Ray had hoped. Their pace was slow; it couldn't be helped. Ray was unfamiliar with this land, and Princess Niamnh had never walked so much in her life. When they settled down for the night, Ray felt antsy and on edge, but they had to rest. The princess had to rest.

The two found a small clearing before the suns had completely set. Setting up camp didn't take much time at all. They worked together to get a fire going. Afterward, Ray had the princess set up their bedrolls and prepare a package of rations while she made "tea". When Ray mentioned she was brewing some, the princess didn't react with the same enthusiasm as she had that morning. Perhaps she just wanted to get to sleep and rest her bones.

A relatable feeling.

What about the handcuffs? Those sat in the satchel to Ray's right. She kept wondering how she would convince the princess to put them on. *It's for your own good, Your Highness.* No, it was for *Ray's* own good.

The princess had been silent for most of the day, which Ray assumed was going to be a normal occurrence. About an hour before the suns had set, the princess started acting a little strange, stranger than Ray had seen thus far, anyway. The princess began glancing around and tilting her head to the side. It made Ray's skin crawl, and she made sure to stay out of arm's reach from her in case it was the Doshara lurking beneath. Or was the princess listening for knights and soldiers to come crashing through the underbrush and rescue her? The king had surely deployed men to find her, but they would be searching the city first or boarding ships. Their first instincts would be to look south, not north. They'd want to blame the Provira for the abduction.

The fire grew steadily as Ray fed it more twigs. They would need its warmth overnight. The princess handed her the ration package. Inside was dried salted fish, dried fruits, and tack biscuits. Ray split the food between the two of them then started gnawing on a biscuit. There were enough rations to last at least ten days, and they needed to travel as quickly as possible over the next few days. Hunting would have to wait until they got closer to Na'roc of North.

Ray let the tea steep for several minutes before handing the mug over to the princess, who had sat down on her bedroll.

"Thank you," Niamnh murmured, wrapping both hands around the mug and raising it to her lips.

They sat in silence for the duration of their meal. The biscuits were terrible, but the fruit and fish were alright. Ray watched the fire crackle and burn, allowing herself to be lulled into a sense of comfort. Around her the wind whispered among the trees, stirring the leaves into a quiet dance. Movement flickered on the edge of her vision, but she assumed it was a tree swaying, or some bugs flitting about.

"What do you hope to see in the flames?" the princess asked softly, but her voice sounded different. Wrong. The pitch was too low, the tone too gravelly. It sounded like she was recovering from a nasty cold, but she had sounded fine just moments ago.

Ray snapped her head up and looked across the fire. *What's going on with the princess?* The princess's bedroll was empty, but there was movement to her left—

"Or perhaps the light just draws you in, like a moth, and blinds you to everything else." Niamnh crouched down beside her, leaning in ever so slightly. Strands of white hair hung in front of her face like a tattered curtain.

Ray threw her body to her right out of instinct, partially to put space between her and the princess and because she had been scared out of her skin at how quickly and silently the princess had moved.

Why's she sound like that? Was the biscuit that dry?

Ray turned and met the princess's gray eyes, and she was shocked by the sudden realization that she wasn't looking at Princess Niamnh; she was looking at the Doshara wearing the princess's skin. Those gray eyes hardened, sharp and cold as steel, brimming with malice.

The gray eyes widened for a moment, eyebrows arching in amusement. "Hello, little moth." A crooked grin split across its mouth, teeth practically glowing against dusky skin.

"H-hello," Ray mumbled, trying to regain her composure.

The Doshara tilted its head to the side. "It's a pleasure to speak with you, Walker. Although it's a shame your lord isn't here with you."

Ray's body twitched involuntarily, a bolt of panic racing down her spine. *It knows about me? About Naro?* "I-I don't know wh-what you mean."

"Don't worry, little moth. It's just you and me talking right now. No other company." It sat up straight, then threw its arms forward and leaned in close. "And I know all about your lord's rules. About not giving away your identity. Who you belong to. But I know that compass you carry."

Ray couldn't stop her brow from furrowing, but after a split second, she forced herself back into a neutral expression. She struggled to decide if it would be better to be honest or continue denying the truth that they both clearly knew. It also left an uneasy feeling in her stomach, hearing the Doshara refer to just the two of them.

What happened to the princess?

The smile slipped from the Doshara's face. "If I wanted you dead, I would have already drawn out your last breath. So, play along. It'll be better for you this way."

As she studied the Doshara, her blood ran cold. The warmth had drained from the princess's face, her skin appearing more gray than brown in the firelight. The Doshara held the princess's body in a rigid pose, her back straight, her chin tilted just slightly to the right, so the campfire illuminated her gray eyes, like flames caressing steel.

All of Ray's fears and worries over the past few days had culminated in that moment. She knew it spoke the truth. Every inhale and exhale were precious gifts it was affording her. But she had given the princess the elixir moments earlier, which was supposed to suppress the Doshara inside of her.

Can I bide my time until it goes away? Or is it possible that the elixir didn't work? "What do you want?" Ray managed to ask without stuttering.

"I want to give you one chance to save your skin. Tell me where to find Naro."

Ray's eyes wandered over the princess's form, watching to see when the elixir would start to kick in. She knew the princess would go limp, perhaps even pass out. She just had to stall for time. "What do you want with him?"

The Doshara laughed, and Ray hoped to never hear the noise again. It was a hoarse, scratchy sound that made her skin crawl. "It's a visit that's long overdue."

"But why? How do you even know about him?"

With jerky, unnatural movements, the Doshara crawled toward Ray on hands and knees. Its steely eyes shone with hunger. Ray caught how its right arm moved slower than its left. The elixir's work?

"I don't like all of these questions, little moth."

Ray leaned back on her arms, prepared to shuffle backward if the Doshara got too close. Perhaps even kick it to keep it away. She also had her daggers, but she didn't want to risk hurting the princess. "If you know the rules, then you know why I'm asking these questions."

The Doshara stopped and nodded thoughtfully, the corner of its mouth tugging upward into another small smile. "Clever, little Walker."

Biding my time. Keep it up. Ray felt her chest collapse under her exhale, her body relaxing just a bit. She opened her mouth to repeat her questions in a more assertive tone. "So, how do you—"

The Doshara was on her in an instant, pinning her to the ground underneath its weight. Too fast for the elixir to actually be working. As she hit the ground, the breath was knocked out of her. An arm pressed against her throat, and she struggled to breathe in. She threw her hands up to claw at the arm when she felt the kiss of cold metal against her cheek. The tip of a dagger—*her* dagger—touched the corner of her right eye.

How did it get my dagger? And why isn't the elixir working?!

The Doshara glared down at her, hunger twisting to malice in its eyes. "One last chance. Tell me where he is, how to get to him, or I'll pluck your eye from your head and make you watch as I eat it."

Ray's mind raced too fast for her to fully process any thoughts. It was very possible, nearly *guaranteed*, that she would die here if she didn't produce a satisfactory answer for the Doshara. Even if she spoke the truth, would it listen to her? It's not like Naro was an easy person to track down, even with her intimate knowledge of the Walkers' safehouses. She wasn't sure if he would even be in the city after the kidnapping. Something else had been going on the night he sent Ajak and Ray into the castle, and she didn't know what the fallout had been. But she had to say *something*, so that she didn't get tortured, eaten, or *killed*.

"H-he's supposed to meet me," Ray choked out, trying to keep her head very still. She gripped onto the Doshara's arm with all of her strength, her own arms shaking from the exertion.

The Doshara let out a quiet hiss, pressing the dagger down further onto her cheek until it broke through the skin. She felt the hot bubble of blood as it welled up underneath the blade and slid down her cheek. Even though the blade was sharp, the prick was excruciatingly painful. She clenched her teeth and tried not to squint. The dagger lifted away from her cheek and the Doshara's arm eased off of her neck, allowing her to suck in a breath of air.

"Where and when?" the Doshara demanded.

"Th-that's the whole p-point of this," Ray responded, her voice hoarse and wavering. "On the edge of the t-tundra. He's gonna meet me and help g-get rid of you." It was a risky endeavor, bluffing to the Doshara like that. Pretending that Naro would be there, waiting for them in Na'roc of North. It was, perhaps, even more dangerous to say that Naro would play a part in getting rid of the Doshara.

But what choice do I have?

Another hoarse chuckle fell from the Doshara's lips. "What a stupid, foolish plan. You expect me to believe that?"

For a brief moment Ray was worried that it wouldn't believe her, but the dagger didn't return to her face. Emboldened, Ray retorted, "You say you know Naro. If you *really* knew him, you'd know I'm not lying."

The Doshara fell silent as it studied Ray. She felt like her skin was being peeled off underneath its gaze, and she wanted nothing more than to crawl underneath a bush and hide. Thoughts and questions continued to swirl about in her mind, which she knew better than to vocalize.

How does the Doshara know Naro? How did it recognize the compass? What happened to Princess Niamnh? Am I only prolonging my inevitable death?

"You'll lead me to him, little moth," the Doshara croaked, its words slurred. It stumbled and caught itself as it climbed to its feet. The dagger fell from its hand and landed next to her leg. The elixir was *finally* kicking in. "Lead me to him, and I'll let you fly free."

Ray stayed on the ground, looking up at the Doshara as it walked over to the princess's bedroll and laid down. For several moments, the only noises she heard were the fire crackling and her own breathing. When Ray felt like she had mastery over her limbs again, she sat up and collected her dagger, returning it to its empty sheath. Across the campfire was the princess, sleeping soundly.

The handcuffs.

Ray fetched them from her bag, careful not to make too much noise. With great care, she picked up the princess's wrists and secured the handcuffs, letting her hands rest on her stomach. The princess didn't stir, which brought much comfort to Ray.

Over the course of the next hour, Ray washed the blood from her cheek, massaged her tender neck, and finished her dinner. Bruises would no doubt color her skin for the next few days, but she was otherwise uninjured. The biscuit tasted a little better this time. She washed it down with water from her waterskin.

Princess Niamnh stirred toward the end of that hour. She rolled onto her side and pulled her knees to her chest. Every so often Ray could hear her sniffling, an obvious sign that she was waking up. Her dinner lay scattered across her bedroll and the ground, long forgotten.

Did she even touch her food?

"Oh, I must've fallen asleep…" Princess Niamnh mumbled as she sat up and rubbed her eyes. "How late is it?"

A frown passed over Ray's face. "It's only been about an hour or so."

The princess looked around her bedroll, noticing the scattered food scraps, and she started to gather them up. "I don't remember this…"

"What do you mean?" Ray asked, the Doshara's words lingering in her head. *It's just you and me. No other company.*

The princess shook her head. "I must've fallen asleep after drinking that tea. Is it a blend for aiding sleep?"

She doesn't know that the Doshara emerged. That, or she's faking it, but why would she do that?

Ray stood and plucked the biscuit from near the princess's bedroll. She gently poked the princess's shoulder, offering her the food. "You should eat."

Princess Niamnh didn't bother to take the biscuit. "I can't."

Ray frowned. "You haven't eaten anything all day. You'll need your strength for tomor—"

"No, I *can't*." The princess raised her chin, so Ray was looking into her gray eyes. All traces of steel and murder were gone; the princess was in control of herself again. "Because of *him*, it's not possible for me to eat."

"Well, that doesn't make sense. What keeps you going, then?" Ray asked, then regretted it almost immediately.

Gruesome tales from her childhood flooded into her head. Dosharas turned men into blood-frenzied maniacs. They killed and ate anyone near them. More recent memories of her time in the castle kitchens bubbled to the surface. That one woman—Jayne?—had told her and Ajak that the princess only ate raw flesh. And lest she forget that the Doshara had threatened to eat her eyeball only an hour ago. She had been lucky that the elixir had incapacitated the princess's Doshara when it did.

Ray must have made a face because Princess Niamnh averted her gaze and responded without directly answering the question. "I'm... not hungry now. Not yet. But tomorrow night I will need something."

"I'll have to hunt," Ray mumbled more to herself than to the princess who nodded anyway. *I'll have to hunt if I don't want to get eaten,* she thought.

The fire continued to burn steadily, warming their small camp. They didn't exchange any other words that evening, and eventually Ray tucked herself into her bedroll. She stared at the fire and let it lull her to sleep, her mind churning with thoughts of the Doshara, Naro, and the princess.

She wished Ajak were here to help.

CHAPTER V: MUNNE

Munne and the guards arrested the woman with the javelin. They brought her back to the castle and kept her in a cell toward the bottom of the massive structure. Two guards questioned her later that afternoon, and Munne convinced them to let her listen in. The woman opened up easily enough, not worried about hiding any plans she and her gang members had concocted.

"We're gonna tear the city apart piece by piece until Naro has nowhere left to hide," the woman promised.

The guards are hanging onto her every word—this can't be a coincidence. Does this Naro fellow have something to do with the princess or the Provira? Munne thought as the woman continued her rantings. She slipped out of the questioning room and made her way to the council room. She didn't know if anyone would be present, but she needed to talk to *someone.*

The council room was empty, but a passing steward paused and asked, "My lady, are you in need of assistance?"

Munne nodded. "Where is Lord Rhorek?"

"I believe he's in his chambers eating dinner," the steward replied. "Would you like for me to escort you there?"

Munne nodded again, and they set off on another winding journey throughout the castle. Rhorek was indeed in his chambers enjoying a meal with his family. He excused himself from the table, and they moved to a small study deeper in his chambers.

"How can I help you, my lady?" he asked.

"Who is 'Naro'?" Munne replied.

Rhorek frowned and stayed silent for a moment. "He's a gang lord and has been a thorn in our sides for many years. Where did you hear about him?"

"We arrested a woman in the streets today for attacking the guards. She claims there's a new gang that's out to get Naro, and that's why there's chaos in the streets."

"I see... That's troubling indeed. And the timing couldn't be worse with the princess's disappearance."

Munne crossed her arms. "I don't think these two events are unrelated. Something else is going on, but we don't have all of the information."

"Historically speaking, the gangs have never tried attacking the royal family or infiltrating the castle. They seemed content to stay within the city instead... But there was a commotion in the Sky District about a week ago when the princess visited her seamstress." He rubbed a hand against his chin, eyes darkening. "Protector's grace, you might be right. I'll gather a report from the prison guards later and determine what to do with that woman."

Munne nodded. A nagging thought tugged at the back of her mind, and she knew she had to voice it. "I have a sinking suspicion that the Provira are involved in this."

Rhorek met her gaze, his expression grim. "Dire news if your hunch is correct. Within our own home..." He trailed off, eyes flickering back to the floor.

She knew his mind was drifting back to the meeting of the Daarian Council back in Elimere, where her father Huntaran had told the council that he planned on parlaying with the Provira rather than renew the fight at the border. If the Provira had found a way to sneak past the frontlines and throw Auora into chaos, the Proma knight-general would be forced to focus on protecting his home rather than bolster the border.

They stood in silence for a little while longer, giving the theory time to bloom within Munne's mind. As more time passed, the more she became convinced that the Provira were behind the gang revolts, and perhaps the kidnapping as well.

What better way to cripple your enemy than from within?

Over the next two days Munne spent almost all her time patrolling the city. She helped extinguish fires, escorted citizens to safety, and listened for any rumors on the streets. She left the castle before sunrise and took her midday and evening meals at the inns. Floating between tables with her tankard of ale, she posed questions to citizens and guards alike about the various street gangs and the general population's opinions of them.

"Drug traffickers, the lot of them," one guard snarled over a plate of fish and vegetables.

"Some of them mean well enough, others're nothin' but trouble," a woodworker mumbled around a mouthful of bread.

Others murmured apologies and excused themselves from her company. It seemed that some of the people were sympathetic to the gangs' plights and wouldn't divulge their true thoughts to her. She heard rumblings about a couple of named groups like the Disciples and the Iron Hawks. No one mentioned the name Naro.

As she broke bread with the residents of Auora, she found herself glancing around for the caravan leader's green and white eyes, hoping that he had made it safely into the city. She didn't know *when* she'd be able to pull herself away from the city's struggles, but she needed to know she had a path forward. *Ely can only protect me from the* Ardashi'ik *for so long.*

Out in the streets there were no further attacks on the guards, but there were more fires to put out. Barrels of water were sent out every hour and smoke hung heavily over the city. Screams were replaced with coughing fits. Munne found herself coughing as she traversed the streets. Even when she returned to the castle late at night, she still couldn't get the ash out of her lungs.

Because she left so early in the mornings and returned so late in the evenings, she didn't cross paths with the other ambassadors within the castle. It was better for her conscience that way. The less she gazed upon Eldo Talltree, the less guilt she felt for disobeying her father's orders and plotting her escape to Kherizhan.

Ely didn't return to her dreams those two nights, which made her stomach squeeze with an emotion she hadn't felt since she was younger and taken with Laralos, her childhood sweetheart. *I miss Ely*, she realized, feeling rather silly for missing a shapeshifting stranger who she could only see when she was sleeping. Though he hadn't made an appearance the past two nights, he did ensure that she wasn't plagued with any nightmares. His handprints lingered on her skin as well, which she drew comfort from.

She wrote another letter and delivered it to the rookery, which would in turn be sent to Elimaine to muster more troops. Though they wouldn't arrive for several weeks, she knew Auora would need assistance in rebuilding what had been destroyed in these riots.

On her fifth morning in Auora, Munne was invited to break her fast with Rhorek and his family in their chambers. His wife Margwen and his daughter Sharanna were in attendance, so their conversations stayed cordial and avoided any discussion about war or the gangs.

"I've been meaning to take my lady wife and daughter to Elimere to visit," Rhorek said in between bites of potatoes. "Although perhaps we'll wait until the spring thaw."

Margwen smiled politely at Munne. "Rhorek has told us wonderful stories about your city's festivals. I think it would be lovely to attend one."

"The valley is a sight to behold, no doubt," Munne agreed. "Although, would it not be a swifter journey to Lithalyon? You could visit any time of the year, and the great tree of Aelrindel is a sight to behold."

Margwen's smile faltered and Rhorek shook his head. "Elimere would be a safer journey," he stated.

Munne understood the implications and spoke no more of the Elviri city to the south. "*Tessalothe* is an enjoyable festival over the summer months. We dedicate seven days to honoring our history and learning something new."

"That would be a pleasant event, don't you think, Sharanna?" Margwen asked her daughter.

The young woman nodded, sparing a glance up from her food. "Yes, Mama. It would be a delight to learn more about the Elviri." Munne could tell Sharanna meant well with her words, but she could hear the hollowness of her heart behind them. Munne recalled that Sharanna had been betrothed to King Nelle's eldest son before he died in the war with the Provira. She was then betrothed to the king's second son, Robyn, but he had disappeared beyond the Wall almost two years ago. She must still be in mourning over the deaths of both princes.

Poor young thing.

They continued their meal in peaceful silence, enjoying the bounty of fried potatoes, smoked fish, buttery biscuits, and tart cadra berry jam. After their meal, Rhorek offered to escort Munne through the castle and show her some of the many Proma heirlooms on display. She was quite enamored with the many suits of armor down one hall, preserved from over two thousand years ago.

"It's truly wonderful that your people have been able to preserve these pieces," Munne said, inspecting one particular suit of armor that had belonged to one of the first Sworn Swords in the line of Nelle.

"Thank you, my lady." Rhorek nodded and gestured towards a longsword hanging above the armor stands. Its silver blade shone in the candlelight, the light catching on the carved runes and lines close to the hilt. The Proma had kept the sword in pristine condition, its guard and hilt polished. "This sword belonged to the first King Nelle nearly three thousand years ago. It's said that he used this sword to cut down Daerion the Cursed in their duel."

The name was vaguely familiar to Munne. The first Nelle had challenged the crown prince Daerion to a duel over his wife's honor. Nelle won the duel, and with it the throne of Promthus.

More Proma arrogance, Munne mused. Not that she would ever vocalize such thoughts. It was clear to her which lineage the Provira inherited their brashness and violent tendencies from. *But if Daerion had any descendants, would they have turned out the same as Nelle's?*

Thoughts of Malion floated across her mind; her ancestor who had suffered from his own violent affliction caused by the *Ardashi'ik*, and she immediately quelled her negative thoughts toward the ancient Proma kings.

"Lord Rhorek!" A soldier ran around a corner and stopped in front of them, out of breath.

Rhorek turned, a look of alarm on his face. "What is it, soldier?"

"The king has requested your presence at once in the council chambers. To discuss the newest prisoner," the soldier explained.

Rhorek and Munne exchanged looks of concern before he asked, "Which prisoner? The woman from the streets?"

"No, sir." The soldier paused for a moment, catching his breath. "Naro turned himself in, just across the bridge. He's being taken down below to the interrogation room at this very moment."

Munne's eyes widened, and she felt a tight squeeze in her stomach. *Could this truly be the man I've been searching for these past few days?*

"Let us make haste," Rhorek said, taking off towards the nearest staircase. The soldier followed quickly behind.

"I'm coming with you, my lord!" Munne called out, hurrying after him.

Within the council room King Nelle, Captain Munhart, and a host of other knights and guards were gathered together. Lords Nathfer and Delsaran weren't present. Rhorek took a seat in between Captain Munhart and Sir Brien Mauntell. Munne recognized some of the knights as Sworn Swords of the king and his family. Others were higher ranking officers in the guard. No one had made any attempt to stop her from entering the room, but it was apparent that she was the odd woman out; no other foreigners or emissaries were present.

"Today is a historic day," King Nelle began, silencing the rest of the room. All attention turned to the king. "And one that I never thought I would see. Someone claiming to be Naro has turned himself in, and we are now in possession of one of the most dangerous men in Promthus."

Murmurs broke out across the room.

"Could it be true?"

"Will we hang him?"

"Surely we'll interrogate him first."

"Does this mean the riots are over?"

The king slammed his hand on the table, drawing attention back to him. "My lords, we must not hasten to any conclusions. While we all wish for justice, we must do what we can to protect our city. We'll question him about his involvement in the riots these past few days, and then we'll question him about his gang after. I need not remind you all that this very well could be a ruse."

More murmurs rippled across the room, and the statement piqued Munne's curiosity. *Has someone pretended to be this Naro in the past? What kinds of crimes has this man committed?*

"Captain Munhart, you'll be the one to question the prisoner. Ensure that no harm comes to him before we've had a chance to gather answers," King Nelle ordered.

The captain nodded. "Yes, Your Majesty."

"The rest of you will be sworn to silence until Captain Munhart has had the opportunity to talk with the prisoner. We must ensure that this... man truly is who he claims to be. We'll reconvene in the morning."

The room stilled. No one dared to voice their thoughts. All the men simply nodded. The vow had taken its hold on the room. The king stood and took his leave. The rest of the room stood as well, watching him and his three Sworn Swords go. Once the king was out of the room, the silence was broken.

"Captain Munhart, when will you speak to him?"

"That rat won't miss a couple of fingers."

"How do we know he's truly Naro?"

Captain Munhart slammed his hand on the table, silencing the discourse. "My lords! Our king gave you all an order: *silence.* Allow me to execute *my* order and meet with the prisoner. I'll have updates for you in the morning."

The captain took his leave and exited the room. Munne heard the other knights and advisors grumble, but she paid them no mind. She had to catch up with the captain and speak with him. She left the room, following the sounds of stomping boots down the hall.

"Captain Munhart!" she called out.

The stomping stopped. The captain stood in the middle of the hall, his head hung low. "Lady Vere'cha, I must make haste—"

"Allow me to sit with you during your questioning." He turned to face Munne. She saw a hundred questions bubbling across his face. She continued on before he could voice any of them. "I wish to help you. This man has clearly caused the city a lifetime of hurt, and he may also be tied to the princess's disappearance. It would be shameful of me to not assist my allies in their time of need, no matter the battlefield we find ourselves on."

Captain Munhart looked her over, his expression relaxing. "I thank you, Lady Vere'cha. I truly do. To be honest," He took a step towards her, his voice dropped to a low whisper. "I worry about the prisoner's safety. If he is who he says, he's the greatest enemy to the crown after the Provira. He's not safe here. Would that I could wring his neck myself, but there are processes that must be followed. We must ensure this isn't a trap. And it just may be that you're the only person who can assist with that."

She understood. She had seen it before with other Proma and other prisoners. The Proma had the tendency to strike first and wave their hands at the reasoning after. That was the Proma's form of justice. She looked upon the captain with a new light, impressed by his ability to curb his desires for the sake of *real* justice.

"You may accompany me to the dungeon and sit in the room with me."

Munne fell into step behind him and the two set off.

The dungeon was in the lowest level of the castle, built from stones stained by the lakes. Munne and Captain Munhart had gone through several gates to get to the cells, each manned by two city guards who were silent as the grave. Within the dungeon there were several rows of cells; Munne couldn't count how many there were. The rows stretched past the flames of the torches that hung on the walls. Munhart plucked a torch from the wall and led her deeper within the cells to a particular one flanked by two guards. The prisoner inside sat in a corner, one knee pulled close to his chest. In the dim torchlight Munne could see that his skin was dark, his hair darker. Though his hair had been pulled back into a ponytail, several loose strands fell across his face. A dirty linen shirt hung loose on his body, the sleeves rolled up to his elbows. His trousers and boots looked even dirtier than his shirt.

As Munne and Captain Munhart approached, the prisoner raised his head. "Hello Captain, my lady," he greeted them with a smile, his voice rich and warm.

Captain Munhart turned to the guard on his left. "Bring him down for questioning."

"Yes, sir," the guard responded, voice muffled by his helmet. There was a hint of disdain in his response, but he obeyed his captain.

The two guards opened the cell and entered, pulling the prisoner to his feet roughly. The prisoner grunted but otherwise said nothing. As the guards passed by Munne and Munhart, she caught a glimpse of a frown on the captain's face.

Munhart spoke true—I can see mutiny brewing in his men's faces. How long will they obey his orders? And just what exactly has this Naro done to warrant such levels of disobedience?

The questioning room was further within the dungeon. Munne was reminded of the lower levels of her father's manor where the books from the Eldest Days were kept. At least the books offered good company. The room felt more like a tomb. For the man calling himself Naro, it very well might be.

The guards took the prisoner into the room and sat him down at a table. They secured pairs of cuffs around his wrists and ankles, which they fastened to a metal loop on the ground. The walls and floor were made of stone. There was only one way in and out, and that was through the heavy wooden door which was now shut. Munhart lit the torches around the room, bathing it in a warm firelight. He handed the torch to one guard and then took his seat across from the prisoner, Munne sitting next to him. There was a wooden table separating the prisoner from Munne and Munhart.

"Thank you," Munhart said to the guards. "Wait outside."

The guards both hesitated. Munne wasn't sure if it was normal for guards to sit in during a questioning, but she was sure they wanted to for this prisoner. After a pause, the two left the room and shut the door behind them. When Munne's eyes fell on the prisoner, she realized he had been watching her the whole time. The corner of his mouth twitched, and the ghost of a smile spread across his face.

In the light she could see that he had bronze skin, and his hair had a deep blue hue similar to the sky as the last of the suns' light vanished into night. Dark circles hung under his eyes, one blue and one green. Her stomach twisted sharply.

Mismatching eyes. Just like the caravan leader I met back in Elimere.

His smile widened.

"I'm told you turned yourself in this morning?" Captain Munhart said, breaking the silence.

The prisoner's mismatched eyes cut to Munhart. He nodded. "Yes, Captain."

Munhart leaned forward, placing his elbows on the table and folding his hands together. "What crimes have you committed?"

The prisoner looked up to the ceiling and chuckled. "I believe the listed crimes are drug trafficking, murdering guardsmen, and being a gang lord, among others."

"May I have your name?"

The prisoner looked back at Munhart. "It's the name on everyone's tongue today it seems."

"So, you're claiming to be Naro?"

The prisoner leaned back in his chair and held up his hands with a shrug. "I may be a crafty fellow, but I have never allowed anyone to impersonate me."

Munne was taken aback by the casualness of his statement, but she was careful not to let her neutral expression slip. Though she hadn't been too certain of the idea that someone was impersonating him, she was surprised by his statement. *How many have tried stealing his identity over the years? How many has he silenced?*

Captain Munhart tensed up beside her. "No, I suppose we have never arrested anyone claiming to be you," he begrudgingly admitted.

Naro's shoulders relaxed, and he dropped his hands onto the table. His gaze turned from Munhart to Munne. His eyes lingered on her pointed ears before meeting her icy blue stare. "And we have a special visitor with us today, do we not?"

"I've been here for several days now," Munne replied curtly. "Though I wouldn't say my presence is special."

"Isn't it?" There was a glimmer in his mismatching eyes. Under his gaze, Munne suddenly felt exposed.

He knows something.

"The Elviri Warlord is here to aid with troubles in the city. Troubles *you* have caused," Captain Munhart accused.

Naro looked back at Munhart and scoffed. "I can assure you that this nasty business with the riots and fires is *not* the work of myself or the Walkers."

"We've arrested some of the more unruly thugs. They're all saying the same thing—that they're looking for *you*."

Naro drummed the table with his fingers, maintaining a neutral expression. "And that's precisely why I'm here in this dungeon, Captain." Munhart leaned back and crossed his arms over his chest. He said nothing, allowing Naro to continue. "It's in our best interests if we work together"—Naro looked between Munhart and Munne—"to deal with those who threaten our city." When his eyes met hers, a chill ran down Munne's spine.

Does he mean the Provira?

"And how can you help the city guard?" Captain Munhart asked.

"Of the listed crimes, I will admit to one: the high lords may sit in their council chambers in the castle and pass whatever decrees they wish, but *I'm* the ruling lord of the streets."

It was Munhart's turn to scoff. Naro's eyes narrowed, and he tilted his chin up. His entire demeanor changed—chest puffed out, shoulders straightened. Despite his filthy and unkempt attire, it was plain to see that there was merit to this man's claim.

Munne allowed herself a small frown. The man perplexed her. *Something I'm becoming all too familiar with in recent days.*

"So, you're claiming ownership over every gang in Auora? Therefore, you *are* responsible for all—"

"Come now, Captain Munhart!" Naro snapped. "Though the king has sought my demise for years, there's no denying that until the deadly athra outbreak, the streets were under control. *My* control. I've had an iron fist over the Syrael Walkers, the Red Court, the Iron Hawks, and even the Disciples."

"Then who lights the fires in the city?" Munhart demanded.

"In due time, Captain," Naro replied through clenched teeth.

"The woman we arrested earlier mentioned a new order, calling them the 'Suneaters'," Munne said, drawing the attention of both men. She heard Munhart's jaw clench, but it was Naro who held her attention, the glimmer resurfacing in his blue and green eyes. "Was this group also under your control?"

"A fitting name, though they don't yet know it," Naro murmured, his voice low enough so that only Munne could hear.

"What was that?" Munhart barked.

"He said that it's a curious name," Munne said to the captain, her gaze not leaving Naro.

Naro nodded. "A curious name for a curious group of traitors. Six nights ago, one of my lieutenants slaughtered an entire Walker safehouse looking for me."

Betrayed by one of his own? Either this man is incredibly dangerous, or incredibly inept.

Captain Munhart perked up at that. "Six nights? Would that have anything to do with—"

"With your princess disappearing?" Naro turned to look at Munhart coyly. "The bastard didn't rebel against me because of some twisted loyalty to the crown. But since you're asking, yes, I kidnapped her."

Munhart's chair flew back as he jumped to his feet. As he reached for his sword, Munne grabbed his wrist. "Lady Vere'cha, unhand me at once," he growled.

"Captain Munhart, need I remind you of what your king asked of you? Sit back down or I will be forced to make you sit," Munne ordered, her voice calm, her other hand dropping to the hilt of her short sword.

For several moments, the room stood still. Munhart glared at Naro, inhaling sharply through his nose. Munne's grip on Munhart's wrist tightened, and she stared at him until he turned to look at her. After another moment, he dropped his hand from his sword, picking up his chair and sitting back down.

After she was content with Munhart's behavior, Munne looked at Naro. A wolfish grin had spread across his face. He indeed wore many faces. Street rat. Royalty.

Predator.

"Sir—"

"Naro."

"*Naro*," she hissed, the name feeling strange on her tongue. "It should go without saying that any of the king's men would be happy to cut your head from your neck without hearing another word. I would urge you to refrain from taunting Captain Munhart and instead tell us how we can help one another."

The grin disappeared from Naro's face. He seemed to look upon her with new regard. "Of course, Lady Vere'cha. I willingly surrendered myself to the city guard because I wish to protect my city from *all* threats."

If only I could sit alone with him and press him further. She knew she couldn't, not with Munhart here. Not yet at least. *But I need to know what threats he's referring to.*

"I think it's apparent that you seek protection here, and that's why you've turned yourself in," Munne said. "And while I understand you hold a certain position of authority among the gangs of Auora, it seems that your authority is lacking in recent days. So, what do you have to offer the crown?"

"The most precious commodity—information."

"About the gangs?" Munhart asked.

"Yes, and about the princess," Naro said with a smile.

The captain's jaw clenched again, but he stayed in his seat. "You'll tell us where you have taken her?" Munne asked Naro.

Naro's face lit up and he grinned again. "Of course. At this point it would be cruel of me not to. I think the king will actually be appreciative of this. She has been spirited away to Na'roc of North to get rid of—No, wait, I shouldn't spoil the surprise. The king will understand what the journey means."

Na'roc of North. The land of Munne's ancestors where the first Elviri traveled and became gods. A land separated from the rest of Daaria for thousands of years. The Elviri had very little written about that land since the Eldest Days. She had never gone beyond the Wall that sat at the border between the frozen tundra and Promthus.

Why would he have sent the princess there? To get rid of what?

"I'm famished. Perhaps we can discuss all of this more tomorrow?" Naro asked, tilting his head to the side.

"A polite way of telling us you're done speaking for now," Munne said with a hint of contempt.

"For now, but not for good." Naro's smile faded. The quip gave Munne a small seed of hope for a future conversation between them. She just needed to find a way to make it happen.

Captain Munhart slowly rose to his feet and moved to the door. He knocked and the guards on the other side unlocked and opened it.

"Yes, Captain?" one of the guards asked.

"Return the prisoner to his cell. We'll continue questioning him tomorrow," Munhart ordered.

The two guards nodded and entered the room, releasing Naro from his shackles and pulling him to his feet.

"I look forward to our discussions tomorrow, Captain, Lady Vere'cha," Naro said on his way out.

CHAPTER VI: SETH

The next morning, an urge bubbled up within Seth to visit his mother's library, so he could feel the presence of her memory. And perhaps bathe. Though he yearned to do both, he awoke in a terrible mood. He didn't want the stewards coming with him or helping him around the pyramid. They were nothing but horrible reminders of his father's control.

The same steward brought in a tray of tea and a bowl of sweet porridge for breakfast. Seth's stomach didn't growl at the sight of food. Last night's meal had been enough to satisfy him for the time being, so he decided to be obstinate and refuse the porridge. The steward tried to set the tray on Seth's lap, but he rolled over away from them. After a moment's hesitation, they placed the tray on the table beside the bed and then returned to their position by the door.

For a few moments, Seth just stared out the window to the rainforest beyond. It was another dark and dreary day with thunder rumbling quietly in the distance. Perfect for reading a book in the library.

"I want to go to my mother's library," he blurted out. He was surprised at the sound of his own voice and how it cracked from disuse.

The steward was startled as well, pushing away from the wall and approaching the bed again. They held their hands out in front of them as if trying to communicate *something*, but Seth couldn't understand them. Watching their gloved hands stretch then collapse, lift up then down, did nothing more than irritate Seth.

What a waste of time. He turned back to the window with a scoff. *Why can't they just leave me alone?*

"You can't," a low voice croaked from behind him.

Seth whipped his head to the side, staring incredulously at the veiled body. Provira stewards were forbidden from speaking in the presence of the Kharis family. Seth could only recall one instance where a steward dared open her mouth around his father, Osza, and Astohi, shortly after Amias had destroyed Seth's legs. They had the poor fool stripped, beaten, and thrown from the top of the pyramid. Though Seth had turned away from the balcony, he still heard the muffled crunch as the body hit the side of the pyramid and slid down into the village below. From what he knew, the Asaszi stewards enforced the vow of silence beyond the presence of the Kharis family, and ensured the Provira didn't speak while wearing their robes and veils.

"Did you just say something?"

The steward crouched down beside the bed, so they were on eye level with Seth. They kept their voice quiet as they spoke, a strange accent curling around their words. They almost sounded... sad. "Your father has forbidden anyone from entering there."

Seth's eyes watered. He had expected his father to do something like that, but to hear it out loud—from a *steward* no less—just twisted the dagger in his heart. Screwing his eyes shut, he threw himself down on the bed and turned away from the steward, pulling one of the blankets up to rub furiously at the tears that began to fall.

He heard the faintest rustle of cloth and then felt a hand rest gently on his side. He turned and lunged at the steward, snatching their wrist and leaning forward so he was close to their veiled face.

Seth snarled. "Don't *ever* touch me—"

"I should have told you sooner," the steward said, a little louder than before. Something about their voice sent a shiver down Seth's spine. He recognized it. He knew the voice, had heard it endlessly in his dreams since returning to the pyramid, but he didn't dare hope—

"*Lisanthir?*" Seth breathed.

The steward turned away from him for a moment, looking at the closed door, then turned back, removing their hood and veil to reveal Lisanthir's face, just as Seth had remembered it. His black hair was pulled back, revealing long, thin pointed ears. His green eyes shone like emeralds.

"Your sister said to wait to reveal myself to you, but I couldn't—I couldn't wait while you lay here in your misery." The words spilled from Lisanthir's lips, his voice no louder than a whisper. He reached out to touch Seth's cheek, and Seth let his head fall into his hand.

"How is this even possible?" Seth murmured, both to himself and to the Elviri. His eyes pricked as fresh tears welled up and threatened to spill down his cheeks.

"I followed you. After *Henayth'mar*, after we..." Lisanthir's cheeks flushed. "I was worried about you. I didn't want things to end so poorly between us."

He's been here this whole time?

Seth was overwhelmed with the desire, the *need* to touch Lisanthir. To be held by him. He let go of the Elviri's hand and threw his arms around his neck, embracing him and pulling him toward the bed. He wept openly, swallowing hiccups and sobs.

"I shouldn't have run. I should've stayed," Seth buried his head in Lisanthir's chest, feeling the Elviri wrap his arms around Seth's back. "I should have *stayed*. My legs be damned, we could've... I could've..." Renewed memories of Lithalyon assaulted him once more. He felt shame burn in the tips of his ears and spread across his cheeks, his chest, his legs...*Even if I had stayed, my legs would've returned to this. To being useless. There's no way Lisanthir would've put up with—*

"It's okay. I found you, it's okay." The Elviri pressed his lips against Seth's hair and the inferno of shame grew all the hotter.

"I lied to you," Seth mumbled. His skin prickled as Lisanthir rubbed his back, just like how his mother used to comfort him after a nightmare or one of his father's experiments.

"You may have called yourself a different name, but I saw the light of your spirit under Aelrindel. I saw a spirit that was kindred to my own, and I couldn't let you disappear as quickly as you had arrived."

Seth squeezed Lisanthir tighter, afraid that if he let go, the Elviri would vanish again, and he'd be alone with his thoughts and broken legs once more. *I don't deserve this. I'm so, so thankful for this. I can't let him go.* So many emotions spun around in his head, leaving him in a dizzy state, so he could only manage to ask one question. "How are you here?"

"Your sister. Without her, I would've been slain the moment the Provira saw me. I'm lucky that she was the one who found me that night."

Octavia did this? Was it her *idea to disguise Lisanthir as a steward?* Memories flooded Seth's mind from the past several days. It had been *Lisanthir* who moved him with gentle touches during the last dinner with his parents and Octavia. Since his mother's death, it had been *Lisanthir* watching over him and trying to get him to eat. *What a fool I've been*, Seth chastised himself, guilt coursing through his body. "I-I'm so sorry, I've been so cruel, putting you through so much, I—"

Lisanthir stroked Seth's hair, and the guilt lessened. "We're together now. That's what matters."

They stayed like that for several moments, arms wrapped around each other in a warm, tight embrace. Tears continued to stream down Seth's face, but he didn't care. Lisanthir was with him alive and well, and he was going to treasure that.

"Seth." The sound of his name coming from Lisanthir's voice filled him with warmth.

Not Calydrian. Seth. My real name.

"I never thought I'd hear you say my name," Seth whispered. "Say it again, please."

The Elviri let out a breathless chuckle. "Seth. Seth, *ebilin*. I need to return to the other stewards."

In an instant, the warm haze cleared from Seth's vision. His tear-stained cheeks felt cold; his hair felt unkempt and unclean. He pulled away from Lisanthir, just far enough to be able to look him in the eye.

Not even the rainforest in bloom compares to the green of his eyes.

"They'll get suspicious if I stay here too long. I've already been getting questioning looks from the Asaszi stewards the past few days. Being unable to speak has been both a blessing and a curse." Lisanthir smiled, raising a gloved hand to dry the tears on Seth's cheek.

He leaned into the Elviri's touch, wishing he could feel the touch of his hand and not his glove. "But I just got you back."

"I'll return, *ebilin*, with dinner. I always do."

Lisanthir pulled Seth forward with the gentlest of touches and brushed his lips against Seth's. Warmth spread from Seth's cheeks down his spine, and he felt like he could melt into his bed.

"I should get out of this room," Seth murmured as Lisanthir stood. "This place doesn't feel as comforting as it once did... and I could do with a hot bath."

Lisanthir flashed him a grin as he donned his veil and hood. "You only need to call out. There're two other stewards outside right now. Just... please, not the library."

Seth nodded solemnly. A flurry of warring emotions surged within and threatened to consume him. He became all too aware of how long he had neglected his body. He needed to bathe, to feel clean and fresh. The yearning for his mother's library only grew with Lisanthir's warning. How he wanted to go there and get lost in her books! But his father— curse him—had shut everyone out.

Seth watched Lisanthir pick up the tray and head toward the door. "Lisanthir, wait," he said as loud as he dared.

The Elviri returned to the bedside. "Yes?"

"What does *ebilin* mean?" There was a pause in Lisanthir's response. *He must be smiling,* Seth thought. He couldn't help but smile in return.

"It means 'dear one'. Used for courtships."

"I see." Seth's cheeks flushed. *Courtships. Is he courting me? What does an Elviri courtship look like?* Other questions raced through his mind, too fast for him to fully process.

Lisanthir chuckled. "I'll see you this evening."

Seth said nothing else, not knowing what to say and not wanting to jeopardize Lisanthir's disguise, so he simply watched the Elviri leave. The room felt darker in his absence, but Seth now had a small candle of hope flickering within.

He decided he would leave his room today after all and called out for the other stewards several moments later to take him to the bathing chambers.

Seth soaked in the stone tub long enough that his skin pruned, and his muscles practically melted beneath his skin. The heat soaked away all of his physical stress, and the lingering feeling of Lisanthir's lips on his pushed away all of the dark clouds looming in his mind.

When he had arrived, the tub had been filled with hot water, scented oils, and flowers. It had been nearly scorching at first, but as he soaked, the water cooled until it was comfortably warm. His skin had turned a bright red, and he was fascinated by how it turned white underneath his fingertips when he pressed against his arms and thighs. Being submerged in the warm water, it was easier to pretend that his legs weren't dead weight. Like he was still whole. And the heat from the bath was enough to melt those bitter feelings, at least for now.

The bathing chambers were built on top of massive furnaces, so the water could be heated without needing to constantly carry around buckets. There was also a section of the chambers with stone chairs and lounges meant for the Asaszi to heat their scales. Thankfully, it was in a separate area from the tubs, so he didn't come across any of the scaled creatures while he was bathing.

Lisanthir is here. In Yiradia. With me. He sank lower into the water, unable to stop himself from smiling. *I don't know how Tav managed it. Sneaking an Elviri into Yiradia, right under Father's nose! I need to ask her what happened. Is she taking care of him and making sure he's following all of Father's inane rules? Lisanthir's ears aren't long enough to completely give away his heritage, but if Father found out who he is...* His cheeks flushed with heat as he thought about the Elviri's appearance and his thoughts pivoted. *He's been taking care of me this whole time, bringing me food and drink, trying to get me to eat... What have I done to deserve such kindness from an Elviri? Why did he follow me back?*

After his bath, Seth returned to his chambers and put on fresh new clothes. He allowed the two stewards—one fully covered, one revealed to be an Asaszi—to enter and clean up the room, taking his discarded clothing to be washed and changing out the silks and furs on his bed. As the stewards worked, he eyed the veiled one thoughtfully, wondering if his Elviri was underneath that black hood and veil. They stood a little too short, though, and their shoulders were too narrow.

Seth lost interest once he decided the veiled steward *wasn't* Lisanthir and chose to sit in his wheelchair by the window and read a book. It was written for children, retelling heroic tales of the Asaszi from the Eldest Days. This particular book was older than his father and had originally belonged to Osza and Astohi. They bestowed it to Amias and Evelyn during one of her first pregnancies. Evelyn had translated the Asaszi text into the common tongue and used the book to teach Seth and Octavia both languages when they were growing up. He had enjoyed it as a child, but today he was simply flipping the pages to pass the time. While the book talked about several heroes from the wars, there were several mentions of the *Tserys*. There were no illustrations of him, though, which Seth found odd.

Eventually the stewards left, and Seth returned to his bed, thinking back on his earlier conversation with Lisanthir. Within his mind, his thoughts pivoted like mirrors and considered the past several days with a new perspective.

Lisanthir is here. Because of Octavia. She must be keeping him safe from Father and the Asaszi. But where is she? Why hasn't she come to visit since Mother's murder? I'll ask Lisanthir when he comes for dinner.

He got as comfortable as he could in bed and continued flipping through the Asaszi book.

Lisanthir returned later in the evening with another tray of food and tea. He didn't remove his veil and hood, but he did sit on the edge of the bed and talk while Seth ate what he could stomach.

"It brings me joy to see you eating again," Lisanthir said quietly. "Though I know a heavy burden still lies in your heart."

"Knowing you're here lessens the pain," Seth whispered. He pushed the stewed fruit around on the plate, raising the fork to his mouth every so often. He had so many questions to ask but he knew he didn't have long until the Elviri would have to leave for other duties. "Where's Octavia been? Have you spoken to her?"

"She's been spending a lot of time with the recruits. Training. I've been allowed to join their sessions on occasion." Lisanthir sighed. "It's both familiar and new. It reminds me of my time in Elimaine during my lifepath rotations."

Seth recalled mentions of lifepath rotations back in Lithalyon when they first met in the library. One of the other librarians had said that Lisanthir recently completed his and had chosen to work in the library. "What exactly are those?"

"Growing up, each Elviri spends several years traveling across the three provinces serving the various factions and learning skills," Lisanthir explained. Seth could hear the smile although he couldn't see it.

"So, you served in the army?"

Lisanthir shook his head. "No, not as a proper recruit. I trained with the soldiers and learned about their lives, but I never left Elimaine. In the province's capital city, Elyr Tym, there's an entire ward dedicated to the students, completely separate from those who are actually enlisted. And when it was time to move onto the next lifepath in the next city, I left."

Seth found himself enthralled in Lisanthir's tales. He wanted to know more, but he knew he would only be able to gather new information in small doses. Lisanthir would have to leave soon, so he returned to the previous subject. "Why has Octavia not come to see me?"

Lisanthir shifted around uncomfortably on the bed. "Things have been rather complicated. Your father has been very demanding of her since... your return."

Seth's stomach clenched. *Has Octavia been given the time to grieve our mother?* A horrible voice in the back of his head told him that Amias wouldn't have allowed it.

"I need to see her," Seth said, dropping his fork. "I need to speak with her."

Lisanthir nodded. "I understand. She and I haven't crossed paths in the past two days, but I'll try to find her."

Seth looked over the tray on his lap. He had eaten roughly a quarter of the food presented to him, but he couldn't muster the energy to eat any more. "I think I'm done for the evening. Could you leave the cup of tea, though?"

"Of course, *ebilin*," Lisanthir murmured as he stood. He picked up the cup and set it down on the table near the bed, then picked up the tray.

Before the Elviri could leave, Seth stammered, "A-Are you courting me?"

Lisanthir turned back to him, raising the veil with one hand and offering him a sheepish grin. "In some regards, we're beyond courting. Under normal circumstances, I wouldn't have been permitted into your room until we'd been openly courting for at least one year, but..." A faint blush spread across the bridge of his nose and painted his cheeks a pale pink.

Based on the heat spreading through his face, Seth was sure he looked very similar. "Well... I-I'm okay with it. If you are. *Ebilin.*" The Elviri word felt foreign on his tongue, his tongue slowly flicking the back of his teeth. It felt... *good.*

Lisanthir's blush deepened as he lowered the veil across his face once more. He shuffled his way out of the room and into the pyramid.

Seth leaned back in his bed, slouched down as far as he could go. He already missed Lisanthir. He couldn't help it. He missed Octavia, too. He had been suppressing that feeling for several days because he hadn't been sure if his sister still cared for him or if she was still alive. It warmed his heart to know she was safe, but he knew he wouldn't rest easy until she came to visit.

Please, Lis, speak to her. And stay safe.

He listened to the forest's idle noises. Leaves rustled in the wind. Birds chirped their songs. Deep within the trees other strange creatures were calling out to each other. The suns had vanished about an hour ago, so there was very little light left in Seth's room. He looked out the window until the room went black.

Seth pulled himself into a sitting position and reached for the cup of tea from the table beside his bed. It had cooled considerably, but he still enjoyed the flavor of the tea. After draining the cup, he returned it to its perch and then sank down deep into his bed.

The next morning Lisanthir brought a tray of porridge and bread for breakfast. He set it on Seth's lap before sitting on the bed beside him. Their discussions were kept to whispers and murmurs.

"They've cut me off from the tea canisters. I suppose there's not enough to go around," Lisanthir explained, his voice apologetic.

"It's fine. I'm surprised they let you bring as many cups as you have."

They sat together in peaceful silence as Seth ate most of his meal. Lisanthir placed a hand on Seth's knee. He felt the weight of the Elviri's hand through the blankets, the pleasant warmth of the gesture wilting underneath the fiery flush of shame. His stomach lurched angrily as his eyes shifted from his porridge to Lisanthir's hand. He tried to reason with his emotions, reminding himself that Lisanthir had been nothing but gentle and loving since learning about his true condition. He had nothing to be ashamed of. Nothing to fear. Nothing to hide—

"They're losing the war," Lisanthir whispered.

It took Seth a moment to realize that the Elviri was referring to the Provira and Asaszi. With great mental strain, he shifted his thoughts to the war. When he had been in Lithalyon, he came to the same conclusion as Lisanthir. The Elviri were not fazed by this war. The Provira were simply nuisances to them. *Should I take comfort knowing that my father's life work has had such little impact on his foes? So many lives ruined...*

The bedroom door swung open without warning. A spasm ran down Seth's spine and his mind was overwhelmed with fear. Lisanthir's reaction was much tamer than Seth's. He merely turned to look at the door and slowly slid his hand off of Seth's knee.

Octavia's form filled the doorway, and Seth's fears vanished. She wore a pair of beat-up leather pants, dusty boots, and a cloth shirt that had been stained with dirt, sweat, and blood. Her dirty blonde hair had been pulled back behind her head, a few loose strands falling across her cheeks. Her pointed ears were on display, the skin still pale with scarring from when their father had carved them with his own dagger. She had just come from training or sparring, no doubt. In her brown eyes, Seth saw the fading embers of adrenaline and pride. Whoever she had sparred with, she had bested them.

The youngest pyredan *in the Provira's ranks. Father's pride and joy. My sister.*

"Tav!" Seth cried out. A knot formed in his throat, and he felt the familiar prick of tears in his eyes.

"It's so good to see you again, brother." Octavia beamed, shutting the door behind her. Lisanthir pulled the tray from Seth's lap and placed it on the nightstand, giving the girl space to approach. Octavia approached the bed and threw her arms around Seth, pulling him in for a tight hug. "I'm so sorry for not coming sooner, I couldn't... So much has changed."

So much has *changed. Where have you been, Tav? Why did you leave me alone with this cold, dark misery?*

All of the words Seth tried to say died in his throat. He simply held onto his sister, thankful to have her back and be able to see her, touch her. They rocked from side to side, Seth's head buried in Octavia's shoulder, Octavia's head pressed against his. He felt hot droplets in his hair. Octavia kissed the side of his head several times. After several long moments, the twins separated.

Octavia looked over at Lisanthir who briefly lifted his veil to show his face. "I need to return to the kitchens," he said quietly.

Seth smiled as Lisanthir adjusted his veil and picked up the tray, leaving the bedroom. He then turned his attention to his sister. "He said you saved him. How'd you do it?"

The corners of Octavia's mouth tugged upward into a grin. "I went back to Marus's stables after you returned to see if Anrak had come back as well, or if anyone had followed you. Marus said no one had, but as I was coming back to the pyramid, your Elviri rode into the village on his own horse."

Seth's cheeks flushed. *My Elviri.*

"In the torchlight, he mistook me for you and called after 'Calydrian'. I took him inside one of the ruined huts and got his story before any of the patrols spotted him. I don't know how he even made it to the city without running into a patrol or sentry. He's lucky none of them saw him as he entered the city, and that it was me he ran into."

"How much did he tell you about...?" Seth asked warily, feeling a twinge of embarrassment curl in the pit of his stomach. Though there were no secrets between the twins, there had also never been any romantic interests in Seth's life.

"Well, he apologized for mistaking me for the handsome man who ran off after they shared several dances at *Henath... Henyth...*" She struggled with the Elviri word.

"*Henayth'mar,*" Seth mumbled sheepishly.

Octavia raised an eyebrow and gave him a smug look. "It was all quite romantic, and he seemed very surprised that his dance partner fled to Moonyswyn."

"I'm sure he was also surprised to find out his dance partner is a cripple," Seth grumbled, leaning back into his pillows and running both hands over his face.

"The biggest surprise was learning who your father is," Octavia murmured, her playful façade fading. "I tried convincing him to return to Lithalyon, but he wanted to stay and help you."

Seth's throat tightened. *Lisanthir would brave this nest of snakes for me. What have I done to deserve that?* "I can never repay you for keeping him safe."

"Don't say that, Seth. There may come a time, and soon."

Hands falling from his face, he gave her a questioning look as she fidgeted on the bed. With one finger she dug at the skin near her thumbnail, her left foot tapping restlessly on the ground.

"I've been a fool," she began, lowering her voice so it was barely above a whisper. "I've followed Father so blindly over the years. I trusted that he was doing what was best for us. I was so wrapped up in my desire to please him that I overlooked so much." Octavia closed her eyes for a moment and inhaled deeply. Her lips quivered. Seth reached out and took both her hands, squeezing them in reassurance. "I didn't listen to your pain. Your hurts. It wasn't until he—" Octavia paused. "She was our *mother*."

Seth nodded, tears running down his cheeks. "And he took her from us," he whispered.

Octavia embraced Seth again. Perhaps one day they could speak of it more, but for now they silently mourned the loss of their mother together. Seth felt the burden of loss begin to lessen, the pain more of a dull ache instead of a sharp jab. It comforted him to have his sister by his side.

"I can't lose you, Tav."

"I'll never leave your side, nor let you leave mine."

They pulled far enough back to look each other in the eye, and Octavia smiled. In that moment, she was as beautiful as their mother had been, even with her puffy eyes and tear-stained cheeks.

"We have to find a way to get out of here." Octavia's voice was barely audible. "We can't stay here any longer."

Seth's heart pounded in his chest, so loud that he couldn't hear his own response. "Where would we go?"

"Anywhere but here." There was little resolve in her voice, just a fleeting protest lashing out at their current situation.

As much as he desperately wanted to escape his father's reach, taking Lisanthir and Octavia with him, he knew—they both knew—that anywhere outside of Moonyswyn would be a guaranteed death sentence. Daaria wasn't a welcoming place for two runaway Provira.

Better to die out there than by Father's hand. At least we would finally be free.

Seth tried to focus on one step at a time, or rather his *lack* of steps. "How would we do it? There's no more elixir. I can't leave."

Octavia's jaw tightened. "I'll find a way. Perhaps Szatisi's been able to recreate the elixir here since she and Father returned from Iszairi. But even if she hasn't, *I'll find a way.*"

Seth studied her face, watching her nostrils flare as she breathed. She had figured out a way the first time. He had to believe in her this time. *What other option do I have?*

"Lisanthir is coming with us."

"Of course."

Seth picked up her hands and squeezed again, taking comfort in her warmth. "I missed you."

Octavia smiled. "I missed you too. Would you join me on the colonnade? It's much cooler out today. I think winter is almost upon us."

Seth nodded, eager to leave his room and feel sunslight on his skin.

CHAPTER VII: MUNNE

When she lay down to rest that night, Munne hoped that Ely would appear in her dreams. She opened her eyes and was in Ceyo's clearing, Ely standing just out of arm's reach.

"Something has happened?" Ely asked, his brow furrowing.

Munne shot him a curious glance. Her summoning had worked, but he didn't seem to know why. "I thought you knew everything in my mind," she said.

He chuckled and averted his gaze. The faintest coloration spread across his cheeks. "Not everything, not unless you are open with *all* of your thoughts. Willingly or otherwise."

"Oh, I see," Munne murmured. She closed her eyes and breathed in deeply, relaxing her shoulders and trying to open her mind to the strange man so he could see the events of her day. She didn't quite know how to allow him entry, but she hoped the effort succeeded.

"You found your quarry," Ely said, his voice closer than before. She hadn't heard him move. "A man named Naro. You spoke to him, and that... unsettled you." Munne nodded. "Are you picturing his face?"

"Yes."

"Hmm, it may help if I—"

Munne opened her eyes, and her body jolted. Ely stood in front of her, his face mere inches away from hers. She inhaled sharply, her gaze wandering from his pale green eyes to his paler skin, then to his clothed chest. A blush crept across her face and ears.

"It will help me see more clearly if I were to take your hand," Ely said softly, taking off one of his gloves. He held his hand out to her.

Munne tilted her head to the side, shrugged her shoulders ever so slightly, and placed her hand in his. Warmth immediately spread from his skin to hers and she felt enveloped in it. Underneath the heat she felt a shiver run down her spine, and for a moment, she forgot to breathe. His fingers curled underneath hers as he tightened his grip on her hand.

Ely turned away and waved his other hand toward the clearing. The air rippled and shimmered, and then the figure of a man appeared. His form darkened then brightened, and Munne was looking at Naro once again. He appeared just as he had in the questioning room, his clothes dirty and disheveled, his hair loosely pulled away from his bronze face. He was smirking.

"I know this one," Ely muttered. He turned to face the illusion entirely, their joined hands slipping to his side. He squeezed her hand, though she couldn't tell if he meant to or not.

"You've seen Naro before?" Munne asked, glancing between Ely and Naro.

"Not in this form..." He trailed off and approached the illusion, letting go of Munne's hand.

Although he had stopped touching her, she still felt like she was enveloped in flames. She shook her head to clear her thoughts and focus on Ely's words. "What do you mean?"

Ely turned to look at her. "You talked to him about Auora? Nothing more?"

"Not yet, but I want to return to the dungeon tomorrow to continue questioning him."

"*Yhryk kanat'yr Nahaesyraellonore?*" Ely spoke in his mysterious language, pacing in circles around the illusion. "Be careful with this one. He's cunning, but he shouldn't hinder your quest in Auora."

"He says he's responsible for kidnapping Princess Niamnh," Munne said, glancing back at the illusion with mismatching eyes. "Can I trust him?"

"He may play games, but he has Daaria's best interests at heart."

And what interests would those be, I wonder? Munne looked back at Ely, who gave her a knowing look. She took a step towards him. "He's like you, isn't he? Something... more?"

After a moment Ely nodded. They stood in silence, the illusion of Naro just out of arm's reach. It brought her little comfort to be correct with her assumption. With mortal men she could understand their motivations and predict their movements. But she had yet to figure out who or what Ely was, nevermind what he was capable of doing. *I know Ely is on my side, but what about this Naro creature?*

"I should let you rest. You'll need all of your wits for tomorrow's questioning."

She reluctantly agreed and the dreamscape faded away, leaving her with a flame's caress on her hand and arms.

Munne returned to the dungeon after eating a light breakfast in the ambassadors' common room. Rhorek accompanied her and Captain Munhart in the questioning room today. The guards had to bring in an extra chair to accommodate him. Captain Munhart sat in the middle chair with Rhorek on his left and Munne on his right.

Naro was escorted into the room after the trio took their seats. He looked even worse than the previous day, but he held his head high. A fresh bruise blossomed on his left cheek. Munne noticed he was breathing heavily for someone who had just walked down a couple of corridors. One of the guards must have roughed him up before bringing him inside the room. She wondered if Munhart or Rhorek were aware of the guard's behavior.

Would they even care? She knew the answer, and it made her grimace.

"Good morning, my lords, my lady," Naro said with a slight grin. There was less bravado in his words. "Lovely day today, isn't it?"

The guards secured the cuffs on his wrists and ankles, then Captain Munhart dismissed them. They exited the room without a word.

"Knight-General Gondamire and I are hoping that this will be a quick meeting today," Captain Munhart said, gesturing to Rhorek beside him. "Give us more information about Princess Niamnh and the gangs in the city, and we'll be swift and merciful with our judgment."

Naro drummed his fingers on the table. "Were I any other wretch in this dungeon, your offer would be most tempting to take. A swift trial and execution would be a reward, certainly, to avoid any more violent urges your soldiers may feel towards me." He leaned back and stretched, tilting his head to the side to reveal another ugly yellowing bruise along his jawline. "But I'm afraid I must decline."

"You would withhold information you already said you would deliver?" Munhart growled.

"On the contrary, I intend to honor my word. You will have your information, but"— Naro leaned against the table, dropping his voice to a low murmur, "I will *not* be beaten in my cell, nor will I be rushed through a farce of a trial just to be hanged and my body dumped in the lakes."

"You would walk free instead?" Rhorek sneered.

Munne looked between Naro and the two Proma. Munhart had dropped a hand to the hilt of his sword, his jaw set. Rhorek had both of his hands in his lap, looking down his nose at Naro.

"Of course not," Naro retorted. "I'll reside in one of your cells, left unmolested by your men, eating two meals a day—not your standard single bucket of slop. After Captain Munhart brings order back to the streets with my help, *then* I will stand trial before your king and submit to his justice."

What courage, Munne mused. Yesterday she would have assumed he was just another prideful, arrogant Proma, but Ely had said he knew Naro, and that the man was cut from the same mysterious cloth as him. *If he's like Ely, then why does he subject himself to the Proma's laws? Why turn himself in? And what kind of magic can he control?*

The room filled with uncomfortable silence. Neither Rhorek nor Munhart had a response to the man. Munhart's grip slackened on his sword. Naro leaned back in his chair, dropping his hands into his lap. His gaze swept across the table and settled on Munne.

They stared at each other for several moments before she broke the silence. "Captain, my men from the Ferilin outpost should be here tomorrow. I'll instruct a few of the triples to take up posts down here to guard your prisoner."

Munhart shifted in his seat to face her, an incredulous look passing over his face.

Rhorek coughed and cleared his throat. "Lady Vere'cha, I mean no disrespect to you or your soldiers, but our men are more than capable of guarding *our* prisoner."

Munne pointed to the bruises on Naro's face and neck. "Knight-General Gondamire, your men have demonstrated that they can't control themselves around this prisoner. I believed the Proma to be honorable men, above the practices the Provira use," she told him.

Rhorek looked between Munne, Naro, and Captain Munhart, his expression bordering between shock and rage. He closed his eyes and tilted his head to the side, as if lost in thought. After a moment, he returned to a neutral expression and got to his feet, beckoning for Munhart to follow. "Come. We must speak."

Munhart didn't budge right away. He opened his mouth to say something, but Rhorek cut him off.

"We'll return for Lady Vere'cha in a few moments."

Munhart grimaced and stood, crossing the room to knock on the door. One of the guards outside opened the door, allowing the two men to exit, and then shut the door behind them.

"I'm glad to know the Elviri are still an honorable people," Naro murmured.

Munne turned her gaze to Naro. Now that they were alone, she looked at him with a new perspective. As if he were like Ely. She searched for any glimmers in his appearance, anything strange. *Besides his mismatching eyes.* "I would have your full name," she said softly.

He cocked his head to the side. "I'm not sure I understand, my lady."

Munne opened her mouth to speak but reconsidered her actions and instead placed her elbows on the table, pulling her sleeves back far enough to reveal part of Ely's imprints on her skin. Naro's eyes left her face, saw the red marks, then snapped back up to meet her gaze.

A crooked grin slid onto his face. "It's really quite the mouthful. Are you sure 'Naro' won't suffice?"

"I would have it all the same," she insisted, folding her hands and resting them on the table.

He cleared his throat before speaking, "*Nahaesyraellonore.*" The name sounded melodic rolling off his tongue, and she realized she had heard it in her dream last night, from Ely.

What touch of magic do you have, Naro?

"Now that we have gone through formal introductions, may I have a closer look?" Naro asked, nodding toward her arms.

Munne pulled her arms back without thinking. She frowned. "May I ask why?"

His gaze continued to shift between her arms and her eyes. "It's been… quite some time since I saw a mark of this kind."

Her stomach churned, unsettled. Pushing the feeling aside, she held her arm out to the man, pulling her sleeve up farther to reveal the entire hand-print.

Naro reached out with one finger and gently pressed it against the red skin. She waited for heat to spread through her body like wildfire, but it did not come. Unlike Ely, his finger was cool to the touch, causing her skin to prickle and gooseflesh to rise. He let out a quiet sigh and spoke, "Most curious…"

"Indeed," she muttered.

Thoughts raced through her mind as Naro held up her right arm, then her left, scrutinizing the red marks. She wondered if Naro was a shapeshifter like Ely and if the form she looked upon was Naro's true form, or if he had another form similar to Ely's. She wondered why Naro's touch cooled her skin while Ely's made her blood run hot.

"Where did you acquire these remarkable imprints?" Naro raised his eyes back to Munne's. She opened her mouth and then shut it, not quite sure how to explain. "From one who can dreamwalk, yes?"

She nodded silently.

"*Most* curious. I didn't think any of us had enough power to walk through dreams anymore."

"What do you mean?" Munne asked, her mouth curving into a frown. "Where do these powers come from?"

Naro cleared his throat and leaned back in his chair, removing his hands from her arms. "Forgive me, Elviri, it isn't my place to divulge any more than I already have. Nostalgia loosened my lips, it seems." His referral to her race rather than her name sent a small chill through her veins. He wasn't like her, the Proma, or any of the other races in Daaria. He was something else.

Munne looked Naro over, not pleased with his response. His demeanor had shifted away from the vulnerable stranger yearning for a glimpse of his home and back to the cunning gang lord who made his home in this city. She knew she had limited time before Captain Munhart and Rhorek returned, and she still had more questions to ask.

"Let us move onto a new subject, then, and speak of the dangers surrounding our cities," she said, regaining her composure. She pulled her sleeves back down, covering Ely's handprints. "Your rebellious lieutenant. Am I correct in assuming that there's more to his betrayal than a disagreement with his leader?"

Naro chuckled. "Aye, a great deal more. His betrayal is tied to this little war with the Provira. He follows their cause, and he seeks to sow discourse in the city because it benefits his true masters."

So, the Provira are *behind the troubles in Auora.*

"Then we must root him out and kill him. Cut off the head of the snake before it can poison Auora," Munne declared, one hand curling into a fist.

"I'm afraid, my lady, that it's too late for that," Naro said and shook his head. "Seeing and knowing things is my specialty, but I'm afraid I didn't see this dilemma until the snake had already struck. The poison is spreading. And it's my responsibility to slow its spread as best I can while others tend to things much worse than a single snake."

Could he be referring to my journey?

"What do you know of Kherizhan?" Munne asked, though her tone conveyed it was closer to a demand.

She caught another glimmer of light in Naro's blue and green eyes. "I know that you must arrive there before the year's end if you are to stop the nest of snakes from poisoning Daaria any further."

Munne felt the air leaving her lungs as her lips parted, but she had no opportunity to reply. Rhorek and Munhart returned to the room, wearing grim expressions on their faces. She looked at them, urging her heart to quiet its beating.

"Lady Vere'cha, we've decided to accept your offer. We'll ensure your soldiers have lodging within the castle," Rhorek announced. The two men took their seats and Rhorek's gaze fell on Naro. "As for you, we'll consider your requests, but we require a token of good faith."

"Of course, good Knight-General." Naro grinned. "Name your token, and I will deliver."

Rhorek and Munhart exchanged glances before the captain spoke. "It would be to our mutual benefit if the rogue forces in the city were culled. Aid us in thinning their numbers and we shall revisit our discussion of your fate in three days' time."

Naro nodded thoughtfully, drumming his fingers on the table. "Very well. A list of locations they could be using as safehouses?"

Munne stayed seated as Rhorek and Captain Munhart gathered their list of locations to raid from Naro, but she didn't pay attention to their conversation. Munne no longer wished to think about the problems plaguing Auora. As the mens' conversation drifted to the state of the city, she excused herself and chose to wander the halls of the castle, her brief discussion with Naro repeating over and over in her mind. She needed to go to Kherizhan. Perhaps in Kherizhan she would learn more about Naro and Ely and the strange magic they wielded.

"*Stop the nest of snakes,*" Naro had said. No doubt he was referring to the Provira who had unearthed something from the Eldest Days from before the Elviri had hunted the Asaszi to extinction.

Perhaps there's a way to end the war in Kherizhan. If that was true, she had to make haste to Kherizhan, all other duties be damned.

Munne's footsteps echoed loudly in the hallways and corridors around her. Her gaze drifted to the paintings, tapestries, and shields on display. After a few hours, her feet brought her back to the ambassadors' quarters. The Barauder had left the quarters to journey down to the shores of the island, and Eldo had gone off to write letters to his kinsmen, leaving Munne alone with her thoughts. She stayed still long enough to fill a goblet with wine, then continued her pacing. Her triple would be arriving in Auora any day now, along with soldiers from the Ferilin outpost. She wished that they'd arrive sooner, but that was beyond her control. She would have to wait. And while she waited, she would pace.

Part of her yearned to speak with Ely again, but that too would have to wait until nightfall. But there was no guarantee that she would see him in her dreams that night. She wanted to share the conversation she had with Naro and get insight from her own mysterious visitor. *At least if Ely doesn't show, the* Ardashi'ik *will be kept at bay for another night. But for the rest of the day, I will* wait.

CHAPTER VIII: RAY

As per Naro's instructions, they arrived on the western bank of the River Thuala on their third day of travel, though it was much later in the day than they were supposed to arrive. They often had to stop for the princess to catch her breath and rest her feet. Even with the Doshara inhabiting her body, she was still a princess. Proma princesses weren't trained to climb and fight, nor were they accustomed to walking several miles in one day. Their slow progress indicated Ray was at least partially correct. Part of Ray didn't mind the slow pace, though, because it meant she got to take in her surroundings and enjoy the forest—somewhere she had never been before.

Another factor of their slow pace that Ray *did* mind was having to stop and hunt for the princess's dinners. She tried to do that as they were moving, listening for any rustles in the underbrush. *Surely it's similar to hunting rats back home. But there's so many other places to hide out here in the forest.* The day before she had only managed to fell one rabbit, which she skinned once they made camp. The princess was thankful but expressed concern that it wasn't enough to satisfy her hunger. Ray didn't like the way that sounded. She would need to do better.

The next day Ray managed to nab another rabbit and she felt rather proud of herself. She passed it along to the princess to hold onto until they made camp for the night. She stayed alert for any other creatures moving around. She had also been keeping an eye on the princess, to see if the Doshara would emerge again, but it hadn't spoken to her since their first meeting two nights prior. Ray didn't tell the princess that she had met the Doshara, and as far as she knew the princess was still blissfully unaware it had even happened. Ray made sure to serve her tea earlier in the day to keep it from resurfacing. So far, the journey had almost been pleasant with its absence. If Ray ignored the fact that she was essentially keeping the princess prisoner, and they were marching for a hostile land.

According to Naro's sunsdial, it was four hours past midday, which meant the suns would be setting soon. The river was wide, and undoubtedly too deep to wade across. There were no bridges this far north. They would have to travel along the riverside to find stones large enough to jump across, or perhaps they would stumble upon a fallen tree they could cross over.

Looking at the sunsdial and compass, Ray positioned herself to move north along the river then set out. Over the past two days the princess had started opening up to Ray and speaking more, and the two had quickly fallen into a comfortable dynamic where the royal would ask the pauper about their travels. Ray enjoyed the discussions, and was pleasantly surprised to discover the princess had a basic knowledge of the land and could explain what several of the trees and plants were. They never discussed their destination though. Both wanted to keep things pleasant for the time being while they still could. It was nice to have someone to talk to.

Princess Niamnh followed closely behind. "How are we going to cross the river?" she asked.

"That's what I'm looking for," Ray responded, throwing a quick grin over her shoulder. Bodies of water, she was more familiar with, even though she hadn't seen this one before. She understood the basics of shipcraft and how to navigate on or around water. She wondered why Naro didn't have them sail up the river and then depart for Na'roc of North. *Why land so far to the west?* Although to be fair, she didn't know what the mouth of the river looked like where it connected to the Hourglass Lakes. *What would Naro do in this situation? Would he swim across the river? Or am I already doing what Naro would do?* She tried forcing a feeling of reassurance upon herself, but it didn't stick.

The two girls navigated their way around trees and shrubs, treading carefully so as not to fall into the river below. Ray realized they were climbing up a small hill, which gave her some degree of hope that they could find a place to cross up ahead.

"Naro could've given us something for this," Ray mumbled as she stepped over a particularly large root.

From behind her, Ray heard a sharp gasp. She turned to look at Princess Niamnh, ready to ask what was wrong. The princess spoke before she had a chance. "Sorry, he's beginning to stir. He doesn't exactly like that criminal's name."

Ray stopped in her tracks, her blood running cold. She hadn't meant to vocalize her thoughts, much less loud enough for the princess—and therefore the Doshara—to hear. And if the mere mention of Naro awoke the Doshara, then Ray needed to sedate it *fast*.

"We should go ahead and stop here for the night."

Princess Niamnh walked past her, eyes fixated on the river. "Are you sure? Shouldn't we try to find a way across?"

The suns were getting lower in the sky. Ray frowned. They *could* keep going until they found somewhere to cross the river. But if they crossed tonight, their clothes would be wet, and they shouldn't be risking sitting naked in the woods after dark while their clothes dried over a fire. They'd be too exposed. It was also possible that Ray would be so preoccupied with finding a means of crossing that she would forget about the Doshara, and it would take over the princess again. She shuddered at the thought. Her bruises had healed but she would never forget the malice in the princess's eyes when the demon had possessed her.

"I think it would be best to make camp now while there's still light. Don't your feet hurt? We can cross in the morning," Ray said.

The princess stopped and turned back toward her, sighing and nodding in agreement. They moved a bit further away from the riverbank, so they'd have enough room for a small campfire and their bedrolls. A routine had been established where the princess would set up their bedrolls and Ray's dinner, and Ray would build the campfire, prepare the princess's dinner, and brew the "tea". It reminded Ray of some of the Walkers' safehouses back in Auora where they would take care of one another. Her heart ached for their company and that sense of belonging. That the ache was dulled when she looked at the princess.

After finishing her nightly ration of fish and fruit, Ray brushed the crumbs from her jacket and then lay down on top of her bedroll. She looked over at

Princess Niamnh who was rubbing her feet. The skinned rabbit sat on a plate nearby, untouched.

"Not hungry?" Ray asked.

"What? Oh, no, I'll eat soon." The princess shook her head. "He's just… stopped talking."

"Is that because of the tea?"

The princess lowered her waterskin and tilted her head to the side. "I can't really tell. I think it's because of the tea to some extent. Either that, or he's so upset about it that he leaves me alone."

"I can't even imagine hearing someone else in my head," Ray murmured. "It must be nice to have some peace and quiet."

Princess Niamnh was silent for a moment. "I rather think not. To hear his voice, feel his thoughts mingling with mine for five years, and then suddenly nothing? It's… uncomfortable."

Ray frowned and kept her mouth shut as she pondered those words. It made her think of Naro, and her chest tightened a little. She squirmed around, the bedroll no longer providing as much comfort as it had before.

"How long have you been a… how long have you been involved in one of the street gangs?" Princess Niamnh asked with slight trepidation.

"How long have I been a criminal, you mean?" Ray retorted with little venom.

"You *did* kidnap the crown princess."

Ray tucked one arm underneath her head and looked up at the darkening sky. The suns had set long ago and now the stars were beginning to twinkle in the gloom. She spoke to those stars, forgetting her place. "He said we'd be saving the city."

The princess inhaled sharply and shuffled around on her bedroll. "Of course, I'm a danger to my family and people because of Daerion. It's because of him my mother is dead, and why my father keeps so many knights stationed in the castle."

The princess's words were dire. No official explanation was ever given for Queen Annalah's death, so it was possible the Doshara killed her. Even more dire that the princess was an idle threat to the king himself. However, Ray couldn't get past the name that Princess Niamnh said. "Daerion?"

"That's his name. Not that he ever told me directly. I only found out during that night when..." She trailed off. Ray heard Princess Niamnh try to breathe in and out, but a sob wracked her body.

"Princess...?" Ray sat up, looking across the fire.

The princess was curled up on one side, knees pulled to her chest. She was crying again, and Ray had a hunch that she was referring to the night of the kidnapping.

"Princess, what happened when we came for you? Who were you with—"

The princess sniffled and breathed in deeply. "Trys. My best friend, my Sworn Sword, my—" Another sob.

Ray and Ajak had stolen Princess Niamnh right out of her bed while she was becoming intimate with one of her knights, Trys. Ray hadn't considered the emotional bond between the princess and her knight, or what had become of him after she and Ajak stole the princess away. Ajak's hands had been red that night. Had he killed Trys, the princess's sweetheart? Ajak always had a flair for the dramatic, but surely, he knew the dangers of killing a knight—in the castle, no less. But the theatrics were over now. He wouldn't be pulling any kinds of stunts like that again.

The tears were heavy and threatening to run down her cheeks. Ray dabbed at her eyes with her sleeve. "He's still alive, I'm sure of it." *Ajak would never kill a knight.*

Princess Niamnh rolled over to look at Ray. Shadows fell over her form, but Ray could see the tears glistening on her cheeks. Her lips were parted, her chest and shoulders rising and falling with noticeable effort. Ray was sure she was in a similar state or would be soon enough.

"He's the only one who—" The princess choked down another sob. "Everyone else either treats me like a prized doll or a mad hound. But Trys... he loves me for *me*. He saw past the crown, past the monster..."

"Princess—"

"Niamnh."

Ray's brow furrowed. "I-I'm sorry...?"

The princess inhaled sharply, then said in a steady voice, "Call me Niamnh. Please. I need someone else to see *me*. Like he did."

Ray's stomach clenched and the tears began to fall. She had spent so many days viewing the girl the way everyone else did—a crown with a monster hidden beneath it. She had been so swept up in her fear of the Doshara that she forgot it was sharing a body with someone with an iron willpower who had played a host to it for so many years.

She overheard Niamnh whispering a quiet prayer to the sky. "Protector, please, let me see him again one day."

Ray didn't know what awaited them in Na'roc of North. She felt so small, and desperately wished Ajak was there to wrap his arms around her and tell her it would be alright. Tell her what to do. But when she thought of his hands, she only saw Naro's bronze skin.

She was truly alone in the forest.

Alone with Niamnh.

The two girls set out shortly after sunrise the next morning. Ray broke her fast with a hard tack biscuit and fresh water from the river. Niamnh drank from the river as well, ensuring their waterskins were full before she washed off the plate from the night before. The princess must have eaten her... meal... after Ray went to sleep. Ray was no stranger to seeing and handling raw meat, but she wasn't quite sure if she was ready to watch someone eat it.

They set out north again, following the riverbank. After almost an hour, they came across a tree that had fallen into the river. It spanned most of the surface, and what distance it didn't cover could easily be jumped. Ray crossed the tree first, taking each step lightly and testing the trunk before placing all of her weight on her feet. Niamnh watched from the western shore.

Soon Ray and Niamnh were reunited on the eastern shore, and they continued east. The princess would sometimes limp, her feet sore, but she never complained. Without saying as much out loud, she increased their number of breaks to give Niamnh time to recuperate.

They had more conversations than on previous days, though they mainly discussed their surroundings and the forest and the wildlife residing within it.

"I've read about these woods, but it's something else entirely to be out here experiencing it for myself," Niamnh said in awe as they both looked at the trees during one of their breaks. "Although most of the lumber for Auora comes from the forests around Trent, there are a handful of mills located on the southern edge of these woods."

Hopefully, we won't come across any of them. Ray couldn't bear to say the words out loud and ruin the princess's mood. It would be better for both of them if she was in pleasant spirits as often as possible. And Ray didn't want to upset her.

"I've never been off the island, actually." Ray was surprised at how easily she offered that information. "Lived my whole life in the city."

"That's something we have in common, although..." The princess's words tapered off into a pause. "Our lives are very different."

In that moment Ray craved a connection, a conversation. "Do you like to read, Niamnh?" she blurted.

Niamnh's face lit up, and she smiled. Ray liked seeing her smile. "Yes, I do. I enjoy learning about the world beyond the island."

"That's something else we have in common, then," Ray said.

"My favorite books are about the Elviri and their culture. Some of their traditions are just so romantic."

Ray had never thought of the Elviri as romantic, but then again, she hadn't thought of anything as very romantic. Ajak had been the closest thing to *romantic,* and, well...

I knew better than to take his words at face value.

"What about you? Which books are your favorites?" Niamnh asked.

Ray thought back to all of the books she'd read over the years. Naro kept a few bookshelves in his house, filled with books from the Elviri provinces, the Imalar Woods, and even the Black Lakes. She had forced herself through several history books and informative texts, but she had a fondness for the make-believe stories.

"Tales of adventure," Ray finally responded. Niamnh gave a thoughtful hum.

As they resumed their walking, they exchanged memories of stories they had read when they were younger. Niamnh regaled Ray with tales of chivalric knights and their lovely ladies, and Ray gushed about treasure hunters.

The air grew colder as the day progressed. Ray pulled her coat tightly around her chest, tugging up on the collar so it covered her neck. It would only get colder from here, she knew that.

This'll be worse than any winter in Auora, she thought with a grimace. When Ray glanced over her shoulder, she caught Niamnh adjusting her coat and gloves as well. *We'll need a big fire tonight.*

They made camp early to give themselves enough time to gather additional kindling and wood. Ray helped Niamnh move some of the larger branches and logs. Soon they had a large fire going, Niamnh was massaging her sore feet, and Ray was preparing the princess's nightly tea.

Ray and Niamnh huddled close to the fire, the princess holding her cup with both hands and Ray chewing idly on a piece of dried fish.

"Damn cold," Ray grumbled.

"And it'll only get colder," Niamnh agreed. "I didn't think it could get worse than the palace gardens in winter..."

Ray let out a laugh and slapped a hand against her bedroll. "With all due respect, Princess, your castle isn't nearly as bad as the docks in the dead of winter."

A look of worry crossed Niamnh's face before she blinked and blushed. "You're right. I-I wasn't thinking."

"It's alright," Ray mumbled, looking away. "This'll probably be worse than anything either of us have seen before. Thank the Protector we have these coats."

Niamnh hummed, but Ray wasn't sure it was in agreement. She decided not to push the princess further and instead stayed as pleasant as she could. They ate and drank in silence until Niamnh climbed into her bedroll and lay on her back. Ray polished off the last few bites of an apple and threw the core into the woods, pleased with the distant thump of its landing.

"How many more days east?" Niamnh called from across the fire.

"Three or four, depending on our going," Ray answered.

She clutched the sunsdial in one hand and fidgeted with its latch. Their going had been slow thus far, which worried her. They had enough supplies to get to the border, but she didn't know how many days they would be traveling across the tundra. Another nagging thought ate at the back of her mind: would the Enthai find them before the Doshara realized she had been lying about Naro meeting them in Na'roc of North?

With a lurch Ray realized she genuinely wanted the Enthai to find them first. Perhaps they would keep the Doshara at bay, perhaps even get rid of him, and then Ray could return to Auora safely. After all, Naro had said she'd be safe as long as she bore the mark of the Walkers. Naro wouldn't send her to her doom. He was trusting her to carry out the mission and return successfully.

He did *mention something about returning, didn't he? That the Enthai would return me to Promthus.* She was sure of it, or wanted to be. A long shadow with dagger-sharp claws and teeth loomed over her thoughts, and she couldn't keep herself from doubting her memories.

It took a while for her to fall asleep that night.

The fire still burned brightly when Ray awoke the next morning. The flames overwhelmed her senses, and she rubbed the painful heat from her eyes. Squinting, she could see Niamnh across the fire, poking at it with a stick.

"Niamnh?" Ray asked, her voice groggy.

"Good morning," Niamnh said quietly. "I kept tossing and turning, so I decided to tend the flame instead."

Ray noticed the fresh pile of kindling and branches next to the other girl. "You went out on your own?"

"Not very far," Niamnh retorted. "Just far enough to get more wood."

"We don't know what lives in these woods," Ray protested. "You could have been attacked!"

"It's fine. I took one of your knives with me."

Ray's head spun. *She could have hurt herself, what was she thinking?* Then it hit Ray—she was more concerned for the princess's wellbeing than she was about her taking a blade and escaping into the woods. Or the Doshara reemerging. *She could've run away if she wanted to. She could've stabbed me in the gut, left me for dead, and been gone from here. So, why didn't she?*

The alarm and confusion must have been evident on Ray's face. The princess winced and said, "I returned the knife. You have both."

Ray patted her hips and back. The two blades were indeed in their sheaths. She mustered her courage. "You could have left. Why did you come back?"

Niamnh's lips pursed. "I told you. There's no reason for me to leave. And more importantly, I don't *want* to."

Ray frowned. She wanted to snap or yell but couldn't find the right words. Silence hung heavily in the air between the two girls. Niamnh continued to tend the flame.

Does she finally want to get rid of the Doshara? Has it offended her somehow, or made her distrust it?

Ray pulled herself to her feet and began pulling on her boots and packing up her bedroll. She wanted to say something. She wanted the princess to hear her questions and understand her concerns. Maybe they could even talk about getting rid of the Doshara, and how much better that would be for her. For everyone.

But she's a princess. How can I get her to listen to me, a street rat?

Ray and Niamnh continued their bouts of silence as they traversed the northern forests. The trees grew thick and dense, but with the coming winter, there wasn't enough foliage to block out the suns. In the distance, birds cawed and chirped to one another. Sometimes they could catch a glimpse of deer in the distance. By the Protector's grace they hadn't come across anything more dangerous like a bear or snow lion. Ray knew very little about the predators of the north, but she knew enough to know that she didn't want to see them.

None except for the Enthai. The dark thought sent a shiver down her spine.

The two hadn't spoken to each other since they broke their camp for the day, and Ray felt tension growing in her shoulders and neck. *How does this princess work me up so much?* She fiddled with Naro's sunsdial to distract herself. It was midday, and they had been traveling for five days. They should be in Na'roc of North in two days' time. *But how will we know? Will the trees thin out? What about snow?*

Ray had seen snow before, but only a light dusting on the streets. She had read descriptions of the northern tundra, but it was difficult for her to imagine.

A land covered in white. How curious.

Niamnh stayed silent during the day, following a short distance behind Ray. Curiosity gnawed at Ray's thoughts. *Is the Doshara talking to her again? Or is he not responding to her?*

Ray realized she had referred to the demon as "he" rather than "it". She grimaced and removed her bow from her back, suddenly overcome with the urge to shoot something. The princess needed her dinner, after all. Ray still had yet to see the girl eat any of the animals she had slain and prepared for her. Every morning the princess cleaned her plate. There were never any bloodstains on her hands or face. Ray wondered how she managed to do that.

Perhaps for the best.

"Ray?" Niamnh called out softly from behind. Ray threw a brief glance over her shoulder to indicate that she was listening. "Daerion wants to know if you can fell a deer for us tonight."

She was thankful she wasn't facing the princess. Her face twisted into an ugly sneer at the mention of the Doshara's name, and the fact that it thought to make demands of her was even worse.

But can I hunt a deer? She was irritated that she was doubting herself, though she knew the doubts were well-founded. She'd never hunted anything like a deer before. At least with the smaller wildlife, she could use her hunting skills from the city—rats, birds, and other creatures.

As the suns sank lower in the sky, Ray did manage to kill a pheasant and another rabbit. No deer for the Doshara today, though. They set up camp in a small clearing, the smoke from their campfire rising into the sky. They built the fire large again tonight; Ray wasn't worried about being spotted. She skinned the rabbit and set its carcass on the tin plate, handing it over to the princess who accepted it without a word. Ray tied the pheasant to her pack, to save for the next evening. Her own dinner consisted of dried cadra berries, an apple, smoked fish, and another hard biscuit. She sprinkled the biscuit with water, then held it over the fire for a few moments to soften it up before gnawing on it.

When she finished eating, Ray stretched out on her bedroll and looked up at the sky. Only the brightest stars shone against the smoke and flame of the fire. Seeing them brought a smile to her face. It reminded her of the constellations painted on Naro's ceiling.

"How much more tea is there?" Niamnh asked, her voice quiet.

Ray raised her head and gave the princess a questioning glance. "For a second cup tonight?"

"For the trip."

"Oh, um… plenty, I think," Ray trailed off, thinking of the sacks of dried petals she kept in her bags. She split them up across each bag, not that that would stop the Doshara if he were to take over Niamnh and search through their belongings. "Why?"

"He wanted to know." Niamnh's response was ominous. Something had changed in the tone of her voice. It was hard to make out because she was so quiet, but it sounded like her voice dropped an octave.

Ray squirmed around on the bedroll, her stomach tightening. One hand idly rested on the hilt of one of her daggers.

Niamnh's face twisted into a confused expression, conflicting with the calm, confident words slipping past her lips. "He says we shouldn't need it once we get to Na'roc of North. To not serve it anymore once we get there. That you'd understand why."

"Niamnh, can you tell him to shut up?" Ray snapped.

The princess was quiet for several moments. When she spoke next, her voice returned to its normal cadence. "You should put the handcuffs on now, I think."

Ray sat up, realizing she hadn't been using them for the past couple of nights. She silently cursed herself as she gathered the cuffs and moved to the princess. "Do you need more tea tonight?" she asked as she secured the princess's wrists behind her back.

"No, I don't think so. I think I can keep him at bay…"

That did little to assuage Ray's fears. "Right, well, you tell him that if he kills me, it'll be real difficult getting back home."

Niamnh closed her eyes, only mere seconds longer than a normal blink, but when she opened them again, they were cold as ice. Ray saw malice in those gray eyes.

"Don't worry, little moth, I'm not going to kill you. You still have a purpose to serve." The low voice spilled from Niamnh's throat. It spoke louder now, its voice scratching at her throat and making the princess sound like a sick creature. "And for your sake, I hope that purpose finds its way to Na'roc of North. Otherwise, I'll have to leave you to meet its natives while I travel back to Promthus."

Ray rolled back on her heels, throwing one hand behind her to stabilize herself. She held her tongue, refusing to lash out in fear or anger. *It's goading me on. I can't let it.*

She stood and brushed the dirt off of her lap. Without saying a word, she returned to her bedroll, poked the fire, and then took a seat. Sleep didn't come easy that night.

CHAPTER IX: SETH

Seth and Octavia strolled along the colonnade together, Octavia pushing his wheelchair from behind. Two stewards shadowed their walk, staying five paces behind the siblings. The forest was lively with many animals singing and shrieking to one another in the late morning. It all sounded so much clearer and louder from up there without the walls of the pyramid muffling their noises. Seth found himself gazing out at the foliage, staring at the numerous hues of green and brown. Birds darted across his vision, leaving blurs of yellows, reds, and blues amongst the leaves. He knew that was life as normal out in the rainforest, but a small part of his mind childishly thought the birds were welcoming him back to the outside world, singing their songs to *him*, showing off their plumage and flight to *him*. His heart swelled at thought, and a small smile danced across his lips.

Beneath the animals' chorus, Seth could hear the familiar low hum of the rainforest. *Of magic*, the Asaszi had said during his youth. He hadn't heard the hum in several days, since before he had escaped to Lithalyon. The ominous noise put a damper on his mood and his joy faltered.

Clouds covered the land, and the two suns were nowhere to be found. Pockets of blue poked through the clouds in certain spots, revealing the sky beyond. It was indeed cooler out, but it was also more humid thanks to the clouds. His hands dampened. He was sure Octavia was also sweating.

"Besides how damp the air feels, it *is* nice out today," Seth said, trying to recapture his good mood. "All those birds and creatures are making quite the racket, though. I don't think they like the turn of the weather. That, or they're saying hello to me again."

Octavia let out a small chuckle. "Funny, I normally tune them out when I'm in the practice yard. It's kind of nice listening to them from up here, though," she responded. "I wish I knew what some of these creatures looked like."

"Perhaps there's illustrations of some of them, maybe Moth—" Seth stopped. He didn't know if he should speak of his mother or her library around the stewards. *Did Amias's lockdown extend to Octavia? Or just me?*

"Perhaps," came Octavia's cool reply.

They had both spent many hours in that room when they were children, so she surely knew that's what he was referring to. She said nothing else on the matter, so either she was unaware of their father's lockdown of the library, or she was choosing not to share what she knew.

Perhaps later she'll tell me.

Seth pushed the thought of books from his mind and allowed the restless noise of the forest to fill his head instead. He listened for one particular song from the familiar kytling, but he couldn't pick it apart from the rest of the noise. He found himself missing the little bird, wishing he could catch a glimpse of its yellow feathers.

"Training's going well," Octavia said suddenly, drawing Seth's attention. "We have a set of new recruits from the past fortnight. Some of them show promise."

Seth raised an eyebrow. *Lisanthir is who she's referring to, surely. This must be how she's keeping an eye on him when he's not tending to me.* "What have these recruits been working on?"

"They've all mastered the basics quite fast. You know, wooden sticks and shields," Octavia explained. She was a *pyredan* now, after all. One of Amias's generals. She'd be expected to train new recruits and ensure they were ready to fight in his war. "Some prefer the shorter sticks, more like swords. A couple prefer the longer ones, though. Could be decent at polearms. We'll be starting with dull blades in the coming days. They certainly know how to handle themselves."

Seth couldn't stop the faint blush from spreading across his face. He was glad to hear that Lisanthir was adapting to the Provira lifestyle. He tried to tune out the gnawing fear that bubbled within, whispering *why* Lisanthir had to learn these things to begin with. *Father's sending all these Provira off to die.*

All the other recruits Lisanthir's training with will be dead before too long. At least Lisanthir isn't being sent to Promthus to fight.

"Wonderful news, Tav," Seth said, his voice strained.

"Actually, I'm due back in the training pit this afternoon. Do you want to come watch a few sparring matches? Then have dinner with me in my chambers after?" his sister asked, the inflection of her voice a little higher than normal. She was excited to share Lisanthir's progress with him and show him a glimpse of her world, but he could tell she was also nervous asking him. When they were children, they had trained together. After his legs were destroyed, though, he stopped attending any of the training sessions and never spoke to her about her own training.

"Sure, it'll be a nice change of scenery," he answered, trying to convey as much warmth and pleasantry in his words. He wanted to go and watch to support his twin. Having dinner with her afterward also meant they'd have time to discuss their plan to escape.

Octavia let out a small sigh of relief and steered his chair toward the inside of the pyramid. The two stewards kept up with them, always five paces behind. "Oh, great! I'll escort you to your room, and then I'll be back in about an hour to help you down to the arena."

Seth made a small noise of agreement. He supposed he could flip through another one of the books in his room to pass the time until she returned. Octavia left him at the entrance to his chamber along with the two stewards. One opened the door for him, and he rolled inside. Both stewards took up their posts on either side of the door, leaving him alone in his room.

True to her word, Octavia returned an hour later to escort Seth to the training pit. She had freshened up a little and had wrapped new cloth strips around her knuckles. Seth guessed that she would most likely be participating in some of the fights before the day was over.

The pyramid was bustling with activity. Provira and Asaszi alike were moving through the corridors murmuring to each other, carrying baskets and stacks of goods to various storerooms or to the kitchens. Several Provira greeted Octavia, asking her about her day and where she was off to. Some even murmured greetings to Seth, which caught him off guard. He had never been very sociable, even when he was a child. Octavia had been his only friend growing up, so it was surprising to hear other people asking after him, speaking to him with fondness.

Do they truly care about me, or do they just see me as an extension of my father?

There were several ramps throughout the pyramid, connecting floors together. Where there were no ramps, Amias had ordered the construction of lifts wherever possible, so Seth could still get around after the accident. He never used them because he chose to stay on the higher floor instead. As the twins descended the pyramid, he noticed that several servants were utilizing the lifts to transport goods to and from the higher floors. That gave him a small sense of relief to see the lifts were serving some purpose after all.

Amias hadn't done anything about the village surrounding the pyramid, though. At the time, Seth was told it wasn't worth the cost and labor. With his new perspective on the war, however, Seth realized that Amias didn't have a choice in the matter. He couldn't afford to do anything as costly as reconstructing a decaying city. Amias, Osza, and Astohi left the common Provira to fix the huts and roads themselves when they weren't training or scouting or fighting.

Seth's wheelchair didn't travel well across the village's roads. His thighs and lower back went numb after a short time due to how uneven and rocky the surface was. He kept his mouth shut, knowing that if he complained his sister would no doubt return him to the pyramid rather than let him endure the pain. He had a feeling she knew what the ruined road was doing to him and his chair, and perhaps she was trusting him to tell her when it became too much. Idly he wondered what "too much" was. The low hum was louder, and he thought he could feel it vibrating within the wheels of his chair and in his lower back.

On the southern side of the pyramid, the other *pyredans* had constructed a semi-permanent camp in a large field in between some of the stone huts. A fence made up of wooden poles surrounded the camp, the tops sharpened into pikes. Laughs and jeers could be heard from within the makeshift arena.

"Are you going to fight again today?" he asked his sister.

"Yes, to show off someone's progress." She patted his shoulder. "Also got a bastard who needs to be put on his ass. He's been stirring up trouble."

Seth pondered how best to respond. Octavia had always been competitive and eager to prove herself to her fellow soldiers and officers. She took to their culture easily enough, so much that it didn't surprise or bother Seth when she became more crass or aggressive.

"Should be a good show then?"

Octavia grunted in agreement.

The area was used as training and sparring grounds with other exits leading back to the village. Weapon and armor racks lined the fence, filled with various training instruments like wooden poles and shields. Some contained dull steel weapons for when the recruits were comfortable with the wooden ones. Today, hardly any of the weapons had been picked up. Bodies filled the makeshift arena, forming a circle around the center where two teenage boys were beating each other with wooden clubs.

"Hit 'im harder!"

"Smash 'im with the butt!"

"Stay on your feet! I'n't over yet!"

Seth couldn't see around the crowd, so he instead twisted his neck to look up at Octavia. Something predatory gleamed in her eyes as she pushed Seth around the right curve of the wall, keeping him between the wooden spikes and the warm bodies. Looking to his left, he caught brief glimpses of the fight between the soldiers and recruits. One boy was towering over the other, raising his club high. The smaller boy wore a shield on his left arm, lifting it to meet the other's club. The crowd surged forward, their screams getting louder. He could no longer make out individual words, but the fight appeared to be reaching its peak. The larger boy was no doubt wailing on his counterpart, which left an uneasy feeling in Seth's stomach. He hadn't visited the arena in several years, and he idly wondered if it was a mistake to do so today.

Octavia stopped pushing his chair and stood on her toes to look over the crowd. She let out a loud shout with the others, pumping her fist in the air. Turning back to Seth, she had a smile plastered across her face. "Dillyn won. Used the leg-sweep I taught him."

Seth returned the smile despite not fully understanding what she meant. *Is she referring to the smaller boy? How did he manage to knock the bigger one off his feet?* "So, um, where am I going to sit?"

His sister inhaled deeply and nodded, gripping onto the back of his chair again. "Right. Let's go find Arcyr'ys."

The crowds filled the center of the ring, making it easier for Octavia and Seth to navigate the perimeter. They went nearly halfway around the arena before they spotted the older Provira sitting with a few other *pyredans* inside of a covered booth, observing the fights with keen interest. The last time Seth had seen Arcyr'ys, it had been at the gathering where Amias killed his mother. His stomach twisted.

"Arcyr'ys!" Octavia called out, raising a hand in greeting. "Cyndaryn! Borros!"

Arcyr'ys rose to his feet, beckoning her over. The man wore his armor, but his helmet had been discarded. He had short brown hair that fell to his chin with eyes to match. A few gray streaks could be seen at his temples. Scars covered his face.

"Kharis! *Both* Kharises!" Arcyr'ys said.

The two other *pyredans* exchanged some words that Seth couldn't hear before they stood as well. Octavia maneuvered his wheelchair to the entrance of the booth. The female *pyredan*, Cyndaryn, pushed the wooden chair closest to the entrance out of the way for the twins.

"We weren't sure if you were coming back for the rest of it," Acyr'ys said with a fond grin, clasping arms with Octavia.

"What, and let Vinse gloat about it? No." She laughed then gestured to Seth. "Besides, I wanted to bring my brother down so he could see how the recruits are shaping up."

Arcyr'ys looked beyond Octavia to Seth. There was no hiding the curiosity in the older man's brown eyes. He knew Seth never made appearances at events. He bowed his head respectfully, pressing the tips of his fingers to his forehead. "Well, welcome, my prince."

"Thank you, *pyredan*. Is it okay if I sit here for the afternoon?" Seth responded.

"Of course. I'll join you two on the end."

All of the *pyredans* began shuffling around the booth. It was cramped having four chairs and Seth's wheelchair within the booth's walls, but if anyone was bothered, they didn't vocalize it. Seth's chair was placed at the end closest to the entrance with Octavia sitting to his right and Arcyr'ys beside her.

Seth leaned over to catch a glimpse at Cyndaryn and Borros, not as familiar with them. Both were closer in age to Arcyr'ys than Octavia with as many battle scars to match. Cyndaryn was a woman who naturally frowned, with pale wrinkled skin and cropped black hair. Borros had a kinder face with sun-kissed skin and green eyes. If Seth remembered correctly, Borros was around his mother's age and had been friends with her growing up.

"Which match is up next?" Octavia asked the others.

"Couple of Enzo's boys," Borros grumbled. "What I heard, not much to look at."

"Practice or punishment?" Octavia replied.

Borros replied with "punishment" as Arcyr'ys said "practice".

Octavia leaned over and shot a glare at Borros. "Let's give them the benefit of the doubt. Maybe they'll do something impressive."

Seth heard Borros grumble again, but he couldn't make out the individual words. It was surely something negative, though.

How Mother ever put up with him, I don't know. A knot formed in his throat as he pictured his mother in her youth, spending time with this boorish man.

"Clear off, clear off!" someone shouted from the fighting ring, pulling Seth's attention back to the arena.

Seth turned away from the *pyredans* to watch as the crowd pushed back around the outer edge of the ring, leaving the center empty except for three people—an announcer and two challengers. The announcer was only a few years older than Seth while the two challengers appeared to be no more than fourteen or fifteen years old. Both carried wooden swords and shields, each glaring menacingly at the other.

The crowd quieted but never fully went silent. Over the low din, Seth heard Arcyr'ys whisper, "Bet you ten coins on the taller one."

Octavia turned to whisper back. "They're the same height?"

Both snickered. Seth rolled his eyes and focused on the fight instead, the looming bloodshed less revolting than his sister's behavior with the older man. The two had always been close ever since Octavia first joined the army. It made Seth's skin crawl how his sister fawned over the older *pyredan*, constantly seeking his favor and attention.

Wooden swords clashed. Shields bashed together. The crowd became rowdy again, but with many more jeers than cheers. Seth understood that the fight was no doubt a form of punishment and meant to serve as a filler in between the more anticipated matches. He wondered when Octavia would be entering the ring herself.

One boy smashed his shield into the other's face, cracking his nose. Blood spurted out, drenching the front of his shirt and creating a small puddle in the dirt. The injured boy let out a loud screech and threw himself at the other, tossing his shield aside in favor of grabbing at the other's clothing and trying to tackle him to the ground.

Seth's stomach churned, dismayed by the brutality of the boys and the frenzied screams of the crowd. It all felt so needlessly cruel. *Is this what the other races see when they look at us?* He blinked slowly, letting his eyes glaze over. The fight became a blur of colors and motions. He wished for a swift end to the fight so they could move onto other matches, which hopefully would be less crude. *At least Tav isn't so cruel.* He hoped, anyway.

The fight devolved into an all-out brawl in the dirt. Fortunately for Seth, he couldn't hear the sound of fists hitting flesh over the roar of the other soldiers whooping and hollering. Eventually the announcer forced his way back into the center of the ring, yelling and waving his arms for the fight to end. The two boys had to be pulled apart and carried off through separate exits.

A horrible thought came forth unbidden in Seth's mind. *Will these two try to kill each other later?* If the recruits were trained the same way as they had been when Seth was a child, the other *pyredans* would encourage each boy to win no matter what the cost. Several recruits had been killed under similar circumstances ten years ago. Seth banished the thought before it could continue on.

"NEXT UP! A dance of demonstration!" the announcer roared, the crowd erupting into overwhelming cheers. Casting a glance over at his sister and the other *pyredans*, Seth saw Arcyr'ys nudging Octavia with his elbow. Her face twisted into a cheeky grin, and she rose to her feet. "*Pyredan* Kharis and her new feather-toed pupil!"

They love her so much, Seth realized, looking back at the crowd. They had all turned toward the booth and were cheering for his sister. She exited the booth, reaching out to shake hands, clasp shoulders, rub elbows with every soldier in her path.

In the center of the ring stood another soldier beside the announcer, already wielding a spear and shield. He was dressed in an outfit similar to Octavia's cloth shirt and pants, except he also wore a tan cloth head wrap that covered his hair, ears, and the lower half of his face. Though he was too far away for Seth to make out his eyes, he had a feeling he knew who stood in the arena with his sister.

Lisanthir. That must be who she wanted to show off today. Is that why she asked me to come down here? Seth's heart leapt up into his throat. Though he knew Octavia wouldn't maim or kill the Elviri, he couldn't help his heart from beating faster, dreading what he was about to see. *Tav's not as brutal as the others. They're calling it a dance. I should just try to enjoy it.* He inhaled deeply and exhaled through his mouth, but his muscles were still tense.

One member of the crowd handed Octavia a wooden shield, and another passed her a dull training sword. She stood on the opposite side of the announcer from Lisanthir, shield raised in front of her chest. He mimicked a similar stance, though his right arm was bent and angling the spear toward her.

The announcer raised a hand into the air, then took a few steps backward. "*P'thy'ks!*"

Seth recognized the word from his childhood when he used to participate in combat lessons: *Fight!*

Octavia immediately lunged forward with her shield, smashing it into Lisanthir's. She raised her sword in her right arm, stabbing it towards his neck. Lisanthir absorbed the shield-smash with his own, allowing the force to push his weight back on his left foot. He rolled his shoulder, angling to the right and thrust his spear into Octavia's left flank behind her shield. She threw her left arm out, slamming into Lisanthir's shield again. She let the rest of her body follow the movement, her hips twisting left as well. Lisanthir's spear struck the empty space where she had been standing.

Seth's hands flew to his armrests, nails digging into the wood. He knew his sister was an excellent fighter, but he had never seen her in action before, not since childhood. And Lisanthir... They had discussed his training with the Elviri army, but he hadn't fully processed that it meant Lisanthir knew how to *fight*. The rest of the crowd was just as impressed, the ground practically vibrating with excitement.

"Yeah, *kytsyrii!*" one soldier close to the booth called out.

Several others pumped their fists in the air, screaming out Octavia's name. Lisanthir and Octavia continued their battle dance, shields clashing together as they tried stabbing, swiping, slashing at each other.

Seth found himself unable to tear his gaze from the fight, but he also struggled to follow along, fearing every blow that successfully landed. *What if Tav hits him too hard and breaks bone? Or if Lisanthir pierces her with his spear?* Seth's eyes gravitated instead to their feet, watching as they kept their weight in their toes, which made it easier to twist and jump away when needed.

A small dust cloud kicked up underneath their boots as they spun in circles, driving the crowd into a heightened frenzy. Seth struggled to see through the haze and reluctantly raised his gaze to the fighters. He had assumed the spear would limit Lisanthir's ability to attack, especially with his sister favoring a sword and pressing in so close to him. Instead, the Elviri used it more like a second form of defense, catching Octavia's sword as she swung down toward his shoulder. Pushing the sword out when she tried stabbing at his midsection.

His sister had Lisanthir completely on the defensive, giving him no time to adjust his stance or make any attacks of his own. Lisanthir held his spear and shield steady and continued to deflect blow after blow.

Is he trying to wait her out until she gets tired? Won't he get tired first with how heavy her blows are? What if she manages to get past his defenses and really hurt him? Seth's stomach churned at the thought.

Lisanthir angled his spear in between them, giving a quick thrust toward Octavia's chest. Rather than push against the spearhead with her shield, she swung her sword to push the wooden weapon away. The Elviri seemed to allow it as his spear was driven far to his right, opening his midsection for further attack. Octavia no doubt noticed and stepped forward to throw her weight against his shield and make him stagger.

Seth's heart pounded in his chest, unable to look away from what came next.

Octavia did indeed move forward, but her step turned to a stumble. The crowd let out a collective howl, which Seth felt roll down his spine. His mind raced as he tried to process what had happened. Lisanthir's spear was in between their bodies again, and Octavia was trying to regain her footing. And he realized that Lisanthir had rammed the butt of his spear into her leg when she tried to step toward him.

He turned the tables on her and has her on the run now. The pit of dread in Seth's stomach melted away, pride swelling up in its place as he kept his eyes on Lisanthir.

Now the Elviri thrust the spear forward, small jabs into Octavia's shield, further keeping her from straightening out. She took several shaky steps to her right, and Lisanthir followed, continuing to poke at her defenses and keep her from bringing up her sword. Every time she tried to slash or stab, he used the shaft of the spear to drive the blade out wide, then resumed thrusting forward.

Round and round they went in circles, trading jabs and swipes. Both the Elviri and Provira raised their shields and rammed into one another, throwing their full weight behind the blows. They struggled to retain their footing, but Lisanthir relented after two heartbeats, pulling his left elbow down and twisting his body so that Octavia stumbled forward under her own weight. Lisanthir leaped away, spinning and raising his shield in the air. With a cry that could barely be heard over the fanatic crowd, Lisanthir chucked the shield at Octavia's back and then immediately ran after her, wielding the spear with both hands.

Octavia turned just in time to see the shield flying toward her. She dropped into a crouch, the metal passing cleanly over her head. As soon as it was clear, she leaped forward with her shield raised high. Lisanthir thrust the spear forward with both hands. Octavia used her shield to deflect the spearhead, then curved her sword out to push the shaft away. Her arm completed a full rotation before stabbing at Lisanthir's midsection. He pulled the spear back to his body, angling it to intercept and deflect the sword swipe.

Their dance continued, trading blow for blow, neither landing a solid hit on the other. The fight lasted no longer than a few minutes, but it felt like a lifetime as Seth watched his sister and his partner spar. It all came to a head when Octavia knocked Lisanthir's spear wide and then landed a heavy blow to his chest with the pommel of her sword. He stumbled back a step, and she swiped out with her leg, knocking him onto his back. She snapped her blade down to press its dull point against his throat.

Her leg-swipe maneuver.

Seth's breath caught in his throat as Lisanthir fell onto his back. He thought Octavia had won. She had clearly bested the Elviri, physically knocking him to the ground. But the crowd was screaming a mixture of both "*pyredan*" and "*kytsyrii*".

He looked at his sister's face for a clue—

Wait, he realized.

Lisanthir had angled the tip of his spear against Octavia's jaw. It was a draw. Seth couldn't contain his delight. He started clapping and cheering alongside the other soldiers. With a glance to his right, he saw Arcyr'ys and the other *pyredans* were also cheering.

How many years did Lisanthir spend in Elimaine training with the army? What else did he learn before becoming a librarian?

The announcer returned to the center of the ring, his hands raised in the air. Lisanthir tipped the spear away from Octavia, and she threw her sword out to the side. She offered her hand to Lisanthir and helped pull him to his feet. Men and women from the crowd surged forward to congratulate the two for their performance, and Seth lost sight of them both, much to his dismay.

"Vinse's got a tough act to follow," Cyndaryn said, and Seth could practically hear her grinning.

"Surprised he hasn't gotten a shank in the back yet," Borros responded.

"I'd do it if I could, but my girl wants to take care of him herself," Arcyr'ys murmured.

An unsettling chill ran down Seth's spine. Hearing the older Provira refer to Octavia as *his girl* made Seth want to... want to do *something* violent. His legs be damned, his sister deserved better.

"How many more until it's me and Vinse?" Octavia asked, pulling Seth out of his negative thoughts.

He turned to her with a smile, but the brightness faded from his face when he saw how red and cut up she was. Bruises would no doubt bloom over the next few days. It appeared that Lisanthir managed to land quite a few blows during their fight. With a jolt of panic, he wondered if Lisanthir was also bruised and bloodied like she was.

"Hey, Seth. Quite a fight, huh?" Octavia placed a hand on his shoulder and squeezed gently, bringing him some comfort.

Arcyr'ys stood and clasped arms with her, his eyes wandering over her form. "Should be three more. Enough time to clean up your blood and dirt," he said.

"Might be more intimidating to stay dirty," Octavia replied with a smirk.

"Your dance partner was something else!" Cyndaryn exclaimed as they all took their seats again. "Where did he come from?"

Octavia shrugged. "Not entirely sure, but I'm thankful he's with us. He's a force to be reckoned with."

"Let's hope Vinse doesn't take an interest in him, then," Borros chimed in with a hearty chuckle.

"After today, Vinse'll be lucky if he can see past his own nose." Octavia smiled, but her voice was dark and filled with something ugly. Something hateful.

Something Father would say.

The rest of the fights blurred together. Seth tried his best to not focus on any one thing, because every time he heard his sister laugh at something Arcyr'ys said, or whenever one of the combatants let out an anguished cry or frenzied scream, his stomach lurched.

Perhaps coming down here was a mistake.

Seth found himself craving Lisanthir's presence. He wanted to talk to him, distract himself from the sparring ring, and take comfort in just being with him. But the Elviri had disappeared after the fight, leaving Seth to fend off his thoughts by himself. For a few moments, his thoughts did turn away from the fights and toward the Provira stewards that served his family.

Do the other stewards know that Lisanthir is receiving combat training? Are any of them receiving combat training? I've never seen any of them wielding any weapons, but it would make sense that Father would want them capable of defending me. But if that's the case, do they wear the veils for training? He felt silly for even thinking that; Lisanthir hadn't fully covered his face in his match against Octavia. Surely the other stewards were also excused from wearing their veils sometimes.

"Next up!" the announcer shouted, shattering Seth's focus.

He blinked and trained his vision on the center of the sparring ring, where two men were clasping arms and congratulating each other on their performances. The announcer shooed them away, then turned his attention to the crowd once more. He raised his hands in the air, and the crowd responded with shouts and cheers.

"Our final match for the day! *Pyredan* Kharis and *Thy'ksiir* Vinse!"

A Provira man a few years older than the twins entered the ring, wearing a leather chest plate and brandishing a pair of wooden clubs. He had dark curly hair cropped just above his jawline, the curls hiding the tips of his ears. An ugly sneer was painted on his face, directed at Octavia as she rose to her feet and left the booth.

"Show 'im your fangs," Cyndaryn called after her.

Octavia threw a grin over her shoulder, but Seth didn't miss how his sister's fists clenched at her side.

Something's wrong. Is Tav truly prepared for this fight?

One of the soldiers offered Octavia a leather chest plate to match Vinse's. She donned the armor then accepted a wooden shield and dulled sword from another pair of soldiers. As she stalked out across the dirt ring, Seth was reminded of the hunting cats in the jungle. Octavia wasn't looking at the crowd or waving to her men; she was a predator eyeing her prey. And Vinse was watching her with similar interest.

Seth's grip on his armrests tightened. The fight would be nothing like Octavia's fight with Lisanthir. They had been showing off their talent and had fought with respect for each other. Whoever ended up on the ground in this fight wouldn't be offered a helpful hand once it's over.

Blood will be shed.

The announcer stood in between Octavia and Vinse with his hand raised in the air. They stood far enough apart that they'd both have to step forward in order to land any substantial blows to the other. The announcer looked over both combatants, giving a slight nod of his head, satisfied with whatever he was checking for. He retreated to the ring of soldiers before lowering his hand and shouting, *"P'THY'KS!"*

Seth heard the first blow land before his eyes registered what was going on. Vinse lunged forward, throwing his whole body against Octavia's shield. She staggered backward underneath his weight, the hilt of her sword hitting his shoulder. He pushed her backward several steps before he relented, pulling himself off of her and swinging his clubs.

The crack of wooden club on wooden shield sounded like summertime thunder. Seth jumped, startled with each hit against Octavia's shield. Vinse gave her no time to gather her composure or straighten out; he was going for a quick victory.

After Vinse hit Octavia's shield four or five times, there was enough of a delay for Octavia to regroup and brace herself for impact. Vinse anticipated this and changed his angle, instead swinging for her sword arm. Octavia recognized the movement just in time to throw her right arm back, outside of his reach. Her left arm crossed further over her chest to defend herself, throwing off her balance. Seeing her weakness, Vinse pressed onward, beating his clubs against her shield.

The two combatants were mere steps away from the ring of soldiers. Men and women were scrambling to make room for the fight to continue, desperate not to get in the way of Vinse's vicious swings. Octavia dropped into a squat as Vinse swung his clubs again. Without anything to hit, his momentum carried him into a stumbling step to the left. Octavia leapt up, angling her shield to slam it into his right arm.

Vinse let out an angry yelp, his grip on the club weakening. It clattered to the ground, and he was left with one weapon. Octavia wasted no time in pressing the attack. She beat the pommel of her sword into his elbow, then his shoulder, driving him back. With the additional room, she began slashing and swiping at him in earnest. He threw himself back and raised his left club to fend off blow after blow, and now they were making their way to the opposite side of the ring.

When they made it to the center of the arena, Octavia followed one of her slashes with her shield, throwing her weight into Vinse. They stumbled a few paces, but Vinse recovered first. He swung his club at Octavia, landing a heavy blow against her sword hand. The sword fell from her grasp.

With an enraged shout, Octavia swung her fist, and it collided with his cheek. The crowd let out a collective shriek as the combat devolved into a brawl. Vinse's head rolled to the side, but he recovered almost immediately, righting himself so he faced Octavia again. He grabbed Octavia's shield with one hand, trying to pull it away from her chest as he drove the butt of his club down toward her face.

Seth saw his sister hesitate for one moment, and that moment's hesitation cost her. The club slammed into her cheek, and she was thrown backward. Both combatants maintained a grip on her shield, which was the only reason she didn't fall to the ground. Vinse saw that and immediately let go of the shield. Octavia fell and hit the ground. Hard.

Arcyr'ys jumped to his feet with a roar. "Shield up, shield up!"

Seth's heart leapt into his throat. Vinse fell upon Octavia, straddling her waist. She limply raised her shield over her chest. He threw aside his club and grabbed the shield with both hands, wrestling her for control over it. With brute force he managed to pull it from her grasp and threw it across the ring. Then he began pummeling her with his fists instead—face, neck, chest, arms. Octavia tried keeping her arms up over her face, but several of his blows struck true.

Seth couldn't see it from where he sat, but he knew Vinse had drawn blood. The crowd had pushed in further, taking several steps to get closer to the brawl. The space in front of the booth remained open, so Seth and the other *pyredans* could still witness the fight. Octavia lowered one of her hands, accepting the vicious hits from Vinse. He was so focused on beating her, pummeling her into the ground, that he didn't see her grab the hilt of her sword. She stabbed at his leg. Though the blade was dull, it bit through his pants and dug into his leg.

Vinse threw himself away from her, but Octavia followed. She twisted onto her side and scrambled to her feet, tackling him into the dirt. For a brief moment, Seth saw her bruised and bloodied face framed by cropped, mutilated ears. There was fury in her eyes. It reminded him of his father, and that scared him. With her back to the booth, Octavia smashed the pommel of her sword into Vinse's face several times before dropping it and throttling the man with both hands. His legs kicked out, and he grasped at her arms, but his strength faded rapidly as she pressed down tighter and harder into his skin.

The announcer burst out of the crowd and ran to Octavia's side, watching with wild eyes as she choked Vinse. When the man's movements slowed and his struggling stopped, the announcer grabbed Octavia's shoulder and declared, "*Pyredan* Kharis is victorious!"

Octavia let go of Vinse and leaned back, throwing her head back. The sparring ring erupted into an overwhelming roar as several of the soldiers ran forward to pick Octavia up and celebrate her victory. Arcyr'ys ran from the booth to her side. Seth lost sight of his sister amidst the crowd, but he couldn't shake the horrible twisting feeling in his stomach.

What has Father done to you, Tav?

CHAPTER X: MUNNE

The rest of the day passed uneventfully. Munne received no summons to join any of the patrols in the city. *Will Rhorek and Munhart begin raiding the safehouses now that they have their list?* The two Proma were certainly eager enough to be rid of the gangs in the city, but they both seemed more levelheaded than their kin. Munne believed that they would wait until they had a plan of action before sending soldiers and knights into the streets.

Ely didn't visit her in her sleep. When she awoke the next morning, she felt a pang of disappointment. She assured herself that he'd show up eventually, and when he did, she'd be able to ask him about Naro, Kherizhan, and himself. She found herself wholly consumed with the desire to learn more about Ely.

Such a fascinating creature.

While she broke her fast, a steward arrived, escorting Araloth and Mayrien, the other two members of her triple, into the ambassadors' quarters. Relief washed over her as she took in the sight of the two Elviri women. Both were garbed in their riding coats. Araloth ran a hand through her short blonde hair, smoothing it back down from the way the winds had blown it about. Mayrien's long brunette hair had been braided and tossed over one shoulder with only a few strands loose from their journey.

"Munne!" Mayrien exclaimed as she joined Munne at the dining table.

Munne leapt to her feet and pulled Mayrien into an embrace, a smile plastered on her face. "It's good to see you both. Thank the gods you're here."

"We met Ethelmar and his troops at the western bridge," Araloth said, a hint of worry underlying her words. "And the journey through the city... What's going on here, Vere'cha?"

"A few events that have altered our course, I'm afraid," Munne responded, breaking free from Mayrien to clasp arms with the older Elviri woman.

"Princess Niamnh has been kidnapped, and the seedy underbelly of Auora has decided to expose itself at the same time."

"And Ethelmar's here to provide support." Araloth nodded, following the logical thought process with ease.

"That, and six of the triples are to take over guarding the dungeons here in the castle," Munne told her.

Both Mayrien and Araloth gave Munne curious looks.

"Aren't those triples better off in the city?" Mayrien asked.

"Under normal circumstances, yes, but there's a prisoner being kept here, and it's in everyone's best interest that he doesn't meet an unexpected end at the hands of his captors," Munne replied.

The other two Elviri women exchanged wary glances. They, too, knew of the Proma's violent tendencies towards their prisoners.

Araloth nodded. "Very well. Ethelmar and his troops stayed across the bridge in the city to help bolster the Proma's numbers. Should we ride out and inform him about the prisoner?"

"Yes, but first, I need to find Captain Munhart or Knight-General Gondamire."

"Captain Munhart was across the bridge with his knights when we passed through," Mayrien said.

Munne shrugged and nodded. "Alright, then let's be off."

The three Elviri found Munhart in the Night Lantern, the tavern closest to the castle bridge. The city guard had turned the tavern into their main outpost in the city, so few citizens were found inside; only the tavern keep and his family remained, serving food and drink to their new patrons. Proma and Elviri soldiers gathered around Captain Munhart at one of the larger circular tables as he was issuing orders. Ethelmar stood at Munhart's side, dressed in his steel blue and silver armor. One sword hung from his left hip and a circular shield was secured across his back, painted with a blue barren oak tree against a silver moon.

Munhart was in the middle of explaining the current situation to the gathered troops. Munne, Araloth, and Mayrien stayed near the edge of the common room, not wanting to interrupt. "Most of the safehouses are in the lower districts, but there are a few higher up that we must target as well."

I was right. Munne nodded at Munhart's words, pleased that he had formed a plan of attack rather than send his men out yesterday with the list he gathered from Naro. *But will the gangs know they're coming? How many will die today?*

For a brief moment, she felt as if she were standing in her war tent near Merrioff, or in one of the ruined farmhouses along the southern border near Moonyswyn with soldiers awaiting orders—waiting for the order to begin the bloodshed and death. How often had she been the one standing in Munhart's place, poring over maps of the battlefield, sending Proma and Elviri out into the fray?

This isn't my fight, she reassured herself. The Proma were her allies, so she felt obligated to assist them, but she knew that Auora wasn't her battlefield. She had to go south to Kherizhan. Still, it pained her to walk away from these men and women and leave them to their fates, especially when she knew she could help turn the tide against their foes. *That's why Ethelmar is here, and why I wrote home to summon more soldiers. Auora will be safe.*

Captain Munhart stood up straight, addressing the crowd. "We move out when the suns are at their peak. Couriers, report to Fennick for your assignments. Deliver your orders with haste. The rest of you, prepare to strike. Knight-General Gondamire will arrive with his knights within the hour."

The Proma and Elviri broke off into smaller groups, the tavern filling with low voices and the creaking and clanking of armor. More than a few mugs of ale were passed around, and the mood gently swung from sober to pleasant. The room became a sea of chainmail and hauberks.

"Captain Munhart, Commander Ethelmar, a word?" Munne asked the two men, approaching them.

They both turned to greet the three Elviri women and bowed politely. "Lady Vere'cha, it's good to see you," Ethelmar said softly.

"I trust your journey went smoothly?" Munne asked the Elviri man.

He nodded. "The majority of the outpost is here. We left five triples behind, and I passed your message along in my letters to Elimaine."

"Thank you." She turned her attention to Captain Munhart. "Did you move against the safehouses today?"

"Aye, Rhorek and I finalized a map of the city yesterday with our *guest*." Munne caught the disdain as he referred to Naro. "But we expect this to take a few days to finish. We've closed entry and exit to the city, and with your men arriving, we'll bolster the numbers on the docks to keep watch for anyone trying to leave."

A pit formed in Munne's stomach. *If the city's exits are closed, what happens after I find the caravan leader, if I can even find him? How will we get out of Auora and journey to Kherizhan?* Her mind raced with other questions and concerns, but she forced herself to maintain a neutral expression and focus on the Proma in front of her.

"Very good. And have we arranged for a small number of triples to take residence in the castle...?"

Munhart's lips curled down for just a moment before he responded. "Not yet, Lady Vere'cha."

"Commander Ethelmar, you're to send six triples to the castle to guard the prison cells," Munne ordered, her gaze shifting from Munhart to Ethelmar.

"At once, Lady Vere'cha." Ethelmar bowed and took his leave.

Captain Munhart remained, gaze drifting across Munne and her companions. "Will you be joining us today, my lady?"

She shook her head. "No, I'm afraid we can't. There are other matters that need my attention."

A look of disappointment crossed the Proma's face, but he didn't vocalize it. "Very well. Thank you for your assistance thus far, Lady Vere'cha." He bowed and excused himself from the table.

"Back to the ambassador quarters, then?" Mayrien asked, her lips curled into a sly grin.

"Yes, we need to discuss the next leg of our journey," Munne murmured, leading her companions out of the tavern and back across the bridge into the castle.

As they entered the main foyer, Rhorek was preparing to depart with his host of knights, all dressed in shining plate armor and equipped with swords and shields. There couldn't have been more than one hundred knights in all, and Munne wondered if they were leaving any behind to guard the castle. Between the war in the south and the search for Princess Niamnh, there surely weren't many men left in the city. Though it appeared most of the men had rallied around the mission to raid the safehouses. Perhaps they saw it as some sense of justice for their missing princess.

The three Elviri stayed out of the knights' way and traveled farther into the castle, retracing their steps back to the ambassadors' quarters. Some pitchers of water and wine had been left on a table inside the common area, along with a platter of buns and sweet rolls. Mayrien plucked a sweet roll for herself while Munne filled a goblet with wine and sat down on one of the couches.

Araloth turned her attention to Munne, standing beside her at the table. "So, are you still set on traveling—"

"East, yes. The same path that we discussed in Elimere," Munne replied, bringing the wine to her lips and inhaling the floral scent. It was risky for them to discuss those plans so openly where one of the Barauder or Eldo Talltree could listen in or interrupt. *Best to keep it vague, just in case.*

Araloth also recognized the danger in having the conversation in the open but continued anyway. "When and how?"

"I'll speak to Rhorek or one of the other members of the council and get a signed letter if I must," Munne muttered. She took a sip of the wine, allowing the flavors to dance across her tongue before swallowing. The wine was a touch on the sweet side, which she preferred. "But they *will* let us depart when we're ready."

"And when will we be ready?" Araloth asked through clenched teeth.

Munne glanced at Araloth then back at her goblet, her fingers fidgeting with the stem of the goblet. "We're waiting for another to arrive in Auora, someone who'll lead us the rest of the way."

Araloth drummed her fingers against the table, waiting for Munne to offer a better explanation. Munne felt like a fool. All of her recent actions went against her decades of training and discipline. Even the lowest ranking soldier knew better than to trust a stranger and put the entire fate of the mission in their hands. She had a responsibility to all three Elviri provinces to act in their best interests and protect them from any who wished them harm. The war with the Provira should be her main and *only* priority, and yet she was planning on abandoning her soldiers, the Imalarii, and the Proma to journey to Kherizhan with a stranger on a whim.

Better this than to end up like Malion, who died by his own hand. Every day I linger here in Auora, I risk the Ardashi'ik *overpowering Ely and dominating my mind.*

"Let's go for a walk, Munne," Mayrien said, standing next to the older Elviri. "And give Araloth some time to eat and unwind from our journey."

Munne cast one last glance at Araloth before turning to leave with Mayrien. She tried to convey all of her mixed emotions in that glance, imploring Araloth to be patient and to trust her, but also to help support her on this strange new path before them. The older Elviri turned her back to the pair, stalking off to her bedchamber without another word.

Mayrien and Munne wandered the halls of the castle, letting the silence sit comfortably between them. Both wore their riding clothes, dark blue coats over leather leggings and thick boots. Mayrien's brunette hair was in a single braid, draped over her right shoulder. A thin scar ran from her jaw down her throat, disappearing beneath the collar of her jacket. Munne remembered when her friend had gotten that scar nearly ten years ago, during one of the border skirmishes with the Provira on the edge of Elifyn. One of the mixed-blood brutes had broken through the frontline of Elviri defenders, charging straight for Munne and her triple. Mayrien had thrown herself in between the attacker and her friend, catching part of the man's downward swing with his sword. The blade carved an ugly line from the corner of her jaw down the front of her chest, and the only reason she wasn't cut clean in half was Araloth attacking the man from the other side and pushing him away from the other two women. All three had taken blows and wounds for each other, but that particular experience had left Munne shaken for several days.

"She'll follow you to the end of the world," Mayrien said softly, catching Munne's gaze. "We both will."

"I don't doubt that. Ever." Munne sighed and shook her head. "In truth, I'm thankful for how much she pushes back against me. It helps guide my steps and ensure I'm making the right decisions."

"And you're sure Kherizhan is the right decision now?" There was no accusation in Mayrien's words, just a genuine question.

"It has to be. I won't allow myself to be corrupted like Malion was. I won't."

Mayrien reached out and placed her hand on Munne's arm, squeezing gently. "And we won't let you. You can't beat us in a fight, anyway," she jested, flashing an impish grin.

Munne couldn't help but laugh at her own expense. "I'm so thankful that I was able to persuade you to join the army with me."

"I needed no persuading." Mayrien's voice softened, the smile fading from her face. "There was no choice for me. I knew I was meant to be by your side, not kept away behind the walls of my parents' home."

"They would've let you join, regardless of your friendship with me," Munne argued, knowing Mayrien came from one of the oldest families in Elimaine with deep ties to the Elviri army.

"If I had been born a man, perhaps, or had a brother. But with just me and my sister, they expected one of us to stay in Elimaine to continue the family line." The two continued their walk through the castle halls but at a slower pace. Mayrien's gaze wandered across the decorations and tapestries lining the walls. "I've told myself before that I would've made the decision to join anyway and wouldn't have let anything stop me... But Tirilyn chose to get married before I had the chance to put my bravery to the test. How thankful I am for that."

They walked past a door where the air was chillier than the rest of the hallway.

"An outdoor walkway, perhaps?" Mayrien said, tilting her head to the side.

"Sounds lovely," Munne replied, tugging gently on Mayrien's arm and leading her outside where there was indeed a covered walkway that hugged the side of the castle. Their view faced northward, toward the forested shores of the Hourglass Lakes and the tundra beyond. "Remember our talks about visiting Rymo-tehp?"

Mayrien chuckled. "That was one thing I could never keep up with you on. Scholarly pursuits weren't my strong suit."

"I seem to recall your excitement about traveling north."

"I was excited by the idea of what creatures we could hunt up there. And the challenge of survival in such a cold, unforgiving place."

Munne leaned against the balcony and sighed wistfully. "Maybe one day we'll go there. After the war."

The Elviri gods had been born in Rymo-tehp, as the histories told it. A castle made from ice, as large as the valley of Elimere, tucked away within the tundra of Na'roc of North. The lands were too cold and inhospitable for the Elviri to build homes and cities, though, so the gods had traveled south to Elimaine and raised their people there instead. Very few had made the pilgrimage to their most holy site, and Munne hoped to one day join that number.

To walk in the gods' footsteps, to stand where Ceyo herself became a god...

Mayrien mimicked her pose, their shoulders brushing. "Are you sure you don't want to run away there instead?" Munne gave her a sour expression, which only led to laughter. "I jest. I know your path lies south. We'll find a way to rid you of the *Ardashi'ik*."

The two stood together in pleasant silence, letting the lake breeze blow their hair around and the coldness seep into their clothing. It felt good to be outside, away from the chaos of the city. The Hourglass Lakes were peaceful. Munne almost envied the Proma for building their homes on this island.

"You know," Mayrien murmured. "I'm surprised your father didn't just call for our troops to withdraw and wait out the Provira dying."

Munne let out a thoughtful hum, her brow creasing. Though she hated the idea, she had to admit that Mayrien had a point. According to several of the royal archivists and scholars, it was only possible for an Elviri and Proma to successfully create life together once every thousand years. Typically, there were no more than a few hundred Provira offspring born in each generation. They would live about two hundred years, though, and would be incapable of creating life themselves. These periods of birth were tracked by scholars in Lithalyon, with the last period occurring a little over two hundred years ago. The cursed half-breeds would all be dying from old age soon anyway, so perhaps that's why Munne's father had sent a Lithuan mindwalker and a Paladin of the Gods to treat with them. But the harm the Provira could cause in the meantime...

"They'd burn down the entire realm of Promthus if we left them unchecked," Munne sighed.

"Shame they couldn't take Moonyswyn with them. Only the gods know why Ceyo didn't allow us to burn the rainforest down at the dawn of the Second Sun." Mayrien nudged Munne's shoulder with her own. "But I digress from our given course. Tell me more about this individual we're waiting on. What do they know about the lands of Kherizhan?"

Munne's brow furrowed, and she shifted her weight between her feet. "Truth be told, I don't know much about this man. I believe he's a Proma, but a strange one with mismatching eyes. He runs a caravan that's apparently traveled to Kherizhan in the past, bringing back trinkets to sell."

"And how do we know he's not stealing these goods from other Proma villages, or even the Imalarii?"

It was a fair question, and one that didn't sit well with Munne. She *didn't* know if he was a thief. But she had to trust what she saw. "When we spoke, he carried a magical trinket—a small coin—that could create fire with the touch of a finger. I've never seen anything like it before."

"Magic?" Mayrien asked, her voice dripping with doubt.

"Magic from an era long past," Munne went on stubbornly. "I won't deny that the man could be dangerous, but I believe that he knows a way into Kherizhan, and that he'll take us there." Mayrien was silent for several moments, staring off across the lake. "I know I'm asking for much from you and Araloth, but this is my path. It has to be."

"He's supposed to be in Auora?" Mayrien asked.

"Yes, but with the city on lockdown, I don't know if he's here or not. I haven't found him yet during my patrols."

"Well, we have our work cut out for us, then. What's he look like?"

Munne couldn't have asked for a better companion.

Mayrien and Munne returned to the ambassadors' chambers not too long after their balcony chat. Convincing Araloth to return to the city took little effort, using the guise that they were going to help refugees. Munne knew that was the primary reason Araloth agreed to go, not because she wanted to help Munne and Mayrien find the caravan leader. They brought their weapons with them just to be safe.

They first went to the Night Lantern to inquire after the city guard, and see if any news had been reported back yet of their mission in the lower levels of the city.

The tavern keeper shook his head. "No news from the guard, but more refugees have arrived. Some have come here, saying that the other inns are full."

"Are any of these refugees a man with mismatching eyes?" Munne asked, an inkling of hope leaking into her words.

"No, my lady, not that I've seen," the tavern keeper replied. "Should I be on the lookout for him?"

Munne exchanged looks with her companions. Mayrien gave her a shrug while Araloth simply frowned. "It'd be much appreciated," Munne said to the tavern keeper.

"Of course, my lady." The tavern keeper bowed his head and returned to his duties.

Munne, Mayrien, and Araloth left the Night Lantern and walked across the street to the nearest inn, the West Breeze Inn. The building stood five stories tall, built from dark stone. A handful of city guards had been left behind to watch over the refuge, allowing Munne and her companions entry as soon as they saw their approach. The first floor was packed with men, women, and children. People had to shout to hear each other over the sounds of laughter, chatter, and children crying. Several men and women darted between tables, juggling plates, mugs, and other items as they tended to the surge of visitors. Proma from all walks of life were in the common room, though most were either craftsmen and women, dock workers, or other families with very little wealth. Very few individuals of the other races were present, except for handfuls of Imalarii scattered across the room.

"Seems likely that your caravan man is here." Mayrien had to raise her voice to be heard over the din.

"One green eye, one white eye," Munne responded, eyes already shifting among the crowd to find the man.

"Did he give you a name?" Araloth asked, not bothering to hide her dissatisfaction.

"Dalys." That had been the name she told the caravan leader to use.

Araloth snorted and split away from Munne and Mayrien. Munne frowned, watching her companion move toward the bar.

"Don't worry. I can keep an eye on her while looking for Dalys," Mayrien said with a smile before walking away.

Munne wandered around the common room, hanging back near the outer walls. She idly listened to many of the different conversations, learning what she could of the city from its citizens.

"The king's knights came out of the castle in force today," one man muttered to his table over a pint of ale.

"They're going to drive out the gangs, no doubt," another one responded.

"So, this is it, then? D'you think the king will remember he's got more people living here than just the rich Sky folk?" a third asked, his voice quieter than the others.

"We can hope," the first grunted.

Munne wandered away from their table, looking for more information. A different conversation at a nearby table caught her attention, and she leaned against the wall for a moment to eavesdrop, her eyes searching the crowd as if she was looking for someone.

Four individuals were huddled together, their voices low. Two were little older than children, boys acting like men, wearing clothing too big for them. Across the table was an older woman with short black hair, perhaps their guardian or neighbor, and a figure with their hood drawn and cloak wrapped tightly around their body. Munne caught sight of stubble on their jaw, as well as a nasty cut on their lip—a third man. That one was several years older than the boys across the table.

"What're we gonna do, now that the boss's gone and the safehouses're getting hit?" one of the boys hissed to the older pair.

"Find any others and keep safe here. *Only* loyal ones," the woman responded, glaring at the two boys. "I'm trying to find us passage out of here as soon as we can."

"What about the lockdown? How can we get outta here with the docks off limits?" The boy's voice rose, and he ended his questions with a quiet yelp. The woman looked ready to jump over the table and clobber the boy.

"Might not need to worry about that," the woman said through clenched teeth. "Definitely won't need to worry about it if you keep talking so loudly."

"Sorry, Sabyl," the boy mumbled, leaning further over the table to rub at his leg.

These four surely belong to one of the gangs. Perhaps Naro's? As much as she wanted to stay and listen to the rest of their conversation, she needed to keep moving. If the caravan leader was there, she had to find him.

Munne pushed away from the wall and continued shuffling through the room, squeezing in between standing patrons and tables. After circling the common room once, she made her way to the bar and ordered a glass of wine to calm her nerves. Mayrien and Araloth arrived sometime later after she had finished half of the glass.

"Any luck?" Munne asked the pair.

Araloth shook her head and Mayrien said, "No one by the name of Dalys here. Are there any other inns or buildings they're sending people to?"

Munne frowned, taking another sip from her glass. "I think there's one other place in this district, but it's closer to the Sky District."

"Pardon, my ladies, but did you say you're looking for Dalys?" a man inquired, stepping in beside Mayrien.

Munne immediately looked to his eyes but was disappointed to see two brown orbs looking back at her. She adjusted her gaze to take in the rest of his form, noting that he was a middle-aged Proma with warm tan skin and brown hair to match his eyes. Long, bushy stubble spread across his cheeks, indicative of him needing a good shave.

"Simply discussing a friend," Munne said with a flippant shrug. She hoped her dismissive answer would send the man on his way, and she could get back to the search with her companions.

"I traveled into the city with a fellow named Dalys," the man responded, raising his mug to the three Elviri. "He mentioned he was due to meet with a friend in Auora."

That gave Munne some pause, her heartbeat accelerating. *Could he be talking about the caravan leader? Would he have been traveling openly using that name?* It seemed too good to be true, so she tempered her expectations before replying. "When did you two arrive in Auora?" she asked, angling her chin so she was barely looking in his direction.

Mayrien and Araloth caught onto Munne's change of tone, and they shifted their focus to the man as well.

"We squeezed in yesterday morning, and it sounds like we were some of the last to cross the bridge. I hear the city guard has ordered a lockdown of the island." He took a drink from his mug. "Most of the others we were traveling with chose to turn back to Ferilin, but this fellow insisted on crossing. Seemed odd, but maybe he was just eager to catch up with family or friends returning from the war." His eyes drifted to the three's attire, riding clothes clearly depicting the Elviri army sigil.

This man knows more than he's letting on. Is he one of the caravanners?

Munne's stomach dropped, and she silently cursed herself for her fumble. In her haste to find the caravan leader, she forgot all about the element of stealth. She had made a point to him back in Elimere that she didn't want any others connecting him to the Warlord of the Elviri. Even if this man was part of the caravan, chances were he wouldn't admit it out loud.

"Well, hopefully he was able to find his cousin, and hopefully you haven't suffered too terribly with what's been going on in the city," Munne said, her words casual and pleasant.

"On the contrary, the city's been quite enjoyable. This inn really comes alive at night." The man nodded his head respectfully to Munne, then took his leave.

After he departed, Mayrien and Araloth pressed in closer to Munne. Araloth watched the man go, crossing her arms.

"I think we need to come back after sunsdown," Munne said quietly so only her friends could hear her. "And we should look out for that one when we do."

"You think he knows your Dalys?" Araloth asked in the same hushed tone.

Munne nodded. "We'll come back, and we'll blend in better."

Glancing first at Araloth, then Mayrien, Munne led the pair out of the West Breeze Inn and back across the bridge into the castle.

CHAPTER XI: SETH

Octavia was carried off to an impromptu celebration with her soldiers, leaving Seth behind in the *pyredans'* booth. Cyndaryn and Arcyr'ys went with her, but Borros stayed to ensure Seth made it back safely to the pyramid. Once inside its walls, a pair of stewards came to collect him and return him to his room. Seth knew he should be thankful for Borros's aid, but he was too distracted with Octavia's savage behavior in the sparring ring, and her abandonment of him after, to mutter any kind of thanks before the *pyredan* left. He never thought his sister was capable of brutally beating someone the way she had beaten Vinse.

Is she training Lisanthir to be that cruel?

Seth pulled himself into bed and stared at the ceiling, listening to the distant noises of the rainforest, that familiar low hum constant beneath it all. The suns had started to set, and Lisanthir had yet to bring dinner to his chamber. Seth figured the Elviri had either gotten caught up with Octavia's celebration, or he had other steward duties to attend to. He tried not to let jealousy overtake his heart, but he found himself losing that battle. He wanted to know that the Elviri was okay, and that Octavia hadn't injured him too greatly during their fight.

After the suns slipped beneath the horizon, one of the stewards knocked on Seth's door before opening it. One of the Asaszi stewards entered with a greeting, and Seth had to suppress a shiver of disgust. "Lord Kharisss, your sssister isss inviting you to her chambersss for dinner."

"Is she here right now?" Seth asked, pulling himself into a sitting position.

"No, ssshe sssent word on her way back to her chambersss."

"Oh. What time is the meal?"

"Now, if you ssso desssire," the Asaszi replied.

Seth nodded. "Okay. I'll be outside in a moment. Please leave the door open."

The steward bowed and left the room. With substantial effort, Seth shuffled to the edge of the bed and swung himself back into his wheelchair. He maneuvered his chair toward the door and departed, one of the stewards trailing behind him. The other set off in the opposite direction, most likely to notify the next pair of stewards that Seth would be in Octavia's room for dinner.

Octavia's room was on the same floor as Seth's, separated only by a few hallways. As he approached her door, the steward stepped around him and hastened to knock on the door in his stead. Behind the stone door he heard his sister's muffled voice as she called out, "Enter!"

The steward opened the door and stepped aside for Seth to enter. The inside of Octavia's chamber was similar to his own with her stone bed up against one wall, four pillars reaching up to the ceiling. Her pillars were wrapped with blue and yellow silks. At one end of the room was a table and chairs, currently bare and awaiting whatever meal the stewards would be delivering. One chair had been pulled away from the table, leaving him space to pull his wheelchair up.

Octavia stood near the table. She had changed out of her training clothes into more casual dress—soft leggings, a long-sleeved teal tunic that fell to her knees, and a brown vest. She had bathed, and her hair was hanging loosely around her face, hiding her ears. The bath had washed away the blood, but dark bruises littered her face and neck. He was sure more bruises were hidden by the tunic.

"Food will arrive soon?" Seth asked as he rolled over to the table. His appetite had reawakened after the past few days, and he was ready to eat again.

"Yes, I sent word to the kitchens as I was returning to the pyramid," Octavia responded. She didn't take her seat across from him. Instead, she paced around the room.

"What's on your mind, Tav?"

"Soon. A little patience, brother."

Seth frowned and continued looking around the room. It was tidier than the last time he'd been here. Her wardrobe was closed and there were no clothes discarded on the floor. Across the room was a large chest where she kept her training weapons and clothes–closed as well.

The door opened and a veiled steward entered carrying a tray of food and drink. Octavia shut the door behind them as she escorted them to the table.

"I can't stay," Lisanthir's voice came from beneath the veil, warming Seth's chest and cheeks. "The Asaszi are getting suspicious of me. They've been questioning my lengthy visits with Seth." He placed the tray on the table and took a few steps back. Two bowls of soup and two glasses of wine.

"Let them question. I'll correct their behavior tomorrow," Octavia growled. Then she let out a resigned sigh, picking up a glass of wine and taking a sip. "But alright. Thank you. We'll talk during practice."

Lisanthir nodded. He turned to leave, but Seth grabbed his hand just in time, giving it a squeeze. The Elviri turned to face Seth and smiled. "Please eat, *ebilin*."

"I will. It's good to see you," Seth murmured. He squeezed Lisanthir's hand one more time and then let him go with great reluctance.

Steam rose from the soup, along with a delicious savory scent. It consisted primarily of roots and herbs, but Seth saw a few chunks of meat floating within as well. He raised a spoonful to his lips, blew on it, and then ate.

"What did that word mean?" Octavia asked coyly, tucking her hand under her chin.

"J-Just a term of endearment," Seth mumbled, feeling his cheeks flush. He shoveled a few spoonfuls of soup into his mouth to distract himself. "So, um, what's all this about, Tav?"

"Our escape plan," she whispered before eating some of her own soup. "It's going to be a lot harder this time. Szatisi is supposed to be going back to Iszairi in the coming weeks, so we may have to wait for her to brew a new elixir and return here."

Our escape plan. Seth couldn't believe the words from his sister's mouth. A small part of his mind also lit up at the mention of the elixir, waking a hunger he had suppressed several days earlier. He wanted to drink it again and feel his knees, his legs, his toes. He frowned. "If she returns with it, she'll be guarding it more closely than before." *And even if she brings a new elixir, who knows if it will work?* The fierce hunger quieted to a dull, throbbing yearning.

"We'll deal with that if we need to." She sounded detached. It was wrong.

Seth set down his spoon and looked his sister in the eye. "Tav, you're not considering forcing your way into her chambers, are you?"

Octavia's eyes were cold, her words colder. "I'll do whatever it takes to get us out of here."

Seth was painfully reminded of her performance in the sparring ring earlier that day. The wild look in her eyes as she threw herself on Vinse and beat him within an inch of his life. A strange buzzing sound filled his ears, and he couldn't tell if it was the forest or his heartbeat.

"Surely we can figure out another way," he said.

Octavia held his gaze for several tense moments before looking down at her glass of wine. She swirled it around in her hand and then set it on the table, her fingers sliding down its stem and lingering on its base. Trembling. Seth could see the faintest tremble in her hand.

She must've noticed him noticing because she changed the topic. "How's your soup?"

Flicking his own eyes down to the table, he stirred his spoon in the bowl before offering her a weak smile. "Tastes alright I guess."

Octavia let out a low hum before raising her own spoon to her lips. They ate together in silence, but the silence was distinctly unsettling. Normally being alone with his sister would bring him some level of comfort, but today he wasn't sure if he was truly sitting with his sister or some shadow of his father.

He mustered some degree of courage, and before it could depart, he asked, "What was that fight all about?"

Octavia didn't look up from her bowl of soup. "What fight?"

"Vinse."

She grunted and ate some more of her soup. Seth watched her hands and arms for any trembling or shaking. She gripped onto her bowl tightly, knuckles pale in color. As he was about to speak again, she opened her mouth. "He thought I shouldn't have been promoted."

"Oh." Seth reached for his wine, noting his own trembling hand. If Octavia saw, she said nothing. The room was silent beside the clinking of utensils and slurping of liquid.

Would Tav get upset if she knew that I *thought she shouldn't have been promoted? But surely, she'd realize it's about Father, not her... So, does this have to do with her pride?* He wanted to talk to her about it, about *everything*, but when he looked across the table at her and saw traces of Amias in her, he was afraid of being honest. *But she wants to escape.*

"You and Lisanthir looked so beautiful earlier," he blurted out, drawing Octavia's attention up from her bowl. She arched an eyebrow, and he stuttered out an explanation. "I-in the ring. You both moved so gracefully, and you were in sync with each other. It was like watching a dance performance." *Not a fight.*

Octavia's lips curled into a small grin. "Your Elviri knows how to move. He was a little shaky on his feet when we first started training, but he's a fast learner."

Seth returned her smile. "He has a good teacher."

The grin fell from his sister's face alarmingly fast, driving Seth into a panic. He had clearly said something wrong, but he didn't understand. His brow furrowed and his grip on his spoon flexed, unsure of whether or not to reach for her hand.

"Tav?"

"You don't mean that," she muttered. "I saw how you looked at me, after... Vinse."

He reached for her hand. He opened his mouth to speak, but the words wouldn't come. *I was scared of you, Tav. Why did you hurt that man like that, Tav? You looked like a monster, Tav. You looked like Father.*

Octavia grabbed his hand and squeezed comfortingly, almost too tight. She turned to look away from him, eyes darting for something to lock onto within her room. "After Osza and Father promoted me, after the... ceremony... Vinse and some of the others started spreading rumors that I got the promotion because I slept with Arcyr'ys, or because Amias is my father. As if I hadn't *earned* it."

Seth's throat constricted underneath a pang of sadness. Although he was reassured that his sister's relationship with the older *pyredan* hadn't gone that far, his heart still broke for her. He thought she had the support of the other soldiers, but he supposed there was always someone lingering on the edge of the crowd, jealous of what they couldn't have.

Were Father and the other older Provira jealous of the Elviri? Is that where all the resentment comes from?

"As soon as word got to me and Arcyr'ys, he offered to fight the stupid *syk'kyth* for me. He didn't understand why that would only make things worse." Octavia's gaze had fixated on the blue silks wrapping around one of her bed's pillars. If Seth hadn't been paying attention to her, he would've missed her bottom lip quivering. She kept her voice composed as she spoke, "Part of me didn't even want to fight him. Just let him continue spreading those ugly rumors. Maybe Father or one of the Asaszi would hear of it and believe it. Maybe they'd do away with 'the youngest *pyredan* in Moonyswyn'."

Seth let out an involuntary gasp as Octavia tightened her grip on his hand. Octavia's eyes widened for a moment, and she let out a small *oh* before blinking rapidly, tears welling up. She let go of his hand and grabbed her cup of wine, drinking deeply.

"I'm sorry, Seth. This is all just so... I've just been so angry, I... If we don't leave soon, I know I'll lash out."

"We will. We just need to think through our options and find something that's safer." The rest of his thoughts went unspoken, but he knew his sister was thinking it as well. *Something that doesn't involve violence. We won't become monsters like Father.*

They were both quiet for a moment. Seth took in the image of his sister; gone was the headstrong woman who had climbed the ranks in the Provira army. At that moment she wasn't a *pyredan* and the favorite of Osza and Astohi, she was a nineteen-year-old girl who was scared out of her mind. She wiped at her tears with the back of her hand, sniffling quietly. She looked small and frail in her stone chambers, so unlike the brutal warrior she had been earlier. When her hand brushed against her ear she jumped.

"I shouldn't have let him mutilate me." Octavia muttered.

Seth had no words for his sister. He wished she hadn't gone through the mutilation either, but the Octavia from a fortnight ago would never have listened to him. A part of him was glad that she regretted it, but mostly he just felt sad for her.

Gone were the days of their youth, when the twins would run around the pyramid chasing each other, blissfully ignorant of the evil ways of their father.

Seth yearned to hear his mother's voice again, to feel her warm embrace. He yearned for the nights where he and Octavia would stay up late at night with their mother in her library, listening to her regale them with tales of noble knights and cunning adventurers.

"All we can do is accept our burdens and shoulder on," Seth said softly. "The weight will be easier to bear if the three of us carry it together."

Octavia laughed breathlessly. "Beautiful words, brother. I hope we can live up to them."

Seth gave her a small smile, taking a sip from his own cup of wine.

Seth's sleep was interrupted by a loud knocking on his door, followed by the stone door groaning as it swung inward. Someone hurried into the room, the heels of their boots tapping on the stone floor.

"Lord Kharisss, your father requestsss your presssence in his experiment chamber," an Asaszi steward hissed loudly, standing at the foot of the bed.

Seth groaned softly and rolled onto his back. He opened his eyes and rubbed at his face, trying to wipe away the exhaustion. Mind still lagging behind with sleep, he asked, "Right now? How early is it?"

He heard the steward flick their forked tongue at the air. "Lord Amiasss Kharisss made a requessst. I am here to sssee it through."

As the Asaszi's gravelly voice filled his ears, he realized he had just done something foolish; he had indirectly challenged his father's orders. Adrenaline shot through his veins, and he threw himself into a sitting position. "I-I understand. I'll be ready in a few moments."

The steward flicked their tongue again out of mild irritation. "Very well. I ssshall be outsssside when you are ready." With that, the steward turned on their heel and left the room, pulling the door shut behind them.

Seth let out a loud exhale and rubbed his face once more for good measure. He should know better than to talk back to the Asaszi like that, *especially* if they were delivering an order from his father.

But what's Father doing in the experiment chamber this early in the morning? Or have I overslept? He turned and looked out of his window, catching the suns' first tendrils of light peeking through the rainforest. The trees' shadows were still long and deep. He hadn't woken up this early in a long time, especially not for one of his father's experiments. *Why does he want me there?*

Pushing his thoughts aside for the time being, Seth pulled himself out of his bed and into his wheelchair. He maneuvered over to his wardrobe, picking out one of his nicer robes. He shimmied out of his bedclothes and threw them onto the bed before pulling the fresh dark blue robe over his head. His limbs were still heavy with sleep, so it took him a few moments longer to pull the robe underneath his hips and thighs. Rather than wrestling with a pair of boots or socks, he simply went barefoot. The robe was long enough to cover his feet, and winter's chill hadn't set in the pyramid yet.

Running a hand through his hair, he twisted his chair around and rolled to the door. "I'm ready!"

The stewards outside pushed the door open, giving him space to emerge into the hallway. Soon he and the two stewards were heading toward the experiment chamber, to the balcony he always perched at. Amias would know to look for him there. Seth wondered if his father would be waiting for him to arrive before starting his experiment, or if he'd be able to slip in unnoticed. Knowing Amias, he would be waiting. Seth's stomach churned unhappily.

Returning to the experiment chamber left Seth with a lingering, heavy sense of dread. Too many bad memories were tied to this place—his legs, his sister, his mother. The balcony was dark and sparse. A few chairs were pushed against a wall, used by the stewards when Seth was required to be here. Light soaked into the stone railing, giving the illusion that the balcony would look upon something beautiful, something warm. Seth knew better. As he rolled his chair over to the railing, he saw that several spellsingers and soldiers were already gathered in the room below. Three platforms had been assembled in the center of the room, each bearing one spellsinger and two soldiers with shields. Panic seized Seth's stomach as he realized he had seen this scene before.

Amias stood in between the three platforms, his arms crossed behind his back. He had been looking at the balcony and knew immediately that Seth had arrived. "Hello, my son."

Seth tried not to flinch. He dug his fingernails into his thighs, trying to push down the nauseous mix of dread and hate that threatened to surge up from his stomach. "Hello, Father."

Even though he was several floors above the main floor, Seth saw Amias's lips twist into an unsettling smile. He looked so proud to see his son back in the room where...

Where he destroyed my legs.

Where he mutilated my sister.

Where he killed my mother.

"I'm glad you're here with us today. I want you to bear witness to this success."

Seth had heard those words from Amias's mouth before, not even a month ago, in this very room. If his toes could curl in disgust, they would have. He wondered which spellsinger or shield-bearer would be the one to "fail" and get executed. *What's he even trying to do?*

Amias turned away from Seth, holding his arms out. "Spellsingers, begin the chants. Shield-bearers, raise your shields. Today we *will* hear the *Tserys's* voice. He *will* speak to us."

Seth's mind raced as he tried to understand the exact implications of what his father said. *He's trying to talk to the dead? What kind of absurdity is this? Does Osza know about this?*

The three spellsingers raised their hands above their heads, their chants starting at a low volume that Seth struggled to hear. The six shield-bearers flanked each of their spellsingers, raising their shields to protect themselves and the spellsingers from the center of the room. Amias stayed put, feet firmly planted on the ground, his head tilted back, and arms outstretched toward the ceiling.

As the spellsingers continued their chants, Seth heard Amias's voice join theirs. The space above the platforms seemed to darken and thicken. Seth recognized the blue cloud from the last experiment as it formed and knew it would soon take on a more defined shape, separating him from those down below.

Something was different, though. Underneath the four voices Seth heard the familiar and strange low hum from the rainforest. *Magic.* The hairs on his arms rose as he straightened in his chair. His eyes darted around the room, trying to determine what was different this time from the last attempt.

Amias and the spellsingers raised their voices from a low rumble to a proud call, loudly speaking the ritual words. Seth knew that they were speaking in an ancient Asaszi tongue, but he didn't know the meaning of the words. It was something the *Zsikui* didn't teach outside of the academies in Iszairi.

Amias hadn't chanted with the spellsingers last time. Is that what's making a difference?

Strands of darkness wove together, forming the familiar dark blue cloud in the center of the room. Seth could no longer easily make out the movements of those on the platforms below, even when he leaned further against the railing. He lost sight of his father, but he could still hear his voice joining with the others.

As the spellsingers' chanting turned to frenzied shouts, the humming became a deep rumble, then a roar. Seth's chair vibrated and he felt it deep in his core. A cold sweat broke along his brow. Something inside of him snapped, and he was overwhelmed with the urge to *run, flee, get away.*

Something is coming.

The center of the cloud darkened, black against blue, and then stretched down toward the floor. Through the funnel Seth could barely make out the shape of Amias, his arms outstretched toward the cloud. A gloomy tendril curled and extended toward his hand. The spellsingers' chants were drowned out underneath the all-out *roar* of magic.

And then Amias touched the darkness.

Silence filled the experiment chamber. Seth's ears rang from the sudden loss of sound. His lips parted and he let out a shaky breath, but he couldn't hear it. Eyes darting around, he tried to make out what was happening on the floor below, but he couldn't see through the black and blue swirl of darkness.

But then the cloud began to disperse, and Seth could see his father down below, hand curled around the fading gloom, a serene smile on his face. His eyelids fluttered to a close and Seth saw his father's mouth move but he couldn't hear the words. He tried to focus on Amias, read his lips and body language, *something* to figure out what had just happened. The longer he stared at his father, the louder the ringing in his ears became.

And then sound returned to the chamber.

"Bring my son down here," Amias said calmly to the stewards on the balcony, his gaze still fixated on the dissipating darkness above him.

Seth heard the steward's footsteps as they approached him. He heard their leather gloves creaking as they gripped onto the handles of his chair. A full-body twitch overcame him as they pulled his wheelchair back and pivoted toward the archway leading back into the pyramid. Despite all of the little groans, squeaks, and taps that filled the air, Seth could only notice one thing—or lack thereof.

The hum is gone. He tried to filter out every other noise, no matter how small, so he could try to find it again. Something inside of him was reeling from the loss. *Where did the hum go?*

When the steward pushed him through the entryway into the experiment chamber, only Amias stood in the center of the room, facing away from them. He must've dismissed the others already. Seth hoped no one would be punished for today's experiment. It seemed to have gone according to plan, but... what *was* his father's plan?

We will hear the Tserys's *voice.*

Amias raised a hand and flicked his wrist away from his body. "Leave me with my son."

The steward's robes rustled as they stepped away from Seth's chair and bowed. "Yesss, Lord Kharisss." Their heels clicked softly on the stone as they left the room.

Seth took hold of his wheels and rolled himself further into the room, approaching the edge of the wooden platform nearest to him. He hesitated to get any closer to his father, at least until he knew what kind of mood the man was in.

Amias turned to face Seth, not moving from his spot in the center of the room. The corners of his eyes crinkled with the remnants of a smile, and for once Amias Kharis resembled the kinder man he had been during Seth's childhood. Seth's heart raced, suddenly overwhelmed by his father's presence.

"It finally worked, Seth." Amias's voice was barely above a whisper, but Seth could hear him clearly as if they were standing right beside each other. Awe and adoration seeped from his every word. "I've heard the voice of the *Tserys* once more, and He is pleased."

Once more? He's done this before? But it should be impossible, the Tserys *has been dead since the Eldest—*

Amias touched his shoulder, and then Seth heard—no, he *felt* it again. He felt the vibration of it in his teeth, the hum filling his ears and drowning out the other little noises like his open-mouthed breathing and the rustle of his father's eyelashes as he blinked expectantly at Seth. "You hear the echoes of Him, too, don't you?"

Seth's eyes snapped to his father, and—*When did he get so close to me?* Amias towered over him, squeezing Seth's shoulder gently. *Fondly.* Glancing to his left and right, he saw the wooden platforms and realized Amias hadn't approached him: *he* had rolled his chair toward his father. Panic flooded his senses, and he couldn't tell if he was hearing his own blood roaring in his ears, or the hum of the rainforest.

The echoes of the Tserys.

"To hear Him so clearly again, after so many years... Today, my son, we are blessed." Amias squeezed his shoulder again. "He told me the secrets of Iszairi and offered me guidance on our next steps. Oh, such wonderful things await us in Iszairi."

"Father, I-I..." Seth was at a loss for words. His father was surely in the midst of one of his mental snaps, where he didn't know who he was or where he was. He must be hallucinating, or perhaps the spellsingers had chanted the wrong words and it somehow damaged his father's mind. Seth was torn over whether or not to indulge his father or try to gently coax him out of his episode.

"It's time for you to know the full truth, especially with your ceremony of devotion approaching. With your sister leading our armies, you by my side, and the *Tserys* guiding our steps, the Provira will be unstoppable." Amias straightened his back and removed his hand from Seth's shoulder. "Come, sit with me. I'll tell you our history."

Amias walked over to the nearest platform and sat on its edge. With great reluctance and overwhelming curiosity, Seth maneuvered his chair, so he was perched beside Amias. Because of the height difference between the platform and the wheelchair, Amias still towered over him. Dark bags hung heavily beneath his father's eyes and wrinkles covered his face, the flickering candlelight of the experiment chamber deepening the jagged curves greatly. He looked ancient and sickly, except for the curve of his lips and the spark of hope in his brown eyes.

"Do you know how the Provira came to be?" Amias asked, his voice gentle. Memories of a forgotten childhood surfaced in Seth's mind when his father would use that same gentle voice to talk to him when he was a babe—when he first joined his father at his workbench.

Seth shook his head, reeling in disbelief that this discussion was coming unbidden from Amias, of all people. He wanted to hear everything his father had to say, so that he could uncover the truth of the experiments and the *Tserys*.

Amias chuckled softly. "I'm surprised your mother kept this knowledge from you. Ah, well... Provira like me were born from a coupling between an Elviri and a Proma. That is a rare occurrence, one that can only happen for a brief period of time every thousand years, where Elviri and Proma across Daaria are able to bear children together. Scholars have recorded these periods of time, dating back to the beginning of the Second Sun. Thirteen generations of Provira..." He trailed off, staring blankly at the ground.

Seth frowned. The Provira had been banished to Moonyswyn nearly one hundred years ago and had created families of their own. It was no rare feat for those families to bear children. Difficult at times, yes, but as he understood it, that was normal. From what Seth's mother *had* been willing to discuss, some mothers would lose their children before childbirth, or shortly after. He knew she had lost children of her own before he and Octavia were born. But perhaps there had been more to it that she hadn't divulged. The thought of his mother hiding things from him left an unsettling feeling in Seth's stomach.

Amias inhaled deeply, straightening his back. He folded his hands together and set them in his lap. "Those thirteen generations were unable to bear children of their own. Discovering that ignited my desire for knowledge, and I made it my life's mission to understand the Provira. I served as a pupil to the royal archivists in Elimere, learning all that I could, about *everything*. While combing through the tomes on the line of the Hunting Throne, I found an ancient journal bearing the most curious markings. When I opened its pages, I heard the most... *enchanting* whisper slip past my ears. Though I did not recognize the words it said, I knew that *it* knew. The answers I sought about the Provira, perhaps about the rest of the world...

"All of the scholars I questioned about it merely waved their hands and said it was the work of the gods." Amias let out a bark of harsh laughter. "Their gods were driven out of this world at the end of the Eldest Days, so what do they know of us? Of their children's children? How could *their* voices be trapped in this journal that had been written a thousand years after the second sun rose in the sky? I asked the scholars in Elimere if the voice I heard could be something magical, something *beyond the gods*, but I was mocked and ridiculed. The kinder ones called me a starry-eyed dreamer. Those less kind called me a blasphemous fool."

Amias's hands separated and squeezed into fists. Seth saw the light leave his father's eyes, replaced with something dark and hateful. For a moment Amias lost himself in his memories, and Seth did nothing but watch his father disappear under the surface, his nostrils flaring with angered breath. Seth was lost to his own memories of his father's rage. He had seen this glare countless times before, after countless failed experiments. He had seen this look when his father killed his mother in front of all the Provira and Asaszi. He wanted nothing more than to yank his chair away and flee this place, but he stayed put, determined to hear the end of his father's tale.

But he wouldn't be the one to break his father's trance. Instead, he sat quietly, hoping he wouldn't draw Amias's attention while rage consumed his thoughts.

After a few moments, both Kharis men returned to themselves. Amias's fists relaxed, and he smoothed out the wrinkles in his gray robe. Seth let out a breath he didn't realize he had been holding. The corner of Amias's mouth twitched into a bitter grin before he continued his tale.

"The Elviri in Elimere wouldn't listen to my words, so I left the valley and traveled to Lithalyon. The southern city had a reputation for being more *lenient* with frivolous pursuits of knowledge, so I decided to try my luck amidst the musicians and poets. They humored me for a time as I tried to learn more about our heritage and how it related to that heavenly whisper, but eventually they, too, cast me out. Fortunately for me, that's where I met Rhono and Berylla.

"The three of us met in secret to discuss our origins, how the Provira came to be. I told them about the voice I had heard inside the archives of Elimere, and they were fascinated, wanted to learn more. Other Provira wanted to learn and discuss as well, and eventually our private little meetings turned into a city-wide political movement. The Elviri tried to silence us, but we would not be cowed. They tried to separate us, force us apart, but we would not break. So, they exiled us from their lands. We took refuge with the Proma, but they wouldn't have us either. Eventually we were on our own, and then the *Zsikui* found us."

Amias turned toward Seth, the light returning to his gaze, his expression soft. Seth remembered that look from his childhood when he'd do something to make his father proud. Once, he would have done anything to please his father and bask in that gaze, but today the sight twisted Seth's stomach and filled him with dread.

"They welcomed us in their lands. When I told them about the voice, they *knew*. They had heard it, too. It was *Him*. The *Tserys*." Amias's lips curled into a gentle smile. "The *Zsikui* gave us everything. They gave me *you*."

"What?" Seth couldn't stop the word from slipping out. His mind raced with what his father could possibly mean, moving so fast that he didn't realize he had spoken until his father chuckled. He froze, the color draining from his face as Amias patted his shoulder.

"One of the gifts the *Zsikui* gave us when we entered Moonyswyn was a concoction that would allow our women to conceive children. Berylla and a few other heroic women were the first to drink the concoction, and we were blessed with the first new generation of Provira. Our *true* descendants."

Mother... her birth was only possible because of the Asaszi?

Amias's hand sat on Seth's shoulder like a stone weight. "In exchange for such a lovely gift, they asked us to partner with them and aid them in unearthing their secrets in Iszairi. In finding a way to restore the *Tserys* to this world. Osza brought Rhono, Berylla, and myself to Iszairi and led us through a ritual and we heard Him, His voice filled my head again, and I knew we were where we needed to be. With the help of the *Zsikui*, we would bring back magic to Daaria and serve justice against the Elviri and Proma who wronged us."

Amias was staring intently at Seth, no doubt expecting some kind of response. Seth tried to swallow, but his mouth was dry. He held his father's gaze for several moments but eventually he broke and averted his eyes, looking down at his lap where his fingers were twisted into his dark blue robes.

"S-So this is all because of Him. It's *for* Him. Th-the *Tserys*." When he spoke, his voice cracked with fear.

"Yes," Amias whispered, his smile growing. "All of my research and experiments, it's been to find a way to free Him from His prison."

The tomb in Iszairi, Seth thought. *All of this so Father can free a ghost?*

Amias pushed himself off of the platform, rising to his feet. Brushing off his robes, he turned to Seth. "He has spoken to me and showed me our path forward. I'll be issuing the orders to the stewards and guards today; we depart for Iszairi in a matter of days. He told me of a day where the ground will tremble around and underneath the last flame, and the rituals we must conduct in its presence. Time is of the essence."

Panic set in and Seth had to maintain control over his body to keep his eyes from widening and a gasp from escaping. It would be tremendously harder to escape from Iszairi, with all of the Asaszi who lived there. The city was further in the rainforest, which would mean a greater distance to travel to flee Moonyswyn. Seth wasn't sure that it would be possible, especially if he was still stuck in his wheelchair.

His father cleared his throat. "He smiles upon us and what we are doing... And He's eager to meet *you*, Seth."

CHAPTER XII: RAY

A light dusting of snow fell during the night. Ray woke up shivering. She crawled out of her bedroll and began working on a fire. As the first of the flames devoured the kindling, Niamnh stirred and stretched. She began shivering too.

"Good morning, Niamnh," Ray greeted her with as much cheer as she could muster.

"I-It's so much c-colder this morning," Niamnh muttered, rubbing her hands and feet together within her bedroll.

"Aye, it's a proper winter now. No more sleeping under the stars, we'll need to set up a shelter at night." The fire was taking longer to spread. Ray frowned. The snow had made everything wet.

She nearly missed the next words from Niamnh's lips. "I'm sorry he threatened you last night."

Ray paused from her work, her eyes fixated on the log in her hands. *So, the Doshara hadn't blocked that from the princess. Had he let the other conversation slip out? Did Niamnh know about my promise to meet Naro in Na'roc of North? I haven't spoken about it any other time...*

"Under normal circumstances, I'm able to keep him from taking over my body like that. That hasn't happened in so long... I'll be more vigilant."

She doesn't know about the night he held a dagger to my throat. Ray grimaced. "It's alright. We'll just be more diligent with the tea."

Ray didn't think she was supposed to overhear Niamnh's next words, but she did, nonetheless. "Maybe everything'll be better without him."

Ray couldn't stop herself from smiling as she continued stacking logs. She pretended as if she hadn't heard Niamnh. Maybe they could talk about it in the evening after the tea had suppressed the Doshara. She was glad to hear the princess was reconsidering her devotion to it. Hopefully, no harm would come to her during... whatever it was that the Enthai would have to do to get rid of the Doshara.

Once the fire was burning in earnest, Ray heated up her morning rations—a biscuit and dried fish. Niamnh crawled out of her bedroll and sat with her hands and feet practically in the fire. Their legs were touching, and Ray felt Niamnh shivering ever so slightly.

"If you don't mind me saying, you always seem so cold, princess," Ray mumbled. Niamnh turned to look at her, a curious look in her eyes. "More than you should be. Even back in the woods—"

"M-my mother always wore heavy c-coats and dresses, after Daerion," Niamnh said, looking back at the fire. "And now I, t-too, have been c-cursed with these chills for s-so many years. I miss the warmth."

Ray watched Niamnh shiver, alternating between rubbing her hands, rubbing her shoulders, and trying to soak up as much heat as she could from the flames. She felt herself sliding closer to the princess, pressing more of her weight against her, and the princess leaning into her touch. The two sat like that, silent, for a long time before it was time to break down their camp and continue their journey.

It took the girls almost an hour to get up and start moving. They were both reluctant to leave the fire and sat with their hands held over the flames a lot longer than they should have. Ray dug through their bags until she found gloves and hooded cloaks. They would need the extra layers today. She considered how much of a delay they had caused by not moving out as soon as possible, but she struggled to care. She would need all the rest she could get if she was going to cross a frozen tundra over the next several days. Niamnh seemed to be doing better with their travels, though, which was a positive.

Trees still surrounded the girls, although they were beginning to thin out. Ray could see more of the sky when she looked up. The two suns shone down on the woods, offering little warmth during the day. As they trudged through the woods, the trees continued to thin, and the dusting of snow turned into blankets laid upon the ground. The winds picked up, growing from a quiet whistle to a low moan. The girls didn't speak for the remainder of the day, but they stayed close to one another, only separating when Ray stopped to hunt. Before the forest gave way to the plains, she wanted to gather as much meat as she could for the princess. She didn't trust that she could hunt as successfully out in the open. She managed to fell another pheasant and two rabbits.

In the late afternoon they could see where the forests of Promthus ended, and the wide open expanse of the snowy plains began.

"Na'roc of North," Ray breathed.

From the forest's edge, she felt like she was standing on the shore of the Hourglass Lakes, its waters stretching as far as the eye could see. Nothing loomed on the horizon to the east except low clouds and the coming darkness. To the south were two mountain peaks covered in snowy trees, and a structure built in the valley between them—the Wall. The single path leading back to Promthus, back to civilization. Naro's instructions bubbled up in her mind.

If you can see the Wall, turn north and travel until it is out of sight. Only then should you turn east again.

Ray twisted to look at Niamnh, to see the princess's reaction to their surroundings. Indeed, she was looking south as well, her eyes fixated on the Wall, her expression blank.

Is she considering making a run for it tonight, and abandoning the mission to get rid of the Doshara? Ray frowned, desperately hoping that Niamnh wouldn't do that. She still hadn't had a chance to talk to her about her feelings about, well, *everything.* She looked back to Na'roc of North, and her stomach dropped. *Will the Doshara come out tonight, demanding to know where Naro is?*

"Let's go back into the woods. Better shelter than out here," Ray said, her voice low. She was afraid to raise it any higher, lest it carry across the plains.

Niamnh nodded in silent agreement.

As the suns set, they made their camp between three large pines. Within one of the packs was a large tarp made from animal skins. Ray hung it between two of the trees, creating a makeshift lean-to for them to rest under. The tarp blocked out most of the wind, allowing her to stoke a fire with relative ease. Niamnh set up the bedrolls next to one another, sheltered by the tarp.

Ray looked at the arrangement and sat back on her heels. They had slept on opposite sides of the campfire for the past seven nights. She had convinced herself that the extra space would give her ample time to wake up and defend herself if the Doshara took over the princess's body again.

What if he slips free tonight? He could strangle me in my sleep and be off for the Wall within minutes, never mind his promise to keep me alive until he found Naro.

But it would be stupid to sleep away from the lean-to. She needed its protection, just as Niamnh did. She would have to accept it for tonight. And keep at least one of her daggers near her head.

Ray finished building the fire and preparing Niamnh's dinner. The princess sat at the end of her bedroll, heating her legs and feet by the fire, cradling the cup in both hands when Ray handed it to her. Beside her was a plate of skinned rabbit. Ray took a seat next to the princess and ate another biscuit. She fished Naro's instructions out of her bag, reading over them once more.

Another four days after that, the forest will thin, and you will be in Na'roc of North. If you can see the Wall, turn north and travel until it is out of sight. Only then should you turn east again. Travel east until you find their villages, or they find you.

Her throat tightened around a lump of biscuit. She forced it down with a swallow, reaching for her waterskin and taking a sip. The Wall was indeed within sight, so they would have to go north. Judging by the distance, it would be at most two or three days before they could turn east again. They'd need to follow the edge of the forest to avoid any kind of detection from the men manning the Wall.

But can I convince the Doshara to go along with this? Maybe if I tell it that Naro told me to go north first... then cross into the tundra and find some kind of landmark...?

As if the imminent threat against her life wasn't enough, it also bothered Ray that there was no estimation of how long it would take to find the Enthai. Naro had been careful with his calculations for the rest of the journey. So why did his instructions end without precision?

Until they find you.

She had difficulty finishing her meal.

Sometime later, Niamnh set her empty cup down then turned so she was facing away from Ray. Ray cocked an eyebrow and watched silently. There was a rustle as the princess removed her gloves. She hunched over, and the sounds of flesh tearing answered all of Ray's unsaid questions. Leaving the princess to her dinner, Ray tended to the fire.

Before she settled down for the night, Ray grabbed handfuls of snow and melted them over the flames in one of their pots. They hadn't come across any streams or ponds during the day, and they needed to refill their waterskins. Once they were full, she fed a few more branches to the flames.

"I need to wash my face and hands," Niamnh said quietly.

Ray nodded and filled the pot with snow once again. After the snow melted, she carefully removed the pot from the fire and set it down beside the other girl. The princess held her hands close to the pot, savoring its warmth, before dipping her fingers into the water and beginning her cleaning ritual.

Normally this was a silent endeavor, but tonight she sighed wistfully and cast a glance over to Ray. "I *do* miss real food. Eating animals like this... it's sick."

Ray hummed, not sure if in agreement or acknowledgement. Perhaps a little of both. "What's your favorite thing to eat? Or, um, what *was* it?"

A smile danced on Niamnh's lips, and something tugged at Ray's heart. Niamnh looked rather pretty when she wasn't thinking about the kidnapping or the Doshara. "My mother's pear and silverberry pastries. She used to eat them all the time, before..." She trailed off and the smile fell away from her face.

Ray's eyes lit up in recognition. "I had one of those! Back in the kitchens. They'd made some for your sister, and there were leftovers in the kitchen, so Ajak and I got to try them."

Niamnh's smile returned, and Ray couldn't help but mimic the gesture. "Protector's grace, what I wouldn't give to eat one of those again. What about you, Ray? What's your favorite treat?"

She fell silent for a moment as she considered all of the treats she had come across, either from Hilthe's cooking or her own quick pocketing at the market. "There's a bakery back in Auora run by a lady named Mingweril that sells all kinds of bread loaves and other goodies for midweek church services. I save up what coin I can to buy one of her braided loaves that's got cadra berries, walnuts, and goat cheese in it. Sometimes she drizzles it with honey." Her stomach grumbled, and she salivated at the thought of the delectable treat.

"Oh, that sounds lovely," Niamnh said softly as she finished cleaning her hands. Once she was done, she tossed the dirty water into the woods behind the tarp, drying her hands on her coat and putting on her gloves again.

Their pleasant conversation gave way to tense silence as their nightly routine continued. Ray held up the handcuffs and Niamnh offered her wrists. Ray helped the other girl into her bedroll, then crawled into her own. After she stopped squirming and adjusting, she realized her bedroll was touching Niamnh's. She could feel the princess's form against her side, radiating little warmth. Ray held still, not wanting to disturb the other girl, in fear of waking the Doshara instead. He hadn't appeared all evening, and with any luck the tea had kicked in and he would be silent throughout the night.

Ray closed her eyes and thought about her last night in Auora. She desperately wanted to curl around the form beside her and pretend it was Ajak, and that they were back in one of the Walker hideouts in the city. She craved his touch. She wished to hear him whisper to her to go to sleep, but instead she only heard the crackling of the fire and the low whistle of the wind.

The winds blew more fiercely the next day. Ray weaved in and out of the trees, trying to avoid the brunt of the wind. She studied the landscape before her, often turning to look south where the Wall loomed on the horizon. Every time her gaze fell upon the stone structure, her heart raced; they were moving too slow. They needed to walk faster. They couldn't risk being discovered. They'd been fortunate thus far with no signs of knights or guards in the woods, but if they ventured too far into the open, the soldiers manning the Wall would most certainly see them.

The snow had grown deeper overnight, though, and would grow deeper still. The girls had adequate clothing—Naro had seen to that—but the cold sapped their strength, and they struggled to carry on. When Ray spared a glance at Niamnh, she noticed the princess had her arms wrapped around herself and she was shivering despite her layers of coats and clothing.

Ray fell into step beside her. "How are you faring?"

"W-well enough," Niamnh responded curtly. "But I must rest soon."

Letting out a sigh, Ray said, "I'm sorry, but we have to keep moving. We can't risk stopping while—"

"While we can see the Wall," Niamnh finished.

Ray kept her mouth shut, refusing to say anything more. Though she continued walking beside Niamnh, she kept her gaze forward and trudged on.

Ray had no luck with hunting that day. She had seen a few small creatures out on the plain, but didn't want to run the risk of being seen. She was also not sure what the best way to hunt these creatures was, being so exposed. They would surely see or smell her before she could shoot an arrow in their direction. The princess still had a pheasant and a rabbit, so there was no reason to worry just yet about the hunt. For now, they just needed to continue moving north.

They made camp within the bounds of the forest again that evening. The lean-to was set up, a rabbit was skinned, and some tea was brewed. Ray considered asking the princess some mundane question about books or perhaps food but decided against it.

Their bedrolls were once again set up side by side underneath the lean-to. Ray grimaced as she finished her dinner and brushed crumbs off of her pants. Niamnh had turned to eat her own dinner, so Ray chose to gather some more wood for the fire. She stayed close enough to watch the princess through the trees, but was far enough away that she couldn't easily hear the sound of flesh tearing and bones breaking under Niamnh's delicate fingers.

The woods were dark. The suns had set only moments ago, and yet it felt like the middle of the night. Ray weaved in and around the trees, gathering sticks and fallen branches that could be used to stoke the fire. To the east she could see through the breaks in the trees out onto the snowy plains. Moonlight reflected off of the snow, revealing the great expanse that they would have to cross in the morning.

Somewhere in that vast open plain were the Enthai. The creatures the Proma warned their children about in bedtime stories. The creatures who undoubtedly played a part in Prince Robyn's disappearance two years prior. The creatures Naro expected Ray to work with to rid Princess Niamnh of the Doshara inhabiting her mind.

Ray shivered from more than just the cold. She was afraid. Seven days ago, she had never left the city-island of Auora. Now she stood on the edge of Promthus about to leave her kin's land behind. Naro had said the Enthai would help her return to Promthus, and she desperately wanted to believe him, but so much had changed since that night in the underground hideout. Never mind that history told of another fate for anyone who came across the Enthai north of the Wall. Not even princes were safe up here.

I need to return to camp.

Ray turned away from the forest's edge and followed the flickering light of the campfire. Niamh had finished her meal and was washing her hands and face.

"Do we have anything else we can use for bedding tonight?" Niamnh asked as Ray set her armful of wood down beside the fire.

"Check my pack. There might be another blanket in there," Ray responded as she fed more kindling to the flames.

The princess did find another blanket, one large enough to cover both of their bedrolls. She pushed her bedroll closer to Ray's and tossed the blanket over both. "I think I'm ready to sleep."

Niamnh offered her wrists up to Ray, who secured the handcuffs and then assisted the princess into her bedroll. She cast one last sweeping glance over their campsite before crawling into her own bedroll, appreciative of the extra warmth from the blanket and Niamnh's body next to hers.

The warm, comforting embrace of sleep had nearly taken Ray when Niamnh stirred beside her. "Ray?"

She could feel the princess's body go rigid, which sent an unpleasant rush of adrenaline through her own body. She was wide awake. "Yes, Niamnh?"

When Niamnh spoke again, it was through clenched teeth. "I'm only going to say this once. I need you to listen, and then never repeat this again. But I need to say this out loud so someone—so *you* hear it."

Ray pushed herself up onto her elbows, looking over at the other girl. Outside of their lean-to, the fire burned low, throwing shadows over everything. She could barely make out Niamnh's face in the dark. She couldn't tell if it was truly the princess talking, or if the Doshara had resurfaced. Her voice had its normal cadence, even if she was straining to speak. Ray would find out soon enough who was in control.

"Okay... I'm listening."

"I've... blocked Daerion out. So, he can't hear this. But—" Niamnh let out a quiet hiss, her body twitching. "I think... I think I do want him gone. I want to taste real food again. I want to be *warm*." Ray felt Niamnh pressing her leg against hers, seeking warmth. "But I'm scared that I won't know how to be alone again. But maybe it's worth the risk."

Ray sat completely still, allowing Niamnh to move her body closer to hers. She chose not to respond, out of fear of Niamnh's control waning, and Daerion resurfacing and hearing whatever she said. She wanted nothing more than to tell Niamnh it would be okay, that it was the right decision to make. But she didn't want to risk raising the Doshara's ire.

After a few moments, Niamnh's body stilled, and her breathing became steady and quiet. She had fallen asleep with her entire right side touching Ray's. Even through the bedrolls and blankets, Ray could feel the slightest bit of warmth radiating from her body. Some part of her wanted to hold Niamnh's hand and share her heat, but the lingering fear of the Doshara kept her hand at her side.

Ray's dreams took her back to Auora, to the lounge in Naro's home. Scents of warm spices and porridge wafted through the house. Lamps were lit in the corners of the room, casting a yellow glow over the dark furnishings. She lay on her side across one of the plush couches, gazing up at the painted ceiling. In her dream the stars moved along the length of the ceiling, swirling around and swimming across the sky.

Somebody wrapped an arm around Ray's waist, their body pressing against her back.

Ajak.

Ray stretched and arched her back into him, reaching to touch his face. His skin was cold beneath her fingertips. The scent of rot swirled around her. She listened for the sound of his breathing, but there was nothing.

"I wish you were here," Ray murmured, her eyes fixated on the swirling stars above.

Ajak's corpse didn't respond.

For a brief moment she felt herself stir and the waking world beckoned to her. "No, I'd like to stay a while longer," she whispered to the stars.

Ajak's corpse tightened its hold on Ray's waist. She idly stroked his cheek, watching two stars twinkle and circle each other. One grew brighter while the other dimmed until it faded into the night.

Halfway through the next day, the Wall slipped out of sight behind the small hills of the plains, and Ray felt her body relax as she realized they were far enough out that no one would see them on the frozen tundra. The edge of the forest curved toward the west, revealing more of the open plain.

"It's time to turn east," Ray said, shuffling around the weight of her bags. The burden had grown a little lighter since they first set out, her ration supplies dwindling. She had about five days' worth left, if she cut down on how much she was eating, before she would need to start hunting for herself as well as the princess.

"Couldn't we make camp in the woods for one more night?" Niamnh asked from behind her.

Ray couldn't deny that she was tempted to agree with the princess. The trees offered protection from the wind, and it was easier to build a fire under their boughs. Though she couldn't help but wonder why Niamnh was hesitating to continue their journey. Perhaps she wasn't ready to part with the Doshara yet, despite wanting her freedom.

"One more night," Ray said. "Only so we can gather what we need for the next part of the journey."

They set up their camp early that day, to give ample time to tend to other tasks. Ray instructed Niamnh to gather kindling and logs for that night's fire and for future fires on the plain. Ray went deeper into the forest to try hunting one last time.

The snow was getting deeper, even within the forest. It crunched under Ray's boots with every step. She winced, worried about how many creatures would hear her coming and flee. She withdrew Naro's sunsdial and checked the time as best she could—two hours until sunset, give or take. She would continue west for another thirty minutes, then turn and head back to camp.

We'll have to ration the remaining game and provisions, Ray thought as she wandered through the woods. She needed to check how much of the herbs were left as well. *If the princess doesn't have her tea, and if we run out of raw meat, will the Doshara try to kill and eat me, despite his promise to keep me alive?*

"Stop being stupid," Ray hissed to herself. As much as she tried to force bravery, fear gnawed at her heart.

It cost her a rabbit that darted away from an arrow that missed its head by over an arm's length. She retrieved the arrow, scowling. Perhaps she should instead be hoping for the Enthai to find them as soon as possible.

She wanted to curse at herself again. Any thought of the Enthai sent a wave of dread coursing through her body. She knew that she was dependent on the Enthai for the mission of Naro's to work, but she wasn't prepared to actually *see* them. But perhaps it *would* be better for them to find her and Niamnh sooner rather than later, so they could return to Auora faster.

Or be killed faster.

Ray was uneasy the whole walk back to camp. With every step and crunch of snow under her boot, she found herself scanning her surroundings, as if a pack of Enthai were going to jump out at her from the trees and kill her then and there.

Niamnh had started a fire and used their tarp to create a small tent rather than a lean-to. Both of the bedrolls must have been inside the makeshift tent already because Ray didn't see them anywhere else.

"Anything?" Niamnh called out to her, seeing her approach.

Ray shook her head and held up her hands. At least she had managed to retrieve the three arrows she fired. Niamnh frowned and returned to the fire.

With the extra sunslight, Ray and Niamnh went through their belongings to see what they had left. They melted snow so they had plenty of water to drink. Ray secured their acquired bundles of sticks so they would be easier to carry. Niamnh drank a cup of tea. Neither girl ate dinner that night, instead choosing to save their food for the tundra.

They sat side by side with their legs touching. They had gotten comfortable with each other over the past few days, and despite Ray's better judgment, she found that she enjoyed the princess's presence. If she pretended the Doshara wasn't lurking inside of Niamnh's mind.

Niamnh shifted to a more favorable position, now leaning against her right arm in a way that brushed against Ray's left.

Deep inside she felt her stomach clench and warmth spread through her torso. Ray recalled feeling this way around Ajak when he devoted his attention to her. If she focused on the campfire and blocked everything else out, she could pretend she was with him again and it was his head that was nearly touching hers. If she allowed her left arm to slide back, she could lean her head closer so the gap would close, and their bodies would be pressed together—

"We're on the edge of the tundra, little moth. Where's your lord?"

All warmth vanished from Ray's bones. The unforgiving cold of the forest seeped underneath her skin, freezing her where she sat. She inwardly cursed herself for allowing her guard to slip. She *knew* that the Doshara would resurface eventually to ask that very question.

The Doshara let out a quiet chuckle that sounded more like a death rattle. Ray felt it move beside her, shifting its weight very slowly and methodically. A hand touched her left and squeezed tightly. She clenched her jaw to keep a hiss of pain from escaping her.

"This isn't—*ah*, the meeting place." Ray managed to keep her voice steady and her body in place, despite all her instincts screaming at her to roll away from this creature and run into the woods. She knew she wouldn't get far and that it would almost certainly end in her death, but it felt so wrong to sit with the Doshara leaning against her as if they were intimate.

"Don't lie to me," the Doshara growled, sending a violent shiver down Ray's spine. She couldn't keep her body from twitching. "I can feel the fear radiating off of your body. You reek of it. You don't want to die, so don't lie to me. *Where is he?*"

Tears welled up in her eyes and she wanted to curse out loud. Instead, she took a deep breath and spoke as calmly as she could manage. "I told you, this isn't the meeting place. He picked a place on the other side of the border."

The grip on her hand tightened and she was genuinely worried that the Doshara was going to break bones. "Where?"

She racked her mind for how she could continue this bluff. *What kind of landmarks existed this far north? What would be a better meeting place than the forest? Did the Enthai have towns or villages?* She prayed her response wouldn't give her bluff away. "A village."

The Doshara growled wordlessly and let go of her hand. It pushed away from her and climbed to its feet to pace around the campfire.

There actually are *villages up here? Would the Doshara even know?*

Ray didn't dare move. She focused on the weight of her daggers on her hips. Wondered if she'd be able to draw one before the Doshara fell upon her. Maybe if it was on the other side of the fire, she'd stand a chance.

It stopped in front of her, and she had to force herself to tilt her chin back to meet its cold gray eyes. "Very well, little moth. The fires won't consume you. Yet."

It returned to its spot beside Ray, slowly stretching its limbs out to mimic how Niamnh had been sitting moments before. When it leaned its head against Ray's, she had to fight the urge to push it away, or vomit, or perhaps both. The only thing keeping her from reacting was the realization that it had blocked Niamnh out of their conversation, and it was putting her back where it "took over", so she wouldn't realize she had lost control.

Should I tell her?

Niamnh yawned and Ray's eyes darted to her face. The malice was gone from her eyes, and she looked genuinely tired.

"Time for bed?" Ray asked quietly. She didn't dare raise her voice, lest it crack and betray the fear that simmered under her skin.

Ray felt Niamnh nod against her. They moved to the tent, Ray securing Niamnh's wrists in the handcuffs. Despite the early timing, it took Ray several hours before she relaxed enough to fall asleep.

CHAPTER XIII: SETH

Amias's tale about the Provira haunted Seth's every thought for the rest of the day. He desperately wanted to see Octavia and Lisanthir and share everything he had just learned. He wanted, *needed*, one of them to challenge Amias's claims and say that he was just a madman. That the *Tserys* really was dead. That the *Zsikui weren't* the reason Seth and Octavia were alive. Octavia was nowhere to be found, though, and the steward that brought his dinner was an Asaszi and not his Elviri.

The serpentine steward sang praises of Amias's experiment from earlier in the day, apparently not aware that Seth had been present for it. "Word hasss ssspread quickly throughout the pyramid. We are ssso pleasssed to hear of Lord Kharisss's successses."

Normally Seth would've tried his best to block out their voice, but it occurred to him that the steward might know more about the plan to relocate to Iszairi. He decided to take that chance and asked his question. "Have you heard any news about us traveling to the other city?"

The steward cocked their head to the side, their tongue flicking out past their bronze scales. "Yesss, we are aware of the planned move. Lord Kharisss isss currently making the preparationsss with hisss ssstaff." Their words left no room for additional questions. He could tell that even if they knew more, they wouldn't easily divulge that information. They did offer one more comment, much to his chagrin. "Your father isss doing great work. Praissse to the *Tserysss.*"

Seth dropped his spoon back into his stew, stirring it out of agitation. He had difficulty finishing his meal and ended up sending it back to the kitchen with the steward several moments later.

The next day, two veiled stewards entered Seth's chamber to bring him his breakfast. One of the stewards was almost assuredly Lisanthir, but because of the other's presence, an Asaszi, Seth couldn't speak to him. Lisanthir placed the tray of food on Seth's bedside table, then picked up the bowl and handed it to him, gloved hands grazing his own for the briefest moment. The contact raised the hairs on the back of Seth's neck, and his stomach curled pleasantly on itself.

Seth let out a noncommittal hum and waved one hand, dismissing the two stewards. He couldn't risk showing any kind of emotion or affection toward the Elviri; he didn't want to risk Lisanthir being discovered. Even knowing that, it still hurt Seth to treat him with such coldness. He looked down at his breakfast to distract himself. The bowl was filled with chilled porridge and fruit.

He picked at the meal over the course of an hour and eventually set the empty bowl on the bedside table. Lisanthir had also brought a carafe of water, which Seth was thankful for. He poured himself a glass and drank, his gaze drifting to the window. Despite the bright sunlight, a chill seeped into the pyramid from outside. He wondered how the kytling was faring in the colder season.

After an hour of trying to relax and enjoy the warmth of his bed, Seth finally decided to get up and leave his room. He intended to find Octavia, and if he couldn't do that, he'd go to the colonnade to get some fresh air. He dug out a brightly colored shawl from his wardrobe and set it on his lap. He also pulled one of the smaller blankets off of his bed and threw it over his lap and legs.

Better to be too warm now than need to come back before heading to the colon-nade, he thought.

He asked the stewards stationed outside his room where his sister was, but neither knew. They both followed Seth as he went to her room and knocked on the door. After waiting several moments with no response, he sighed and decided to go to the colonnade.

Is Octavia somewhere with Arcyr'ys? As soon as the thought bubbled up, Seth was filled with disgust and put effort into thinking of other places his sister might have been. *Maybe she's training with her soldiers, or training Lisanthir today. They moved so gracefully together during their sparring match. I'm so thankful she's helping him, helping us.*

Us.

Seth's cheeks flushed as he emerged outside, the thought of him and Lisanthir together bringing him such joy that he forgot how to breathe for a moment. He couldn't stop the smile from spreading across his face, thankful the stewards were behind him and that there was no one else around.

The colonnade was empty, which was normal. Seth was used to having the space all to himself, so he wasted no time beginning his lap around the pyramid. At one point he had to stop and wrap his shawl around his shoulders, and he was glad he had the foresight to bring it with him. On the northern side of the pyramid, he caught sight of the kytling flying among the trees in the village. He stayed put and watched the bright yellow bird for a few moments, pleased that it seemed to be doing well. He wished he could say the same about himself.

What did Grandmother know that she was hiding from Father? Seth tried to remember what he could of Berylla's notes that he had found hidden within various books in the Great Library of Lithalyon. He remembered she had written something about the *Tserys* and Osza, but he couldn't recall her specific words. Instead, he tried thinking about something else, but he couldn't get past his grandmother. *What happened to her? She must've died before Octavia and I were born, but neither of our parents ever talked about her. None of the other Provira or Asaszi have talked about her, either.*

A hand touched his shoulder, and he felt his chair being pulled backward. Seth's whole body spasmed, and he snapped his head to the side, a flurry of hope, alarm, and fear swirling inside of him. The feel of the gloved hand was different from his Elviri's touch. The veiled steward standing beside Seth was also too short to be him.

Seth exhaled loudly, trying to get his heartbeat under control. "What is it?" he snapped, hands clenched in his lap.

The veiled steward shrugged their shoulders and nodded their head back toward the pyramid. Standing at one of the archways was the second steward as well as a green-scaled Asaszi dressed in silken finery. Seth didn't recognize the Asaszi, but judging by their attire, he assumed that they were one of Osza and Astohi's courtiers, which meant the Asaszi royalty were in Yiradia again. His heart thudded even louder, roaring in his ears.

What are they doing here?

The steward moved their hand to the handle on his chair and turned him so they could push him back inside.

As the two of them approached the pyramid, the Asaszi bowed their head in Seth's direction, their green scales glittering in the warm sunslight. "Greetingsss Lord Kharisss. Our queen hasss requesssted your presssence for dinner thisss evening. Your father and sissster will be in attendance."

Seth nodded. If Osza was the one arranging the meal, he knew he couldn't miss it. He wouldn't be allowed to miss it. He wondered what the Asaszi queen wanted with his family, and every possibility filled him with dread. At least with his father, there had been a period of Seth's life where he hadn't been afraid of him and had created a few nice memories with him. Seth had always been afraid of Osza. Seth's mother had acted as a barrier between him and the Asaszi when he was growing up.

The realization that it was going to be his first time being around Osza without his mother hit him hard. He became painfully aware of his quickening breath and became desperate to get away from the Asaszi courtier. He wished the steward would push his chair faster and take him away to his chamber, so he could escape the Asaszi's golden gaze.

"We'll sssend for you at sssunset," the Asaszi said as Seth was pushed past them. They stayed on the colonnade as the two stewards returned inside with Seth.

The stewards stayed with Seth for the rest of the day, looking after him as if he were a small child. They took him to the bathing chambers and subjected him to a multi-hour cleaning and pampering session that he hadn't endured in *years,* since before the war had escalated and drained all of their resources and wealth.

Seth was filled with guilt as he soaked in the heated tub. Scented oils had been poured into the water and several flowers with yellow and white petals floated on the surface. One of the stewards scrubbed him all over with a bar of floral soap and a washcloth while the other tended to his hair, brushing out all the tangles and pouring more oils over his head. He wasn't unaccustomed to that level of care from the stewards, but it definitely left him feeling uncomfortable. For most of his baths, the stewards only helped him undress and climb into the tub; they didn't go to those lengths, not anymore.

Eventually the scalding water cooled to a comfortable warm temperature. Looking down at his chest and arms, Seth's skin was bright red. It was a miracle he hadn't burned or blistered. The stewards lifted him from the stone tub and began dressing him in one of the finest outfits from his wardrobe. They slid on a pair of dark brown pants that billowed around his legs. Even if his legs were working properly and his muscles strong again, there would still be room for another pair of legs within the garment. Seth felt like a child being dressed, unable to do anything on his own. He knew they were doing this to ensure he was presentable to Osza, but it irritated him, nonetheless. Although it could be challenging sometimes, he *was* capable of dressing himself.

Next came a long-sleeved teal tunic that fell down to his knees. The steward held the garment in front of him to show that he would need to slide his arms into the sleeves from behind, then they moved behind him to hold it up. Wriggling around awkwardly in the arms of the second steward, Seth managed to slide into the tunic. The first steward circled around in front of him and fastened the metal clasps running from neck to navel on the tunic. When Seth swallowed, the collar pressed snugly around his neck, trapping him inside the garment.

Now that he was mostly dressed, it was easier to finish the outfit with a gold sash tied around his waist, drawing the tunic closely around his lithe form. The last piece the stewards shuffled him into was a sleeveless blue robe that was dark as the night sky. They maneuvered him back into his wheelchair, and he was thankful to be out of their grasp. His armpits hurt. The stewards continued to flit about, brushing his hair and fastening other accessories to his body along with a pair of wooden sandals. One steward fished one of the yellow flowers from the tub and patted it dry before sliding into his hair over his left ear. It took them a few moments to fidget with his hair and the flower before they were content with the appearance. Ultimately, they decided to push his hair behind his ears, showing off the pointed tips.

This wouldn't be nearly as bad if it was Lisanthir doing this. Seth's face flushed with embarrassment at the thought. It wasn't an unpleasant thought, just... *At what point in an Elviri courtship do the two see each other in the nude?*

One of the stewards ran their hand down Seth's chest, smoothing down the robes and ensuring he looked his best. If he didn't look too closely, he could almost fool himself into thinking it was Lisanthir's hand, but he knew better. The heat of arousal and embarrassment faded into an unsettling emptiness as he forced himself to focus on what was coming next—a dinner with his father and Osza.

Whatever gods are out there, please help me and my sister get through this.

The stewards brought Seth to his father's dining chamber, which had been elaborately decorated in preparation for the meal. Swaths of silks and flowers hung from the stone walls. In the center of the table was a beautiful stone art piece that was equal parts decoration and candleholder. A few candelabras had been brought into the room and placed against the walls, filling the room with a warm golden glow. The table was set for five, which was one seat fewer than normal. Grief seized his heart as he stared at the empty place where his mother's chair had been.

No one else was yet in the room, which Seth took solace in. That gave him time to be moved into one of the stone chairs at the table without his father or the Asaszi watching. After being lifted into his customary seat on the left side of the table, one steward smoothed down his clothes while the other removed the wheelchair from the room.

No easy escapes tonight, Seth thought bleakly. *Hopefully, there will be plenty of wine.*

Amias and Octavia entered the room together a few moments later, both looking like royalty. His sister wore an outfit similar to Seth's except her outer robe was bright gold with a dark blue tunic underneath. Her hair had been pushed back behind her ears as well, to show off the new points with flowers nestled behind them and all throughout her blonde locks. Seth much preferred this look to the dress she had worn to her ceremony, although he wished she was allowed to hide her ears. Knowing what he knew now, he was sure she felt the same way.

Amias was dressed in flowing black robes with gold embroidery stitched into his sleeves and chest. His graying hair was smoothed back out of his face, the candelabras' flames dancing in his brown eyes. The finery had shaved off several decades from Amias's appearance, making him look like a much younger, saner man.

His gaze snapped to Seth, and he smiled warmly. "Hello, Seth."

"Hello, Father," Seth said, trying his best to keep his voice from wavering or showing any signs of weakness.

Amias walked Octavia to the seat beside Seth and pulled the chair out for her. She accepted the seat graciously with a polite smile. "Thank you, Father."

Amias sat at the end of the table opposite the doorway, his gaze fixed on the threshold. Seth knew he was waiting for the arrival of their hosts, Osza and Astohi. "Bring the wine," Amias told the stewards.

One of the stewards left the room, returning a short while later with another steward, both bearing jugs. One contained wine, the other water. The steward with the wine filled the cups around the table before standing against one of the walls. Looking around the room, Seth realized that all of the stewards tending the dinner were Asaszi, which he found curious.

Without waiting for the queen or her consort, Amias raised his glass and tipped it toward his children before drinking deeply. He let out a satisfied noise and set it back down.

Why is Father not waiting for the Asaszi? He always does... Seth looked closer at Amias. *Is this because of his most recent experiment? Talking to the Tserys? Wouldn't he want to brag about that to Osza?* Despite his rebellious action and show of confidence, Amias was still staring at the entryway, looking rattled.

The two Asaszi royals arrived a few moments later, Astohi leading Osza into the room. Both were covered in jewels and precious metals, and little else. Astohi held his chin high, allowing the candlelight to flicker across the gold scales that ran from his chin to his lower abdomen, a stark contrast to the dark green scales that covered the rest of his body. Secured around his waist was a belt made from gold, holding up a piece of black silk that wrapped around him and fell to his knees. Beside the silk garb, the only other things the serpentine man wore were gold bracelets and necklaces dripping with green and red gems.

Osza wore a necklace that appeared more like a dress, though it did very little to cover her body. Emeralds and pieces of jade were woven into the golden chains and patterns that fell down her chest. Her black hair tumbled down her shoulders and back. Atop her head was a gold crown with a large topaz gem in the center. The metal was shaped and twisted to resemble two serpents with their mouths open trying to devour the jewel.

Astohi helped his queen take her seat then took his own on her right directly across from Seth. The Asaszi's tongue flickered out in his direction, tasting the air before reaching for his cup. His eyes darted down, saw the cup had already been filled, and then drank deeply. Osza merely sat and watched the others around the table.

Seth had never seen so many gemstones before. The Asaszi had never flaunted their wealth before, not to that degree. There was something special about this dinner, even more important than his sister's permutation ceremony. He just wished that he knew what the reason was, so he wouldn't be surprised in the middle of the meal.

As if they had been summoned by the thought of food, a parade of stewards and servants entered the room carrying steaming platters and dishes. They circled the table, stopping to add portions to everyone's plates before setting the dishes down in the center. Two kinds of fish, a few roasted pork ribs, and a plethora of cooked vegetables and roots had been piled onto Seth's plate. Despite his nerves, the food looked and smelled delicious, and he was actually looking forward to eating what he could. He just needed to be mindful not to eat too much.

After all of the servants had set their dishes down and stepped away from the table, Osza picked up her fork and took her first bite of food, signaling to the others they could eat as well. Seth wasted no time digging into a small pile of stewed greens, enjoying their savory flavor.

The room was silent for several moments as everyone ate, but all good things had to come to an end. The Asaszi queen was the one to break the silence. She set her fork and knife down to look up at Amias. She actually didn't speak for a few moments, just observed him while he ate and drank. Seth noticed almost immediately since he sat next to the Asaszi woman. He tried his best not to stare at her, but he wanted to understand what she was thinking, why she was staring at Amias that way. There were no traces of anger in her gaze that he could see, but she wanted something from him. While she may be patient for the time being, eventually the snake would strike.

"Amiasss, have your troopsss returned from the border?" Osza asked, her tone light and airy.

Seth looked at his father without moving his head. Intriguing as that was, he didn't want to draw any attention to himself. Amias raised his chin as he chewed on a piece of fish. He took his time with finishing the bite and swallowing, then replied, "They've returned to Moonyswyn, yes."

The corners of Osza's mouth curved downward for just a moment before she returned to her neutral expression. "Were they sssuccesssssful with capturing the Elviri?"

Amias nodded, setting down his fork and picking up his cup of wine. "They were, yes. The prisoners are being sent to Iszairi." He raised his cup to his lips and drank deeply as Astohi's hood flared, snapping a couple of the golden necklaces around his neck. Seth's entire body twitched out of fear, his fork rattling on his plate.

Osza turned to look at Astohi. Though Seth couldn't see the expression on her face, it was enough to ease—or perhaps threaten—her partner into calming himself down. She blinked slowly, her tongue flicking out to taste the air. Her voice was deceptively calm as she turned back to look down the table.

"You *dare* go againssst your ordersss?" Her eyes widened for a moment as if daring Amias to step into the trap she had laid out for him.

Amias didn't flinch at the Asaszi's words. He took his time with his drink and then set it back on the table gently. He licked his lips. "I follow the orders of the *Tserys*. He spoke to me this morning, and I did what He asked of me."

Seth watched the Asaszi queen blink again, just as slowly as before. Whatever thoughts swirled in her head, she didn't show them on her face. The dining hall was silent, except for the sound of Seth's heart beating in his ears and the constant low hum that hid underneath everything else. Everyone had stopped eating, too angry or too afraid to break that silence. He didn't realize he was staring at Osza until he saw Astohi move out of the corner of his eye. The Asaszi man had turned his attention to Seth, glaring at him through narrowed slits. Seth's stomach dropped, and he looked down at his plate again, eager to avoid that predatory stare.

Osza let out a quiet hiss. "You did not inform usss of thisss."

"I am informing you of it now," Amias responded coolly.

Fear gnawed at Seth's stomach. He thought that Amias and Osza working together was terrifying enough. But with the sudden rift rapidly growing between them, Seth was scared of what kind of repercussions this would have.

Please let Octavia and I get through this unscathed.

"What did the *Tssserys* inssstruct you to do with the Elviri?" Anger began to seep into Osza's voice. Seth dared to take a peek at her posture, keeping his chin tilted down toward his chest. The Asaszi queen's back was rigid, her hands in her lap. She raised her chin, so she looked down at Amias.

"He revealed to me one of the rituals needed to open the Tomb."

Osza hissed again and leaned forward ever so slightly. Anger dissolved into intrigue. Perhaps she and Amias weren't so divided after all. Or perhaps the queen was capable of looking past the conflict for the greater good.

No, nothing good can come of this.

Amias didn't miss the Asaszi's interest in his words either. "I have begun preparations to move my work and my family to Iszairi in three days' time. From there, I—" He stopped for a moment and then altered his words. "*We* will take the next steps to opening the Prince's Tomb."

Was the slip intentional, or is Father trying to further divide himself from the Asaszi? Looking down the table at his father, Seth could tell he was in full control of his mental faculties. Amias was playing a dangerous game with dangerous predators.

Osza simply nodded and picked up her glass of wine, raising it toward Amias. "We will sssecure Yiradia and journey back with you."

Amias returned the toast, then both drank deeply, eyes locked over the rims of their glasses.

Seth drank enough at dinner to suppress his fears while around his father and the Asaszi. There was very little chatter for the rest of the meal, and eventually Amias allowed Octavia and Seth to leave. Two stewards followed the siblings like shadows.

"Do you want me to help you to bed?" Octavia asked quietly as they navigated through the corridors. She leaned against the handles of his chair, pushing him along.

"Could you?" He was exhausted from the stress of the dining hall, and he wanted to spend a few moments alone with his sister. He'd missed her, and he needed to talk to her about, well, *everything*.

Octavia made an affirmative noise. As they turned the corner toward Seth's room, the sound of hurried footsteps chased after them.

"*Pyredan* Kharis?" a nasally voice called out.

"Yes?" Octavia stopped near the door, turning to face the newcomer.

Seth turned his head to look behind him. A Provira soldier stood nearby, panting quietly. The poor kid must've run through the pyramid looking for Tav. "*Pyredan* Wynn sent me to look for you. He wanted to discuss assignments."

Octavia let out a soft growl. "And it can't wait for the morning," she grumbled, mostly to herself.

The soldier assumed she had been talking to him, so he responded. "He insisted."

Octavia looked back to Seth, and their eyes met. She looked tired and sad. She wanted to retreat into solitude with him, he knew that, but Seth also knew she had to commit to appearances for now. If Arcyr'ys wanted to see her, she was going to go, even if she didn't want to.

We need to get out of here.

"It's okay, Tav," Seth whispered. "Maybe tomorrow morning."

His sister reached for his shoulder and gave it a squeeze. The touch was one mostly of comfort, but she squeezed just tight enough to reflect her own fear. Seth endured the twinge of pain, meeting her eyes to silently reassure her that everything would be ok.

We will *get out of here.*

"Alright, alright. Is he in the pyramid or the village?" Octavia asked the soldier, letting go of Seth's shoulder.

"The village."

The two walked off together, leaving Seth with his two shadows. He dragged his chair to the door and opened it. One of the stewards moved to follow him inside, but he raised a hand. "Not tonight." The stewards assumed their posts outside his door.

His room was dark with only the faintest slivers of moonlight reaching through the window. Letting out an audible sigh, Seth started tugging at his clothes, suddenly eager to get out of this finery and into his bed. He rolled his chair over to his wardrobe so the moonlight could guide his movements. First went the sash tied around his waist, thrown to the floor.

He reached for the flower in his hair, but a quiet voice stopped him. "May I help?"

Seth twisted in his chair and saw Lisanthir standing behind him, his veil discarded. His eyes widened as he took in the sight of the Elviri, unmasked, a few loose strands of black hair falling across his face. How Seth wished the moon was fuller, so he could see the green of Lis's eyes.

"H-how...?" Seth asked.

"Your room needed cleaning, and only the Asaszi stewards were allowed to tend to tonight's dinner." Lisanthir smiled, reaching out with a gloved hand to pluck the yellow flower from Seth's hair. "I didn't think they'd miss me tonight. Too busy making sure the food was perfect."

"The food was rather good," Seth murmured, a blush creeping across his face. His stomach twisted with a mixture of pleasure and fear. He didn't want to talk about the dinner with Lis, but the Elviri needed to know what had happened over the past two days. He wished Tav hadn't been called away, but he would figure out a way to ensure all three of them were caught up with recent events. "Sorry that my sister isn't here. Arcyr'ys needed her for something."

Lisanthir's brow furrowed. "What do you mean?"

"You two planned this so we could all talk, didn't you?"

The Elviri let out a nervous laugh, setting the flower on the window sill beside his gloves. "Oh, ah, no... I haven't spoken to her since training this morning."

Seth watched as the moonlight and shadows danced across Lisanthir's features. The Elviri's cheeks had turned a bright red, and... *Oh.*

Seth turned his head back toward the wardrobe, running a hand through his hair. "Oh, I see."

"But she wanted to talk tonight? Do you know what about?"

Seth shook his head, removing the small pieces of jewelry the stewards had fastened around his wrists and neck. "I'm not sure. I assumed she had news about our plans."

"The last we spoke, she had been trying to find a way into Priestess Szatisi's chambers, though she didn't say why." Lisanthir stepped closer, holding out a hand to take the trinkets.

Seth passed them over and tugged on the dark blue robe to pull it off next. He was impressed with the Elviri's pronunciation of the priestess's name; there were Provira soldiers who didn't have as strong of a grasp on the Asaszi language. "Szatisi created an elixir that restored my legs. *Temporarily.*" He spat the last word, staring down at his feet. The overwhelming urge to rip the wooden sandals off and throw them out the window bubbled up within him. But he couldn't do it.

"Oh," Lisanthir mouthed softly. He kneeled down next to the wheelchair, the black steward's robes pillowing around his knees.

"Did she say anything else about Szatisi?" Seth asked, his voice frail. *Did the priestess ever find out what happened with the first elixir?*

"No, nothing. I'm not sure if I'll see her tomorrow, but I'll try to talk to her."

"She's supposed to come see me tomorrow morning," Seth murmured. He had gotten the robe off of his shoulders and was pulling it out from underneath his thighs.

Lisanthir reached out and took the robe from Seth, folding it up and setting it aside. "Even better. If I don't see her, I'll try to come see you instead."

Seth's stomach twisted sharply with glee, but then he tempered his emotions. "I-I don't want you getting caught—"

Lisanthir took Seth's hand in his and squeezed gently. "Nothing and no one in Daaria can keep me from your side, *ebilin*."

"*Ebilin*," Seth echoed, placing his other hand on top of Lisanthir's. Before his bravery could escape him, he managed to ask, "Why did you follow me out of Lithalyon? A-And stay, even after learning what I am?"

Lisanthir cast his gaze down to their hands, a shaky laugh passing his lips. "The goddess Lithua herself must've spurred me on because I just couldn't imagine letting you slip away. I've never been particularly brave, thus why I chose to study in Lithalyon rather than join my brothers on the frontline, but I've always been restless. My mind wanders to far-off places and times, always wanting to learn more and experience more. And when we met, I felt like I could do all of that with *you*."

Seth wanted to reply, but words failed him. *We're kindred spirits. Gods, how good it feels to have someone like him by my side.*

Lisanthir continued, "Chasing after you is the bravest thing I've ever done, and I don't regret it. Calydrian intrigued me, but Seth stirs a part of my heart that I've never felt before. Being here with you, in a place that I thought was lost to the Eldest Days, I think I can brave any danger we face."

Seth brought their joined hands to his lips and kissed the top of Lisanthir's hand. "Running away to Lithalyon was the bravest thing I've ever done. I'm glad I did it. I'm glad I met you."

Lisanthir laughed quietly, the joyful noise warming Seth's heart. "It's late. You must be tired."

Despite the shock and stress of the day's events, Seth wasn't tired at all. His skin felt like it was on fire, and he wanted nothing more than to bask in Lisanthir's presence for as long as he could. He wanted to be greedy and selfish and stay up all night committing the Elviri's appearance and voice to memory. But he did want to get out of his elegant clothes and into something more comfortable. The collar of the tunic was tight around his throat, and he thought he'd break out into a sweat if he kept it on any longer.

"Could you help me out of this tunic?" he asked with a breathless chuckle.

Lisanthir flashed a look that sent his pulse and his mind racing. He tried to unearth all of the thoughts and emotions behind it but couldn't get past the heat growing inside of him. The Elviri kissed his hand again and then let go, instead reaching for the metal clasp near his throat. The hairs on the back of his neck stood on end and he was sure his cheeks were bright red, but he tried to ignore how flustered he was underneath Lisanthir's touch.

After the third clasp was unfastened, Lisanthir lowered his hands and leaned back, his eyes meeting Seth's, and he asked, "Would you like something to replace this?"

Seth felt more of his skin heat up from the blush. "Um, one of my sleep shirts, yes."

Lisanthir nodded and stood up, turning toward the wardrobe. He opened one of the doors and reached within, pulling out a few garments before settling on a sleeveless green tunic that Seth often wore to bed.

Seth fidgeted with the next fastened clasp. There were only two left, and though he had been enjoying Lisanthir's touches, the thought of the Elviri continuing to undress him made him want to curl up and melt away. He couldn't tell if that was a good feeling or not, so rather than risk getting overwhelmed any further, he unfastened the clasps himself.

When Lisanthir turned back to him with the green tunic in hand, Seth reached out for it. He was worried he'd have to say something, make up some excuse for finishing removing the shirt himself, but the Elviri only smiled and gave him the garment. "I'll get your bed ready while you change."

Seth didn't realize he had been holding in his breath. He exhaled as quietly as he could, waiting until Lisanthir walked around him before shrugging the fancy tunic off his shoulders. The cool winter air kissed his skin, raising gooseflesh all over his body. He hadn't realized how cold it had gotten outside. For a moment he considered trying to pull and tug the long garment out from underneath his seat, but he decided against it. Once he was in bed, he could reach over and throw it toward his wardrobe, and let the stewards deal with it some other time.

Seth pivoted his wheelchair back toward his bed where Lisanthir was still arranging his blankets and furs. Watching the Elviri, he couldn't help a smile from spreading across his face. He found himself yearning to have that every night, to be in the presence of his *ebilin*.

When Lisanthir was finished, he looked up and returned the smile. There was suddenly too much space in between them, and Seth needed to touch Lisanthir. He needed his Elviri to hold him. "C-Can you help me onto the bed?"

Lisanthir had picked him up before, but Seth hadn't *known* that it was his gentle hands on his sides guiding him into his wheelchair. He craved that now, and the Elviri was by his side in an instant.

"Wrap your arms around my neck," Lisanthir murmured, kneeling beside the chair. His hands brushed against Seth's sides as he lifted him up. Seth leaned into the movement, his arms snaking around Lisanthir and holding onto the Elviri. He kept his gaze fixed on where the Elviri's pale skin slipped beneath the collar of his black robes, his heartbeat pounding in his ears. With strength that Seth both found admirable and was envious of, Lisanthir lifted him out of the wheelchair and pivoted gracefully to set him down on the nest of blankets and furs.

Lisanthir twisted within Seth's grasp to sit beside him on the bed, one hand lingering on his waist. That touch acted like an anchor for Seth, grounding him in the moment. He dragged his fingertips along Lisanthir's upper back, savoring the heat, committing the feeling to memory. He was so wonderfully, painfully happy, but a quiet voice in the back of his head told him it couldn't last.

"Stay with me." Seth's voice was barely above a whisper, afraid that his words would shatter the moment, but also afraid that if he didn't say anything, the moment would come to an end regardless. He wanted to be selfish and keep Lisanthir here with him *forever*, but he would be satisfied if it was for just one night.

Lisanthir's mouth curled into a soft smile as he leaned closer, brushing his lips against Seth's in a silent response. A promise: *I'm not going anywhere.*

After several kisses and shared breaths, Lisanthir pulled back. Seth was reluctant to let him go, but he let his arms fall away from the Elviri's neck. He watched Lis bend over to tug at his shoes, a few loose strands of dark hair falling across his face. Seth found himself wanting to push the strands behind

Lis's ear. And perhaps let his hand linger on his cheek. Feel how soft his skin was beneath his fingertips...

"You don't have to wait for me," Lisanthir murmured, drawing Seth out of his reverie. He blinked a few times and saw the Elviri was giving him a lopsided grin as he fiddled with the front of his robe. "Go on, get comfortable."

Seth let out a breathless chuckle as he began shuffling backward in the bed toward the wall. He tugged one of the blankets out from underneath his hips and draped it over his legs before sliding down and resting his head against the pile of pillows. Lisanthir finished unfastening the front of his robe and slid it off his shoulders, revealing a loose shirt and pants that appeared to be made from the same black material. The Elviri reached up to untie the leather ribbon in his hair, letting it tumble down across his shoulders. He threw the ribbon on top of his robe and then approached the bed again, raising a few of the blankets to slide in beside Seth.

Seth's whole body felt like it was on fire. He wasn't sure how he'd be able to sleep underneath *anything* with Lisanthir beside him, but he made no move to toss aside the blankets. Instead, he pulled one up to his chin, tucking himself in so that the only part of his body not covered was his head. He watched Lisanthir as he adjusted the blankets and got closer to him until their thighs were pressed together.

Lisanthir lay on his side facing Seth, his head propped up on one hand. "Get some rest, *ebilin*. I'll be here beside you."

This... I want this. Now and always.

CHAPTER XIV: MUNNE

CASTLE AUORA: DAY 28, MONTH 11, YEAR 13,239

As the two suns dipped below the horizon, Munne and her companions returned to the island of Auora in a change of clothes. Mayrien and Araloth had brought with them a large pack of clothing meant for wearing around a campfire, which suited their purposes that evening. All three women wore some hat or accessory with their hair to hide their pointed ears so onlookers couldn't immediately tell that they were Elviri. They left behind their swords as well, so as not to draw attention to themselves.

Before they entered the city, Munne stopped to talk to the guards at the bridge. She made sure to make eye contact with all six of the ones standing on the bridge and introduced herself and her companions, so they would recognize her later when they returned to the castle. Though she recognized several from her patrols into the city, they all looked exhausted, and she couldn't trust that they'd easily remember who she was later that night.

The West Breeze Inn was indeed livelier than it had been earlier in the day. The common area was even more crowded than earlier if that was possible. As soon as they entered the building, Munne, Mayrien, and Araloth shuffled their way through the crowd toward the bar to order themselves drinks. There was enough space between two men for Araloth to squeeze in and wave down the barkeep. Munne and Mayrien stood behind her, trying to leave as much room for other patrons as possible to move about. As the barkeep poured them mugs of ale, Munne glanced around the room to see if she could spot the Proma from earlier that day.

"Three silvers for the drinks," the barkeep called out as he handed the mugs to Araloth who passed two of the mugs on to Mayrien. The older Elviri dug into her pockets and handed over the specified coin.

Mayrien passed along one of the mugs to Munne. "Find either of our boys?"

"Not yet," Munne said over her shoulder, raising her voice to be heard.

"Should we find a table, or linger here by the bar?" Araloth asked, squeezing in between the other two women.

"I don't know if there's even a table for us *to* sit at," Mayrien said with a snicker and cast a glance around the room.

"True enough, but let's try to get one if we can," Munne responded.

The three each took sips of their ale, the taste less enjoyable than what they were used to back in Elimere.

Ale is ale, though, and it'll help keep me calm tonight, Munne thought.

"Not many kin here," Mayrien said and took another sip of her ale. "Probably better that way, though."

"Perhaps they left before we got here," Araloth suggested, leading the group through the common area.

"Or perhaps there's another refuge in the city where they've flocked to," Munne said as she turned her torso to avoid bumping shoulders with a passer-by.

As the trio neared one of the staircases leading up to the inn's rooms, a voice called out to them from one of the nearby tables, "Cousin! Over here!"

Munne turned toward the voice, an eyebrow arched in confusion. She met the gaze of two mismatching eyes, one green and one white, and her heart leapt into her throat.

He's here!

Mayrien bumped into Munne from behind, cursing as some ale sloshed out of her mug. "Vere'cha, can you not—"

"He's here," Munne breathed, her voice barely audible over the noise in the inn.

"Lead us to him," Araloth replied, placing her hand on Munne's back.

The caravan leader sat at a table nearby with four other men and women, waving at Munne and her companions. The Proma from earlier that day sat alongside the caravan leader, raising his mug at the three Elviri. He wore the same dark blue tunic as before, his brown hair swept back out of his face. Across from the caravan leader were two women and one man, all of whom stood up to make space for Munne and her companions.

As she approached, Munne recognized that one of the women was an Elviri, her pointed ears poking out from underneath her blonde hair. The other man and woman were Proma with darker complexions. Everyone was dressed modestly, blending in with the other citizens of the inn. Nothing about the group's appearance indicated that they were travelers. They looked as if they were born and raised in Auora and had never stepped foot off the island.

Curious that one of our kin sits at this table, Munne mused. *Although I suppose it makes a little bit of sense. Having an Elviri as part of the caravan would make traveling through the Elviri provinces easier.*

"My new friend told me you were looking for me earlier today," the caravan leader continued with a crooked smile on his face. "I apologize. I was in my room resting. The goings-on in the city have left me with a strange sleep schedule, I'm afraid."

"What matters is that we were able to find each other," Munne replied with an easy smile. The sentiment was genuine even as thoughts of her homeland and her people raced through her mind. *He's here, which means my journey to Kherizhan is about to begin. I pray that I'm making the right choice in saving myself.*

"Indeed! I hope your travels were safe, cousin." The man's continued use of the term brought Munne a small bit of comfort. "And well-met to your own traveling companions!"

Mayrien raised her mug of ale in acknowledgement with a grin. "Well met."

Araloth mimicked the gesture. "It's a terrible shame what's happening here. If only we knew; we could've met in Ferilin instead," said the older Elviri, setting her own mug on the table. While her tone was friendly enough, Munne understood the bite behind Araloth's words and that they were directed at her.

The caravan leader and his companions all nodded and murmured their agreements.

"I don't think I've met your friends," Munne said, glancing around the table. "And I have introductions of my own to make."

"In due time, cousin. Let's enjoy our drinks, rest our bones, and be thankful we're not out on the streets tonight." He took a long drink from his mug of ale.

Munne wanted to frown, but she composed herself. She needed to be patient. The inn was so crowded that anyone could overhear their conversation, so perhaps there was wisdom in waiting. But she didn't want to wait *too* long.

"How long will you be in the city?" she asked.

The man looked at the brown-haired Proma to his right then at his female Elviri companion. "Not quite sure with the lockdown going on. We'd like to get moving as soon as the bridges are open again."

"Hopefully it'll only be another day or so," was all she offered in return, hoping he understood the undercurrent of her words. *Can I convince Captain Munhart to let us leave before the lockdown is lifted?*

The caravan leader looked at his other two companions standing next to the table. "Can you two go gather up something to eat for us and our guests? We'll be up in the suite where it's quieter."

"Sure thing, boss," the man replied, leading the woman off to the bar.

The caravan leader turned his gaze back to Munne and the others. An easy smile slid onto his face, the corners of his mismatching eyes crinkling. "I apologize. That was presumptuous of me. Would you like to join us for dinner in our suite upstairs?"

"Of course, we'd be delighted to," Mayrien answered before Munne could. Her face lit up with a cheery grin. "Sounds like a much better place to enjoy a fine dinner and finer company."

Munne couldn't help but let out a small chuckle. Mayrien could always be counted on to play along with whatever antics they found themselves in. The same couldn't be said for Araloth, but the older Elviri was doing her best to appear cordial.

"Excellent! I'm sure there's other patrons who'd like to have this table. Come, let's go." The caravan leader stood and led the way to the staircase farthest from the bar. Sure enough, within moments of their departure, a family claimed the table for their own, setting down cups and plates to finish their meal.

The group climbed up three flights of stairs before the caravan leader turned and led them down a hallway. He fished a key from a satchel on his hip and unlocked one of the doors, pushing it open and inviting the others inside. Munne watched his two companions enter first then crossed the threshold herself. Though she and her triple had left their armor and swords back in the castle, they were far from unarmed. She had sheathed daggers in each boot and knew her two companions had done the same. They were also no strangers to improvised weapons, and Munne felt confident that if this meeting turned hostile, she could land a heavy hit with her mug of ale before drawing the daggers from their sheaths.

The interior of the suite was well-lit and well-decorated. They walked into the common area, which was little more than a dining area and fireplace. In the center of the room was a round wooden table and eight chairs. The small stone hearth already had a fire lit in it. Flanking the fireplace were two small windows covered by dark curtains. A clay vase stood in the center of the table, filled with greenery and a few white flowers. Sconces hung on the interior walls, bathing the room in a warm glow. Both walls had a door in the middle, presumably leading to bedchambers beyond.

The caravan leader's two companions chose the two seats closest to the entrance. Munne walked around to the side closest to the fireplace, wanting to keep her back to the windows so she could survey the whole room. And so she wouldn't feel trapped between the three caravanners in the room and the ones still to join them.

Mayrien and Araloth flanked Munne on either side, setting their mugs down on the wooden table. The caravan leader closed the door behind them then moved to sit beside his Elviri companion.

"Now that we have a little peace and quiet, we can make proper introductions," he said with a warm voice. "It's a pleasure to meet you ladies. As our mutual friend knows, Dalys isn't my real name but a suitable alias. You may call me Tethe."

Munne tipped her mug in Tethe's direction, watching the way the firelight flickered across his white eye. "Tethe. It's good to put a real name to your face." Though, she had her doubts that 'Tethe' was genuinely his real name.

"With us are Yvanna and Ormes, and retrieving our dinner are Jion and Adalia," Tethe said, gesturing to the Elviri and Proma sitting beside him. Both offered smiles to Munne and the others, although Yvanna's looked strained.

"I can't say I've seen many kin take to the wilderness with Proma, but it's good to meet you." Mayrien nodded toward Yvanna with a grin.

"Truth be told I feel more comfortable out in the wilderness than in cities like here. These sorts of places make me feel cramped and uneasy," Yvanna responded, some of the tension slipping from her appearance. Munne could sympathize with the other Elviri's plight. The walls of her father's manor and the steep slopes of the valley often felt more like a cage than a home.

"Where are my manners? Forgive me, let me introduce my own companions," Munne said, putting on a show by sighing with disappointment then gesturing to her friends. "Beside me are—"

"Two friends who are very interested in where she travels," Araloth interrupted, her steady gaze leveling with Tethe.

Munne clenched her jaw and shot an angry glare at the older Elviri that went unseen by her target. Tense silence filled the air for several moments before Tethe let out a sharp laugh and nodded. "Your friend preferred discretion back home, and I can respect that. As I'm sure you can respect our own discretion. But please, for our sake, what would you have us call you?"

Araloth looked at Munne and Mayrien, her face a blank slate. She was waiting for a direction provided by one of the other two women.

He knows who I am. Should we even bother with fake names or pretending otherwise?

"We're past the point of false identities, I believe." Munne carefully picked each word before speaking, eyes drifting from Araloth to Tethe. "And it's in our best interests to be honest with one another if we're to leave Auora together."

"Well said, my lady," Tethe responded with a bowed head.

Another bout of silence filled the room as all eyes fell on Munne. *Perhaps "Tethe" is some form of his real name, then. Or perhaps he cares not for honesty. We'll have to keep a close watch on this man and his lot.*

"Do you still carry the trinket from our first meeting?" Munne asked, breaking the silence once more.

Tethe reached into one of his pockets and fished out the small black disk, handing it to Yvanna. "Be gentle, my dear. No unnecessary friction."

Yvanna smirked and reached out to hand the disk to Mayrien who accepted it with a wary eye. She held it up to her face, inspecting the blue gem and turning the stone all about.

"Rub it gently and then pull your finger back," Munne muttered to her friend.

Mayrien tossed a skeptical look at Munne then returned to the disk. Holding it in her left hand, she rubbed the blue gem with a single finger then slowly pulled it away, a tendril of blue flame stretching from skin to stone.

"By the gods," Mayrien gasped, eyes widening in shock.

"What trickery is this?" Araloth demanded, slamming her fist on the table and staring daggers at Tethe.

Munne snapped her head to the older Elviri, hand outstretched to grasp her shoulder. "*Etilith*, please—"

"It's no trick, fair Elviri," Tethe replied, unbothered by the outburst. "Your friend knows, this is a relic left behind from the Eldest Days. Magic."

"Magic!" Araloth spat. "We're wasting our time here; we should return home before anything—"

"Ara—nngh, *etilith*, stand down!" Munne ordered, grabbing Araloth's shoulder and forcing her friend to pivot and face her.

Araloth's green eyes were bright with fury. Munne inhaled sharply through her nose and met that furious gaze. To back down now would be to admit defeat. She couldn't return to Elimere, not if she wanted to be rid of the nightmares. To learn the secrets of Ely and Naro. To find *something* in Kherizhan that could turn the tide of the war against the Provira. To keep herself from going insane and taking her own life. She needed Araloth to back down and stand by her side.

"My fingertip burns," Mayrien murmured, her voice soft and calm. She was in awe of the disk, Munne could tell. She shared the sentiment. "How do you make the flame go away?"

"Tap your finger against the gem once more," Tethe told her.

Araloth was the first to break away, her eyes shifting to Mayrien. Munne watched the older Elviri for any trace of anger in her expression. Araloth seemed to be focused on Mayrien, her fury vanishing. Her brow furrowed and she kept glancing between Mayrien's face and hands.

When Munne turned her head to look back at Mayrien, her friend had set the disk back on the table, the blue fire gone. Yvanna plucked the disk from the table and handed it back to Tethe. Ormes's gaze followed the disk from Mayrien to Tethe, shock and awe plastered across his face.

Is this his first time seeing the disk? Does Tethe not share his trinkets with his companions? Yvanna has clearly seen the disk before.

"When do you leave for Kherizhan?" Munne asked Tethe, drawing the attention of everyone at the table.

Before Tethe could respond, someone knocked on the door. He turned to Ormes and nudged the man gently with his elbow. "Help them bring the food inside."

The Proma hesitated to get up, still clearly focused on the magic disk. Yvanna scoffed and rolled her eyes, crossing her arms over her chest.

"Ormes," Tethe murmured darkly, his tone a clear warning to the man.

Finally, Ormes rose to his feet and opened the door where the other two companions, Jion and Adalia, were standing with two large platters of food. As soon as he opened the door, the two entered with haste, placing the platters on the circular table and immediately unloading the dishes. The spread wasn't as lavish as the food Munne had been eating in the castle, but it smelled delicious enough and she knew she'd enjoy it. There were three loaves of crusty bread, two large roasted fish, a small cauldron of stewed roots and vegetables, and a large pitcher of water.

Jion and Adalia prepared plates for the table, handing the first plate to Munne, who accepted it and set it down. The fish smelled delicious, but she chose to wait until Tethe and his companions had been given plates of their own. She wanted to trust the man but knew it would be foolish to do so blindly. Araloth and Mayrien had even less of a reason to trust him, and they too chose to wait to eat until their hosts did.

After the three Elviri were served, Adalia set a plate down in front of Tethe, Ormes, and Yvanna before she prepared her own dish and sat down beside Jion. Tethe gestured to the food, inviting everyone to partake. His companions did so without any further persuading, all eating with fervor.

Munne watched them for a few moments before picking up her own fork and knife. She glanced at Mayrien, who also began eating, and then turned her head to look at Araloth. The elder Elviri disguised her mistrust easily enough, maintaining a neutral expression as she surveyed the table, but her hands were in her lap, her plate untouched. It was plain to see that Araloth wasn't pleased with the sequence of events. Munne owed her friend several drinks in the future and perhaps some sparring matches to let Araloth let out her anger and frustration on her in battle.

"Not the best I've had in Auora," Ormes grumbled around a mouthful of fish. "But given the circumstances, it's not bad."

"The spices help disguise the age of the fish. Not as fresh as I'm used to," Jion replied.

Munne watched him carefully, trying to get a read on the Proma. His skin was much darker than his companions'. He was dressed like a man accustomed to the higher districts in Auora with bronze beads woven into his black hair and fine stitching on his dark green tunic. She didn't think he had been with Tethe in Elimere, but she wasn't certain. She didn't recall much about the others in the tavern because she had been so focused on Tethe's mismatching eyes.

"So, you're all members of the same caravan? Do you travel together across Daaria?" Mayrien asked, her voice pleasant.

Jion and Adalia nodded. Ormes looked to Tethe, while Yvanna didn't raise her eyes from her food. Tethe was the one to respond. "Yes, fair Elviri. We make up the Moon's Wares. We've been traveling together for several years, although Ormes only recently joined our crew. He also has his sights set on Kherizhan, you see."

Mayrien nodded thoughtfully, tearing off a small chunk of bread and nibbling on it. "And do you often travel to the southeast?"

Tethe cracked a small smile, cutting at a piece of fish. "Often enough to have charted the best paths. There's certainly still plenty of the region that we're unfamiliar with, but fortunately the Olaava had several cities spread throughout the mountains."

A small thoughtful noise escaped Mayrien as she raised her wine goblet to her lips. Munne knew her companions cared little for history, but the mention of the ancient, long-gone race was a surprise. The idea of this group of travelers having been to the barren wastes of Kherizhan multiple times was impressive, let alone being able to map out where the Olaava used to live.

If it was true.

Gods, please let it be true.

"Isn't that dangerous with the war going on in the south?" Araloth asked, her voice stern. "Or does your path take you through the Imalar Woods?"

"Not within, but certainly around," came Tethe's reply before he took a drink from his own goblet. "That border doesn't have as many eyes on it as Moonyswyn's."

Munne ate a forkful of vegetables, letting the flavors meld in her mouth. A part of her felt guilty hearing his words. If she had stayed true to her course, she would have been bolstering defenses along the edges of the Imalar Woods. She could still pass the order on to Ethelmar and ensure the Imalarii would be protected, but it wasn't the same. She would carry the guilt in her heart knowing she was choosing to personally abandon her allies at a time when they needed her most.

But if I don't follow my own path, there will be nothing left of me to protect my allies.

"When are you planning on leaving Auora?" Munne blurted out, drawing all eyes to herself. "I realize the city is under lockdown. But when were you planning on leaving?" *I can't wait until this lockdown is lifted. We must leave immediately if I'm going to rid myself of the* Ardashi'ik.

Tethe held her gaze, his expression blank. Firelight cast an eerie glow across his green eye, turning it gold. "When would you propose, my lady?"

"Perhaps I can work something out with the captain of the guard to let us leave sooner." She could feel Araloth glaring daggers in her direction. Mayrien was throwing looks of concern her way too, no doubt.

"I'm humbled by your offer, my lady." Tethe bowed his head. "Under ordinary circumstances, we would be forced to wait out the lockdown."

"Is your wagon safely kept somewhere?"

"Alas, we lost the wagon during the evacuation of the Crafting District. We still have two chests of goods. It's our normal practice to bring the more valuable items into our rooms when staying at an inn," Tethe explained.

Munne took a sip of wine, mulling over some ideas in her head. *How will I get these five out of the city? No doubt I could convince Captain Munhart to allow my triple to leave, but what about these Proma?*

The path forward visualized in her head; she needed to talk to Ethelmar and Captain Munhart, as soon as possible. "Well, the night is young. I must see to a few arrangements before the hour grows too late. My friends and I will return soon. Be ready to leave at a moment's notice."

"Of course, my lady. We'll await your word." Tethe stood and bowed to the three Elviri.

Munne led Araloth and Mayrien down the stairs and through the common room of the West Breeze Inn.

"We're leaving tonight, aren't we?" Araloth asked as they departed the inn and headed for the Night Lantern.

"If all goes to plan, yes," Munne replied. "I've spent too much time here as it stands. The longer we wait, the greater—" *The greater the chance I'll meet a fate like Malion's. The greater the chance I'll kill my loved ones and then myself.* "—the greater the danger we put ourselves in."

From the looks she received from Araloth and Mayrien, Munne knew her friends had heard the words she refused to speak.

CHAPTER XV: RAY

As the two suns rose in the sky, Ray found herself standing on the edge of Promthus looking out into the wild unknown of Na'roc of North. Her breath caught in her throat as she took in the vast white expanse that seemed to stretch on forever. She felt like she was standing at the edge of the world. *Is this how Prince Robyn and all of the others felt when they traveled north of the Wall?* She had half a mind to ask Niamnh if the prince had ever told her about his journeys. It was no small secret that the prince often went north on hunting expeditions. However, she kept her mouth shut. The prince had disappeared almost two years ago, no doubt surrounded by hardy men trained to survive this far north. *Then how come he never came home?* Naro's words seared across her memory. *Until they find you.* The Enthai must've found the prince and his companions. *But did they kill them? What other explanation is there? And what hope do we have for survival out here?*

Winds from the north blew all around her, whipping strands of her hair across her face. Snow covered the land, stretching far across the horizon. She pulled up the hood of her coat, tucking loose strands of hair behind her ears. On her back was her main pack of supplies. She had secured a large bundle of sticks to the underside of it. Other smaller packs were secured to the belt around her waist, including her quiver and waterskin. She carried her bow in one hand, and her daggers sheathed at her sides.

Princess Niamnh stood beside her, hands tightly gripping the straps of her own pack. The princess was similarly carrying several supply packs and bags. Her hood was already drawn, and she had a scarf wrapped around the lower half of her face to keep warm. Her gray eyes were bright against her brown skin. Ray looked more once to the south where she could only see mountain peaks in the distance. The Wall was out of sight, so they could finally continue east.

The two girls exchanged wary glances. Ray took the first step, snow crunching softly under her boot. She looked around as if expecting the Enthai to leap out from the ground at that very moment to capture her and the princess. She knew the thought was absurd, but she couldn't help getting caught up in how surreal it was to be entering such a vast, open land. And covered in snow.

How far did Prince Robyn travel before getting captured and killed? Her mouth went dry, the cold seeping through her clothes and chilling her bones.

"What are we looking for, now that we're here?" Niamnh asked, voice muffled underneath her scarf.

Ray considered her response. She couldn't tell the truth because then the Doshara might try to lash out and attack her. She couldn't trust that Niamnh could control him, not after he slipped out *again* last night without her knowing. She had to continue her bluff that she had told him. Not to mention she had no idea how Niamnh would react if she found out they were seeking the same creatures that had killed her brother.

"We're looking for a village of some kind. We should find it today or tomorrow," Ray told her. Her stomach twisted at the half-truth, but she couldn't afford to be honest. Not yet, perhaps not ever.

Niamnh hummed in acknowledgement, and they set off.

Protector, please let there be some crumb of truth in what I said. Please let us come across an actual village. Or let the Enthai find us first.

They were able to set a decent pace for most of the day. Though the wind howled and blew, it didn't burden the girls. The journey got their blood flowing, so they were able to move with decent speed. It helped that they weren't stopping to hunt. Ray doubted she would find anything to hunt in those lands anyway. Her stomach pinched at the thought of food. She had eaten half of a biscuit that morning. She was no stranger to the scarcity of food, and she had been mentally preparing herself for the days to come, but she was concerned for Niamnh.

That thing will keep her sated, Ray realized, or at least hoped. Once again, fears of the Doshara trying to kill and eat her flitted across her mind. She waved a hand in front of her face, brushing both the snow and the thoughts away.

Around midday the snowfall became heavy, and their pace slowed. When Ray looked behind them, she could no longer see the forest. They were completely surrounded by the white frozen tundra. Niamnh was to her left. Ray instinctively reached out and grabbed her hand, ensuring that they didn't get separated. She felt Niamnh grip her hand tightly.

Their pace was slow and they had nowhere to stop. The land stretched out all around them with no trace of trees or even a small hill to camp up against. As the suns began their western descent, Ray started to worry. Though the snow had tapered off in the later hours of the day, it was still falling heavily enough that they wouldn't be able to light a fire.

"Look out for any hills!" Ray called out to the princess who only nodded in response.

As Ray whipped her head from side to side, searching for some kind of shelter, she felt panic bubbling from within. *Am I going to die tonight? After coming all this way?* Inside of her chest, her heart threatened to break free from its cage. The terror got her blood pumping, for whatever good that would do. Her thoughts turned to Niamnh who no doubt was experiencing a far greater terror. She had to do whatever she could to ensure the princess's safety.

Niamnh grabbed her shoulder and pointed at something to their left. Even squinting, Ray could barely distinguish the shape from the snow around it, but it certainly looked like it might be a small crest of land. They adjusted course and made for the bump in the distance.

"Thank the Protector!" Ray exclaimed, letting out an exhausted sigh.

The small crest turned out to be a rather decent shelter with enough height that the girls could lay down beneath it and cover themselves with their bedrolls and heavy sheets to insulate themselves. Ray doubted a fire could be built, and she didn't have the strength to try, so instead she settled for helping Niamnh set up a makeshift tent.

As she watched Niamnh crawl into the tent, Ray's eyes widened, and she let out a panicked gasp. *The tea.*

She fumbled for one of her bags, quickly drawing out the pair of handcuffs. She crawled into the tent after the princess and held them out in the space between them.

"Oh," Niamnh breathed. "I don't think you have any reason to use those here." Though her eyes darted around the tent, Ray realized the princess meant the strange land.

"What do you mean?" Ray asked.

"He's been... disturbingly absent. Even with the elixir's effects waning. Normally I can feel him stirring, even if he chooses not to talk to me. I think there's something about this place that has caused him to retreat."

Ray listened carefully to Niamnh's words. The princess spoke in the same cadence as she had earlier in the day. It didn't sound as if anything was stuck in her throat, or that her words were garbled. Still, perhaps the Doshara had gotten crafty and realized how different the words sounded when he spoke from her mouth.

She couldn't take any chances.

"Please, just for tonight," Ray begged, the handcuffs gently shaking in her grasp.

Niamnh looked at the cold metal and sighed to herself, holding her hands behind her back. She allowed Ray to secure the cuffs to her wrists, then help her into her bedroll. Ray secured the tent flaps, closing them off from the outside world. She ensured the blankets were wrapped tightly around their bedrolls, and she crawled into hers and pressed her body against Niamnh's so they could share each other's warmth.

Night passed slowly, and Ray wasn't entirely sure how much she had slept, but she got up as the suns began to rise. She still didn't know if the princess had spoken the truth about the Doshara being "absent", but she was still alive, breathing in fresh, frigid air. Golden sunslight reflected off of the snow with such brightness that Ray had to shield her eyes and squint to see. It didn't look like any additional snow fell overnight to their benefit. All she could see was snow in every direction. Their little shelter was the only distinct shape within sight.

Ray fished Naro's sunsdial out of her coat pocket and oriented herself to the east, toward the rising suns. "Are you awake, Niamnh?"

"I d-don't know if I was e-ever asleep," Niamnh replied with chattering teeth. "C-Can we p-please get moving?"

Ray grunted in agreement and helped the other girl to her feet. They broke down the tent and packed up the blankets, and soon they were trudging through the snow again. It was difficult to judge how much distance they had actually traveled within Na'roc of North. Snow surrounded them on all sides, and there were very few landmarks to distinguish where they were at. Ray hadn't seen a single tree that day, and she grew worried that they hadn't brought enough kindling and logs for a fire, let alone multiple fires across several days.

Even if I wanted to summon the Enthai, how would I go about doing that? Should I just start screaming for help? Even if she could abate the guilt gnawing at her insides, Ray didn't want to test that idea, lest she scare Niamnh.

Around midday, the girls caught sight of several dark forms on the horizon. As they got closer, Ray realized she was looking at several single-story buildings made from gray stone. Her heart leapt into her throat, and she felt her legs moving faster.

Protector's grace, it's real. A real damn village!

Niamnh shuffled along faster as well, and about an hour later they arrived on the edge of the little village. There were maybe ten or fifteen buildings altogether, and most were small circular huts. Only three of the buildings were larger, all of which were in the center of the village. As Ray and Niamnh walked between the buildings, fear mingled with curiosity.

"Who lived here?" Niamnh asked, marveling at one of the huts.

Did Prince Robyn ever come across this place?

The stone stood sturdy against the cold winds. None of the huts had any windows, only singular door frames. Most were missing the doors themselves, although a few had some shattered remains of wooden doors propped against the wall.

Ray poked her head inside one of the huts and was unsurprised to see it was completely cleared out. No furniture, no decorations, nothing indicating that it had once been a home, nor any signs that travelers had stopped here in recent years. "I don't know, but whoever it was, they're long gone."

They continued exploring the village, slipping in and out of the huts to see if anything still remained. Each hut had a small opening carved into the roof where Ray imagined smoke would vent out of.

But what kind of fires did these people build? There's no trees within sight.

One of the larger structures in the center of the village had a small stone staircase wrapped around the exterior. It looked sturdy enough, so Ray took a chance and climbed up to the roof. She left Niamnh below to explore the interior of the building. The rooftop was enclosed by a short wall that stood no taller than her hip. Gazing out onto the plains, it was clear that it was a lookout post when the village had been inhabited. If anyone tried to approach the village, they'd be spotted immediately. That would explain the lack of walls or fences around the huts; no one could sneak up on the place.

Ray stared at the snowy plain for several minutes with only her thoughts for company. *Protector, please let the Enthal find us soon. If not today, then tomorrow.*

Their rations were dwindling. If they stayed in the village, they'd starve. The Doshara would realize she had been lying, and it would kill her and eat her before returning to Promthus to hunt down Naro. She wondered if she could continue to bluff by saying Naro was late and that he had instructed her to go on without him. That would at least get them moving again, but for what? They'd starve either way. At least in the village they'd have shelter from the wind and snow.

Ray descended the stairs and entered the building proper. Niamnh was kneeling on the ground near the far wall, her attention solely on whatever she was holding. "What'd you find?" she asked.

The princess sat up straight and held up the item—a slab of stone, darker in color than the surrounding walls. "I think it's some kind of record from when the village was inhabited."

"Can you read it?" Ray asked, walking over to Niamnh. It was surreal hearing her footsteps fall on real flooring again after so many days in the wilderness. The building had no windows, so the interior was silent save for their movements and speech.

"No." Disappointment seeped through Niamnh's words.

"I'm surprised to see anything left behind here after exploring the rest of the place."

Niamnh's next words were very quiet. "What if they left it as a warning?"

Ray's skin prickled, and she forced herself to speak with levity to distract herself from the fear gnawing at her stomach. "Well, then they should've left something we could understand."

A frown crossed Niamnh's face as she climbed to her feet and handed the slab to Ray. She took it and immediately began her own inspection. The slab was the length of two hands and as wide as one. It was heavy, similar to the weight of a cooking pot. Markings were carved into the slab—definitely some kind of text—but in a language Ray didn't know. Not that she expected to understand it when the princess couldn't. She tossed around the idea of bringing the slab with them, to see if Naro could decipher it when she returned home. But could she risk the extra weight?

She immediately regretted that thought, nearly cursing out loud. Of course she couldn't risk the extra weight when it was likely she'd be dead in a matter of days.

"What should we do?" Niamnh's voice cut through her thoughts.

Ray blinked a few times, feeling the weight of the slab in her hands. "Let's get a fire going."

"We're staying here?"

"For now," Ray murmured. Every muscle in her body tensed. The lie was easy enough to tell, but it was pulled from her throat like a barbed arrow. "We're waiting for someone."

Niamnh didn't respond, but Ray could see the princess's confusion and concern all over her face.

Can't eat anything tonight. Need to save the rations. Ray didn't think she'd be able to eat even if she wanted to, not with how guilty she felt for keeping the truth from Niamnh.

Ray left the large building and returned to one of the smaller circular huts that had a mostly intact door. Underneath the vent in the roof was a small divot in the floor, presumably where a fire should be built. Kicking away the thin layer of snow, Ray took her pack off and got to work building a fire. Without the wind blowing around her, it was easy to coax the flames to life, and soon the hut began to warm up. Smoke rose from the vent, and she wondered if the Enthai would see it.

Maybe they'll be upon us by nightfall, and we can get this over with. I don't know how long I can keep this bluff up if the Enthai don't find us. Maybe it would be better to just let the damn Doshara kill me and get it over with.

Ray shook her head.

No, it wouldn't be better for that thing to kill me. I'll keep the bluff up, no matter what. I just need to figure out what to do if the Enthai don't show. How many days do I let pass before we move out again? What will I tell the Doshara that'll keep him from attacking me?

Niamnh entered the hut a little while later after exploring the village. The two unpacked their belongings and set up a makeshift bed near the fire. They sat down and let the flames thaw their hands and feet, taking turns inspecting the carved slab.

"The smoke's visible outside," Niamnh said quietly.

Ray let out a hum of acknowledgement. She didn't know how to respond. She could hear the fear in the other girl's words with how the smoke was acting like a beacon drawing others to their location. In truth she was afraid of that as well, but she couldn't admit that. And she couldn't very well tell the princess that she *wanted* them to be found.

"I'll go take a look around again before the suns go down," Ray said.

Grabbing her bow and quiver, she bundled up and left the hut, shutting the door behind her. The building with the staircase was a short distance away from their hut, like most of the buildings in the village. Above her the sky glowed a warm orange color, the suns already on their descent below the horizon. No snow had fallen that day, and the sky was clear of clouds, signaling an evening free of snow. She would be able to see far across the plain. Hopefully, conditions would remain the same in the morning and she could climb the staircase again to see if anyone approached.

Nothing could be seen around the village. No matter which direction Ray looked, the snow stretched on to the horizon. If anyone had seen the smoke, they were still a long way away. She planned on keeping the bow and quiver close to the bed that night, along with her daggers. Hopefully, she wouldn't need to use them.

She stayed on top of the building for several long minutes, walking in slow circles to look out in all directions. When the golden sky faded to a dark blue, she descended the stairs and returned to her temporary home. Inside, Niamnh had continued to feed the fire—not that there was much else to do—and as a result the hut was pleasantly warm. Ray wasn't planning on taking off any of her layers, but it was nice to be able to comfortably feel her fingers and toes.

Ray sat down beside Niamnh and dug through their packs to prepare a cup of tea.

"I haven't felt him all day," Niamnh murmured. "I really don't think we need to worry about the tea or handcuffs here."

Ray's hands tightened around the pouch containing the dried leaves and her gaze fixated on the ground. She didn't want to look at Niamnh. Though the girl's voice was in her normal cadence, Ray didn't want to turn and see coldness in her gray eyes.

"It'll be dangerous if we don't," Ray responded weakly.

"I can control him." Niamnh's response was firm. Full of confidence.

I wish I could believe in that confidence. Maybe she could. She wanted to.

Ray let go of the herb pouch and turned around. Niamnh's gaze was hot like a fire, the flames dancing across her pupils. The fur lining of her hood hugged her face, her dusky skin warm against the white and brown furs. Her lips were drawn tight in a determined line.

Ray let out a quiet sigh and felt her body relax from head to toe. "Alright. Okay." *I can believe in her.*

Niamnh gave a small nod, nothing more than a slight tilt of her chin, and then she turned back to the campfire. Ray sat beside her, removing her cloak and gloves as the night grew darker and the hut grew warmer. Niamnh eventually removed her hood but kept the heavy coat and gloves on. Without much else to do, Ray laid down on their makeshift bed and stared at the ceiling. If she let her vision unfocus, she could pretend there were stars painted on the stone. The room was much too cold to be Naro's lounge, even with the fire roaring beside her.

"What I'd give for some porridge or pudding," Ray muttered under her breath. She found herself desperately missing Hilthe and the other kitchen ladies as her stomach growled. *No food tonight. Save it for tomorrow, or the next day. Just keep drinking water.* She took a swig from her waterskin.

Ray lost track of time. Eventually Niamnh stood up and approached the bed. Ray shifted over to let the princess have the side closest to the fire. She brought the hunting bow with her, setting it and the quiver down beside the bed. Her daggers were still sheathed on her hips. Niamnh lay facing the fire, her legs pulled up towards her stomach.

When she spoke, her voice could barely be heard over the crackling of the fire. "Who are we waiting for?"

Ray froze. *Did the Doshara tell her what I told him?* She didn't want to risk getting caught in a web of lies, so she gave a half-truth instead. "Someone helping us along the rest of the way." Lying was getting easier to do. That brought her some small amount of comfort. She'd need that skill when she returned to Auora.

"I hope they get here soon."

"Me too."

Ray returned to the rooftop the next morning to look out upon Na'roc of North. It must have been a town hall, or some other important building. It wasn't much now, but at least the roof served a purpose. The sky was filled with gray clouds, heavy with snow. Small flakes had already begun to fall as she walked from their hut to the center structure. There was nothing but white snow on all sides, and more on the way. She climbed off the roof before the snowfall got heavier.

Back in the hut, she allowed herself half of a biscuit for breakfast. She washed it down with the rest of her waterskin. Gathering up a pot of snow from outside, she set about melting and refilling the waterskin. They'd run out of firewood by the next morning. Perhaps Ray could cut up some of the wooden doors around the village and use them as fuel for the fire. She'd probably break her daggers in the process, but she had to try.

Niamnh continued lying on the bed, dozing in and out of sleep. She was still curled up on her side, the blankets pulled tight against her body. She hadn't eaten anything the day before either, and all they had left was one rabbit. Ray wanted to give the other girl as much time to rest as possible; she knew that once Niamnh was awake, she'd be hungry. And the Doshara might try to poke out of whatever hole he'd been hiding in.

Ray sat near the door and watched the snow fall through the cracks in the wood. Though the sky was dark, the flurries that fell from the sky were few and far between. She wished she could return to the rooftop and keep watch up there, if it wasn't so damn cold.

Eventually Ray did leave the hut and returned to the rooftop when she couldn't stand sitting still anymore. She pulled her cloak on, swung the quiver across her back, and held tightly onto the hunting bow. She made sure not to disturb Niamnh as she slipped past the wooden door and closed it behind her. She paced on the rooftop to keep her legs warm. When her fingers started to go numb, she flexed her grip on the bow and raised it up in mock fire. There was nothing to see across the plain. No creatures—Enthai or other-wise—stirred in the snow. The Doshara would have to make do with the remaining rabbit. A thin column of smoke rose from their hut, the only sign of life in sight.

"Please be somewhere close," Ray whispered, willing her voice to travel across the snow.

"Who are you calling out to?" Niamnh's light voice carried across the rooftop from behind her.

Ray spun around, her grip on the bow tightening. The princess stood at the top of the stairs, slowly picking her way over to where Ray stood. Her hood was drawn, her arms wrapped around her torso.

"By the Protector, you scared me," Ray grumbled, shaking her arms to rid herself of her anxiety. "Are you sure you want to be out here, Niamnh? You look like you're freezing."

"Is he close? Your lord?" Niamnh went on, ignoring Ray's question. She stared into Ray's eyes, her own dark as stone. "Surely, he is. Why else would you keep us here?"

Ray frowned, tension drawing her muscles tight again. Was the Doshara emerging? "It's safer to wait here than to be out there—"

"Or," Niamnh interjected. "Or are you keeping me here so that the *Enthai* can find us?" The accusation hung heavy in the air.

Ray didn't respond right away, and that decision damned her.

Niamnh continued her approach, invading the space in front of Ray. She uncrossed her arms and jabbed a finger into Ray's chest. "Those things killed my brother, and you would hand me over to them?"

Ray's mouth went dry. The Doshara *wasn't* emerging, which she should be glad for, but hearing the anger and pain in Niamnh's voice twisted Ray's heart. "Niamnh, I've told you from the very beginning what I'm here to do."

"I thought you wanted to help me!" the princess cried out. "Not have me killed."

"Niamnh—"

"You're trying to kill me. You and your wicked crime lord must be plotting with the Provira to overthrow my father. Oh, by the Protector, how did I not realize this sooner?" The princess abruptly turned from Ray, dragging her feet through the snow to put as much space between them as she could.

"Naro and I would *never* work with those mixed bloods!" Ray snapped, catching up to Niamnh. She placed a hand on her shoulder and forced her to spin around, both wobbling to regain their balance in the snow. "We have honor; we would never betray our people!"

A cold laugh ripped through Niamnh's mouth. "Thieves and scoundrels don't know the meaning of 'honor'."

Ray's cheeks flushed with hot anger. "Why are you acting like this? Now, when we're in this horrible place?"

Niamnh had no immediate response. Her face twisted into an ugly smile, teeth as white as the snow beneath their feet. Ray felt the hairs on the back of her neck stand on edge, and it didn't occur to her until a quarter of a moment before that she was in danger, and she was looking at the Doshara wearing Niamnh's skin once more.

The Doshara lunged at Ray, knocking her onto her back and into the snow. The hunting bow fell from her grasp as lithe hands wrapped around Ray's neck and squeezed. "You *lied* to me."

The snow softened Ray's landing, but she was slow to grasp the hands around her neck. She tried to pull the fingers away, loosen the grip, do *something*, but she couldn't breathe. Blackness crept into the edge of her vision.

Protector help me.

Ray gasped, struggling to get air into her lungs as the Doshara squeezed the life out of her. She was no longer looking into Niamnh's eyes and seeing Niamnh's kindness. All traces of the girl were gone, and in her stead was the Doshara and its cold fury.

With a final burst of energy before she lost sight of the princess's face, Ray let go of Niamnh's hands and pulled a dagger from her hip, striking the hilt against the princess's head. The blow was heavy enough to distract the Doshara, and it loosened its grip around her neck.

Dragging in a ragged breath of air, Ray twisted her body to the left, throwing the Doshara off of her. She scrambled to her feet, brandishing the dagger in front of her body. "Kill me, and you'll never find Naro."

As the Doshara propped itself up on its hands and knees, it let out a cackling screech. "For three thousand years, I've always found my way back to the bastard, and I'll do it for another three thousand if I have to."

Three thousand years? Fear seized Ray's heart, a fear so raw and primal that she couldn't help but freeze. *Three thousand years... Naro?*

The Doshara lunged at Ray. She had two heartbeats to decide if she'd keep the dagger raised and drive it into the princess's body to fend the Doshara off, or lower it and find another way to subdue the creature.

The Doshara moved one heartbeat faster than her, and the dagger was swatted out of her hand as it grabbed her wrist and arm and swung her around. She went flying into the snow again, and the demon was upon her in moments, trying to strangle her once more.

Ray was prepared that time and immediately raised her arms to intercept its grasp. They grappled with each other, swatting and punching through one another's defenses. Ray jabbed at the Doshara's neck with pointed fingers. It let out a sharp gasp and gurgle, leaning backward. She used the momentum to sit up and push at the creature, trying to get it off of her lap.

The Doshara fell to the side without much resistance, and Ray took the opportunity to leap to her feet. She fell upon the Doshara immediately, pushing it down into the snow. She straddled its chest and grabbed its chin, holding it still so she could punch it across the face with a closed fist. Ray delivered a couple more blows to further disorient the demon before she wrapped her hands around its throat and throttled it.

Maybe if I can knock out the princess, the Doshara will go away. Then I can handcuff it. Keep the damn thing from killing me. She gritted her teeth and hoped. She didn't want to hurt Niamnh, but she had to defend herself. She had to *live.*

Ray felt the strength leaving the princess's body as the Doshara's grip on her arms weakened. She didn't relent; she kept her grip tight around the princess's throat. She waited until the gray eyes closed, and the princess's arms fell to either side. Ray kept her grip strong for three more heartbeats, ensuring the princess was unconscious.

Ray removed her hands from Niamnh's neck, leaning back and lifting her weight off of the princess. With wary eyes, she climbed to her feet, her breathing labored. "By the Protector, and the Elviri gods, and whatever else is out there... what am I going to do with you?"

She needed to get the Niamnh's body into their hut before the Doshara stirred again. With a sharp inhale, she decided to fetch the handcuffs first, and then carry the princess down the stairs. Maybe Niamnh would come to her senses and regain control over Daerion.

I can't have both of them against me. I need Niamnh in control, and I need her to listen to me.

Dragging her feet through the snow exhausted her. She needed rest, preferably in front of a warm fire. They only had one or two logs left, and maybe a fistful of kindling. Not enough to stoke the flames beyond a smolder. Still, it would be better than sitting outside.

I definitely need to try breaking some of the remaining doors down and use that wood for the fire. But later. I need to rest right now.

Ray was caught up in her own thoughts as her foot touched the first step on the stairs, wondering how to survive the night. She heard the crunching of snow and thought it was her own feet but realized too late that it was someone else moving, their footsteps lighter than hers—faster than hers.

A heavy weight crashed into her from behind, and she threw her hands out and grab at the rooftop to keep herself from falling down the stairs. Cold steel kissed the back of her neck, drawing an ugly line in her skin. Warm blood spilled from the wound, sticking to the collar of her coat. She let out a pained yelp, her grip on the rooftop tightening. Something else—some*one* else—tumbled down the stairs beside her, and as she turned her head a horrible wave of nausea washed over her.

Princess Niamnh's body lay at the foot of the stairs, one of Ray's daggers at her side, blood coating the blade. Ray scrambled down the stairs, her legs shaking so badly she thought that she might collapse.

She can't be dead. She can't be. Did Daerion pull the dagger and attack me? Or, she thought with a horrible lurching feeling, *did Niamnh do this herself?*

She fell beside the princess and reached out to touch her face, her fingers trembling. Niamnh was lying face-up in the snow, her white hair splayed out underneath her head. The princess's eyes were closed, her lips parted. Ray leaned down and listened closely to see if the princess was still breathing.

Quiet, ragged breaths.

Thank the Protector she's still alive.

Ray let out a long sigh of relief, throwing her head back to stare at the sky. Her breathy exhale turned into a loud hiss as the skin around her wound shifted and squeezed underneath her hair and coat. Raising a hand, she reached behind her head to press her fingers against the wound. It was nothing more than a scratch, which brought her great relief. If Ray hadn't thrown her body up against the building, the blade would have cut deeply into her neck. She was lucky to be alive. She allowed herself a few moments to catch her breath and calm her nerves before picking up the dagger and sheathing it, climbing to her feet.

"Handcuffs," she murmured to herself. "Handcuffs and rest."

This time Ray chose to bring the princess's body with her to the hut rather than retrieve the handcuffs and come back. She stood at Niamnh's head and slipped her hands underneath the princess's shoulders, lifting her upper body out of the snow. Underneath the princess's head was a small puddle of blood, dark red against a pure white backdrop. Panic seized Ray's heart, and she recoiled at the sight.

I need to patch that up as soon as I get her back to the hut, Ray thought. She gritted her teeth, mustered her strength, and dragged Niamnh's body through the snow back to their hut. Niamnh's head lolled back against Ray's torso, smearing droplets of blood across Ray's coat.

"I'm sorry, Niamnh," Ray whispered to the unconscious girl. *Sorry for so many things. Sorry for lying to you. Bringing you here. But I have to do it.*

The fire was still crackling and burning when Ray entered the hut with Niamnh's body, but it was very nearly extinguished. She didn't know if she had the strength to go out and break any of the doors down. Or if it was even a good idea to leave Niamnh alone in the hut in her current state.

She dragged the princess over to their bed and threw the blankets over her body. After, Ray moved to their supplies and dug through the various sacks until she found bandages and the handcuffs. As much as she wanted to tend to Niamnh's wounds first, she took the necessary precautions to bind her wrists.

Ray lifted Niamnh's head and gently touched the back, feeling for knots or any other major injuries. Her fingers came away wet with blood. With a grimace, she rolled the princess onto her side and retrieved one of their waterskins. She washed Niamnh's hair and probed for the laceration. It took several moments to finish cleaning off the blood and locating the wound, and she soon had the princess's head wrapped in cloth. Ray stood and moved to the wall opposite the princess. With great effort, she slid down the stone until she was sitting, her knees drawn up to her chest. She withdrew her daggers from their sheaths and watched Niamnh as she slept.

Protector keep her safe... and keep me safe, too, from the Doshara.

With weary eyes, Ray leaned her head back against the wall, ignoring the sting of her own cut. Her mind was bombarded with thoughts and fears for the following day—the lack of food, warmth, and safety. She found herself hoping and praying that the Enthai would find them soon. She hoped Niamnh would regain some sense and keep the Doshara at bay.

CHAPTER XVI: MUNNE

Elviri and Proma soldiers mingled together inside of the Night Lantern, although their numbers were much smaller than they had been that morning. Munne understood that these men and women were merely resting or tending injuries, and would be returning to the fold within hours, or perhaps minutes. She recognized a couple of the Elviri not wearing their armor, instead sporting plain tunics and robes that had splotches of red and brown all over from tending to the wounded. The scent of blood and sweat mingled with roasted fish, leaving an odd clenching in Munne's stomach. The common area was quiet, a stark contrast to the lively inn they had just left. Small clusters of soldiers were murmuring to each other over tankards and plates of food. A few injured soldiers were groaning and panting softly, their wounds too much to bear.

All of the tables had been moved around. Some were pushed together to form makeshift beds, while others were up against the walls to make space for cots and bed rolls on the ground. It was strange seeing the tavern transformed into a makeshift infirmary. It made sense given the proximity to the castle, but...

Surely they would've been better off fortifying one of the houses of healing somewhere else in the city. If they have any? They must. Perhaps there just aren't any close enough to the castle to defend reliably.

One of the Elviri noticed Munne's triple entering the building and leapt to her feet, quickly crossing the room to block them from moving further inside. "Halt, this building is off-limits to citiz—"

"At ease, Muirwen," Munne said softly, raising her hand to stop the Elviri nurse. "Is Ethelmar here? We need to speak with him."

"Apologies, Lady Vere'cha," Muirwen gave a small curtsey. Loose strands of her black hair fell into her face. She swept them away as she straightened up. "It's unexpected to see you out of your armor. Yes, Ethelmar and his triple returned less than an hour ago. He should be around here somewhere. He wanted to speak with some of the soldiers."

Munne nodded, understanding Ethelmar's choice of actions. She would do the same thing if she were in his position; she'd want to comfort the injured men and women and ensure that they knew their lives mattered. Ethelmar had trained under Cesa just as she had, and that brought her some small degree of comfort knowing her mentor was being honored here in Auora. "Thank you. And thank you for your work here."

Muirwen curtseyed again and left the three to return to tending the injured.

"What do we need from Ethelmar?" Araloth whispered.

"Horses and armor for our traveling companions," Munne responded in the same low voice.

Araloth let out a quiet growl. Munne disregarded her friend's animosity, looking around the common area for Commander Ethelmar. She found him kneeling beside one of the makeshift tables, speaking quietly with the injured Elviri resting on top of the table. Munne led her friends to the two men.

"Hello again, Commander," Munne greeted Ethelmar, her gaze sweeping over the injured man beside him. He had been stripped of his armor and had bandages wrapped around his midsection, bright red blood blooming underneath. The man's fate was grim, and chances were he wouldn't see tomorrow's sunrise. Abdominal wounds often resulted in death. Munne grimaced, a wave of sympathy crashing over her.

"Our Warlord graces us with her presence," Ethelmar murmured to the injured Elviri, a small smile spreading across his lips. The light of that smile didn't reach his eyes.

"It is... an honor," the injured Elviri rasped, coughing in between words. Beads of sweat formed along his dark hairline, his flesh sickly and pale.

"No, friends, I'm honored to be in *your* presence," Munne replied, kneeling alongside Ethelmar. She placed her hand gently on the injured Elviri's shoulder. "What's your name?"

"F-Fiomyr, my lady." Another horrible cough. Fiomyr's body seized, his head and limbs curling ever so slightly inward. Pain was written all across his face.

Through his spasm, Munne kept her hand steady on his shoulder, acting as an anchor for the man. "Fiomyr, thank you for protecting our allies in their hour of need," she said softly, giving his shoulder another reassuring squeeze.

Fiomyr gritted his teeth, trying to relax his body. His legs uncurled first, stretching the length of the table. His right hand hovered over his bandages, the left returning to his side with a clenched fist. As his head rolled back onto the cushion beneath it, he turned to look at Munne. His green eyes were glassy and bloodshot, and his lips parted to take in shallow breaths. He raised his right hand and tapped it gently against his chest.

"Th-thank you, my lady. I live and d-die for our provinces, our p-people."

"Azrael smiles upon you," she whispered through a smile of her own. She turned to look at Ethelmar. "I would speak with you, when you are able." Ethelmar nodded in reply. Munne rose to her feet and bowed before the two men. "Rest easy, friends."

As she walked away from Fiomyr and Ethelmar, her stomach twisted with both dread and relief. She still held the loyalty of her soldiers, even on their deathbeds.

Will they still be loyal to me after they've learned of my disappearance? Will some abandon the Proma in search of me? The nauseating feeling of dread spread throughout her body, and her foot faltered as it hit the ground. *I'm dooming my people by going to Kherizhan.*

Araloth was by her side in an instant, placing one hand on her back and the other on her right arm. "Come, let's find somewhere to sit while we wait."

There was seating at the bar, where the tavern keep was wiping down the counter. Araloth led Munne to one seat, then took the one on her right. Mayrien sat on her left, placing a hand on Munne's shoulder. Munne leaned into their touches, seeking comfort and stability from her friends. Seeking warmth. Her hand reached up to caress her left arm, the fabric of her coat separating her from the remnants of Ely's imprints.

"Water, please, if you can," Araloth said quietly to the tavern keep. He grunted in response and moved away to fill their mugs. "Munne, are you alright?"

"I have to be." Munne tried to be mirthful with her response, but there was no fooling her companions.

Araloth frowned. "How can we help?"

Munne wanted them to reassure her that she was making the right decision, but she knew Araloth would never say those words. If the older Elviri knew Munne was wavering with her resolve to go to Kherizhan, she would leap upon that opportunity to persuade her to return to Elimere. No, that couldn't happen.

I have time. My people think I'm going to the Imalar Woods. It would take several weeks for word to get back to Elimere that I didn't arrive. I can use that time to get to Kherizhan and learn what I can. Perhaps even send word to Eldo and his fellow guild leaders that I'm alright, that I'll honor my father's deal once I've been cured from these nightmares and no longer pose a threat to those around me.

Munne closed her eyes for a moment, rooting herself in her companions' touch. When she opened her eyes, she was able to smile. "You already are, by being at my side."

The tavern keep set three mugs of water down in front of the Elviri before resuming his cleaning. Munne picked up her mug and took several gulps before letting out a loud exhale.

"I was just thinking that our dinner was overly salted," Mayrien quipped, taking a drink of her own water. Munne and Araloth both let out chuckles and snorts at the remark.

I will return from Kherizhan.

The three friends sat at the bar for another ten minutes or so until Ethelmar approached them. He cleared his throat to announce his presence, bowing politely when Munne and the others turned to face him. He looked disheveled, his black hair fraying from the simple knot on the back of his head. Though he had removed his gauntlets and leg-guards, he still wore his hauberk, which was covered in dirt and blood. Dark circles clung to his green eyes.

"You summoned me, my lady?" Ethelmar asked.

Munne rose from her seat and set her mug of water down on the counter. "Yes. Have you set up a private room for yourself here? We need to speak."

He nodded and led the trio towards the back of the tavern, heading up a staircase to the second floor. There were five rooms and another staircase waiting for them up above. Ethelmar pushed open the second door on the left, revealing a room with two beds, a hutch, and a small table and chairs.

"Tomas, the owner of this establishment, is letting us use these rooms for some of our soldiers. The remainder are either resting down below, or across in the castle," he said.

We should repay this man for his services. It's no easy feat, housing a small army in one's home or business.

Munne sat at the table, Mayrien and Araloth hovering nearby. Ethelmar closed the door once they were all inside, then sat down opposite Munne. "How can I be of help?" he asked.

"You've done so much already," Munne murmured, turning to look at her friends, then back to the commander. As she pieced together a plan, she shifted uncomfortably in her seat. A seed of dread planted itself in her stomach and quickly took root. "And yet I would ask more from you still. Do you remember what I told you about the mission my father gave to me? To travel to the Imalar Woods?"

Ethelmar nodded, brow furrowing. "Yes. I'm assuming you're unable to leave Auora because of what's going on, and you wrote to me to assist with resolving this conflict quickly so you could continue on your journey?"

"Yes, exactly," Munne replied, jumping in at the end of his sentence. "And I'm grateful for your expedient arrival. Now I need to bargain with the Proma lords to leave. But before we leave, I have a... request."

Ethelmar waited patiently for her to continue.

Can I truly ask this of him? Of my men and women? The dreadful plant sprouted and spread throughout her innards. She did *not* want to vocalize her request. *But how else will I get the caravanners out of the city?* "I... would like to take some of the clothing of our deceased with me, to provision the outpost we have in Trent."

The frown on Ethelmar's face grew deeper. Deceased Elviri were always returned to Elimere with all of their belongings for their family members to sort through and do with as they saw fit. Soldiers were buried in their armor, an honored tradition since the Eldest Days, so she wouldn't have dared to request those pieces go with her to the east. But the riding gear and other articles of clothing... She didn't even want to ask for that, but she couldn't think of another way to get the caravanners out of the city before the lockdown was lifted. Munne could only imagine the thoughts racing through Ethelmar's mind. Surely, he thought she was mad for requesting such a thing. But she was the Warlord, *his* Warlord, so she had reason to do that. And that's nothing to say of Araloth or Mayrien's reactions to her request!

Ethelmar's expression softened, and after a few moments he finally nodded. "If you require it, then I can arrange it. When are you hoping to leave?"

"Tonight, if possible," she said, mustering as much bravado as she could. She felt anything but secure with the decision, especially to rob the dead of their belongings, but she had to do this. *I have to get to Kherizhan.*

"I-I see," Ethelmar stuttered, taken aback by the suddenness of it all. "I'll work with Vinya to get this taken care of as soon as possible. How much clothing? And you're going to meet with the lords now?"

Munne nodded, unable to vocally respond. She tried to swallow and force the growing knot out of her throat. She managed to croak out, "Just one chest or crate. And as soon as you can."

Ethelmar bowed his head to her and rose to his feet. "Then if you'll excuse me, we'll get everything ready for your departure." He gestured for Munne and her friends to exit through the door, and he followed behind them.

Araloth and Mayrien were silent as they descended the stairs and crossed through the common room with Munne. It felt like they were two angry shadows trailing behind her. Ethelmar split away from them and sought out Vinya, a member of his triple. Munne kept her gaze focused on the door ahead, not allowing it to stray and look at her injured soldiers. Seeing their weakness would make her falter, and she couldn't afford for that to happen, not now.

Her friends held their tongues as they approached the bridge to the castle. The same guards were flanking the pathway as before, so they recognized the three Elviri immediately.

"Have Captain Munhart or Knight-General Gondamire returned from the city?" Munne asked the Proma.

"Knight-General Gondamire did. Captain Munhart hasn't yet," one of the men replied.

Munne nodded and set off for the castle, her two shadows following behind. Rhorek most likely would have returned to his suite in the castle, so she set course for that location, hoping she remembered the way. Several moments later, she was knocking on the heavy wooden door to his room. Rhorek cracked it ajar to see who was there.

"Knight-General, we need to speak," Munne said quietly.

A wave of concern spread across his face and the door swung open wider as he took in the sight of Araloth and Mayrien in the hallway. "Of course. Just a moment." He shut the door, and she heard faint footsteps as he retreated into his suite.

Munne turned to look at her companions while she waited. As soon as her eyes locked with Araloth, the elder Elviri dropped her neutral façade and glowered at the Warlord. Mayrien's gaze was no less stern.

"This is a blasphemous plan!" Araloth snapped, crossing her arms over her chest.

Munne hung her head with a sigh. She knew in her heart that Araloth was right, but what other choice did she have? *The nightmares could come back any night. How much longer can Ely protect me from them? From the* Ardashi'ik?

Araloth didn't continue; she let the shame hang about Munne and suffocate any kind of response she might have had. Rhorek returned to the door moments later, wrapped in a fine fur robe and holding a candle dish. The flame from the candle flickered across his face, deepening the circles around his eyes. He looked exhausted. Munne was sure that she and her companions looked the same.

Rhorek stepped out into the hallway, looking past the three Elviri to see if anyone else was around. When he was satisfied with the emptiness of the corridor, his gaze returned to Munne. "Has something happened?" he asked.

"No, I'm here for a request. A personal request," Munne responded, raising her hands in front of her chest. "I need to leave Auora."

A flash of relief crossed Rhorek's face before the corners of his mouth curled down into a frown. "My lady, I apologize, I forgot you were due to travel to the

Imalar Woods. In the morning, I can have some of my knights escort you and Eldo Talltree to Trent."

Munne's eyes widened ever so slightly at the mention of the Imalarii. She hadn't considered where he fit into her plan. Well, perhaps she had; he had *no* place in it. "I appreciate the offer, Knight-General, but I think it would be better if my triple and a select few other soldiers went ahead of Master Talltree, so I can rally some of the forces at the outpost in Trent to return to Auora to aid you and your men."

Rhorek was silent for a moment as he digested the request.

"It wouldn't be wise to have both Lady Vere'cha and Master Talltree travel together through the city," Mayrien chimed in, drawing the attention of the others. Munne had to calm her nerves and stop herself from raising her eyebrows in surprise. "If the envoy is attacked, we'd run the risk of the Elviri Warlord *and* a head Imalarii guild master getting injured or killed. It would be better for Master Talltree to stay within the castle until the situation has calmed down here."

After another moment's consideration, Rhorek said, "Very well, we'll arrange a group to escort you to the bridge in the morning."

"Knight-General," Munne interjected, grinding her teeth together before letting out an exasperated sigh. "Our intention is to leave tonight, as soon as possible. I believe me and my men stand the best chance of getting through the city in small numbers under the cover of darkness."

Rhorek's silence was deafening. Small beads of wax rolled down his candle as he stood in the hallway, shadows flickering across his face. "Lady Vere'cha, I don't think this is a good idea, but I trust that you know what you're doing," He took in a deep breath and blew the air out slowly. "Alright, I'll help you depart this evening. Let me prepare some correspondence for the guards along the Golden Path."

Relief washed over Munne. She felt her legs wobble for a moment, and she feared she'd collapse under the weight of her mission. She breathed in deeply to steady herself. "Thank you, Knight-General. I appreciate your trust."

"I'll be just a moment," Rhorek murmured, slipping back into his chambers.

"We'll go gather our things," Mayrien said, gently taking Araloth's arm and steering her back towards their own chambers. Anger flared up in Araloth's eyes for a moment and she resisted Mayrien's pull, but ultimately acquiesced and let the younger Elviri lead her away.

Munne was thankful for her friends' departure, but the silence of the corridor left her feeling uneasy. She closed her eyes and continued to take deep breaths, trying to center herself and calm her nerves. Behind her eyelids, she saw flickers of light, illuminating the passageway. The colors and material were all wrong. She caught glimpses of rock and dirt, not chiseled stone.

The caverns.

Her hands darted to her arms, and she held herself, feeling the faintest warmth from Ely's fading imprints.

Munne returned to the ambassadors' chambers with four sealed letters from Rhorek's desk—one for each of the two barricades within the city, one for the city gates, and one for the eastern end of the bridge outside of Trent. Araloth and Mayrien waited within, dressed in their riding clothes once more, and their gear already packed into backpacks and saddlebags. Araloth handed Munne her bags, anger still lingering in her eyes. Munne held that gaze, letting her friend's anger penetrate her skin and heart.

Gods bless Araloth, I don't deserve her love and friendship. She could endure Araloth's acidic words, so long as the woman continued standing by her side, which she clearly intended to do.

Munne returned to her bedroom and changed into her own riding clothes, eager and fearful of the journey before her. She tucked Rhorek's letters into one of the pouches that hung from her belt beside her left sword. When she exited her room, Mayrien and Araloth began picking up their belongings and heading for the hallway once more.

"Talltree and the Barauder?" Munne murmured as she followed her friends.

"Resting in their rooms, I believe," Mayrien responded with a low voice. "We tried to make as little noise as possible, and no one came out to investigate."

Munne nodded. They made their way through the castle corridors one last time. Munne took in the sights of the Proma's relics and ancestral weapons, feeling honored to be in their presence.

Generations of allies… I'll find a way to end this war with the Provira, and ensure your memory is honored. Just let me solve this crisis first. Let me heal myself, so I can protect you.

Their horses were kept on the same level as the bridge. Two guards stood outside the stables, allowing Munne and her companions entry once they recognized the Elviri. The trio wasted no time in saddling their horses and securing their bags before taking their leave.

As Munne left the stable, one of the guards called out, "My lady, where are you going?"

"I have urgent business beyond the city," Munne replied over her shoulder, urging Alathyl to move faster. She didn't want to hear the guard's response.

The city was dark. Very few lights could be seen from the island beyond the initial cluster of inns and taverns closest to the bridge. The smell of smoke lingered heavily in the air. Distant shouts and cries could be heard from farther into the city, more than likely from the Crafting District and below. Munne wondered if Munhart and his men would fight through the night, or if they'd rest and return to it in the morning. If it were her leading Ethelmar and their Elviri forces, they'd stay out in the streets until each hideout was overturned.

Will Ethelmar continue even if the Proma pull back? A pang of sadness hit her, raising gooseflesh along her arms and neck. A gust of wind blew around her, the scent of the lakes briefly mingling with the smoke from Auora. She wished she could stay behind to follow Ethelmar into the city and aid their allies. As Warlord, it was her sworn duty to protect her men and her allies. *And here I am, breaking that oath, fleeing in the middle of the night.*

Munne stopped outside of the Night Lantern, dismounting from Alathyl and handing the reins over to Araloth. "Mayrien, can you go to Ethelmar and retrieve our luggage? Let's all meet in the stables beside the West Breeze Inn."

Mayrien nodded and dismounted as well, leaving Araloth to lead the three horses into the stables as the younger two Elviri went their separate ways. Munne entered the West Breeze Inn with her head held high and her gaze searching for Tethc or any of his companions. The room was less crowded than before, but the bar was still full of patrons, several laughing and jeering boisterously. Munne searched that crowd for any of the Proma from earlier, frowning when she couldn't see them. They needed to leave the city with the utmost haste; she thought she had conveyed that sufficiently enough when meeting with the caravan earlier in the evening. She started to pace around the room when someone tapped on her shoulder.

Munne turned to see Ormes who had changed out of his dark blue tunic in favor of a plain leather riding coat. "Pardon, my lady, is it time?"

"Yes, gather the others and meet me in the stables," Munne ordered in a hushed tone. As almost an afterthought, she added, "With haste." She didn't wait for Ormes to respond. She turned and exited the inn, her feet carrying her to the structure attached to the inn. Two torches framed the door, which had been left slightly ajar.

The inside was dimly lit from a few more torches burning low. Araloth stood in the center with their three horses. On either side were stalls filled with other horses, all snorting and snoring softly. Mayrien hadn't yet appeared with the goods from the Night Lantern.

Munne hovered by the entrance, resting one hand on the hilt of her short sword as she leaned out to watch the streets. *Much better than trying to make conversation with Araloth right now.*

From where she stood, she could see the bridge to Castle Auora along with the entrances to the Night Lantern and the West Breeze Inn. Proma and Elviri soldiers were coming and going from the Night Lantern in various states of injury. More arrived than departed, which left Munne with great concern.

Is the fighting going well, or are they being overrun by the criminals and thugs?

Mayrien emerged from the Night Lantern, working with another Elviri to carry a large sack to the stable. Munne's throat tightened, and she parted her lips to take as deep of a breath as she could. Her hand slipped away from her sword hilt, her fingertips ghosting over Ely's imprint. Drawing strength from the heat, she pushed the stable door open to allow Mayrien and the other Elviri enough room to enter.

As they entered, Munne recognized the other Elviri to be Vinya. She was older than Munne by at least two hundred years, but she still retained her youthful grace. Very few wrinkles marred her face, and she was just as strong as any of the younger soldiers. Spots of brown and red could be seen in her silver-blonde hair. She must not have had a chance to bathe since returning from the lower tiers of the city.

"Good evening, Lady Vere'cha," Vinya said, huffing quietly as she led Mayrien towards one of the stalls containing some Elviri steeds. With one deft hand she opened the stall and entered. The two raised the sack and secured it onto a brown-and-white horse.

"Thank you for your assistance, Vinya," Munne replied, following the two women to the stall. She fought the urge to fidget with her sleeves.

As Vinya finished securing the rope and patted the horse gently on its neck, the stable door opened wide to reveal Tethe and his companions all dressed in the same nondescript leather and cloth riding clothes.

Vinya turned to Munne with a questioning stare, speaking in their native tongue. "*Illyn ae et'na maralyth?*" *Why are these people here?*

Munne looked at the caravanners then back at Vinya and shrugged, hoping she was convincingly nonchalant. "*Dyrin'ae illya caryos,*" she responded in turn. *These people love their horses.* She tried her best to pretend like it was normal for them to be here.

Vinya frowned, looking between Munne and the Proma again, and then nodding. She was clearly not pleased to see the Proma, but their presence here was doing no one any harm.

"Thank you again, Vinya," Munne said warmly, stepping toward the woman and extending a hand. Vinya clasped arms with Munne, her hand wrapping around and squeezing near Munne's elbow. She returned the gesture, hoping her small smile and reassuring touch would be enough to placate the woman.

"Be safe, my lady." Vinya let go and left the stable, casting one more glance over her shoulder. The Proma, to their credit, had started drifting through the stables, stopping to admire or coo softly to some of the horses.

After Vinya left, Tethe approached Munne and Mayrien, bowing his head politely. "Are we ready to depart?"

Munne shook her head. "You and your companions need to change. Use the clothing in this sack here." She turned and pointed to the luggage Mayrien and Vinya had brought. "You're departing with us as a small retinue of Elviri soldiers escorting my triple to Trent."

"I see. Very well," Tethe replied, pointing and gesturing for Yvanna and Jion to join him in the stall with Mayrien.

Ormes and Adalia hovered nearby but gave the others their space with the horse. Mayrien helped loosen the sack and distribute the clothing—all riding gear from deceased Elviri. Seeing it pass into the hands of the Proma, even to Yvanna, brought a painful squeeze to Munne's stomach. These clothes should be going home with their owners, not southeast with a group of strangers. The families of the deceased wouldn't have allowed it.

What would Father think of me at this moment? Cesa? Or even Ceyo? Munne frowned, flooded with shame. *Even if they knew what was at stake, would they forgive me for breaking so many customs and traditions?*

It took very little time for Tethe's group to remove their jackets and coats and replace them with the Elviri ones. They each pulled on a pair of gloves and a hood to complete the ensemble, and if Munne didn't know any better—and didn't look too closely—she would assume they were common soldiers in her army, which meant the Proma at the barricades and gates wouldn't know any better.

"Come, we need to be on our way," Munne muttered, going to her steed, Alathyl.

As Munne mounted her horse, Tethe and the others saddled up and mounted horses of their own, and she led them into the center aisle. Mayrien led the packhorse out of its stall and tethered it to her own steed with a rope. Araloth waited for Mayrien to mount her horse before she handed over the reins and mounted her own steed.

"Won't Vinya be watching us?" Mayrien whispered to Munne as they exited the stables.

"It's likely, but we have to trust that *she* will trust us," Munne responded, knowing it was a silly answer. Of course Vinya would be watching, and of course she would report to Ethelmar that Munne and her triple left the stables with five strangers. Munne could only hope that they wouldn't ride after her to demand answers as to who these people were, or where they were going. Or why they were wearing Elviri clothing.

Beside the guards at the bridge, no one else was on the street when the party emerged from the stables. That brought Munne some small relief, but knew she still had to *leave* the city. Rhorek's sealed letters sat on her left hip inside a satchel.

I hope these men trust their knight-general as much as my men trust me. Munne prayed silently to Azrael as they made their way to the ramp leading down into the Crafting District.

CHAPTER XVII: SETH

Though Seth and Lisanthir found comfort with each other that night, and the next two nights, no progress was made with their escape plan. They instead laid in each other's' arms, told stories from their childhoods, and listened to the sounds of the rainforest. Seth was able to identify most of the birdcalls by sound alone, which Lisanthir was impressed by.

Octavia didn't show the next morning, nor the next. Seth didn't see his twin at all until the third morning, but the fear had already taken hold. Lisanthir had just gotten out of bed and was putting his robes on when Octavia slipped past the door and came inside, closing the door behind her. Seth heard hesitation and fear in each footstep that fell on the stone floor.

Or am I just projecting my own concerns?

When Octavia spoke, all of his fears were confirmed. "We're too late."

Seth struggled to push himself into a sitting position, his hands catching on the silks trapping him against the bed. He inhaled sharply, his chest squeezing around his heart as it thumped wildly. Lisanthir was by his side in an instant, his steward's robe haphazardly fastened.

"There's nothing we can do?" Seth asked.

Octavia opened her mouth but hesitated. Her jaw quivered as her breath hitched. "H-He's preparing for our departure. Right now," she said.

It felt as if Seth's soul was leaving his body. *Perhaps it'd be better to throw ourselves from the window. If we live, we could limp away into the forest before anyone notices. If we die, at least we'll finally be free. Just a few fleeting moments of flying, being weightless, just like the kytling, before it abruptly ends—*

Octavia threw herself onto the bed and wrapped her arms around Seth's neck, dragging his thoughts back into the stone chamber. She wept, burying her head in his shoulder. Tav, his gallant, brave, strong sister, had crumbled under the bleak outcome. Seth's mind raced, desperately trying to come up with *something* to reassure both his twin and himself that they could still escape. He enveloped her in an embrace, wincing under her tightening grip. "Maybe during the journey, we can—"

"He won't let us out of his sight!" Octavia snapped.

"W-We could try outrunning them," Seth offered, regretting the words as soon as they passed his lips.

Octavia pulled far enough away from him to shoot him an ugly glare. Even if they tried running, they wouldn't make it far. The wheelchair would be left in Yiradia, to be replaced by another once they arrived in Iszairi. Octavia would have to carry him if they tried running while on the road. They would try, and they would get caught, because Octavia would never abandon him. Not to mention the danger they'd be putting Lisanthir in. If Amias and the Asaszi found out an Elviri infiltrated their lands, Lisanthir would be killed.

"We have to do something," Seth whispered. He felt the familiar prick of tears in the corners of his eyes. "We can't just... We have to get out..." *Curse my legs, and curse Father for doing this to me.*

"We can't, Seth, we can't," Octavia muttered, her voice bordering on mania. "I couldn't figure it out fast enough, and now you're going to suffer for my failures."

Seth cradled her face in his hands, leaning forward to rest his forehead against hers. Touching her was like touching fire. But he needed to get past the hysterics and bring his sister back from the edge.

"Please don't shoulder this burden alone. Lis and I are here, too, and the three of us will figure something out. We *will*. If we must make our escape from Iszairi, then so be it. Perhaps we can escape to Kherizhan."

His sister sniffled several times, the tears still falling steadily down her cheeks. She didn't pull away from him nor did she scoff at his words. "Getting lost in those mountains might not be a bad idea," she mumbled, her voice cracking.

Seth let out a breathless chuckle, wiping away the tears from her face. He tilted his head back to kiss her forehead. "The Asaszi would never cross the border to hunt for us."

"How far is Kherizhan from Iszairi?" Lisanthir asked quietly. Seth turned to look at the Elviri who hovered over the siblings with such care and concern on his face that it made Seth's heart ache.

"The city and coliseum were built in the shadows of Kherizhan, but there are no roads or paths leading into the mountains," Octavia replied, and Seth heard the contemplation in her voice. She plucked Seth's hands from her face and held them in her lap.

Maybe Kherizhan is *the best path forward.* Seth clung desperately to that thought. *The Asaszi always told us how dangerous those mountains were. They're afraid of that land. If we manage to escape into the mountains, then perhaps they won't follow us. We'll be free.*

"Do you know if Szatisi is coming with us?" Seth blurted out.

Octavia's eyes drifted up to his, and her brow furrowed. "I think so."

He smiled, his heart thumping loudly in his ears. "Then let's go to Iszairi."

She caught onto the plan, squeezing his hands tightly and nodding her head. "Okay. Yes, okay. To Iszairi. Let's get you ready to go."

Lisanthir and Octavia helped Seth out of his bed and into his wheelchair. Working quickly, the three of them got most of Seth's clothing and books packed into a chest. He changed into clothes more appropriate for travel, and Lisanthir disappeared underneath his steward's veil and gloves.

Much to Seth's surprise, there were no stewards standing outside of his door. He turned to Octavia to ask, but she spoke before he could. "I sent them away. Although perhaps in hindsight that was foolish because now I have to carry your chest to the stables." She let out a self-deprecating laugh.

Lisanthir placed a hand on her shoulder then pointed to the chest. He stepped over and grasped the handle on one side, then waited. She let out a quiet *oh* and stood on the opposite end, and together they picked up the wooden chest.

With Seth leading, the trio made their way through the pyramid and to the stables down below. On the ground floor, a pair of soldiers spotted them and ran to assist Octavia without being asked. His sister allowed them to carry the chest the remainder of the way, and Lisanthir gravitated to the handles on Seth's chair.

Outside, the rainforest was alive with buzzing, crying, and chittering, the suns barely peeking out above the treetops. The cold seeped through Seth's clothing and into his bones. He crossed his arms and tucked his hands into his armpits to retain whatever warmth he could. The village surrounding them was just as active as the forest with Provira and Asaszi helping prepare the traveling procession for departure. The two soldiers carrying Seth's chest split away to join the other soldiers and servants carrying crates and barrels.

The traveling procession was made up of two carriages, several pairs of mules hitched to carts, and a swath of soldiers on horseback. Amias and the twins would be expected to travel together inside one of the carriages, the other no doubt reserved for the Asaszi queen, her consort, and the high priestess.

Is Osza already inside her carriage, or is she still within the pyramid? A small shiver ran down Seth's back, neither answer bringing him any comfort. At least he wouldn't be sharing a carriage with her or the other Asaszi. *No, I'm just going to be sharing a carriage with Father.*

His father stood near their carriage, speaking to a small gathering of servants. As they approached, Seth caught the end of his father's tirade. "...on the road, you may stop for Queen Osza, but otherwise we only stop every four hours. We'll ride through the night to get to Iszairi as soon as possible. And once we are on the road, *no one* is to disturb me."

Gooseflesh spread across Seth's neck and arms. He couldn't help throwing a fearful glance at his sister before their father caught sight of them.

"Children!" Amias called out, stepping away from the servants. He approached them and placed a hand on each of their shoulders. "We leave very soon. Only a few things left to do." His eyes darted to the Asaszi's carriage, and a grimace briefly passed across his face before he smiled.

"Hello Father," Octavia said softly, forcing a smile. "Are we traveling with you, or with the Asaszi?" Seth was impressed. His sister was completely composed as she spoke. He wished he had that talent.

Amias's grip tightened on Seth's shoulder, telling him all that he needed to know before their father spoke. Amias lowered his voice. "With me, of course. Though I will warn you now that I will be spending the journey communing with the *Tserys*. I've instructed the servants to stop every four hours, which should be sufficient for your needs. I'm not to be disturbed. Is that clear?"

The threat was evident, even for his children. Seth tried to swallow, but his mouth was dry. He nodded, as did Octavia.

"Good. Go ahead and make yourselves comfortable. We depart as soon as the Asaszi grace us with their presence." Amias removed his hands from their shoulders and headed back to where the servants and soldiers were climbing into saddles and securing their luggage.

Octavia and Seth's eyes met. Her mask was still impeccable, although he started to see fraying along the edges as her nostrils flared with a sharp inhale, her eyes narrowed ever so slightly. They were going to be stuck in a carriage with their father for two days, unable to speak or comfort each other. At least Amias would also be silent.

This is the best outcome for us. At least we're not riding with Osza, Astohi, and Szatisi, Seth thought.

The trio approached the carriage. Octavia leaned down to pick Seth up, and he wrapped his arms around her neck. Lisanthir held onto the chair's handles to keep it from rolling backward. His sister's muscles strained under his weight as she straightened up and moved to the carriage steps. The Elviri stepped around the chair and reached up to open the carriage door, allowing Octavia to climb its steps and set Seth down on one of the padded benches. When Octavia pivoted to sit beside him, he could hear her labored pants.

"I hate these carriages," Octavia grumbled in between breaths. Seth's lips curled into a small grin, and he patted his sister on the shoulder.

From outside, Lisanthir shut the carriage door and suddenly the twins were alone inside the wooden interior. They sat with their backs to the front of the carriage where the driver would be seated. To their left was the door with a small window carved in its upper half. Across from them was another padded bench where their father would be sitting. To their right was a second window with a view of the stables. Though they could still hear the sound of the village from the windows, they felt isolated from it all.

Octavia turned to look at him, pushing back a strand of loose hair behind her ear. "Are you going to be comfortable here? Do I need to fetch a blanket?"

Thoughts of his bed and Lisanthir came unbidden in his head. *I'd be more comfortable with him sitting with us, his arms wrapped around me—*

"Is he coming with us?" Seth blurted out, suddenly in a panic. He had assumed that Lisanthir would be included in the procession to Iszairi, but only a handful of stewards would be making the journey. A new staff of stewards would be waiting for them in the other city.

Octavia frowned and it was her turn to touch his shoulder. Her voice was barely above a whisper when she spoke. "Yes, I requested he come with us as a soldier if he wasn't going to be one of the stewards accompanying us."

Seth crumpled underneath her touch, leaning his head against her shoulder. "Thank you, Tav."

She patted his thigh. "I wouldn't dream of separating you."

The carriage door opened, and Amias climbed inside, his arms filled with blankets. Seth bolted upright and Octavia slid her hand into her lap, squeezing her hands between her thighs. Amias took a seat opposite his children and handed them two of the blankets, keeping the last for himself.

"It's unusually cold for being so far south, but no matter. These should suffice until we get to Iszairi," their father said.

"Thank you, Father," Seth mumbled, accepting the blanket and unfurling it across his lap. It was thick and cozy, and he was genuinely thankful to have it.

"Will we be leaving soon?" Octavia asked.

Amias grunted an affirmative noise. "All of the servants have their orders. They'll prepare a midday meal and a dinner for you. You two should be comfortable for the day. You'll sleep in the carriage tonight. We should arrive by sunsdown tomorrow."

Seth's brow furrowed at his father's words and how he was excluding himself from all of those actions. *He still needs to eat and sleep, even if he's talking to a ghost. Why is he speaking so strangely?*

Amias reached into his robe and withdrew a small vial of dark liquid. Before Octavia or Seth could react, he uncorked the vial and drank its contents. He let out a quiet sigh and then leaned his head back against the wall of the carriage, his eyes closed. His hands went slack and quietly thudded against the bench, the vial falling to the floor. Within a matter of seconds, his body stilled, and his breathing deepened. Octavia leaned forward and picked up the vial. She held it up so they could both inspect it, but no trace of its liquid contents remained.

The twins exchanged a worried stare as the carriage lurched forward and began their journey to Iszairi. *What did he drink? What's it doing to him?*

Though it pained Seth to be in forced proximity with his father for two entire days, the silence brought him some comfort and allowed him to dwell on thoughts of escape. He worked his way through several different plans over the first day of travel, analyzing their strengths and weaknesses. He hadn't been to Iszairi since childhood, but he could still visualize the ancient Asaszi city in his mind. While the center of Yiradia was its pyramid, Iszairi was built around a massive coliseum, connected to a pyramid even larger than Yiradia's. Several smaller pyramids surrounded the stone marvel with many more buildings sprawling out from there. It was apparent that it had been the capital of the ancient Asaszi civilization. They had kept the city in pristine condition, unlike Yiradia. The roads were traversable, and the rainforest was kept at bay along the edges of the city. Seth never really understood why Amias kept his family in Yiradia when the conditions in Iszairi were so much more favorable.

True to Amias's word, the carriage stopped every four hours to give Seth and Octavia time to relieve themselves and stretch their limbs. Seth's wheelchair had been left behind at Yiradia, so Octavia had to carry him into the forest and hold him up. He hated subjecting his sister to this, but she said nothing.

Better her than one of the stewards.

During their second stop, the servants took extra time to prepare a meal for the twins along with the rest of the procession. Octavia found a large boulder to set Seth on top, and they ate a bowl of fresh greens and fruit while chatting quietly. They couldn't discuss anything they wanted, so they stuck to very mundane subjects like the weather, the condition of the paths in the forest, and the various noises they heard. The stewards hovered near Octavia and Seth, ready to swoop in and assist with his care if called upon. His twin kept them all away, though, and took care of him herself.

Seth wished that she would let some of the stewards near, though. Just Lisanthir. *But it'd be suspicious if I started asking after the stewards just to see if he's among their ranks, and it'd put him at risk. Besides, Tav said he might be traveling among the soldiers and not the stewards.* He knew Octavia was doing the right thing by keeping the others at bay, but he missed his Elviri.

The Asaszi didn't emerge from their carriage during the first day. Seth wondered if the Asaszi trio considered too good to walk amongst the trees. It was a childish thought, but his opinion of the Asaszi was so low that he didn't mind being a little childish. Anything to bring a little comfort and light into his dark days.

"Ready to keep going?" Octavia asked softly.

Seth cast one long, lingering look at the rainforest before turning to his sister and nodding. "The sooner we go, the sooner we get there."

Octavia grunted in agreement and climbed to her feet. She exchanged glances with one of the servants and nodded her head before reaching to pick up Seth. She took her time climbing back into the carriage and setting Seth down on the bench opposite their father, doing her best to make as little noise as possible.

After his sister sat down beside him, Seth gathered up one of the blankets and threw it across both of their laps. His gaze naturally landed on his father who had his head lolled back against his bench, still in the same trance from that morning. Amias's mouth moved in voiceless words, his hands still resting on either side of him with his palms facing up. Though his eyes were closed, Seth saw his father's eyes moving underneath his eyelids. The sight disturbed him greatly. At least he was silent, but...

Is he actually speaking to the dead? Did Szatisi make this potion for him, or did he make it on his own? Does Osza know about this? The questions swirled around in Seth's head, interrupting other thoughts of what to do in Iszairi. He had never seen his father in such a state before. *It's like he's asleep, but he isn't, not really. Would he wake up if Tav and I talked to each other?* Seth didn't want to take that risk.

The remaining stops came and went, and soon the suns were setting. The twins got as comfortable as they could on the bench, keeping their shuffling around to a minimum to avoid disturbing their father. The sounds of the rainforest eventually lulled Seth to sleep.

The second day was much the same as the first. Amias was still in his trance, having silent communion with whatever was listening to him. Seth curled up underneath one of the blankets and tried keeping his hands warm. The forest was quieter, though. He assumed most of the animals were seeking warmth themselves or perhaps had nested for the cold winter. His thoughts drifted back to the last three nights in Yiradia with Lisanthir in bed beside him.

It'd be nice to spend the winter just like that. Seth mourned what couldn't be.

Octavia kept her entire right side pressed against him so they could share body heat. She had her own blanket wrapped around herself, but still, she shivered underneath. With any luck, the suns would warm the forest, and they'd get a reprieve during their midday rest. That's what Seth hoped for, anyway.

Their father continued his communion throughout the second day. At some point between their midday meal and the next scheduled rest, the carriage came to an unexpected halt. Octavia jerked forward out of a semi-conscious state and looked at Seth with wild eyes. He pulled a hand from his blanket and placed it on her shoulder, squeezing gently to reassure her that everything was okay.

The Asaszi are emerging from their carriage, no doubt.

A few moments later, one of the servants cracked their carriage door open and looked at Octavia, asking the unspoken question of if she and Seth wanted to stop for a while as well. His sister shook her head, and the servant shut the door as quietly as possible. Neither one of them wanted to be anywhere near the Asaszi right now, so Seth was thankful for her making that decision on their behalf.

Without the rumble of the wheels on the cobbled road, Seth could more clearly hear the noises of the rainforest. Today, the creatures were quieter than normal, and underneath their calls and shrieks he could hear *it*—the hum. When the procession began moving again, Seth realized that the hum wasn't just present, but it was also getting *louder* the closer they got to Iszairi.

A nauseating wave of dread crashed over Seth, and he had to drop his head into his hands to keep himself from vomiting. For the first time, despite all of the wild ideas and theories that had been running through his head on the journey, he wondered if they had made a mistake in traveling deeper into Moonyswyn. Perhaps they *should* have tried throwing themselves from the pyramid in Yiradia or making a run for it during one of their breaks. Perhaps during the next break, he could convince Octavia to pick him up and just *run*.

But what about Lisanthir? The soldiers would catch us anyway. I'm nothing but dead weight. At least Octavia could leave me behind and escape on her own.

Seth tried coming up with an escape plan that would ensure all three of them got free, but when the carriage stopped again, he had nothing. Octavia took in a deep breath, picked him up, and climbed out of the carriage.

The forest surrounded them on all sides, blocking out the suns' light. Trees lined the road, their roots disrupting and dislodging the smooth stones they had been traveling on. Several of the servants and soldiers disappeared into the forest to relieve themselves. Those who remained behind murmured quietly to one another.

Is Lisanthir among them?

Seth's veiled stewards trailed after him and Octavia as she tried finding somewhere suitable to set him down. With no small hills or large boulders in sight, she had to settle for a spot amidst the tree roots. Octavia took her time crouching down, one knee after another, then leaned forward to set Seth down in between a pair of thick brown roots.

As Seth adjusted himself on the forest floor, he whispered to his sister, "We have to get out of here."

Octavia stiffened, her hands lingering on Seth's upper back and knee. "Did Father say something?" she said under her breath.

He shook his head, watching as the stewards stopped at a tree that was just out of earshot. They leaned against the tree and stretched their limbs, but otherwise their focus was on the siblings. Seth couldn't risk any of them overhearing his words, but he also needed to find Lisanthir.

"Do you hear the hum?" Seth asked.

They were both silent for a few moments. Octavia leaned back and cocked her head to the side, brushing her hair behind her ear. Her eyes narrowed as she hunted for the sound.

"Beneath the bird calls," he hissed.

After another moment, he flicked his eyes away from the stewards to his sister's face, where he saw recognition. Her mouth formed a small 'oh'. "What is that?"

"The Asaszi call it magic. Father says it's the *Tserys*."

Octavia frowned. She swayed on the balls of her feet, her hands fidgeting in her lap. "Do you know which way is north?" He shook his head again. "Do you know which one *he* is?"

With another sweeping glance over the stewards, Seth shook his head with remorse. *If Tav or I called out for assistance, would Lis push his way forward, or would one of the other stewards beat him to it? Not worth the risk. What if Tav and I run now, would Lis be able to get away while they search for us? But then what happens if he's caught...*

"I don't think we can, Seth." Octavia's voice was barely a whisper.

He parted his lips as he inhaled sharply. He felt the rising onslaught of tears coming, but he had to maintain his composure. He couldn't break down in the middle of the forest. He couldn't let the others see him like that. Then they would know something was wrong.

But I don't want to go. It felt like his stomach was full of rocks, dragging him down into the depths of all his darkest thoughts. *Nothing good is at Iszairi. He is at Iszairi. We need to run.*

And above it all, the rainforest continued to hum.

Eventually one of the Asaszi servants approached them and told them it was time to go. When Seth looked at his sister, he saw she had been crying. He hadn't even heard her over the hum. Something similar to guilt stabbed at his stomach, and it squeezed tighter around itself. It *hurt*.

"Coming," Octavia called out softly, not even bothering to look at the servant. The servant nodded and turned back toward the procession. The stewards shuffled away one by one. Tav inhaled deeply through her mouth, the noise barely audible. She looked at Seth and leaned over to pick him up.

He wrapped his arms around her neck and hugged her tightly. "I'm sorry," he murmured, the words spilling from his lips before he could consider them.

Octavia tightened her grip on him and rested her head against his. Her tears clung to his hair, but he didn't mind. She took another deep breath and then whispered a few words of encouragement to herself. "Okay. We have to go. We'll be okay."

"We will, Tav," Seth replied quietly. "We have to be."

They arrived in Iszairi a few hours after the suns had set. As they approached the city, their path was guided by lit torches. The road smoothed out and widened as they entered the city proper. There were no fancy gates or walls like Seth had seen at Lithalyon; they were just suddenly within the city, surrounded by buildings. Above the torchlight he could see the shadowed forms of the pyramids rising above it all like stone giants. Townsfolk were returning home for the evening, shuffling along quickly but giving the procession a respectful berth on the roads. Several stopped to mutter and stare.

Peeking out the window of the carriage, Seth saw that the majority of the townsfolk were Asaszi with only a few Provira scattered amidst their ranks. The unbalanced ratio surprised him a little; he thought there would be more Provira present, especially with the academies in desperate need for new students. A year or two ago, his father had been bragging about how successful the Provira had been in their studies and had remarked to Osza that they competed with the Asaszi in terms of natural talent. The Asaszi queen had held her tongue, but perhaps she took that as a threat and had been working to undermine the Provira's efforts in Iszairi.

A cruel thing to do to your allies, Seth thought bitterly. Not that he wanted the Asaszi as allies. *But who else do we have?*

The procession stopped outside one of the pyramids. From within the carriage, Seth couldn't tell which pyramid it was, but he assumed it was the *Tserdanii*, the largest of the pyramids in the city, and the home of Osza and Astohi. The few times Seth had visited Iszairi in his childhood, he remembered staying in a guest suite within the great pyramid.

Seth and Octavia sat in the carriage for several moments, exchanging concerned glances. Their father was still under the influence of whatever elixir he had drunk the day before, and there was no telling when it would wear off. He had instructed everyone not to disturb him, but he hadn't given any instructions on what to do when they arrived. None of the servants had come to open the carriage door, so perhaps he had said something to them after Octavia and Seth had climbed inside the carriage. His sister shrugged and reached for the door.

"Eager to escape?" Amias's raspy voice filled the space, caged in by the wooden walls.

Seth saw Octavia flinch. He tensed, all senses heightened as his eyes shifted from his sister to his father. Amias hadn't fully opened his eyes yet; he was just watching the siblings from under heavy eyelids.

Their father leaned forward and cleared his throat. "It'll be good to get out and stretch our legs. I've always disliked how cramped these carriages are." His eyes flicked to Octavia's hand, which had frozen on the door handle. He arched an eyebrow. "Well?"

"I-I apologize, Father," Octavia stuttered, opening the door and gesturing for Amias to exit first.

Amias let out a quiet grunt then climbed out of the carriage. He took a few steps away to give his children room to exit as well and began stretching his arms up and around. Within their wooden box, Octavia and Seth could do nothing but stare at each other. Fear gripped the twins, but within the nest of snakes, they could only push all of the fear, the rage, the despair, deep down within themselves. They had to be brave if they wanted to escape.

Octavia carried Seth out of the carriage with her chin held high. Though he had his arms draped around her shoulders, Seth kept his back straight and his face composed. Within moments, one of the stewards was at their side with a wheelchair kept within the city ready for Seth. It was much nicer than his chair in Yiradia with several carvings and flourishes in the arms and back. Octavia set him gently down in the chair and then took her place behind, her hands on the handles.

They were indeed outside of the *Tserdanii*. Where the lone pyramid in Yiradia was a foothill in the plains, the *Tserdanii* was a towering peak in a range of grand mountains. In the daylight its beige stonework would glitter underneath the suns. The great pyramid stood beside the coliseum with underground tunnels connecting the two landmarks. The network of tunnels also connected the *Tserdanii* to the academies and other pyramids. If it weren't for its foul inhabitants and history, Iszairi would indeed be a city of beauty.

But nothing compares to Aelrindel and the city of Lithalyon.

"Greetingsss Lord Kharisss," a deep rattle called from the ramp leading up to the entrance of the *Tserdanii*. "Your quartersss have been prepared for you."

"Thank you, Taszo," Amias turned to face the Asaszi approaching them. "See that my children are escorted inside. I must speak with Queen Osza first."

"Of courssse," Taszo murmured, bowing.

The Asaszi's blue scales glittered in the torchlight, almost blending in with the dark robes wrapped around his lithe body. He stayed bent at the waist until Amias had walked off toward Osza's carriage, then stood straight and turned back to the *Tserdanii* where a host of Asaszi servants stood waiting. He spoke to them in their native tongue, the words sounding like little more than hissing and spitting to Seth's ears.

Two serpentine women approached the siblings, beckoning for them to follow. As they climbed the ramp into the great pyramid, Seth looked over Octavia's shoulder to see Taszo stalking off to the host of servants and stewards who had traveled from Yiradia. He hoped that Lisanthir's disguise would hold, and that he'd be safe from the Asaszi.

"Welcome back to Iszairi, *py'tseras*," one of the female servants said in a joyful tone. Long black hair swept down her back, a stark contrast to her orange scales. "It hasss been a long time sssince your family visssited."

"Thank you for the warm welcome," Octavia replied without a hint of distress. She sounded more like a *pyredan* than a young girl. "Has dinner been prepared for us?"

The second servant nodded, her green scales rippling with the movement. "Fresssh meat from the foressst."

Seth's stomach growled. He was looking forward to the meal. The pyramid had been built with ramps connecting the floors together, which made travel much easier for Seth. He idly wondered why Yiradia hadn't been built to the same standard, and he considered trying to research it in one of their libraries at a later date. Not that the information would do him any good.

"When will our belongings be brought to our quarters?" Octavia asked.

The green-scaled servant tasted the air with her tongue. "After dinner."

"Excellent, thank you."

Their quarters were roughly halfway up the height of the pyramid on the eastern front. The siblings shared an entire wing on the floor consisting of separate bedchambers, a dining chamber, a bathing room, a study, and a lounge. Amias had a separate suite of rooms elsewhere in the pyramid, which Seth was thankful for. The Asaszi servants led them into their dining chamber where the table had been set, and their meal was waiting for them. Two sets of dishes were laid out, but one chair had been removed. Octavia pushed Seth up to the table, then took her seat next to him.

The Asaszi stood in the doorway. The orange-scaled servant asked, "Isss there anything elssse we can do for you, *py'tseras*?"

"That will be all, thank you." Octavia's reply was curt, and she didn't lift her eyes from the table as the Asaszi left.

The siblings filled their plates with roast boar and charred vegetables and poured dark wine into their goblets. The meal was simple but luxurious, a stark contrast to their meals in Yiradia. Silence filled the room as they ate and drank. But perhaps that wasn't the right word. Underneath the scraping of forks and clinking of glasses, the forest's low hum persisted.

CHAPTER XVIII: RAY

The scent of roasted meat stirred Ray from her slumber. Her head bobbed back and gently bumped against a stone wall. She opened her eyes and immediately regretted it as pain and bright light seared across her vision. She raised a hand to rub at her eyes, trying to banish away the remnants of sleep.

When she removed her hand and her vision unblurred, her heart nearly beat out of her chest. Every inch of her skin prickled and every muscle in her body tensed. In front of her were two creatures with white fur, garbed in coats and pants made from other darker furs. Bushy tails protruded from underneath their coats, idly swishing back and forth. Small, rounded ears perched on top of their heads. She couldn't see their faces, but she could see the sharp claws protruding from their paws. They were hovering over Princess Niamnh, chittering and barking softly to one another.

Enthai. Ray's body spasmed as she choked down a scream. Her hands flew to her mouth, forcing herself to stay silent. Panic coursed through her veins, making her heart pound so quickly and loudly that the sound rang in her ears. *What are they doing to Niamnh? How long have they been here? Are we safe? Can they hear my heart? Smell my fear?* With a lurch she remembered her injury on the back of her neck. *Can they smell my blood?*

Both creatures' ears twitched, and they turned to look at Ray. Beady black eyes stood out against white fur, along with muzzles that no doubt hid sharp teeth. Their faces reminded her of foxes, but much larger and more threatening. A whimper tore through her throat, and she felt her mouth turn dry.

I don't want to die here.

The Enthai on the left let out a quiet bark then made a strange coughing noise. It crossed the hut to stand in front of her. Up close she saw several scars and scratches along its muzzle, bits of fur missing from its skin. With a scratchy, warbling voice, it spoke. "Fear not, Walker. We are here to take you to Mother Shade."

Ray lowered her hands from her mouth, her jaw hanging open. "Y-You know me?"

The creature reached out with one paw and poked her coat, dragging its claw against the blue lidless eye on her chest. "The mark of the Many-Faced One. Yes, we know you." Its nose twitched as it sniffed the air around her, its face twisting into an expression of confusion. "But where is your master?"

It must be talking about Naro. But what, or who, is the "Many-Faced One"?

"Naro wasn't able to—" She paused, her throat seizing and squeezing shut. It took all of her energy to keep her voice level when she spoke next. "He sent me. To look after the princess."

She stared into the Enthai's dark eyes for several silent moments. It didn't move its claw from her chest. Ray felt naked under its gaze like it was peeling back every layer she wore, and every layer of skin after that. For a brief moment she thought she saw hunger in its eyes, but she blinked, and the creature's face became unreadable.

Are the Enthai more like me, or a dog? Ray knew how to read people, but she didn't even know the basics of the creatures, much less any nuance in their behaviors or mannerisms. She could've been staring into the face of her killer, and she wouldn't know until it attacked her.

The Enthai spoke again in a warbled voice. "Eat. Then we leave."

She started to ask about her injury, her hands slipping to the back of her neck to feel... no dried blood, just a small line of scabs. The flesh was tender to the touch, but otherwise everything seemed okay. Just sore. With her own wellbeing accounted for, her eyes darted from the Enthai to Niamnh and then back again. "What about the princess?"

"We tend to that one. You, eat." The Enthai turned away from Ray and returned to its partner by the princess.

Ray let out a shaky breath, watching as they knelt down beside Niamnh and did... she couldn't make out exactly what they were doing, which kept her heart pounding in her ears. They resumed their quiet barking, communicating in a way that she couldn't understand.

Naro's really made contact with these creatures? How did he even find them?

After several moments of concentrating on the two Enthai, Ray eventually tore her eyes off of them and looked toward the firepit. While she had been sleeping, the creatures had built up the fire, so it warmed the hut fully. Beads of sweat formed along her hairline. The creatures had also cooked a few skewers of meat, hanging them across the flames. There were three skewers in total, each holding two small carcasses that had been skinned so she was unable to tell what kind of creatures they were, but her stomach didn't care. She desperately needed food.

Pushing herself off of the wall, Ray crawled over to the firepit and grabbed one of the skewers. Her head spun as she moved, and her stomach lurched and grumbled. The meat looked as if it was fully cooked through, so she wasted no time grabbing one of the skewers, nearly burning her hands in the process, and tearing into one of the carcasses. The meat was very lean and tasted like smoke, but she didn't care. It was the most delicious thing she'd eaten since leaving Auora.

Ray devoured both carcasses in a matter of minutes and was soon sucking the fat and juices out from underneath her fingernails. Her stomach, awoken by the fresh meat, growled and demanded more. She stared at the other two skewers of meat and wondered if they were meant for her or not. With a brief glance over her shoulder to see where the Enthai were, she reached for a second skewer. Only one of the Enthai hovered over Princess Niamnh. The other had moved while she had been eating. Her heart beat faster, the sound ringing in her ears.

When a furred paw touched her shoulder, her whole body flinched violently. The creature's claws pressed lightly against her shoulder, holding her in place. It let out a soft bark. "Drink," it said.

Ray twisted in the opposite direction, looking at the Enthai. In its other paw it held out a waterskin to her. *Her* waterskin. She took it from the Enthai, uncorked it, and drank. And drank.

Blessed Protector, I'm thirsty.

She gulped down several mouthfuls of liquid before the acrid flavor hit her. She wretched, liquid spewing from her mouth.

"*Drink,*" the Enthai growled. Its claws dug deeper into her shoulder, the pain stealing the focus from the foul liquid in her waterskin.

"*What?*" Ray sputtered, wincing and trying to pull her shoulder away from the creature. The Enthai dragged her toward the waterskin with an iron grip. "It tastes foul," she whined, wrinkling her nose.

The creature only growled in response and held her still. Ray raised the waterskin back to her lips, fingers trembling. Her throat tightened. She tried to swallow but had to fight the urge to vomit instead.

Just get it over with, she told herself. Inhaling deeply, she raised the waterskin to her lips and drank. Ray swallowed before the taste could settle in her mouth. She continued to drink and swallow until she couldn't stand it. She dropped the waterskin and doubled over.

Or tried to.

The Enthai tightened its grip on her shoulder and slapped its other paw across her face to keep her from spitting the liquid out. Its fur tickled her nose and irritated her eyes. It smelled like dirt and wet musk, which only made her feel sicker. Drool and water dribbled from her mouth. The Enthai must have felt it, too, even with its thick fur because it tilted her head back to keep the liquid in.

Just. Swallow.

Her body fought back. Her throat closed up, and for a moment, she couldn't force anything down. Her eyes watered and tears streamed down her cheeks. Her vision blurred, the Enthai looking more like a white cloud than an animal. The Enthai's grip suddenly tightened on her shoulder and the creature stumbled forward a step. Blinking rapidly, Ray caught sight of the ceiling.

When did I look up? Or... oh, I'm not sitting anymore. She blinked again, trying to focus her vision but struggling. Her lower back was touching the floor now, and the Enthai struggled to keep her sitting up. *Or is it trying to help me lay down?*

Ray blinked again slowly. She swallowed. The horrible taste in her mouth was still there, but she couldn't... she didn't...

She closed her eyes to blink again, but that time her eyes didn't reopen.

Harsh cold wind shocked Ray into consciousness. A startled scream tore out of her before she could gather her bearings. The sound of her voice was lost in the wind. She was moving fast, but she was laying down. Above her was an open gray sky, as an Enthai staring down at her. It had a hood drawn over its head, protecting its ears from the wind. She couldn't tell if it was one of the two she had met in the abandoned village. Its fur was white just like the other two with the same dark beady eyes. Shortly after making eye contact, the Enthai looked to its right and let out a string of short barks, presumably to another Enthai nearby.

Ray shivered uncomfortably. As her body moved, she felt restraints wrapped around her, holding her down. Glancing down toward her torso and legs, she saw she was strapped to a sled which was being dragged across the tundra by a pack of wolves. Her body had been covered with several blankets and pelts, and she became aware that the only cold part of her body was her face.

Silent awe settled over her as she watched the eight canines run tirelessly in the snow. They were larger and furrier than any dog Ray had ever seen before. Their pelts were predominantly white with streaks of gray and black across their sides and heads. They could very easily blend in with the tundra, especially if it were snowing. She heard other yips and howls on the wind, but she couldn't tell if it was another Enthai or the wolves.

Do the wolves understand the Enthai's barking?

She looked to her right and saw another sled beside her, an Enthai standing on the end, and she recognized Princess Niamnh laying across it. The girl's eyes were closed. Ray's heart skipped a beat, fear digging its claws into her. She wondered if the princess was sleeping, or if she had been similarly drugged back at the village.

Ray's eyes watered from the buffeting wind, and she had no choice but to close them, her tears frigid against her cheeks. *How long have we been traveling? How much further to go? Protector please let them take us somewhere safe.*

She focused on the warmth surrounding the rest of her body, trying her best to ignore how cold her face felt. Her eyelashes stuck together and to her skin. Even if she wanted to, she couldn't wiggle her hand free to rub at her eyes or shield her face. She just had to focus on the other parts of her body.

Sleep easily overtook Ray again. She hadn't even noticed that she had fallen back asleep until she felt something pawing at her legs and pulling away the pelts and blankets. With much difficulty she opened her eyes and blearily looked around. Her neck turned with only minimal soreness, more from stiff muscles than the dagger slash across the back. They were inside a structure of some kind, but she couldn't tell what it was made from. Certainly not wood. The walls were gray and featureless, smooth, with no decorations or markings of any kind.

"Up," the Enthai at the foot of the sled barked at Ray.

Her attention snapped to the creature. Its hood had been pulled back and she recognized the scars and scratches across its muzzle.

So, we did travel together.

Ray pushed herself up into a sitting position and immediately regretted it. Her head swam, and she had to throw a hand back to support herself and keep herself from falling down. Her other hand cradled her forehead, fingers pressing into her skin as if to keep her head in place. Her entire face felt numb and warm. She knew the feeling well from spending hours on the docks in Auora, wind lashing against her skin. She was thankful to be within shelter and let her body try to warm itself up.

The Enthai let out a quiet hoot, its coat rustling as it moved around. She felt a paw take hold of her upper arm as the creature tugged her into a standing position. They stood together as she swayed, waiting for her vision to clear and body to stabilize. As she tried to orient herself, she realized that the Enthai stood no taller than her shoulder.

"Thank you," Ray whispered, voice cracking from disuse. A tiny sliver of panic shot down her spine. *It feels like I haven't spoken in days. How long were we traveling?*

"Come. You need nourishment." The Enthai maintained its grip on Ray's arms as it led her off of the sled and out of the building.

The cold hit her first, followed by bright winter light. She raised her free arm to shield her vision, peering out from squinted eyes. The Enthai pulled her around the side of the building, the light quickly falling to shadow. The building—which was more like a small hut now that Ray was outside looking around—sat at the front of a ravine. Stone cliffs surrounded them on three sides. Behind them was the vast open tundra. Curious gray and white totems stood at the entrance to the ravine, each taller than her. Patterns resembling wolf and fox faces were carved into the totems. Turning back to the direction the Enthai was leading her, Ray took in the sight of the ravine and the mountains beyond.

"I didn't know there were mountains up here," she murmured, her voice lost in the wind.

"There is much you do not know," the creature growled in response. "We need to get underground."

"Underground?" It appeared as if they were walking straight toward a wall, a dead end. "There's tunnels here?"

It let out a loud huff. "Tunnels. Yes."

Her hand immediately went for Naro's sunsdial in her coat pocket, and she was pleasantly surprised to feel its weight resting against her leg. She felt around for her other belongings, equally surprised to feel her daggers in their sheaths.

They didn't take my blades away? Do they not consider me a threat? Or do they just not care? Not that she was planning on attacking the Enthai—no doubt they'd cut her down because she so much as drew a blade.

Halfway through the ravine, the Enthai pulled Ray to the left around a protruding boulder. Behind the large rock was indeed a tunnel dug into the cliffside wide enough for one person to enter, and no taller than the creature standing next to her. Ray would have to hunch over, perhaps crouch down, to get inside. The Enthai wouldn't have that issue.

Is this where they live? How far north are we? Fear squeezed her stomach. *Has Naro been here before?*

"The tunnels get taller further in. Can you walk on your own?" the Enthai rumbled, leaning in close so she could hear it over the wind.

"I-I think so."

It nodded and then nudged her forward with a paw. The gesture felt... gentle. She couldn't tell if it was because of the creature's fur, or if it was trying to be careful with its touch. Either way, she had no desire to provoke the creature into more hostile actions, so she started forward on her own, ducking to keep her head from hitting the ceiling of the tunnel. Her vision spun and she threw a hand out to brace herself against the wall. The surface was surprisingly smooth and not at all jagged like the cliffs behind her.

Ray made it several paces into the tunnel before the daylight no longer reached her and it became increasingly more difficult to see the path before her. She made do for a few more steps, but soon panic began to take root inside of her. She couldn't stand not being able to see her surroundings.

"Calm yourself," the Enthai's voice rumbled behind her. She felt the weight of its paw settling on her upper back between her shoulders. "Keep your hand on the stone. Go slowly until it gives way to another tunnel. The ground will tilt up soon. We climb into the mountains."

Ray nodded, trying to process the creature's instructions—trying not to focus on the way her heart pounded in her chest, or how the tunnel walls pressed in on all sides. With the Enthai guiding her, she wouldn't get lost in the tunnels. She wouldn't need to see where she was going. If she could just trust it—

How can I trust this creature? She blinked, more to clear her mind than anything else. *I have* to trust it. *If I'm going to survive out here, I have to trust the Enthai.*

Ray felt her feet shuffle forward, one at a time. One step at a time. She felt herself blinking, but couldn't see the difference between her eyelids and the rocks around her. The air smelled... *sharp*. The only smells that accompanied them in the tunnels were musky fur and sweat—nothing else to indicate life or warmth or *anything*. She felt her steps growing shorter as the ground angled up. Climbing. It wasn't too steep. She just needed to keep taking one step, and then another.

"The rock is taller here. No need to crouch."

She frowned, letting the Enthai's words soak in. *The rock is taller.* With very careful, deliberate movement, she straightened her back and let herself stand at full height. She didn't collide with any rocks.

I can trust this Enthai. Her steps became more confident.

Images swam across Ray's mind, looking more real than the tunnels around her. If it weren't for her hand touching the stone, tethering her to this cold forsaken land, she could almost convince herself she was back in Auora. She saw Naro's house, the constellations painted on his ceiling. She could see the staircase climbing to the second floor. If she adjusted her step, it almost felt like she was on those stairs. But no, it was too dark to be Naro's house. It was more like... that circular staircase hidden deep within Auora. The one she had climbed with Naro and Ajak several days ago.

Several lifetimes ago, she thought with a grimace. *Or perhaps this has all been a dream, and I'll wake up in one of those beds on the second floor of Naro's house, and Ajak will be there, and we'll go downstairs to get some porridge and cadra berries together—*

She blinked, and Niamnh's face flashed across her vision, the princess's gray eyes bright underneath a blue sky and two yellow suns. White hair framed her warm brown skin, and Ray felt compelled to reach out and brush a strand of hair behind one of her ears. But even though she felt herself raising her hand up toward the princess, she couldn't see her own pale skin. Niamnh's brow furrowed, and she was devoured by shadows, and Ray was back in the cold tunnels with an Enthai's paw pushing gently against her back.

"Where is Niamnh?" Ray asked, her voice echoing down the tunnel. As soon as the words left her mouth, her heart lodged itself in her throat, and she found it extremely difficult to swallow. She needed to know where the princess was, but she was also terrified of the Enthai's answer.

The creature let out a quiet grunt. "The one you traveled with." It was as much a statement as a question, and Ray found herself nodding frantically in response.

She immediately chastised herself. *Can this thing even see me nod my head? I should speak up and—*

"Ahead. Kept separate because of Doshara."

Ray tripped over her own feet and had to throw her other hand out to catch herself. It hit her all at once—the realization that the Enthai spoke her language, and it took her until *now* to figure that out. She had also somehow forgotten about Daerion. The proximity to creatures with claws and teeth sharper than her daggers might have had something to do with it.

Behind her, the Enthai paused and waited for her to straighten herself out.

"Naro told me that your people would get rid of Daer—the Doshara. Has that already happened?"

Another grunt, followed by a strange hacking noise. "No. We bring you to Mother Shade first."

Ray's mind clouded with confusion and dread. Naro had never clarified *how* the Enthai would do it. But this was the second time they had spoken of "Mother Shade", and Ray found herself wondering who or what that was. *Are they an ally? Or a greater danger than the Doshara? Does Naro know who—or what—this is?*

Her thoughts abruptly stopped when the stone wall under her hand suddenly curved and disappeared under her touch. She stopped in her tracks, her heart pounding in her chest. "Wh-where...?"

She heard the Enthai shuffling around behind her, sniffing the air. Her skin prickled at the sound, no doubt amplified by the lack of other sounds or sights. "We go meet Enesse and your princess. They are ahead. I will lead. Take two steps to your right." The creature dropped its paw from her back.

With a shaky breath, Ray slid her right foot to the side. She expected to feel the tunnel wall, or some other barrier, but hit nothing. With a crumb of courage, she pulled her left foot over and then took one more step to the right.

The Enthai stepped forward, moving in front of her. The rustle of its coat over its fur filled the space around them, such a loud indicator calling out to whatever else was in the tunnels. "Put your hand on my shoulder. I will lead." Though the creature gave the instruction, it didn't wait for her to act. It took hold of her hand and placed it on its shoulder.

Ray clamped her hand down on the coat, digging her fingers into the animal hides. If it bothered the Enthai, it made no noise of discomfort or irritation. It started walking away and Ray struggled to match its pace. Because of the height difference, Ray had to adjust her gait, so she didn't bump into or trip over the smaller creature. It seemed to be mindful of her struggles and walked with longer strides, so that she wasn't moving as awkwardly. Its tail rested against her left leg, pushing back against her if she started drifting too far to the left.

Naro's dogs back home had often pressed against her legs and guided her into his home after recognizing her scent. *How kind of it to lead the way like this,* she thought with only a fraction of sarcasm. She really was thankful for the guidance, but the sarcasm was more of a defense mechanism than anything else. The Enthai's gesture was reminiscent of Naro's dogs, but it felt... wrong. With his dogs she knew that she was safe. And although the Enthai hadn't tried killing her yet, a small part of her mind kept whispering that she was going to die here.

Several long minutes later—or at least what Ray *thought* were minutes—the Enthai slowed down and started hooting softly into the tunnel. Some distance away there was a responding yip. The Enthai picked up the pace again and Ray was forced to walk with a wider stance to avoid stepping on the creature's paws. Its tail immediately pushed against her left leg, correcting her course.

"We turn, and then you stay still," the Enthai said over its shoulder. It wasn't a question, simply an announcement. It turned to the left, and Ray squeezed tighter on its shoulder, following closely.

Ray could hear other bodies moving around in the tunnels ahead, their claws scraping on the rock and their coats rustling against fur. She couldn't easily make out how many there were, especially once they started barking at each other. She felt reasonably confident that she could pick her escort's voice out from the others, though. It sounded like they were in a larger space, a chamber perhaps. Not a cramped tunnel.

The Enthai stopped after a few more steps and nudged at her hand with its paw. She dropped her hand from its shoulder, and it moved away from her. Panic began to fester and swell within her at being completely isolated within the darkness.

What if they leave me here and take Niamnh away? Could I find my way out of here?

Although the tunnels had felt rather straightforward, Ray wasn't entirely sure if she could get out of the chamber and follow the tunnels back the way they had come. It was possible she could get lost and die down there without ever seeing the two suns again. It took an enormous amount of restraint to keep herself breathing normally. She forced herself to focus on the Enthai and their noises. Proof she wasn't alone. That maybe she *would* get out of here.

"Here, take," another Enthai said to her, its voice higher pitched than her escort's. Fur brushed against her hand, and something was pushed into her grasp. It was round, perhaps a cup. She wrapped both hands around it, finding it to indeed be no larger than a normal cup. The Enthai barked another order at her, guiding her hands up towards her face. "Drink."

With the creature's assistance, she raised the cup to her face and brought its rim to her lips. It tugged her hands upward, tilting the cup back slowly to control its liquid contents. All of her muscles were tense as she braced herself to get splashed or doused in... whatever it was. No distinct scent came from the cup. Perhaps it was just water. It had been quite some time since she had any. And if the Enthai hadn't killed her yet, it wasn't likely that they'd do it now. Not with a poisoned drink.

When the liquid within the cup sloshed against her mouth, she parted her lips and drank deeply. It had a distinctly floral taste—unexpected but certainly welcome—so she didn't hesitate to consume the entire contents in a matter of a few gulps. When she finished, the Enthai pulled the cup from her hands and walked away, and she was left panting and licking her lips.

Within a few moments, the creature reappeared and pressed another cup to her hands. It was a little easier lifting and drinking from this one. Its contents didn't taste or smell like much of anything either, which made it easy to finish off. She hadn't realized how thirsty she had been. Her stomach was suspiciously quiet, but she didn't want to dwell on that thought and hastily pushed it away. Whatever the Enthai were giving to her, it was refreshing and a marked improvement over what they had given her back in the village.

Ray's eyes watered, so she raised her hands to wipe away the tears. As she rubbed at her eyelids, light sparked and flashed behind the skin. When she lowered her hands, there was nothing but darkness. But after a moment, she could make out the rough edges of the others standing in the room. She jerked her head back and rubbed at her eyes again only to be met with the same scene, except the shadows were getting sharper, more well-defined. There were three Enthai in the room, all standing a short distance from her. They all wore similar coats made of fur and pelts, their hoods lowered. Their eyes shone like beacons amidst the darkness. Ray managed to squash the whimper in her throat, but her pulse quickened, nonetheless.

Predators in the dark. "What did you—?"

"One for nourishment. And one so you can walk on your own," one of the Enthai responded. It was the same one who had led Ray here; she recognized the lower timbre of its voice. "Enesse will lead. Follow her."

The creature on the far left growled quietly and skulked past Ray, heading toward the exit. *Enesse. These creatures have names? How strange.* Ray committed the name to memory, matching it with the lithe body that moved beside her. A female. Her snout was narrower than the other two, her fur tinged with more browns and grays around her eyes and mouth. Ray wondered what the others' names sounded like.

"Kohda, bring the other girl," the first Enthai barked at the third.

"Yes, Keitri."

Enesse, Kohda, and Keitri. Ray couldn't tell if the other two were male or female. When she turned back to face them, her breath caught in her throat as the two Enthai parted to reveal Princess Niamnh sitting on her knees.

"Niamnh!" Ray called out breathlessly, moving for the other girl.

The princess looked up from the ground and her jaw dropped. "Ray?" she responded, her voice cracking from disuse. She climbed to her feet and met Ray in the middle of the room, throwing her arms around her torso and hugging her tightly.

Ray's mind spun wildly as she grounded herself in Niamnh's embrace. *She's alive. She's here. She's... not mad at me?* "Are you okay?" Ray murmured into a tangle of white hair and furred collar.

For the first time she realized that they were still wearing their traveling gear—heavy coats, cloaks, gloves, boots. Niamnh still had her scarf wrapped around her neck. Ray squeezed her arms tighter around Niamnh, seeking out the princess's body through the many layers of clothes. The movement forced the air from Niamnh's lungs and she drew in a sharp, pained breath, but the princess made no move to withdraw from the embrace.

"I-I think so. Mostly, anyway," Niamnh whispered. "They've been giving me many potions... one potion let me see in this darkness."

"I got the same." Ray couldn't stop the smile from spreading across her face. She kept her head nestled against Niamnh's shoulder. "How's your head?"

"I'm okay. Sore, but okay."

From behind the princess, one of the Enthai let out a low growl.

"W-We should move," Niamnh said softly, pulling away from Ray's embrace.

An involuntary grumble slipped past Ray's lips, but she knew the princess was right. Neither of them wanted to make the Enthai angry, so they let go of one another and turned to the exit where Enesse was waiting. The other two Enthai shuffled up behind them, and they were off to traverse the tunnels once more.

Now that she could see in the dark, Ray took in every detail of the tunnels that she could. The ground was made of smooth stone with dust and pebbles blanketing the edges of the path. There was about an arm's length of space between her head and the roof of the tunnel. White and yellow shards of *something* were lodged in the stone walls, smoothed down so that they blended with the stone. No wonder she hadn't noticed them before. Now, though, the difference in color was so obvious she couldn't help but stare.

"What's in the walls?" she whispered. Her voice carried through the tunnels, and she winced at the volume.

"*Eikkis*." Kohda's low rumble sent shivers down Ray's spine.

"Bones of the dead," Keitri elaborated, voice quiet and full of... *sorrow*? "Pieces of the ones who cross Ekerrin's Guard." Ray wasn't familiar with what the "guard" was.

"Bones of Proma you've killed," Niamnh hissed under her breath. The accusation hung heavy over the party.

The Enthai, for their part, didn't react to the princess's words. Ray tensed, expecting one of the creatures to snap or lash out but no one did.

"We are guardians of Na'roc, little *rhiekka*," Enesse said with cold detachment. "We do what we must to keep Doshara from escaping."

Ray couldn't stop herself from glancing at Niamnh, watching for some indication that Daerion was inside her mind, simmering just below the surface. Though she could see the hatred and fear in Niamnh's glare, her gaze was her own. Ray wondered if the Enthai had given Niamnh some kind of potion to suppress the Doshara.

"Is that how your kind justified killing my brother?"

Keitri let out a quiet huff that sounded very much like a sigh. "The princeling was dead when we found his camp."

So, Prince Robyn did *die north of the Wall.* Ray frowned, her heart aching for Niamnh. *But the Enthai didn't kill him?*

"Lies," Niamnh breathed, the edge on her words slipping into another emotion Ray was entirely too familiar with—*denial.* "He went north with several armed men. *Good* men. They wouldn't have turned on their prince."

"Perhaps not when sound of mind," Keitri replied.

"What do you mean by that?!" Niamnh snapped. Ray tried reaching out for the princess's hand, but Niamnh pulled it away.

Kohda growled behind them, which Keitri answered with a breathless bark. The noises reminded Ray of two dogs sizing each other up and fighting over scraps of food. She understood they were communicating with one another, but that knowledge did little to calm her nerves. She felt like cornered prey, waiting for the feeding frenzy to begin.

Protector guide us.

"Do your guards not tell you what happens beyond Ekerrin's Guard?" Enesse asked, and Ray couldn't tell if the female was mocking them or genuinely asking the question.

"I beg your pardon?" Niamnh blurted, voicing Ray's own thoughts.

Enesse stopped and turned to the two Proma girls, black eyes flickering dangerously in the darkness. Ray's stomach lurched. Keitri slid by the girls to stand beside the female Enthai, looking them over with a critical gaze. He was searching for something.

"With the Dosharas," Enesse said, as if that was enough of an answer.

Does she mean this is where the Dosharas come from? Thoughts spun wildly in Ray's mind as she tried to piece everything together with what she'd been told growing up. No one in Auora truly knew where the Doshara came from, only that the vengeful spirits could jump into any body and drive the person to madness. As for Na'roc of North, all that was known about the land was the snow and the Enthai.

"How did you acquire yours, little *rhiekka*?" Kohda growled, placing his paws on Niamnh's shoulders. Ray took a step back from the two, letting out a startled gasp.

Niamnh steeled under the Enthai's touch. "Why don't you ask him?" she replied coolly.

Is she still defending him? Even after all of this? Something inside of Ray's mind ached at the thought, and she grew weary of the whiplash of emotions.

"All will be known by Mother Shade," Keitri said with an air of resigned finality, turning to continue down the tunnels. Kohda's grip turned into a gentle shove, pushing Niamnh forward.

Enesse approached Ray, but she gave the Enthai no opportunity to touch her as she followed after the others.

She heard Keitri's quiet bark speaking to Niamnh. "After speaking with Mother Shade, I can show you to the princeling's bones."

After several moments of silence, Niamnh's quiet voice carried down the tunnel, its venom faded. "I'd like that."

CHAPTER XIX: MUNNE

Passing through the barricade between the Market and Crafting Districts was easy enough. The men accepted Rhorek's letter with no question and allowed Munne and the others through. No doubt they had seen several other Elviri pass through as they aided Captain Munhart on his raid of the lower districts to smoke out the criminals who had caused all of the chaos and violence in the city. They didn't question who the other five people were who rode behind Munne, Araloth, and Mayrien. To their credit, Tethe's group behaved as inconspicuous as possible, eyes focused on Munne, backs straightened, and hoods drawn to cover their ears. They passed well enough for Elviri soldiers.

But I'm leaving my real soldiers behind, a dark part of Munne's mind whispered to her. *And instead I'm sneaking away, stealing from the dead, to what end?* She squeezed her eyes shut for a moment, forcing an image of Ely to surface in her mind. *To save myself from the* Ardashi'ik.

The barricade leading from the Crafting District to the Golden Path proved a little more difficult to pass through. The lead guard accepted Rhorek's letter easily enough, but his scrutinous gaze fell over Tethe and the others for several long moments.

"What's the status of the lower districts?" Munne asked, trying to draw his attention back to her.

"More smoke but less chaos," the guard replied without looking at her.

If I were staying, I'd teach this man a lesson in respect. She clenched her jaw, quelling the urge to swing her fist at him. "That's good to hear. Now, if you'll excuse us, we must make haste to Trent."

"Of course," the guard muttered, taking a few steps away from the party, his eyes still locked onto Tethe. Munne shot a look back at the caravanner, pleased to see that he stared ahead, not allowing the guard to distract him. "There's not much light down there. You'll want to take some torches."

"Gladly," came her curt response.

The lead guard gestured to a couple of men behind him, who rose to their feet and handed off their torches to Araloth and one of the caravanners. As soon as the guards started to step back to the barricade, Munne wasted no time in spurring Alathyl on, descending the road that wrapped around the city-island.

As they went lower into the city, Munne realized the guard was right. Smoke hung heavily over these lower districts, creating a haze over the road. The two torches only provided enough light for them to see the buildings flanking the road and nothing else. She listened carefully for any noises beyond the occasional coughing and their horses' hooves clopping along the stone road. There was some distant shouting, but it was muffled underneath the smoke.

Like traveling through a cave, Munne thought. Her vision darkened and her heart pounded in her chest. *Not those caves. Never those caves.*

"The stars are far away from us," Mayrien murmured, startling Munne and pulling her attention back to the city of Auora.

Munne snapped her head back to regard her friend. Mayrien had her head tilted up, looking toward the sky. In the flickering torchlight, Mayrien fought against the haze to keep her eyes open wide. Munne couldn't help but raise her chin as well, suddenly craving a glimpse of the stars for herself. In the Elviri lands it was typical for the stars to be obscured by trees, but out on the Hourglass Lakes, it was odd not to see them. Only the shape of the moon could be seen through the smoke, its light struggling to pierce it.

Would Nole hear us if we prayed to him now? The stars were often associated with Nole, the wayfaring god. The thought of being separated from her gods sent an uncomfortable shiver down Munne's spine. She knew it was a ridiculous notion, knew that neither clouds nor rain nor rooftops could prevent the gods from hearing them. But these were strange times, with stranger things to come.

"Once we're on the bridge, we'll be able to see them again," Munne replied quietly, eyes watering from the smoke.

They encountered no other living creature on the Golden Path. Munhart and his men must have used other means to get to their destinations, which made sense. Criminals wouldn't traverse such open ground like the main roads.

The downward-sloping road leveled out for a few strides and then sloped upward. Ahead was the gate to the city proper, which opened onto the road connecting the east and west bridges to the island. There were no true walls surrounding the city, just the waters of the Hourglass Lakes. As such, the gate to the city was simply a massive stone arch welcoming all into Auora. Carved into the stone were reliefs of ships, crowns, swords, and other imagery representing the Proma city-island. The arch reminded Munne of the entry arch into Elimere, though the arch stood much taller and was flanked by guard towers.

The guard towers were only half as tall as the arch itself, with beacons atop both so there was enough light to see who came and went from the city. The towers were connected to the bridges, preventing anyone from circumventing the gate and climbing directly onto the east or west roads. Any who wanted to avoid the front gate would have to leap off the island and into the icy waters below. Barricades had been hastily constructed, blocking over half of the road under the arch. Guards swarmed the area, some carrying torches while others carried shields and blades. Quiet conversations rippled across the force as they watched the city and the bridges. Looking up, several men were stationed around the beacons, short bows in hand.

As Munne and her party approached, several of the guards walked out to meet them. "Halt! Who goes there?" one of the guards called out, pointing his spear in their direction. A few men behind him took their places in between the barricades, preventing the party from riding onto the bridge.

Munne raised a hand, signaling for the party to stay put. She continued forward to meet the lead guard. "I am Munne Vere'cha, Warlord of the Elviri. I'm carrying a letter from Knight-General Rhorek Gondamire stating that we are allowed to leave Auora and travel to Trent."

The guard stood to her left, his spear angled toward her leg. No doubt his intention was to skewer her leg and drive his spear further into her horse's shoulder, preventing them from running if she made any attempt at passing him. Munne idly wondered if she could draw her short sword and cut the head of the spear off before he could make his move.

Something to practice, perhaps, but not needed here.

For a moment, the guard's gaze broke from her, dropping to look across where another two guards stood. One had a torch raised, casting her in its warm glow. The other wielded a sword and shield.

"The letter is in the satchel on my left hip," Munne said with a steady voice, leaving her hands on Alathyl's reins. "May I retrieve it?"

The spear bearer locked eyes with her again and nodded his head. Inhaling quietly through her nose, Munne reached down with her left hand and withdrew the second-to-last letter from the pouch. She extended it toward the guard on her left. Keeping his spear steady, he took the letter in his other hand. Another guard appeared behind him, torch raised high. He passed the letter along, repositioning his shield to cover his body once more.

The second guard looked closely at the seal before breaking it and unraveling the paper. He read its contents and then spoke, "The seal does belong to the Knight-General. She's allowed passage."

The first guard relaxed his arm and tapped the butt of the spear into the ground twice—a signal to the others to lower their weapons. "Thank you for your cooperation, my lady. Be careful of the lake breeze this evening; it's rather chilly."

Munne couldn't stop the chuckle from slipping past her lips. *What an odd thing to say, considering the circumstances. I suppose he's just trying to be friendly.* "Thank you."

She clicked her heels against Alathyl, and the horse started forward again, the others following closely behind. The guards cleared out from the barricades to allow them passage. At the bridge they turned left, east, towards Trent.

A cold breeze kicked up from the lake and blew all around them as they went, sending a shiver down Munne's spine. *The guard wasn't wrong. Winter is upon us.*

The bridge to Trent loomed in front of them, shrouded in darkness. As Munne's eyes adjusted to the open night, no longer hampered by smoke or city lights, she urged Alathyl into a brisk pace. She wanted to be within the walls of Trent as soon as possible, which would take a little over an hour. Under normal circumstances, torches would line either side of the bridge, guiding travelers to or from the island. However, with the city under lockdown, the Proma had stopped patrolling the bridge on horseback. Instead, they were sailing on the lakes, small lamps and torches bobbing in the distance. As such, the torches on the bridges remained unlit.

Ahead the lights of Trent beckoned to them like a lantern in the dark. Glancing north and south, there was nothing but the lakes. The waters were calm that night, lapping gently at the stone bridge. Above was the night sky, filled with cold light from hundreds of stars. Yet as she gazed upon them, Munne felt further away from her gods than ever before. The sight of the heavens did nothing to quell the growing storm within her mind.

How could I let these Proma dress themselves in my dead comrades' clothes? What kind of Warlord am I? What kind of Se'vi *will I become?* She grimaced, tightening her grip on Alathyl's reins. *Perhaps the other nobles are right, and I'm not worthy enough to take my father's throne. What will become of the Hunting Throne? The line has never been severed. I would be the one to end it all...*

Munne's eyes stung, and she felt a tear spill down her cheek. She chose to let the wetness dry on her skin rather than raise her arm to wipe it away.

Her mental beratement continued over the next hour, but she managed to swallow her sadness and maintain a stoic exterior. She tore herself down, questioning every decision she had made since she left Elimere—and a few decisions from before that.

At least if I free myself from these nightmares and return home, I won't be a danger to my people. But could I live with the guilt of knowing what I did to cure myself? All of the lives I would've forfeited in the war with the Provira, the people I wouldn't have defended? They'd never let me become Se'vi. *They won't let me continue serving as Warlord. I'll become an outcast.*

Maybe it would be better to end it all, as Malion had. Somewhere far away, where the only lives at risk would be my own and my triple.

Torches could be seen in the distance. The end of the bridge was in sight. Munne breathed in deeply and said to the others, "Trent is up ahead."

"What are your plans once we're within the city?" Tethe asked.

"You and your company go rest for the night. We'll meet on the southern road just before dawn," Munne responded, weariness creeping into her voice.

There were no further replies from the others as the shape of the eastern gate appeared from the gloom. Surrounding the bridge was another outpost similar to the one on the western edge of the lakes. Beyond that was the city of Trent. A faint glow outlined the city's walls and buildings.

A pair of guards approached the party on horseback, torches raised high. "Who goes there?" one of the guards called out.

"Munne Vere'cha, Warlord of the Elviri, traveling to Trent," Munne responded, her voice gravelly and laden with exhaustion. She fished Rhorek's last sealed letter from her satchel and extended it toward the left guard as they neared. He rode alongside her and took the piece of paper, unraveling it with one hand. After digesting the words on the paper, he looked back up at her and bowed his head.

"Thank you, my lady. I didn't realize the Elviri had come to assist the city. Truth be told, we're still in the dark about what's going on," the guard said quietly, tucking the letter into his tunic. "We know the city is under lockdown and why, but we don't know much else."

"Knight-General Gondamire and Captain Munhart are doing their best to ensure the city is safe for its citizens again," Munne replied, offering a sliver of kindness. "My men and women from Ferilin are at their side, and Auora's gate should be open again soon."

"You must have important business to attend to if you're allowed passage during the lockdown," the guard said, the realization hitting him abruptly. "Apologies, my lady. We won't keep you any further."

"Thank you," Munne replied, shifting her focus to the road before her. As soon as the guards backed away from her, Munne spurred Alathyl onward, eager to be off the water and within the walls of Trent.

Trent's western wall bumped up against the watch-post at the bridge. Several guards paced around at the city entrance, but none moved to stop Munne and her companions as they passed by. The city of Trent was more lavish than Ferilin and even rivaled the higher districts in Auora. Musicians, artists, and other creative minds flocked to Trent to make lives for themselves, some carrying on to the city-island to mingle with the nobles and the royal family. The building styles mimicked Auora's with buildings standing five, six, or even seven floors high. The buildings were made from timber rather than stone, courtesy of trade agreements with the Imalarii. The number of theaters, music halls, and studios nearly rivaled those in Lithalyon. The war with the Provira hadn't affected Trent the same way it had with the other major cities in Promthus.

They passed several inns and taverns, music and laughter mingling in the air. Some of the music even sounded pleasant. Munne turned to face the others as they passed through an open square, speaking loud enough for Tethe and his companions to hear, "This is where we'll split ways for the night. I'll see you all again before dawn on the southern road. Remember your station." Her last remark was pointed, her gaze drifting across their clothing.

Tethe bowed his head and offered a small salute. "Of course, my lady." He led his companions toward one of the inns along the edge of the city square.

Munne turned to Mayrien and Araloth, nodding to the road on the opposite side of the square. "Let's get to the outpost. We need rest."

"Are you not worried about one of them following us?" Araloth asked quietly, not even bothering to hide her disdain and suspicion.

"Why would they?" Munne snapped, exhaustion seeping through her bones. She wanted to be done with the day, to collapse into a bed, and slip into unconsciousness. If she was lucky, she may even get some rest. *Traitors don't get lucky, though.*

"Even if they do, the sentries will alert us," Mayrien reasoned to try to diffuse the tension between the two women. "Come, let's be away."

The three Elviri continued on through the streets of Trent, mindful of their surroundings. The city was lively, much like Auora had been prior to the lockdown. Despite the late hour, many taverns were still full of patrons who drank and sang to one another. Several groups spilled out onto the streets, laughing and pointing at each other. Munne averted her eyes at more than a few alleyways where couples were making the most of their revelry.

Thank the gods for the outpost. I don't think I'd be able to sleep in this city even if I wanted to. But then Munne was hit with a pang of sadness. The people were living their lives, enjoying what they had while they could. Although they celebrated it differently from the Elviri, it was a celebration, nonetheless.

Will the Elviri celebrate like this if I manage to find an end to the war? Not if they learn of what I did to end it. The thought left her squirming in her saddle, her stomach clenching tightly on itself.

They passed silently through the central part of Trent and continued on to the southern gate. The main road took them through a few marketplaces, all silent and still for the evening. Empty wooden stalls lined the roads, with no indication of what goods were sold here during the day. No doubt merchants and craftsmen would return in the morning to dress up the stalls and fill them with goods both baked and crafted. If it had been any other kind of trip, Munne would've ensured that she had time the following morning to walk the rows of stalls. Alas, she had no time for such luxuries.

I have to get to Kherizhan.

The Elviri outpost stood just beyond the southern wall of Trent. The war hadn't impacted the eastern shores of the Hourglass Lakes the same as it had in the south and west. As a result, the outpost had far fewer soldiers inhabiting it. The outpost itself consisted of three large buildings tucked behind a tall wooden wall with three guard towers stationed along the eastern, southern, and western edges.

As Munne, Araloth, and Mayrien approached the entrance to the outpost along the eastern wall, they heard a sharp whistle from up above. The sentry in the guard tower had spotted them. "This outpost is for Elviri only. Turn back strangers!"

Munne cast a glance at Mayrien, silently requesting she deal with this instead. Munne wanted nothing more than to lay down and forget the rest of the world for a few hours, so she could be alone with her thoughts.

Mayrien picked up on the subtle signal and raised a hand in greeting. "At ease, *etilith*, we're no strangers."

The sentry lowered their bow and stared at the trio, clearly trying to put together who they were. The gate to the outpost groaned and swung inward, revealing another trio of Elviri wielding swords and torches. Even in her exhaustion, Munne appreciated the discipline of her people and their abundance of caution. Even if it was currently preventing her from finding a private room and locking the door behind her.

"It's Lady Vere'cha and her triple," one of the Elviri whispered, sending a rippling murmur through the group. He cleared his throat, raising his torch higher so their faces were caught in the light. "At ease and let them in!"

The trio moved back, and the gate swung open wider, giving Munne and her companions enough space to lead their horses inside. The gate shut behind them, and the outpost buzzed with quiet excitement.

"We weren't expecting you, my lady," said the same man, holding his torch aloft as Munne dismounted from Alathyl and handed the reins to the woman standing at her side. "If we had known, we'd have—"

Munne held her hand up to cut him off. "It's alright, we're only here until dawn. We've important business to attend to in the east," she told him.

It wasn't a lie, which was the only thing keeping the knot in her throat from squeezing tighter and cutting off her breath. *What does it matter if I tell the truth or lie at this point? The trust has already been broken with my father and with the soldiers stationed in southern Promthus.*

"Of course, my lady. How can we be of assistance?" he continued, following her as she made her way to the lodging cabin. It stood three stories tall, the top floor reserved for the current commanding triple and guest chambers for any other high-ranking officers that may cross through the outpost. Munne intended to claim one of the rooms for herself with walls and a door separating her from the others.

"Nothing is needed from you or the others. We're just here to rest and then continue onward in the morning." The man's silence spoke volumes to her. *They just want to help their Warlord. They've put their trust in me because they don't know any better. They don't know what I've done to get here, or how I will abandon them at dawn. Should I tell this man and the others? Should I let them continue believing in my falsehoods?*

Munne pushed her way inside the lodging cabin and climbed the stairs as quickly and quietly as she could. She didn't want to wake any of the other soldiers currently in their beds. The fewer people who saw her and spoke to her, the better.

Before Munne could open the door to her private chamber, Mayrien grabbed hold of her wrist. Munne stopped and inhaled deeply before turning to her companions.

"We ride out again at dawn?" Mayrien murmured.

"Yes, as we've told the caravanners and these soldiers," Munne responded, her voice low and raspy. The events of the day weighed heavily upon her, pushing the air from her lungs and the words from her mouth. She kept her gaze locked on Mayrien, not wanting to look at Araloth and see the inevitable frustrated disappointment on the elder Elviri's face.

I'll have days, if not weeks, to see that look as we travel to Kherizhan. I don't need to see it tonight.

"Alright. We'll be ready at first light," said Mayrien as she squeezed Munne's wrist gently. "Sleep well, Vere'cha."

"You as well, both of you." Munne's eyes darted across Araloth's features for a fleeting moment, catching a hint of rage and some other emotion in her green eyes. Denying herself a moment to consider those emotions, Munne pulled away from Mayrien's grasp and retreated into the private chamber, shutting the door behind her.

For the first time, the shadows surrounding the forest clearing felt more welcoming than the clearing itself. A shiver coursed through Munne's body as she paced in a circle, eyes drawn to the darkness. She thought she could see twisting paths hidden within the boughs of the forest, leading to other strange places. Fingernails dug into palms as she squeezed her hands tightly at her sides. The pinching brought her a small crumb of comfort. She deserved the pain, deserved the darkness and the shadows, she needed only step beyond the clearing and—

"You reached out for me?" Ely's voice flooded the clearing, driving the darkness back further into the trees.

Munne spun on him, fist raised and swinging before she could register his exact shape or presence. Ely caught her hand in his, and her whole body was flooded with searing heat. It burned away the shadows that had crept across her vision, exposing her thoughts and fears so plainly that she shivered and staggered under the weight of her own guilt.

She blinked rapidly, trying to clear her gaze so she could see Ely clearly. She realized with horror that had her aim been true, and if he hadn't stopped her, her fist would have collided with his jaw. He caught her hand a hair's breadth from his face, the back of his own hand no doubt brushing against his nose. His gloves were gone. His hands matched his face, pallid with a twinge of green.

Eyes downcast, she tried to sputter out an apology, "I-I'm sorry, I—"

"You've nothing to apologize for," Ely murmured, lowering their hands but not letting hers go. "I regret that I couldn't come to your aid sooner…"

She blinked again, registering the first words he had spoken to her. "'You reached out to me'," she echoed, looking up at his face, his pale green orbs burning into hers. "What do you mean? I-I don't remember calling for you."

His lips pressed tightly together for a moment before he responded, "You didn't summon me by name, but I could feel your pain today while you were awake. But I can't reach you in the waking world."

My pain. My shame. My series of false steps and errors. She parted her lips to respond but instead came a choked sob. Her vision blurred once again as hot tears welled up and spilled down her cheeks.

"I'm here now, though, and I can help. I can—" Ely stopped himself, instead choosing to take action. He reached out and took Munne's other hand in his, squeezing gently.

Warmth spread rapidly from her fingertips to her toes, to the tips of her ears. Her eyes fluttered closed, and she wanted nothing more than to melt into his touch.

But I don't deserve this comfort. I deserve what lies out there, waiting, in the darkness—

"Munne." Ely's voice nudged through her thoughts, and she felt his breath near her ear. "Clear your mind of these doubts. They'll only bring you harm."

Her lip quivered and she shut her eyes tighter. "I've already brought harm to my people by abandoning them to travel east. A Warlord should share in her soldiers' misery."

"You haven't abandoned them, you're traveling to save them," Ely argued, and she felt another wave of warmth spread across her skin. "What you do in Kherizhan will save more lives than if you remained to fight against the Provira."

"I've defiled the dead and lied to the living," she pressed on, gritting her teeth and stubbornly ignoring his words. "I've broken my vows as Warlord, and I'll never be welcome home again. The gods don't even spare me a glance. I've failed my people."

"Heroes must make difficult choices."

"I'm no hero," Munne spat, finally opening her eyes to glare at Ely. "I'm a woman doomed to either die by my own hand, or by the hands of my enemies, in a land far away from my people."

Warmth enveloped her once again. She blinked and her head was leaning against Ely's chest. The rough fabric of his robe itched against her cheek, but she found the touch soothing. Grounding. His arms were wrapped around her, one hand pressed against her back, the other cradling the back of her head.

Her words echoed in her mind: *I'm no hero.*

As the dark thoughts swirled violently in her head, she could feel Ely reaching through to her. "*You are. You will be. You always have been. Just like your goddess Ceyo was during her lifetime.*"

Just like Ceyo. What a daunting and comforting thought. Trembling hands rose and rested lightly against his back. Munne had only ever felt his hands before. Though he wore a thick robe, she could feel the heat from his skin radiating through the fabric. Comforting. *That* was the touch she'd been craving earlier in the night, when her friends had tried comforting her at the Night Lantern. She closed her eyes again and felt all of her defenses crumbling underneath Ely's touch. She openly wept, digging her fingers into his back, clinging onto him like an anchor.

CHAPTER XX: SETH

When Seth awoke the next morning, Lisanthir was floating about his room, unpacking the chest they had brought from Yiradia. He rolled over in his bed to watch the Elviri work, admiring the quiet domesticity of it all. The black steward's robes stood out among the warm brown stone walls and floors, his veil discarded somewhere within the room. Lisanthir currently stood in front of a beautiful wooden armoire, organizing the clothes within. Once he was content, he turned and crossed over to a low table that the chest had been set upon. Seth couldn't see inside of it, so he couldn't gauge how much there was left to put away.

"I was wondering how long you would sleep for," Lisanthir murmured playfully, casting a quick glance at Seth as he passed by the foot of the bed. He tucked a loose strand of black hair behind his ear.

"Good morning," Seth replied, stretching his arms over his head.

He pulled himself into a sitting position, leaning back against the stone headboard. Like in Yiradia, the bed was built from stone and had four pillars reaching to the ceiling. Also like in Yiradia, the pillars of Seth's bed were bare, but he was sure his sister's pillars had silks wrapped around them. The blankets were more comfortable in Iszairi, and the room was well insulated against the cold outside. There were no windows or exits to the outside, and the only light sources were a couple of sconces on the wall, the flames burning brightly.

"How late is it?" Seth asked.

"It's almost midday. Some of the other stewards left fruits and baked goods for you in the dining chamber." Lisanthir plucked a tunic out of the chest and shook it out before returning to the armoire.

Seth frowned. He hadn't intended to sleep for so long; he had gone to bed shortly after dinner with Octavia the previous night. "Is it safe for you to not be wearing your veil?"

Lisanthir hung the tunic up in the armoire then turned to Seth, a small grin on his face. "Your sister's outside. She'll stop anyone coming in long enough for me to put the veil back on."

Seth laughed, and it felt *good*. "And not that I'm ungrateful for your presence, but are there any other stewards here?" He was used to always having two shadows, even if there were doors separating them from him.

"No, the stewards follow different orders here," Lisanthir said, a confused look passing over his features. "Is this not what you're accustomed to in Iszairi?"

The smile faded from Seth's face and his brow furrowed. "What orders were you given?"

Lisanthir sat down on the edge of the bed. "Taszo told me that I would be your, what's the word..." The Elviri spoke a few words, first in what Seth could only assume was his native tongue, then he said something in the Asaszi language that he *did* recognize—*kiipyrss*.

"They assigned you to be my live-in caretaker?"

Lisanthir nodded, reaching for Seth's hand. Seth couldn't believe their luck. Out of all the stewards and servants within Iszairi, *Lisanthir* would be the one by Seth's side day and night. A wave of relief came crashing down around him. He took Lisanthir's hand and squeezed it tightly.

Maybe we do *stand a chance at escaping,* Seth thought.

Not long after, Seth pulled himself out of bed and changed out of his sleep clothes. He and Lisanthir left his bedroom and spent some time with Octavia, all three grazing from the spread of sliced fruit and pastries. They kept their conversations lighthearted, discussing things such as the difference in food between the two cities and the little luxuries Octavia had found in their suite.

"Not much has changed since I was here two summers ago," Octavia said with a lingering smile. "I'd like to visit the coliseum one more time, I think."

Lisanthir perked up at the mention of the coliseum, which Seth found curious. "You want to see the coliseum?"

The Elviri nodded. "The history of this place, the things these stones have seen...I-I'm sorry, I understand this place doesn't hold the best memories for you two, and I understand we need to leave as soon as possible, but—"

"But this place is important to you," Seth blurted out, remembering the life Lisanthir lived back in Lithalyon. He had studied the Eldest Days and the wars between the Elviri and Asaszi in depth. The Elviri was no doubt overwhelmed with the realization that he was walking around in the same place his gods had walked thousands of years ago. Seth wondered if Lisanthir had ever dreamed of finding the place.

Or if he ever could've imagined coming here under such dire circumstances.

"Yes." Lisanthir's eyes found his, and in that green gaze, Seth saw the depth of the Elviri's yearning.

Did I have this same sense of wonder when I entered Lithalyon? Explored their libraries, saw Aelrindel? Of course he did. Seth was overwhelmed with the urge to kiss Lisanthir.

Octavia cleared her throat, shifting the attention of the room to her. Seth felt a blush creep across his face as his sister spoke. "Perhaps we can figure something out. But for now, the balcony has an extraordinary view of the coliseum, and the city beyond it."

Seth yanked on the wheels of his chair and headed out of the dining chamber, beckoning for the other two to follow. "Come on, we can go sit out there at the very least."

"You two go ahead," Octavia said as she stood. "I'm going to wander around and get familiar with the place again."

"Be safe." Seth brushed his hand against her arm as she moved past him.

"You do the same," Octavia called out over shoulder, and then she was gone.

Lisanthir joined Seth, and the two moved further into the siblings' suite, passing the door back to Seth's bedchamber and entering the study. The room was sparsely furnished, containing only a single bookcase, a pair of comfortable-looking couches, and a table in between them. To their right was the threshold leading out onto the balcony. The room was colder than the rest of the suite, and Seth couldn't stop a mild shiver from running through his body. The coliseum could be seen even from the room, its beige stones practically glowing underneath the suns' light.

Lisanthir's stride grew as he emerged from the study onto the balcony, leaving Seth behind inside. His hands gripped the railing, an audible gasp escaping him. "It's beautiful."

Seth only had eyes for Lisanthir, though. The way the sun warmed his pale skin, a faint breeze rustling his black hair... Seth smiled warmly. *Yes, you are.* He took his place beside the Elviri, letting his hands rest in his lap.

"History was made here. The Elviri overthrew their captors *here*. And it's in such pristine condition, as if no time has passed..." Lisanthir's face lit up as he pointed to something in the distance. "The pyramid across the way, that houses one of the academies, does it not?"

Seth tore his eyes off of his Elviri to follow his gesture. There were several pyramids flanking the coliseum, but none stood taller than the *Tserdanii*. Two of the smaller pyramids indeed housed the academies, while others served as homes for the Asaszi courtiers that served in Osza's court. Seth had never been inside any of the other pyramids. He had been too young the last time he visited, and his father had kept the family sequestered away within his suite the entire time.

The particular pyramid Lisanthir was pointing to was built out of red stone, its color contrasting with its surroundings. If Seth remembered correctly, the academy libraries and classrooms were within that pyramid. Beside it was a pyramid of similar height, built from gray stone, where the living quarters for the students were housed.

"The largest library in Moonyswyn is in there," Seth murmured.

"How does it compare to the Great Library back home?" Lisanthir replied, tilting his head so he could gaze upon Seth.

Back home. Seth's response caught in his throat. *Our home.* After a moment he managed to force out, "I'm not sure. I haven't been inside before."

Lisanthir placed a gloved hand on Seth's cheek and stroked it fondly. "Perhaps we can find a way. You found a way into Lithalyon, after all." The Elviri offered him a smile, and he couldn't help but return the gesture, leaning into his touch.

"What else in the city do you want to see?" Seth asked, gently guiding the conversation in a different direction away from the memories of Szatisi's potion and his legs magically restored. He took Lisanthir's hand and lowered it to his lap, clasping it between his two hands.

Lisanthir looked out at the city again. "The coliseum, of course. And if the Asaszi keep any relics anywhere, I'd be interested in seeing them, if they let us. I also remember reading tales of underground passages connecting the coliseum to other structures within the city. Perhaps even this pyramid."

Seth knew of the underground passages, though he hadn't traversed them. He couldn't recall if Octavia had been allowed to either, but it might be worth mentioning to her later, when she returned to their suite. As for the relics... "I believe they keep their relics inside of the red pyramid."

"Oh," Lisanthir muttered, his smile fading away. "Well, we should be focusing on our escape first and foremost. Being here means nothing if I can't share my knowledge with others back home."

Their conversation faded away to nothing, but the sounds of the city could still be heard in the distance. They eventually returned inside, Lisanthir donning his veil now that Octavia was gone and couldn't give warning if someone came to visit. Seth perused the bookshelf and plucked a volume he had read often as a child—a study of the flora and fauna of Moonyswyn. He brought the book out into the center room of the suite and positioned his chair beside the other chairs.

Lisanthir bent over and pushed the veil aside, kissing the top of Seth's head. "I need to finish unpacking your belongings. Let me know if someone stops by, or when dinner is brought up."

"Of course." Seth threw a smile over his shoulder before returning to his book.

In the late afternoon, a knock at the door disturbed Seth from his reading. He let out a sigh and called out, "Enter!" *Hopefully, Lis heard me.*

The door to the suite opened and Taszo entered, his blue scales glittering in the candlelight. He wore a black tunic and trousers with a golden silk robe layered on top. Last night Seth assumed Taszo was one of the servants working in Iszairi, but based on his attire, he must have a higher rank. Or perhaps he's one of Osza's courtiers. If that was the case, Seth had several questions as to what business the Asaszi had with visiting him, unless he was looking for Octavia...

"Greetingsss Lord Kharisss," Taszo said warmly, offering a respectful bow to Seth.

"Hello Taszo. Are you looking for my sister?" Seth asked, unable to completely mask the wariness in his voice.

"Not today," the Asaszi replied and clasped his hands behind his back. "Queen Osza hasss sssummoned you to her chambersss. I am here to essscort you to her."

Under Taszo's golden gaze, Seth froze with fear. *What does Osza want with me?* He racked his mind trying to recall the past few days, what mistakes he or Octavia may have made, and what word could have possibly gotten back to the Asaszi queen. *I thought we had been careful with our planning and what we said around everyone else. Did someone overhear us talk about escaping? Does Osza know I ran away to Lithalyon?* His chest tightened painfully, his heart pounding against its cage.

Taszo raised his eyes from Seth and said, "Good. Come, bring Lord Kharisss along."

Seth's chair began moving forward, and that movement broke him free from his mental stupor. He snapped his head back and saw Lisanthir holding onto the handles of his chair, pushing him toward the door. Relief and fear warred within him—he was thankful for Lisanthir taking action to keep Taszo from asking questions but afraid of what awaited them in the queen's nest.

Seth wanted to hold onto Lisanthir's hand and draw strength from the Elviri, but he knew he couldn't. They followed Taszo without a sound, climbing higher within the *Tserdanii*. Osza's chambers took up the top three floors of the pyramid. With each passing floor, the pit in Seth's stomach grew. Thank the gods for Lisanthir pushing his chair. If Seth had to tug on the wheels himself, he didn't think he could do it. He wouldn't have been strong enough to pull his weight up over and over. He would've let go and fallen down the center of the pyramid.

"Our queen wissshes to ssspeak to you of your father'sss work," Taszo murmured as they neared the first floor of Osza's suite.

That brought Seth some relief, but he was still confused as to what Osza would want to talk to *him* about. He hadn't worked directly with his father in several years. He was just an observer, a shadow on the wall.

The doors to Osza's suite loomed ahead, flanked on either side by Asaszi soldiers brandishing curved swords and shields. Images of dragons, wyrms, and snakes had been carved into the beige stone, all circling around a serpent devouring two suns.

"*You* can wait here. I will take Lord Kharisss the ressst of the way," Taszo hissed to Lisanthir, holding up a hand to stop them.

The Asaszi's orders caught both of them off guard. Seth jerked forward in his chair as Lisanthir stopped abruptly to avoid colliding with Taszo. Without waiting for the Elviri to move out of the way, Taszo grabbed onto the handles and pushed Seth away. Seth wanted to look over his shoulder at Lisanthir or offer some kind of reassurance that he'd be okay, but he couldn't do either. He couldn't show any kind of weakness in front of the Asaszi, and he couldn't let them know about his *ebilin*. His hands twisted into the fabric of his tunic, the only kind of control he had at that moment.

One of the soldiers hooked the handle of his sword onto his belt, then pulled the stone door open. If he weren't paralyzed with dread, Seth would have appreciated the beauty and antiquity of Osza's suite. Murals covered the walls, depicting people and scenes from history. Seth recognized none of the Asaszi, but he could assume that they were previous rulers. Several relics were on display within the halls as well, ranging from simple pottery to intricate jewelry.

One thought managed to squeeze its way in between the other fears circling in his head. *Lisanthir would have loved to see this.*

Beyond the entryway was a foyer with a staircase leading into the very peak of the pyramid, as well as multiple thresholds leading to other rooms. The pit in his stomach grew as he considered the stairs and where exactly Osza planned on meeting him. He hoped it was on the current floor, and that he wouldn't have to ascend those stairs.

Mercifully, Taszo pushed Seth through the threshold beyond the stairs into a room filled with plush pillows and chaises. Arches on the opposite wall let out onto a large balcony, the suns' fading light bathing the room in a golden glow.

"My queen, I've brought Lord Kharisss," Taszo called out, coming to a stop in the middle of the room. Seth flexed his grip on his tunic, searching the room for the Asaszi queen. He didn't see her among the pillows, but movement on the balcony caught his eye.

"Thank you, Taszo," Osza's raspy voice came from outside. Her arm was extended out from a stone bench with a high back. "Bring him to the balcony."

His wheelchair began moving again toward Osza. Outside the air was cold, but the direct sunslight made it bearable. More chairs and benches filled the balcony, all facing toward the city. The *Tserdanii* stood taller than any other building in Iszairi, even taller than the trees surrounding the city, and as a result, the city and the forest could be seen from the balcony. Beige, brown, and red stones filled the skyline with the forest's dark green treetops serving as a border. Torches were being lit down below, bathing the buildings in golden light. To the right was the coliseum, its round shape dominating the view. It was a breathtaking sight, one fit for a king or queen.

"You may leave usss, Taszo," Osza ordered from her seat.

She lounged against a stone chaise, her legs outstretched on the bench. As Seth looked upon the queen, he felt his cheeks flush with shame as he realized she was wearing hardly any clothing. Her black hair was draped over her shoulders, covering the gentle curves of her chest. Secured around her waist was a golden chain belt with a long piece of black fabric hanging down the center of her hips, covering the space between her legs. Though Seth knew Asaszi anatomy was different from his own, he couldn't help but avert his eyes, which drew out a light chuckle from Osza that sounded more like a hiss than a laugh.

"Yesss, my queen," Taszo murmured, bowing to her before returning inside.

Seth watched him go until he disappeared from view, and even after the Asaszi was gone, he didn't let his gaze return to the Asaszi queen, which she noticed. "You would not look upon your queen?"

Seth tried to swallow around the knot that had formed in his throat. "A-Apologies, Queen Osza, I-I just wasn't expecting…"

"Look upon the sunsss," she said quietly, and he gladly twisted his head up toward the sky to watch the two suns as they descended below the tree line. "Even in thisss unusssual cold, sunsssdown isss the perfect time to warm my scalesss."

"Of course," came his reply. *What am I supposed to say to her?* He saw her moving around out of the corner of his eye.

"I can hear how fassst your heart isss beating." Osza's voice was very low and very close to his ear. Seth started to turn his head back toward her, but stopped when he felt her hand touch his shoulder. It was just a graze of her fingertips, but underneath that touch he felt himself turned to stone. If it weren't for the beating of his own heart, he might have believed he had died. "Tell me, *Ssseth*, how are you enjoying Iszairi ssso far?"

He swallowed again, painfully, then parted his lips to mutter, "I-It's been… pleasant enough." He cursed himself for such a terrible response, but he didn't know what else to say, how else to lie.

Osza touched his other shoulder as she crossed behind him, digging her nails into his tunic for a brief moment. "Are you not enjoying having your pet ssso clossse to you?"

Seth's eyes widened. *She knows about Lisanthir.* His heart threatened to pound and break out of his chest.

Before he had the chance to control his facial expression, Osza swooped down in front of him, kneeling on the ground in front of his wheelchair and placing her hands on his thighs. His body jolted upright, the chair rolling back ever so slightly, but the Asaszi followed it.

Gods, he's downstairs with those guards. They might've already killed him. Oh, gods, what have I done?

Osza's golden eyes were wide, the corners of her mouth curled upward in a devious grin. She drank in his reaction, savoring his fear. She dug her nails into his thighs, holding him in place. When she spoke, her voice was warm and almost playful. "Fear not, *py'tsera*, he ssstill livesss. Royalty, like *usss*, are allowed our play thingsss."

Seth's dread turned to confusion, and it must have shown on his face because Osza pressed even closer, one hand trailing up his stomach and onto his chest. Gooseflesh spread across his neck and arms. His body flushed with heat under her touch, but his mind howled that it was all wrong. "I—"

"It *isss* normal, you know, to *crave* your other half..." Something changed in Osza's voice. Her gaze dropped from Seth's eyes to his chest where she watched as she flexed her hand, stretching her fingers out then curling them in.

Seth wanted to scream and run. Or try to, anyway. *How did she find out about Lisanthir? About how I feel about him? What does this creature know of love?*

"The Asaszi crave it, too, dessspite all of the warsss and sssuffering," Osza continued. "It isss curiousss, isss it not, how we all rely on the Elviri. Come from the Elviri. Dessspite their flawsss and weaknessses." She dug her nails into his tunic, a dull pain spreading through his chest underneath her touch.

What's she speaking of? His head throbbed painfully, his body tense and aching. He tried to focus on her words and make sense of it all, but he couldn't get past how heavy his tongue was in his mouth, nor the taste of bile rising up his throat. "Wh-what are you going to do to him?" Seth asked, his voice nearly shattering under its own weight.

Osza flicked her eyes up, meeting his once more. Whatever strange feeling had caught her, it was gone now, leaving only a predatory playfulness behind. "Nothing at all, *Ssseth*. He isss yoursss, asss befitting a *py'tsera* of Pyredessi."

Pyredessi. The name of the Asaszi lands from the Eldest Days, from before the creation of the Proma. When the Asaszi had dominion over Daaria. *That's what Osza seeks from this war with the Elviri and Proma. Dominion. But does she know how badly we're losing? That Pyredessi is nothing but a land lost to history?*

"Even a *py'tsera* who sssteals from hisss High Priessstess." Osza's nails pressed down against his chest. The playfulness was gone from her voice, leaving only a threatening hiss. "But the *py'tsera* isss fortunate that hisss queen undersssstands the theft wasss out of eagernessss, and not *ssspite*."

Seth froze, his mind reeling from her accusation. From the truth of it all—from Lisanthir's presence in Iszairi to the elixir theft. The snake had him cornered and now he would face his punishment. *We've been so careful... How did it come to this?*

"Szatisi isss preparing you a new elixir, my *py'tsera*. And we pray that thisss one will have more *permanent* resultsss." Osza removed her hand from Seth's chest and raised it to his cheek. "We have a bright future together, *Ssseth*. While you wait on the elixir, take time to explore Iszairi. It *isss* your new home, after all. I give you the freedom to explore anywhere you desssire." The Asaszi queen rose to her feet, letting her nails drag along Seth's cheek before slipping away.

She's sparing us. She's not going to kill Lisanthir. The dread in his stomach shrank, broke into smaller pieces, underneath the sudden relief from Osza's words. *He's safe.* He bowed his head to the Asaszi queen, trying to remember the right thing to say. "Th-thank you, Queen Osza—"

"It isss under my mercy that your pet livesss. But I am not the only ruler you mussst abide by," Osza said, her tone darkening. "Your father doesss not know about your pet. If he did, I would imagine it wouldn't end well for the Elviri."

There's her threat, and her unspoken offer. I abide by Osza's will, and she keeps Father from discovering Lisanthir's true identity.

Seth cast his gaze up to the Asaszi queen's face, then down again at her feet. The two suns had dipped below the tree line, and the shadows grew longer, darker. The balcony became cold, and he had to suppress a shiver. He tried to keep the fear and disappointment out of his voice but shreds of it slipped through. "I understand, Queen Osza. What would you ask of me?"

"For now, nothing. Enjoy your time in Iszairi. I will call upon you again *sssoon*. You are disssmissed." Osza turned away from him and walked to the edge of the balcony, looking out over her city.

Seth wasted no time tugging his wheels and returning to the inside of the pyramid. As he passed into the foyer, Taszo emerged from one of the other rooms within Osza's suite. He didn't touch Seth's chair, but he did follow closely behind and stepped out to push open the great stone doors as Seth left.

Outside, Lisanthir waited off to the side, perfectly at ease as a steward or soldier would stand. When Seth and Taszo emerged, Lisanthir waited for Seth to approach him before moving behind and taking hold of the chair's handles.

Taszo stayed in the doorway, nodding his head politely to Seth. "Good-night, Lord Kharisss."

Seth managed to return the gesture as Lisanthir pushed his chair away, and they descended the pyramid to their suite.

This is bad. Bad. Who's been watching us? How do they know?

Octavia was waiting for them when they returned to their chambers. As soon as Seth and Lisanthir entered the suite, Seth let out an enormous exhale, and his hands shook.

"Seth, what's wrong?" Octavia asked, rising to her feet and rushing to his side.

Lisanthir closed the door behind them and fell to the other side of Seth's chair, ripping his veil from his face. "*Ebilin*? What did that snake say to you?"

"What snake?" Octavia pressed, concern painted all across her face.

"Osza," Lisanthir replied.

Octavia's eyes widened ever so slightly, then she turned back to her brother and grabbed hold of his left hand. "Osza summoned you?"

Seth nodded weakly, raising his free hand to his face and covering his mouth. His breath was warm against his fingertips. "She knows."

"What does she know?" Tav prodded.

His stomach churned and he thought he might be sick. "About Lisanthir. And the potion."

Octavia's grip on Seth's hand tightened so badly, he thought his bones might snap.

"We were so careful," Lisanthir whispered.

Seth winced as Octavia flexed her hand again. She let out an angry growl. "It was the stewards. I should've known better, I shouldn't have—" Tav jumped to her feet, letting go of Seth's hand and storming off.

"Tav?" Seth called after her. He started to maneuver his chair around the furniture and follow her, but Lisanthir stood in his way. "Lis, move, please—"

"What did Osza say to you? Are we in danger?" Lisanthir's words tumbled from his lips.

Seth's gaze shifted from the doorway Octavia disappeared through to Lisanthir crouching down in front of his chair, his green eyes wide with fear.

Seth took the Elviri's hands in his. "She... She said she won't do anything about it. About *you*. So, we're okay. For now. But she's expecting *something* in return for not telling my father about you."

Lisanthir's eyes shifted away from Seth's, glancing around the room then down to their clasped hands. "She didn't say what?"

"No, she—"

"Of course she didn't." Octavia's voice cut through Seth's. She emerged from her room, arms crossed over her chest. "She's doing this to toy with us. If she knows Lisanthir is an Elviri, she *will* kill him, it's just a matter of when."

Seth chewed on the inside of his cheek, then spoke again. "She also said she's having Szatisi make me another elixir." He kept his gaze focused on his sister, even as Lisanthir gasped quietly, his fearful expression gave way to something akin to hope.

Octavia's face twisted into a sneer. "Szatisi was going to do that anyway because Father ordered it."

"But we wouldn't have to steal it this time," Seth argued. "Once I get the elixir, we could escape—"

"We need to get out of this gods-forsaken snake pit!" Octavia snarled, throwing her hands in the air. "We can't play Osza's games, or Father's. We need to *get out*."

Octavia hadn't been as tense earlier in the day. She must have seen something earlier when she left to scout the city. She was afraid of Amias and Osza, but something beyond them had to be influencing her mood. "What did *you* find out, Tav?" Seth asked quietly.

Octavia inhaled through her nose, then began to speak very slowly, trying to control the wobble in her voice. "The Elviri envoy Father had talked about, back in Yiradia? I know where they're being kept. And I know what Father plans on doing with them."

CHAPTER XXI: RAY

Time passed differently in the tunnels beneath Na'roc of North. Ray wasn't sure if they had been traveling for minutes, hours, or days. They didn't encounter any other Enthai in the tunnels, either. Not that Ray had a firm grasp on how many Enthai existed, but it disturbed her that she hadn't seen any others beyond the three that were traveling with her.

As they traveled farther into the tunnels, the bone murals grew larger on the walls. Flecks of white grew into strips, swirls, and eventually entire mosaics. Her stomach churned uncomfortably at the sight.

So many dead Proma.

The air grew colder as well. Shivers ran down her spine as she wrapped her arms around her midsection. They must be approaching the surface again. She tucked her chin down, trying to burrow into her coat.

"Where are we going?" Niamnh asked quietly.

"Mother Shade's temple," Keitri responded with a rumble. "Just beyond these tunnels is Her valley."

Light began to seep into the tunnels from a distance, and it distorted Ray's vision. Everything became lighter, the colors of rock and bone blurring together. She squinted, trying to sharpen her focus but it only strained her eyes and gave her a headache.

"Who is 'Mother Shade'?" Ray murmured to the Enthai.

"You will know when you see."

The words lingered in Ray's mind even after tendrils of sunslight snaked through the tunnels and led them to the surface. She raised a hand to shield her eyes from the blinding white snow, pausing in her steps to regain her composure. Back in Auora she had been exceptionally talented at orienting herself, always knowing which way was up and where the suns were, but after gazing upon the landscape, a sense of dread coursed through her. They had emerged onto a snowy plain with a gigantic square structure looming ahead. Turning behind to look at the tunnel mouth, she nearly tripped over her own feet. The entrance was no more than a small mound on the ground with the frozen tundra beyond.

Weren't we traveling underneath a mountain range? What kind of strange place is this? And has the snow always been this blinding?

Kohda placed a paw on Ray's shoulder and gently pushed her forward. "Turn back. Straight ahead to the temple. Your eyes will adjust."

Ray rubbed at her eyes with the back of her hand and turned to focus on the temple. It towered over them, taller than Castle Auora itself, with enormous pillars holding up its rooftop. She couldn't immediately tell what it was made from—something both opaque and shining. Like snow that had been packed with glass. It wasn't quite white, though. The more solid parts of the building were tinged with the faintest beiges, reds, and yellows. Almost like tree bark.

Or bones.

All instincts told her to turn back and run into the tunnels. But she couldn't leave Niamnh behind. But she couldn't go on, not to this place of death.

How many died to construct this?

Kohda prodded her shoulder again, but her feet stayed firmly planted in the snow. The Enthai growled. "Move."

Ray shook her head, unable to muster any words. A hand took hers and squeezed. Looking down, Niamnh's gloved hand was wrapped around hers. Meeting the princess's eyes, Ray saw an equal mix of dread and hope.

Hope?

"We must continue on," Niamnh whispered, the corner of her lips curling up into a small smile.

How can she feel hope in a place like this? Something angry curled around Ray's stomach and squeezed. *I need to be strong with her. For her.* She adjusted her hand so that they were properly clasped together. With the barest of nods, she started forward again.

The two girls trudged through the snow together, not daring to let go of one another. Keitri took the lead with Enesse falling in line beside Kohda at the rear. The three Enthai left their hoods down out here in the open, which Ray found curious. They clearly didn't feel threatened by the cold or any potential enemies in this place.

Kohda had called it a temple. *Temple to who?* Even as the question bounced around in her mind, she knew the answer. Whoever "Mother Shade" was, she resided inside. Ray tightened her grip on Niamnh's hand.

Surrounding the temple were stairs on all sides, strangely devoid of any snow. In Auora the churches and shops hired children to sweep away the dirt and snow to keep the places presentable to the rich folk. Ray wondered if the Enthai made their children sweep the snow off of these stairs. She nearly laughed out loud at the absurd thought—furry creatures even smaller than her guides with brooms clasped in between their paws, pushing the snow away. From what little time she'd spent in Na'roc of North, snow fell often enough that those little creatures would have to be outside day and night to keep the stairs so clean. The humor quickly faded into sober questioning as she realized that it would be an impossible task to do. The stairs were *too* clean to have been swept.

Naro's voice echoed in her head. *"You've seen the magic."* Looking at the temple of bones, Ray knew immediately that she was looking upon something magical.

Has Naro been here?

As they drew closer to the temple, Ray had to tilt her head back to see the top of the building. In between the pillars were walls made from the same off-white opaque shiny material. Up close she could see that the temple was indeed made from bones and... *ice*. Her jaw nearly dropped. It glistened as if freshly frozen, but that would be—

"You've seen the magic."

Keitri led the way up the stairs, casting glances over his shoulder the whole way. Ray stopped at the bottom of the stairs, wondering in awe and fear if the surface would be slippery. Without any hesitation, Niamnh took her first step onto the stairs. As she climbed to the third, she tugged on Ray's hand, a silent order to keep up.

Inhaling deeply, Ray took her first step onto the stairs. The surface was solid under her foot, not at all slippery like she had been afraid of. She followed the princess up the stairs before her confidence wavered, her eyes glued to her feet.

At the top of the stairs an entryway stood in the center of the temple wall. Intricate runes and symbols had been carved into the frame surrounding the threshold. The opening led to a set of doors nestled further into the building made from the same bones and ice as the temple itself. Keitri led the group toward the doors, bowing his head as he passed under the threshold. Part of Ray didn't want to pass the threshold. She wanted to turn and run back into the tunnels. Find a way out of the frozen hell. Whispers surrounded her, urging her to do just that.

"Leave."

"Run."

"Away from Her."

A high-pitched yip brought Ray's mind back to her body. She shivered and spun around to look at Kohda and Enesse.

"Do not listen to them," Enesse growled. Ray must have made a face. "They are Dosharas. They want you away from Mother Shade, so they can steal your body."

Fear gnawed at her stomach. *Blessed Protector, keep these demons away from me. I don't want to die out here.* She found the courage to step under the runes and symbols carved into bone. Though they were still outside and not within the temple proper, the cold of the tundra didn't feel quite as harsh. The girls wouldn't freeze to death. They would be... *safe?*

"Come." Keitri's low rumble sent a shiver down Ray's spine. He pushed open one of the doors, revealing an interior lit with a warm glow.

Niamnh squeezed her hand, and they entered together.

The interior of the temple was grand. No other word could describe it. Rows of towering pillars stood to either side of the entryway. Fire pits had been dug out in front of the pillars, flames burning brightly and warming the temple to a comfortable climate. Both the pillars and the walls had been carved from ice, their faces smooth and glistening against the fires. Though simplistic in design, Ray had never seen anything quite so beautiful or awe-inspiring, and she had visited the churches and theaters in the Sky District. As the group walked between the pillars, Ray noticed that neither the pillars nor the walls were sweating from the heat.

Carved into the wall opposite the entrance was a massive mural. Her eyes flickered around, trying to take in every scene presented. Battles between people and all manner of creatures were depicted. Flying overhead one such battle were two beasts Ray had never seen before. They looked like snakes with wings. In the center of the mural was a hooded figure with glowing eyes and outstretched arms. It shared no similarities to the Enthai, but instead looked more like an Elviri or Proma. Or maybe it was something older than the races that inhabited Daaria.

Mother Shade?

"She is below," Keitri said softly.

Ray tore her eyes off of the mural to look at the Enthai. He stood to their left, his body pivoting to reveal a doorway she hadn't noticed before. She wondered how much more of the temple there was to see. Looking back to Niamnh, she saw the princess was still staring at the mural, her lips parted in awe.

"Niamnh, we need to go," Ray whispered to her.

Niamnh blinked and shook her head, pulling herself from her reverie. She nodded her head, letting Ray take the lead as they followed Keitri toward the next threshold. Beyond it was a small staircase that twisted downward. Another memory of the hidden stairwell in Auora bubbled within Ray's mind. The flames here weren't blue but normal orange and yellow.

At the bottom of the staircase was a room that reminded Ray of the churches in Auora. It was no doubt a foyer to another room of worship with two sets of doors carved with runes on the walls opposite the staircase. There were other doors in the room, but none looked as beautiful or important as the center two.

Another pair of Enthai were in the foyer, which caught Ray off guard. They wore nothing more than belts and sashes around their waists, and Ray felt like she needed to avert her gaze. It was a silly notion because these creatures' bodies weren't like hers. They were covered in white-and-gray fur, more like a fox than a Proma or Elviri, and revealed nothing intimate.

The two Enthai looked over at Ray and Niamnh and their ears flattened. They scurried away through one of the side doors, their nails clicking on the floor.

Ray's brow furrowed as she watched them go. *What's that all about...?*

"Through the doors," Keitri muttered from beside them. "She waits."

Ray and Niamnh exchanged a wary glance before crossing over to the carved doors. Ray placed a hand on the ice and pushed. Stepping into the worship chamber, Ray was bathed in warm glowing light. It didn't hurt her eyes like the frigid snow or blinding suns had up above. She felt like a ship drifting toward a beacon in the night, being led to safety. Her senses dulled and she relaxed her shoulders, as if being wrapped in a loving embrace. She was safe here, she could finally—

Niamnh's scream pierced through the fog. Ray's senses sharpened, heart pounding in her ears and she looked down at her hand where Niamnh's should have been joined with hers.

Where is Niamnh?

Ray turned away from the light to look back toward the door. Niamnh had fallen to her knees on the threshold, trembling hands cradling her head. "Niamnh...?" The princess's name fell from Ray's lips in a hushed whisper.

An ethereal woman's voice filled the space in and around Ray's mind. *"Bring the girl forward."*

Ray couldn't tell if the woman had spoken out loud or if she had heard the voice in her head. Keitri and Kohda appeared on either side of Niamnh, taking hold of her arms and raising her to her feet. They led her further into the room, the princess thrashing and screaming in their grasp.

"Stop! *Stop!* I can't—*agh! MAKE IT STOP!*"

Something thrashed inside of Ray's heart, pushing her to run to Niamnh's side and free her from the Enthai, but her feet wouldn't carry her over to the trio. She merely turned in place to watch as Niamnh became enveloped in the warm light. If she squinted and focused on the center of the glow hard enough, Ray could make out the vague shape of a hand, one like hers and not like the Enthai's, reaching out of the light. Long slender fingers brushed against Niamnh's forehead, and the girl's screams were abruptly silenced.

Tendrils of light crawled across the ethereal hand and over Niamnh's face, surrounding her with a silver-white aura.

Something in Ray recoiled at the sight. *Dangerous.* A wave of awe washed over her, pushing the warning away. *Beautiful.*

The aura surrounding Niamnh shimmered and shifted, rapidly changing shape. It stood taller than the girl, and within moments, the aura took the form of a man. The Enthai pulled Niamnh away from the ethereal hand and out of the light. She slumped over in their grasp, barely able to stand on her own. At that moment, whatever spell Ray had been under was lifted, and she ran for the princess, pushing one of the Enthai out of the way to wrap Niamnh's arm around her neck to support her. Both creatures handed the princess over to Ray, taking a few steps away from the girls to fall to their knees, their heads bowed reverently toward the center of the room.

The room dimmed considerably, and when Ray turned back to the center of the room, she was looking at two figures cloaked in silvery-white light. The rest of the room had faded away into darkness, the Enthai vanished from sight, and she couldn't make out any other details beyond the figures. The one closest to her was the man who stood with his back to the girls. He stood a head taller than them both, dark hair falling to his shoulders. Clad only in a plain gray robe, his entire body glowed with what she could only describe as moonlight. He was much too pale, much too otherworldly to be a living, breathing creature like her.

This isn't a living man, Ray realized.

Behind the man was another robed and hooded figure who stood even taller. Twice as tall as the man. Giant and awe-inspiring. As Ray laid eyes on the mysterious figure, she immediately knew this was the same figure in the mural in the upper hall of the temple. She couldn't make out any details from underneath her hood, even standing so close to her towering form.

Mother Shade.

"Daerion Valha, you have been out of my sight for far too long," Mother Shade said softly, voice reverberating through the chamber.

Ray tore her gaze off of the woman to look at the man again, panic bubbling within her stomach. *This is the Doshara that's been inside Niamnh?*

"Not long enough," the man snarled, lunging toward the woman. Niamnh stirred and twitched at the sight, and Ray immediately shifted her weight to better hold the girl back.

Mother Shade merely held a hand up to Daerion and touched a pale finger to his forehead. Her glowing skin was the same moonlit white as her robes, devoid of any color. The man let out a blood curdling shriek and fell to his knees. "*How far you've traveled...*" she murmured, lowering her hand back to her side.

Daerion grunted and gnashed his teeth as he struggled against whatever it was the woman had done to him. "I should've gotten on a boat, left this thrice-cursed land—"

"*You wouldn't have,*" Mother Shade murmured gently.

Daerion continued on as if she hadn't spoken. "I *should've* left, after killing that old fool and his other child—"

"*But Nahaesyraellonore wouldn't have—*"

Daerion roared with unbridled rage, drowning out the rest of Mother Shade's words. He lunged forward again, making it two steps before she touched his forehead again and forced him to his knees once more. She didn't remove her fingers from his skin.

"Don't... speak... that name..." Daerion hissed through gritted teeth, muscles visibly straining as he pushed his head against her touch.

Mother Shade lifted her head to look past Daerion at Ray and Niamnh. With the woman bending forward, it was easier to see underneath her hood, except... there was nothing there except two white flames where Ray assumed her eyes would have been. "*Curious that you would travel with one of his flock...*" Daerion snarled wordlessly. "*I saw why, Misguided One. But it's curious all the same. Does she know?*"

Ray's legs trembled as she gazed upon the two white flames. She struggled to follow their conversation, but she had a hunch they were referring to Naro, or at least the Walkers. She'd never heard of that other name... *Nahae... Nahaes... What a mouthful.* "I know Daerion knows about the Walkers. But beyond that, I-I..." She trailed off, mouth running dry.

"*Oh, child... It goes beyond mere knowledge. He was part of your 'Syrael Walkers', many times over.*"

Ray's jaw dropped as she looked between the ethereal woman and the Doshara. She was drowning underneath a sea of questions, and she had no idea where to begin. *That explains how he knows about the Walkers. So, maybe that's why he would know about Naro. But before Niamnh, the Doshara was inside her mother, so how would he know about Naro?*

"In the *past*," Daerion spat.

His words from several days ago resurfaced in her mind. *"For three thousand years, I've always found my way back to the bastard."*

Mother Shade tilted her head down to look at the man.

"Naro isn't a Proma, is he? He's not... not mortal like me," Ray blurted, drawing the attention of everyone in the room. She felt Niamnh shift and turn in her grasp to face her, but Ray couldn't bring herself to look at the girl's confused face. On the edge of her vision, she saw Daerion's shoulders shake with laughter, but Ray kept her gaze focused on Mother Shade.

"*Naro,*" Mother Shade repeated as if sampling the word to see how it felt on her tongue. "*No, he is Nahaesyraellonore.*"

Daerion's voice was little more than an exhale of air. "Many-Faced One." The same title the Enthai had used when she first met them. From the shadows of the room, Ray thought she heard other voices echoing Daerion's—*the Enthai? Or other Dosharas?*

She always had an inkling of understanding that Naro was magic-touched. Normal people didn't have visions like his, not even the fortune tellers who profited on their "talents". But to hear how Daerion and Mother Shade were referring to him using a strange name, a stranger title...

What is Naro?

Mother Shade removed her fingers from Daerion's forehead and instead extended her hand to Ray and Niamnh. "*Come forward, Princess of Auora, and let me see what you have seen.*"

Niamnh's body trembled in Ray's arms, and Ray couldn't help but tighten her grip on the other girl. To protect her.

"*Fear not, little Walker. I merely wish to share her eyes and ears.*" Then, to Niamnh, she said, "*It won't hurt. Come.*"

After a few moments, Niamnh let her arms drop from around Ray's torso and took a step toward Mother Shade. Ray was reluctant to let her go, but

Niamnh had already made the decision to go, so she let her hands fall to her side. Ray saw the tremble in each step she took, knowing she had to be mentally warring with herself to keep moving. Niamnh lifted her hand, reaching for Mother Shade's, but as the two were about to touch, Daerion sprang to his feet and lunged for Niamnh. The girl let out a startled scream and Ray took a step toward them to... what? Attack a spirit?

A burst of light filled the room and for just a moment Ray felt like she was staring across the Hourglass Lakes or the frozen tundra. The room stretched on, no end in sight. Just as quickly as it struck, it disappeared and all she could see were the illuminated forms of Daerion and Mother Shade.

"Daerion Valha, I forbid you from binding yourself to another mortal being." Mother Shade's voice was like a sudden clap of thunder following a strike of lightning. The floor shook beneath Ray's feet, and she struggled to stay standing. ***"Instead, you shall be bound to me until your end."***

Daerion's hand fell through Niamnh's body, and he stumbled forward. Bewildered, he tossed his head from side to side trying to make *something* make sense. Niamnh stepped away from the Doshara toward Mother Shade.

As Ray's eyes wandered from the man, she saw Niamnh and Mother Shade had their hands clasped together, and a faint silver-white aura surrounded the princess. Ray's jaw dropped at the sight, overwhelmed by the beauty of the two women.

"He won't hurt you, or anyone else, again," Mother Shade murmured to Niamnh, who only stared at the Doshara with horror and pity. As Mother Shade's gaze turned to Daerion, she straightened her back and raised her free hand toward him. *"I will summon you when I'm ready to hear what you have to say about the past two hundred years. Now leave us."*

Ray saw a look of resignation flicker across Daerion's face before he rose to his feet and simply disappeared. It was as if she blinked, and he was gone.

Niamnh and Ray turned their attention to Mother Shade again. The princess was the first to speak. "What are you?"

"One of the last guardians of Daaria," Mother Shade said quietly. *"What Nahaesyraellonore should have been, before he got swept up in his games on your island."*

Ray's head jerked back involuntarily as she processed the woman's words. "How old are you? Both of you?"

"*Old enough to have seen your ancestors' bones wither and fade to dust underneath one sun. Let's leave it at that.*"

A few moments of silence filled the room. Ray simply stared at Mother Shade, trying to take in and understand what this woman could possibly be. That Naro could be... That Naro *was* something like her. *Timeless. Ageless. Dangerous.*

Niamnh parted her lips to speak. "What did—"

"*Little princess, do you feel it?*" Mother Shade's voice drowned out Niamnh's. The woman let go of her hand and placed it gently on top of her head, stroking her white hair. Niamnh looked around the room and then back to Mother Shade, shaking her head wordlessly. "*Something stirs within you. Something... ancient. Watch, observe what it can do.*"

Mother Shade's hand fell from Niamnh's hair, clutching at her robes and lifting to reveal silver-white feet. She lifted one foot and took a step forward, moving with such reverence that Ray knew that something important was happening, but she didn't understand what it was.

The warbled howls of the Enthai startled Ray as they became visible again, prostrating themselves on the ground, their ears folded flat against their heads. From outside the worship chamber, several other Enthai echoed the howls with shrieks and yips of their own. The noise sent an ice-cold knife down Ray's spine and gooseflesh rose along her skin.

Protector's grace, what's happening?

Niamnh was in a similar state of confusion and terror. As Mother Shade moved from the center of the room toward the Enthai, the princess had taken several steps backward away from the towering figure.

The ethereal woman knelt down in front of Keitri and extended a hand to touch his head. "*Chieftain, escort the princess to our guest chambers, then send word for your finest riders and dogs. We travel tomorrow.*"

Keitri let out a low croon. Seemingly satisfied with his response, Mother Shade removed her hand from his fur, and he rose to his feet. He let out a soft bark in Kohda's direction, and the two moved to Niamnh's side. Keitri gestured toward the exit, and the princess hesitantly moved in that direction. Her eyes met Ray's, and she could see the plea on Niamnh's face: *come with me.*

Ray tore her eyes from Niamnh to look at Mother Shade, who had pivoted in her direction. A feeling settled over Ray's body compelling her to stay. *What could Mother Shade want with me?*

After Niamnh and the two Enthai had left and the doors shut behind them, Mother Shade spoke to Ray. "*You have more questions.*"

So did she, Ray thought as Niamnh's face flashed across her mind.

Mother Shade extended a hand out to Ray. "*Come, I would have you and I share memories.*"

"Will you tell—will you *show* me what you're guarding Daaria from?"

The ethereal woman didn't respond. Ray swallowed nervously and closed the gap between them, reaching out to take Mother Shade's hand. Her vision went white, then black. She was no longer in the worship chamber beneath the temple of bones in the frozen tundra; she was standing on the edge of the Hourglass Lakes, staring up into a summer sky where one sun lingered high above her.

One sun?

Suddenly she was hurtling across grasslands and farms, deep into a rainforest, into a village with stone buildings and pyramids. Sweat beaded at her hairline and down her spine. Wherever it was, she was boiling from the inside. High above, the one sun beat down on her mercilessly. A hideous shriek split the air, drawing her into one of the pyramids. Deep in its bowels she saw a beautiful Elviri woman with fiery red hair chained to a stone wall, a giant scaled beast crawling on the ground toward her.

With a single blink of her eyes, the vision changed. She was outside again, now in the middle of a stone coliseum. Chaos surrounded her on all sides. Snake-like people were hissing and screaming, slithering across the many rows of seats to try to get out of the open. They were pushing each other aside, trampling over any who fell to the ground. Anything to avoid being outside. Anything to avoid being killed by what was flying overhead. Ray lifted her gaze to the one sun in the sky and saw a dark shape against its surface, growing larger as it plummeted toward her. She dropped to the ground, arms wrapped around her head to protect herself.

"What terrible beauty!"

"Kill me, but spare the child!"

When Ray lowered her arms and looked around her, she was deep within a forest, not entirely unlike the northern shores of Promthus. She weaved through the trees, leaves and grass crunching underfoot. It was dark with barely any moonlight to guide her.

A feminine voice cut through the silence, her words little more than a hiss of air. "I cannot stay."

"But what about *us?*" a male voice responded, desperation hanging on his every word.

Ray quieted her steps, so the grass was silent as she moved closer to the pair. Peeking out from behind a large oak tree, she saw a man and woman standing together in a clearing, the man gripping the woman's hands tightly. Most of his appearance was obscured with his back turned to Ray, but from the way he carried himself, she assumed he was a noble. There wasn't much to go on because he had a dark cloak wrapped around him. As Ray's eyes drifted to the woman, she had to stifle a gasp. The woman's arms and cheeks were covered in golden scales.

Asaszi.

She had only ever heard of the Asaszi through ancient history books—evil creatures from the Eldest Days. A near-forgotten memory, especially with the threat of the Provira looming overhead. Ray absorbed every detail of the woman, trying to commit the vision to memory. Her hairline started nearly atop her head, her ashen brown hair pulled back into a single braid that fell down her back. Large round gold eyes stared at the man in front of her, the color nearly identical to her scales. Instead of round pupils, though, she had black vertical slits like a serpent. The center of her face and throat were a pale creamy color, a little lighter than Ray's own skin. The Asaszi woman was dressing in an unassuming black robe, but it couldn't hide how swollen her belly was.

She's with child?

"The child's not safe. You've seen how the queen and her consort look at me." Though the woman's words were unhappy, she sounded more melancholic than anything.

"But *she* was the one who brought you here. She would never—"

"But *he* could."

Before the couple could continue their discussion, Ray was dragged out of the forest and went hurtling across Daaria once more. She returned to the rainforest, to the same coliseum from before, and found herself looking out at another battlefield over the edge of a wooden shield. Staring her down was a massive hulking half-Elviri brandishing a terrifying curved greatsword, hatred gleaming in his gold-green serpentine eyes. He wore a golden helmet shaped like a serpent with a flared hood, the jaws parted to reveal his face. An elaborately decorated leather girdle and skirt hung from his waist, covering a pair of golden scaled boots. Patches of matching golden scales covered his torso and arms, exposed and shining in the sun's light.

Is this the Asaszi woman's child?

"*Grandsire,*" the half-Elviri sneered, angling the sword to sweep out at her.

The title sent her mind spinning. In her other hand, she was holding a longsword, steel shining in the daylight. Her gaze flickered to the blade, and she caught her reflection; she wasn't herself in this vision. She was a man with loose strands of dark red hair hanging in front of olive skin spattered with dirt and blood. His face twisted into a snarl, his brown eyes bright with fury.

A glint of sunlight caught on the blade and blinded Ray for a moment, and when her vision returned, she was looking directly at the sun—*suns*—as the sky lit up brighter than the brightest summer day. The shape of two orbs seared across her eyes and lingered long after the sky returned to a pale blue.

She tilted her chin down to avert her eyes from the suns, and once more she had been carried off to a new scene. In the distance, she saw a woman standing in an open field of grass whose gaze was still fixed on the sky, a pair of horns curling against her head. Something was happening to the woman; her clothes and skin were turning black, the darkness spreading across her body until only pale white hands and feet remained. Not even her face was spared by the shadows.

Ray tried to call out to the woman, but no sound came from her mouth. She started running toward her, reaching out to help her, overwhelmed with the need to reverse whatever dark spell had overcome her. The woman tilted her head down and turned toward Ray, stopping her in her tracks. Rather than two eyes against a face, she was staring at two fiery orbs of light piercing through a plane of shadow.

Mother Shade.

Ray was thrown out of her mind, out of the visions, and onto the floor. She hit the ground, and it painfully pushed all of the air from her lungs. Panting for breath, she stared at Mother Shade with new understanding and new questions. A soft glow surrounded the woman, bringing a little illumination to the rest of the room. Darkness still swirled underneath her hood while the white robe hid her fiery orbs.

"That is what we were supposed to protect Daaria from," Mother Shade said softly, her voice sending vibrations down Ray's limbs.

Ray climbed to her feet, keeping a sizable distance between her and the ethereal woman. "But what was that?" she asked.

"Visions of the past, and warnings for the future if we don't make haste tomorrow."

The cryptic message didn't sit well with Ray, and she frowned, wishing Naro were here to help her make sense of it all. He had always been honest—

I didn't know what he was before today. How much of the truth has he actually told me over the years? With these new revelations, she wasn't sure if she could trust Naro anymore. Her chest ached and for the first time since her mother died, Ray felt truly alone.

"Earlier you said something ancient was stirring within Niamnh. Does that have something to do with whatever you just showed me?" Ray asked the woman, trying to regain some level of confidence.

"Yes, that which grows within her will determine if history will repeat itself or not. A gift granted to her by Daerion."

Ray's skin prickled with gooseflesh. "What has he done?"

"It remains to be seen if he's doomed us all or saved us." Mother Shade raised her hand, signaling Ray to stop from responding. *"But that is why we must depart tomorrow and make haste across the tundra. I know you have more questions, but there's nothing else I can answer tonight. My answers wouldn't satisfy you."*

Ray doubted that very much, but she chose not to argue back. Instead, she mumbled out, "Fine. I suppose you'll send me off to bed now."

Mother Shade didn't immediately respond, which made Ray shift her weight between her feet uncomfortably. After several moments she said, *"Chieftain Keitri will be waiting for you outside. He will escort you to chambers that have been prepared for you and the princess."*

"I, um... thank you," Ray responded. She patted her thighs, rubbing her hands against her pants to dispel her sweat. To bow or not to bow; she wasn't sure. As she stepped back toward the door, she offered Mother Shade an awkward little half-bow.

"Rest easy, Ray Finnegan," Mother Shade said, and Ray swore if the woman had a face, she would have seen a smile there. *"We will wake you when it's time to depart for Rymo-tehp."*

That name sounded familiar, but she couldn't place where she had heard or seen it before. She wanted to ask Mother Shade about it, to at least learn what or where Rymo-tehp was, but a gentle compulsion from within pushed her to leave the room. With a final glance over the woman's figure—hooded, robed, and glowing softly with light—Ray turned and exited the worship chamber, her head swirling with questions.

Who were the people Mother Shade showed me? Are these the kinds of visions Naro has? How does any of that play into what's happening right now with Ni-amnh? Those were all visions of lands to the south, not up here. Amidst the serious questions, she also had some absurd thoughts as well. *Surely there's not actually a pair of horns underneath Mother Shade's hood...*

Keitri was indeed waiting for her outside. His tail swished to the side and pointed toward one of the side doors, and he led her deeper into the temple.

"What's at Rymo-tehp? And what *is* Rymo-tehp?" Ray blurted out to the Enthai as they turned a corner. She watched as Keitri's fur prickled and stood on end, but he didn't respond. If it weren't for his physical reaction, she would've thought he hadn't heard her.

He's choosing to ignore me. She frowned. *Did Naro know we'd be sent to Rymo-tehp next? Is this all part of the plan he laid out?* The thought didn't sit well with her, but she didn't know what else to think. If Naro was the same type of creature as Mother Shade, then maybe they'd been working together this whole time, and he meant for Ray and Ajak to arrive here with the princess. *Why else would we've been searching for the Enthai?*

Ray and Keitri didn't speak as they continued through a maze of hallways illuminated with candlelight. Keitri finally stopped outside one door and let his tail drag across its surface. "Your princess is inside. We've already brought food and drink for you."

"Thank you," Ray said quietly. Her stomach growled quietly as she thought about what kind of food would be waiting for her. *What kind of food can grow this far north?*

She parted her lips to ask again about the next day's journey, but the Enthai turned and left before she had a chance to speak. She took a deep breath and placed her hand on the door, pushing it open. To her surprise, it had no locking mechanism on the inside or outside. The room within was warmly lit by several candles. Two large piles of furs were piled against each side of the room to be used as beds, she supposed. In between the furs, Niamnh sat on the floor with a spread of dishes before her. The girl had removed all of her outer layers of clothing and was sitting cross-legged in a large billowing shirt and a pair of doeskin leggings, shoving all kinds of food into her mouth. Her physical appearance didn't change after Daerion was expelled from her body. She still had the same warm brown skin and silver-blonde hair, but her eyes were shining brighter than before.

When Ray opened the door, Niamnh's head snapped up as she was slurping down a spoonful of broth. She swallowed and set the bowl down, scrambling to her feet. Upon closer inspection, Ray saw there were tears running down Niamnh's cheeks.

"Ray! You're okay!" Niamnh said.

The relief in Niamnh's voice and the way her face shone brightly upon her entry melted away a lot of the tension in Ray's body. Her small smile turned into a large grin as the other girl wrapped her arms around her torso and squeezed tightly.

"Why're you crying?" Ray asked softly, hugging her back.

Niamnh let out a shaky laugh, pulling away to rub at her eyes. "It's just all so *good*. Anything's better than the past six years, but this is... even better than anything that came before." She returned to her seat on the floor, gesturing for Ray to follow.

"You didn't wait for me to start eating?" Ray teased, sitting across from the other girl.

The spread before them was truly impressive considering they were in the middle of the tundra, and winter was upon them. She could hardly identify what any of the dishes contained beyond simple descriptions like meat, fish, vegetables, and fruit. The sight of produce caught her off-guard, and she wondered exactly how fresh it was. The vegetables had been boiled and served in various different broths, while the fruit—mostly berries, with a few slices of what looked like apples or some other hardy delicacy—was served plain.

"The Enthai said you'd be a while, and I wasn't sure how long *to* wait." Niamnh picked up a bowl from the ground and handed it over.

Ray frowned, inspecting the contents of the dish with chunks of boiled meat in broth. "A while? How long was I?"

"I'm not entirely sure. An hour, perhaps more?" The princess plucked a few berries from another bowl, popping them into her mouth. She let out a quiet moan and picked up a few more.

Ray stared at her bowl of soup, worry plastered all over her face. Small wisps of steam rose from the bowl, filling her nose with a delicious scent. Her stomach let out a furious growl, but her throat had seized up.

Very quietly, she said, "I was only with Mother Shade for a few moments."

"What were you two doing?" Niamnh asked in between mouthfuls of berries. She had caught onto Ray's distress and lowered her handful of berries back to the bowl, focusing instead on the other girl.

Ray tilted her head to the side, digging her fingertips into the wooden bowl. "She showed me... *something*. Some kind of vision."

"What did you see?" Curiosity seeped through Niamnh's words.

Looking up, Ray saw that the girl was leaning forward over the food to better hear her speak. Her cheeks flushed under the princess's attentive gaze. "A lot that I didn't understand. She said that she showed me the past, and that those visions were also a warning about the future... I-I don't know."

"When she touched me, it was like we were watching my entire life play out in front of us. My childhood, my brothers, my mother's death... But I did catch glimpses of other things through her eyes. None of that made much sense to me either," Niamnh said, eyes wide with wonder. "But you saw the past?"

"Like I was living it out," Ray mumbled, suddenly overheating underneath all of her clothes.

She set the wooden bowl down and tugged at her coat, desperate to cool off. After her coat went her gloves, boots, and tunic, until she was stripped down to a pair of leggings and her linen shirt. The clothes stuck to her body, soaked through with sweat. She rubbed the back of her hand against her forehead, then wiped it on her thigh.

How can it be this hot when we're surrounded by snow and ice?

"That's so fascinating," Niamnh murmured, pulling herself back from hovering over the food. "But you don't know what you saw?"

Ray only shook her head. The glow of curiosity faded from Niamnh's face, and her eyes drifted back down to her bowl of berries. Glancing around the rest of the offerings, Ray opted to try a bite of the boiled greens.

Right before she shoved a stalk in her mouth, she asked, "How, um… how are you doing?" *How are you now that Daerion's not inside of you anymore? How are you now that you have your life back all to yourself?*

Niamnh chewed thoughtfully on another berry. She swallowed, inhaled deeply, and responded, "The silence was deafening. I'm glad you're here with me now."

A blush swept across Ray's cheeks, turning them bright pink. "Me too."

"Now, tell me what you think of those vegetables. I've never had anything like them before."

CHAPTER XXII: SETH

Seth and Octavia had never before considered the worth of an Elviri's life, let alone a group of five Elviri. For Seth, that had all changed when he had visited Lithalyon mere weeks ago. However, he was still under the impression that his sister loathed the Elviri, as many Provira did, even with the doubts she cast against their father and after helping keep Lisanthir's identity hidden. When she told Seth and Lisanthir of the Elviri envoy being kept prisoners in Iszairi, the ritual Amias planned to use them for, and her desire to *free them...*

Octavia was finally free from their father's grasp.

But is it too late? Seth thought. *Can we even escape ourselves, let alone with a group of starving, wounded Elviri in tow?*

Lisanthir hadn't been at the dinner event when Amias announced his intentions to take the envoy to Iszairi. He sided with Octavia immediately, pledging his support to free the other Elviri without any other consideration. Seth's heart ached, and he knew they needed to try, but something small and dark whispered in the back of his mind that it was too risky, too dangerous.

But we must try... Mustn't we?

A pair of Provira stewards brought dinner to their suite later in the evening. Lisanthir had to don his veil to ensure his identity wasn't revealed to them. Even though Osza knew about him, they couldn't risk Amias finding out. Osza had her own ulterior motives for keeping the Elviri alive but with Amias there was no guarantee for Lisanthir's safety.

The trio picked at their meal as they sat together stewing on their next steps. The Elviri were being kept underneath the coliseum, which only the soldiers had access to. Octavia would be able to gain access to their cells, but their escape routes would be monitored at all times by other Provira and Asaszi soldiers.

"Could you use your rank to get them out?" Lisanthir asked, eyes fixated on Tav as he stirred his bowl of soup.

"Perhaps, but I—"

"Could I help you? If I disguise myself as a soldier again?" Lisanthir continued, his utensils abandoned.

"It's a possibility, but"—Octavia looked at Lisanthir, then to Seth—"I don't think it would be wise for you to help."

Lisanthir clenched his fists, the first sign of anger Seth had ever seen from his *ebilin*. The Elviri didn't respond immediately. He must have been processing what Tav said and perhaps was thinking of another solution. Some other way to break his kin out.

"Do we know when Father plans on conducting his next ritual?" Seth said softly.

Octavia shook her head, lowering her gaze to her wine goblet. "If he's decided on a date, the soldiers haven't been informed. I don't know if he'll need any of them for the ritual, like he did for the ones back in Yiradia."

As Octavia spoke, the low constant hum underneath all the other noises grew louder and louder. When she stopped speaking, the hum filled the entire room and Seth couldn't hear his fork scraping on his plate, or his heart beating in his chest.

"It'll happen soon," Seth whispered, unable to hear his own voice.

Lisanthir and Octavia spoke at the same time.

"What?"

"What do you know, brother?"

The trio exchanged glances. Seth couldn't tell if they had heard one another, or even his own words. He opened his mouth then immediately shut it and winced. The hum punctured his mind, vibrating underneath his skin. He wanted to get away from it but knew of no escape. He was trapped in Iszairi until he and his loved ones could escape.

I hope my mind will stand strong until we get out.

"He'll tell us soon. He'll want us there." Seth grimaced, looking at Octavia. He knew Amias's hubris. He knew his father would want to flaunt his connection to a dead man in front of Osza. Not just any dead man—the *Tserys*.

"Do you think he'll deliver the announcement himself?" Octavia's voice was frail, like she was a child hiding a secret.

Seth pursed his lips and shrugged. "I haven't received a personal invitation from him in years, but now that he's claiming to hear the voice of a dead man in his head? And his attempts to push back against Osza? I don't know."

"Even if your father were to come here himself, do you think he will be scrutinizing me?" Lisanthir's voice was eerily calm. A glance at the Elviri told Seth that he was still holding back his anger if his clenched fists and rigid posture were anything to go off of.

"If he thinks you were placed here by Osza? Yes," Octavia replied.

Lisanthir drummed his fingers against the table, going silent once more.

"But he may be distracted if he thinks his children are excited for the news," Seth said slowly, the words feeling like a betrayal on his lips. For years, he had forced himself to be passive around Amias, not revealing his disgust for his father's work. Amias also had Octavia supporting him until very recently. *Could we be convincing enough with our performance and fool Father? Is Octavia capable of lying to his face right now?*

Octavia nodded, a grim expression on her face. The candlelight danced across her brown eyes. The trio finished their dinner with little other conversation. Octavia was the first to leave the table, muttering a quiet goodnight before disappearing into her room. Seth and Lisanthir stayed at the table for a while longer, discussing the differences in the foods they had eaten over the past month.

"I can't say I've ever eaten lizard before," Lisanthir murmured, pushing a piece of charred lizard meat around on his plate. "Though it tastes similar to a particular chicken dish back home. How come the kitchens in Yiradia don't prepare dishes using lizards?"

Seth snickered, covering his mouth with his hand. "It's mostly the Asaszi who eat it, and usually they eat it raw," he said. "I think the Provira here have just adapted to what the kitchens keep stocked. Did you actually like it?"

Lisanthir stabbed the meat with his fork, raising it to take a nibble. "It's not the worst thing I've ever eaten."

"Oh? What dish holds that title?"

Casting one more thoughtful glance over the piece of lizard meat, Lisanthir set his fork back down on his plate. "The boiled greens back in Yiradia."

A full-bellied laugh erupted from Seth. "They're an acquired taste, for sure."

"It's baffling that that dish is served for your family," Lisanthir continued, his face twisting with exaggerated disgust. "Is that something else the Asaszi prefer that the Provira acquired a taste for?"

"Gods, no. Not even Osza likes them." Seth laughed. "I think my father likes his vegetables cooked that way because he thinks it's how nobles and kings eat them."

The two continued to laugh, and Seth felt comfortable. He knew it was only temporary, but that evening he had let the outside world disappear focusing on Lisanthir. He savored the warmth pooling his stomach, and the easy smiles that crossed his face.

Eventually they left the dining chamber and returned to Seth's room to prepare for bed. Seth changed into his sleep clothes, then climbed into the bed with Lisanthir's assistance. He let his hands linger around Lisanthir's neck. The Elviri let out a quiet chuckle and pressed a chaste kiss to Seth's forehead.

As Lisanthir pulled away, cold seeped into Seth's clothes and skin. The evening was coming to an end, and soon he'd be alone with his thoughts and the memories of the day's events. Seth was about to ask Lisanthir where he would be sleeping tonight but stopped himself when he saw the Elviri taking off his steward's robe and folding it up.

He's sleeping in here. Giddiness surged up within him as he shuffled to one side of the bed, leaving the other half vacant for Lisanthir. A blush crept across Seth's face as he watched the Elviri undress and change into his own sleep clothes.

When Lisanthir turned to face Seth, his lips curled into a wide grin. "May I blow out the candles?" Seth nodded, and he moved to extinguish the flames in the candelabra before slipping into the bed. "Sleep well, *ebilin.*"

"You too, Lis."

Sure enough, the next day Amias summoned his children to share the midday meal with him. The summoning was delivered on a piece of paper, handed to Octavia by a Provira steward. Their father had simply written instructions to meet him in his chambers at midday. No explanation was provided, but Seth knew it had to do with the *Tserys*. What he wasn't expecting was for his father to tell them that he was struggling with what to do next.

"The prince was clear with His vision, yet it eludes me in the waking world," Amias said through gritted teeth. His stare was directed at Osza who sat at the opposite end of the table from him.

Seth also hadn't been expecting his father to summon Osza to the meeting.

"Tell me what the *Tserys* sssaid to you," Osza replied calmly, not bothered in the least by Amias's outward distress.

The inhale and exhale from Amias could be heard all throughout his dining chamber. Octavia sat to Amias's right, with Seth beside her. The twins looked between Osza and their father as the conversation continued. The food on the table went neglected, growing cold.

"He told me of something ancient yet fresh that would herald a new generation, something that would shake and part the stone holding Him back."

To Seth it sounded like it could be either a clever riddle or senseless babble. His father's brows knitted together in frustration. When Seth turned to look toward Osza, he was surprised to see her looking so calm and collected.

"I know of what you ssseek." Osza practically purred, folding her hands in her lap.

"Tell me of it," Amias demanded, his face twisting with disbelief and outrage. "If you know what the *Tserys* speaks of you must tell me."

Osza's tongue darted out and tasted the air. All playfulness was gone in an instant. When she spoke, her voice was cold. "You forget your ssstation, Amiasss. I will sshow mercy thisss once because it isss the will of the *Tserys*."

Seth dared to look back at his father. Amias's brown eyes widened for a moment before he regained his composure. He cleared his throat and bowed his head. "Of course, Queen Osza. My apologies."

Silence filled the dining chamber as Osza considered Amias's apology. Her tongue flickered out a few times, giving away nothing with her facial expression. Amias kept his head bowed but raised his gaze so he could look the Asaszi queen in the eye.

"I will take you to what the *Tserys* seeksss. Your children may join usss." Osza's gaze flicked first to Octavia, then to Seth. Underneath her golden stare, he once again felt as if he had been turned to stone.

"Of course," Amias said, unable to completely mask the displeasure in his voice. "When might we go, Queen Osza?"

"After our meal isss finished. The ssspread looksss too delightful to let go to wassste," Osza hissed, picking up her utensils and politely tucking into the plate before her. Seth and his family had no choice but to partake as well, lest they be seen as rude guests to the queen.

True to her word, after they finished eating Osza beckoned for them to follow her out of Amias's suite. Amias followed the Asaszi queen closely, the heels of his boots clicking on the stone floor. Octavia took hold of the handles on Seth's chair and pushed him out, following their father. Lisanthir trailed behind them, acting every bit the shadow he was supposed to be.

"Fetch a torch, sssteward," Osza called over her shoulder. The Asaszi didn't look behind to see if Lisanthir was following her orders, nor did she slow her stride. Fortunately for Lisanthir, torches lined the walls of the stairwell, so he was able to grab one and catch up to the others rather quickly.

Osza led the Provira family down into the bowels of the pyramid, descending beneath the surface of the earth. Seth knew enough about the *Tserdanii* to know there were tunnels underground. The entrance to the underground network was hidden within the center of the pyramid, tucked behind several locked doors. Osza carried the keys to the doors within her robes, not stopping to explain anything to the others. Seth couldn't tell if the keys were a secret that not even the stewards knew about, or if she knew the steward shadowing them was Lisanthir, who most assuredly would *not* know of Iszairi's secrets.

Regardless, the Asaszi queen opened the doors without a sound, locking them once more after the others crossed the threshold. Lisanthir's torch was the only source of light, filling the chambers with a warm yellow glow. Cobwebs filled every corner and crevice, dust covering the ground. Though the stone floors and walls were the same color as the rest of the pyramid, the long shadows of the tunnels made these lower halls feel more menacing. The air tasted stale, and the scent of dust and mildew filled Seth's nostrils.

How long has it been since someone's been down here?

Osza stopped at the threshold of one tunnel and held her hand out. Amias turned to look at Lisanthir and opened his mouth to snap or snarl at the Elviri, but Lis was moving before the words ever left Amias's mouth. Lisanthir handed his torch to Osza and then took a few steps back, bowing his head politely.

Seth heard the Asaszi queen's tongue slither out of her mouth and flick against the air before she started walking away. "The tunnelsss were not carved to be sssmooth," Osza murmured, her voice echoing down the corridor.

Seth swallowed nervously. He felt Octavia slow her pace, his sister no doubt scouring the floor in front of them for bumps or other obstacles. The queen's pace stayed the same, as did their father's.

Though Seth and Octavia never lost sight of their father and the queen, they certainly lagged behind. Osza hadn't been wrong. The tunnel was bumpy and difficult to push the wheelchair through. Several times Seth was tempted to tell Octavia to just stop and pick him up, but without knowing how far Osza wanted to travel, he wasn't sure if his sister could bear his weight for that long.

Perhaps Lisanthir could help, and they could take turns carrying me? He hated himself for thinking about it, but he also didn't want to face the wrath of Amias or the Asaszi queen if they failed to keep up. *But she wanted us to come with her, so surely, she won't leave me and Tav behind.*

Osza and Amias followed a natural bend in the tunnel, and then they were out of sight. Octavia tried to navigate the wheelchair through a spread of sharp rocks that were too large to kick out of the way. Osza's torchlight lingered, but it was quickly overtaken by shadows.

"Tav, just pick me up," Seth whispered. "Or let *him*." Octavia merely grunted in response.

Darkness encroached on them. Seth felt it closing around him, smothering the light from his eyes. He clenched his jaw and hissed, "Damnit, the light's almost gone. Just *pick me up*."

His eyes hadn't fully adjusted to the darkness, but he knew the shadow moving in front of him was Lisanthir. He held his arms out, waiting to feel the Elviri's body move closer as he leaned down to pick him up.

"Get his other arm," Lisanthir said, his voice barely any louder than the rustle of his clothes. Seth wrapped his arms around Lisanthir's neck as he was lifted from the chair. The Elviri spun him around in his grasp, tugging on one arm. Seth felt Lisanthir's breath against his ear. "Let go, Seth. We're both going to carry you."

Lisanthir and Octavia's bodies began to take form as Seth's eyes adjusted to the darkness. With some reluctance, Seth loosened his grasp on the Elviri and allowed him to maneuver his body around.

Octavia was at his side in an instant, grabbing his left arm and wrapping it around her neck. She raised her voice just a little. "Carefully. One step at a time. I'll lead."

Seth felt his body tugged ahead and to the left as Octavia began walking forward. She prodded the ground with her foot, feeling for any rocks jutting out or dips in the floor. Lisanthir followed at an angle, his side brushing against Seth's.

"Come, children, we are at our dessstination," Osza called out from further ahead.

"Coming!" Octavia responded, forcing confidence into her voice. She moved faster, forcing Lisanthir to pick up his pace as well. The three of them hobbled together down the tunnel and around the bend where Amias and Osza stood in front of a tunnel wall.

Seth saw something predatory flash across Osza's golden eyes when she saw them approach, but she said nothing. Amias hovered nearby, his arms crossed—clearly displeased and impatient. If he was mad about the way his son was being carried, he didn't express it.

Will he try to punish us for this later?

"Take the torch," Osza commanded, holding it out toward the trio. Octavia swiftly bent her knees and picked Seth up in her arms, allowing Lisanthir to hasten over to the Asaszi queen. He took the torch and retreated a few steps, giving Osza space to extend her arms out. She began speaking in her native tongue, and Seth didn't recognize any of the words.

She must be speaking in an ancient dialect, he thought. He tried to commit the nuances of her hisses, vowels, and clicks to his memory, but she spoke too quickly for him to follow along. *Does Father know the words she's speaking?*

The tunnel began to shake all around them, masking Osza's voice. Beneath the rumbling of stone and the Asaszi's chant, Seth heard the incessant hum growing louder. It filled the space around him and *within* him. He felt the hum in his fingertips, spreading throughout his arms and into his chest. Before them, a crack formed in the middle of the wall in front of Osza. She took a step forward and placed her hands on the stone, giving it a push as she let out a piercing shriek. The noise cut through the stone and the hum, and then the two halves of the stone wall swung inward.

A hidden door.

Osza looked over her shoulder and beckoned Lisanthir forward with a finger. The silent demand was clear—give her the torch once more. The Elviri handed it over, then returned to his place behind the family. The Asaszi called out softly to them and took a step into the revealed passageway.

"Come."

Amias was the first to follow, Octavia not far behind.

The stonework here was older and different from the rest of the *Tserdanii.* More crude in their making. The walls were the color of mud, something Seth hadn't seen before in either Yiradia or Iszairi. Perhaps the stone and earth were different this far below Iszairi. But that thought perplexed him. Shouldn't he have seen bricks and stones the same color before if the Asaszi had dug down that deep?

The passageway opened into an enormous room—no, a natural cavern. Stairs had been carved along the wall near the tunnel, leading down to the cavern floor. Several other tunnel mouths littered the walls of the cavern, but where they led, Seth didn't know. In all his reading, he had never heard mention of a cavern like it before buried underneath the *Tserdanii.*

"What is this place?" Amias asked, his voice echoing throughout the room.

"We walk in the ancient hallsss of dragonsss," Osza murmured with reverence. The Asaszi queen held the torch with both hands, casting her gaze upward to the cavern ceiling.

Dragons! Seth's breath caught in his throat. He'd heard tales of the magnificent creatures from the Eldest Days who used to roam Daaria. Some of his favorite childhood stories were about dragons and the legendary figures who tamed them. The dragons had made their homes in the caves of Moonyswyn. Their wyrm offspring were prized possessions of the Asaszi rulers. It was even said that some ancient Asaszi kings and queens mated with their wyrms. A chill in his blood tempered his excitement as he recalled that his mother was the one who had passed along many of those stories.

Seth followed Osza's gaze up and his breath was taken away. On the ceiling, a mural had been carved of two dragons breathing fire above a crude representation of the *Tserdanii* and the coliseum. Shadows danced along the rock from the torchlight, making the dragons' wings appear to flap and move.

"Tell me, Lord Kharisss, what do you know of the dragonsss?" Osza asked Amias, fixing her golden gaze upon him.

Amias was staring at the ceiling mural as well. He spoke quietly. "When the second sun rose, the last of the dragons died."

"Ssso sssay the legendsss."

"What else do we have besides our legends and myths?" Amias retorted, though his voice distinctly lacked any bite.

"Truth," the Asaszi queen responded. "Come, follow." She descended the ramp, the orange glow of the torchlight surrounding her figure. Amias cast a glance towards his children before following, but Seth couldn't read his expression.

Octavia's breathing grew more ragged as they followed Osza and their father. Seth squeezed his arms gently around her neck, drawing her attention. He raised his eyebrows and nodded his head back toward Lisanthir who trailed behind them. His sister's mouth formed a tight line, and she huffed a heavy breath out of her nose.

Come on, stop being so stubborn, Tav. Let him help.

Osza led Amias down one of the tunnels, its dark maw devouring the torchlight from the cavern.

Octavia walked faster. Seth could feel the strain in her muscles. Her chest heaved and her lips forcibly parted so she could suck in air. He untangled his arms from around her neck, placing one on her shoulder and squeezing none too gently. She gave a nonverbal hiss in response.

Lisanthir was by her side in an instant, placing one hand on her back. She jolted underneath the touch, whipping her neck to the side to look at the Elviri's veiled face. Tav looked at the tunnel where Osza and Amias had disappeared and came to a sudden stop. She lowered Seth's legs to the ground, keeping her other hand on his back. With her left hand now free, she clutched onto his arm still wrapped around her neck. Lisanthir understood immediately and wasted no time taking hold of Seth's right arm and slinging it around his shoulders. The trio hobbled after Osza and Amias, their movements much easier with how smooth the cavern floor was.

Seth had lost all sense of direction underground. The tunnel they were now traveling through seemed to stretch on forever. The cavern behind them quickly disappeared into the darkness, leaving them in a small pocket of light from Osza's torch. His sense of time vanished as well. Realistically they couldn't have been down there for more than an hour, but there was no telling how quickly the suns were crossing the sky up above.

After a particular curve in the tunnel's path, the righthand wall took on a different appearance. It was no longer carved directly from the ground as the rest of the tunnel had been. Its surface was rigid and bumpy, like that of the pyramid's stonework. Its coloring was a little darker than the rest of the tunnel, though Seth couldn't make out the exact color in the torchlight.

"The Tomb of the Prince!" Amias shouted, his words echoing loudly in the passageway.

"Yesss," Osza whispered, her own voice barely audible over the echoes.

Seth's brow furrowed. He had never been to the Tomb of the Prince before, but it was his understanding that the tomb was accessible from the coliseum in Iszairi. *Why did Osza take us through this secret route if she meant to take us here?* He knew better than to vocalize his question, lest Osza or his father snap at him for stepping out of line.

Amias asked the question instead. "But then, why...?"

"It isss not the tomb we ssseeek," the Asaszi queen replied, her words leaving Seth more confused than before.

She stepped around Amias and placed her hand upon the jagged stone of the tunnel. She whispered something to the earth, which Seth could neither hear nor understand. After a moment, Osza stepped away from the wall and the passageway was filled with harsh grinding as part of the wall slipped away, revealing another dark gaping maw.

The queen handed the torch to Amias and commanded him, "Enter."

Amias took the torch, his eyes wide with wonder. As his foot fell across the threshold into the exposed room, he let out an audible gasp. "Suns above, *what is this?*"

"Ancient yet fresssh," Osza quoted, gesturing for Octavia, Seth, and Lisanthir to follow Amias. "That which will herald a new generation."

"It will shake and part the stone holding Him back," Amias finished breathlessly.

As the trio maneuvered their way into the room beside Amias, they all let out hisses and gasps of disbelief. Octavia's shoulders sagged and Seth's feet dragged across the ground. The room, which was a massive cavern even larger than the previous one, was filled with the bones of an enormous dragon. Seth's eyes raked over its form, taking in each vertebrae of its tail, body, wings, and skull. Its teeth were the size of a full-grown man. Several bones were cracked and discolored, yet it lay on the ground in one piece, as if the great beast had simply curled up within the cavern and expired.

How deep underground are we that these bones are so well hidden? How old is this dragon, and when did it die?

"Long have we waited for the *Tserys* to give thisss command," Osza hissed gleefully, standing beside Amias. She stared at the skeleton with a dark hunger in her eyes. It frightened Seth, sending a shiver down his spine. "Long have we waited for Him to sssummon the dead."

Summon the dead?

Amias turned to look at Osza, his face twisted into a grimace. "You *knew* about this?"

"Of courssse, Lord Kharisss. There isss *nothing* in Iszairi that I don't know about." Though she didn't turn to look at them, there was a clear second meaning to her words, a threat issued to Seth and Lisanthir. "Praissse be that we are working together to free the *Tserys* and ressstore His resssplendence to the world."

Seth saw fear in his father's eyes. It lasted only a moment, but it was enough. He was afraid of the Asaszi queen's power. *We all are.*

"Yes, Queen Osza. Praise be," Amias echoed before turning back to the dragon skeleton. He took a step towards it, his fingers twitching at his side. His fear had dissolved underneath his curiosity. Seth could practically see the questions and theories mulling over in his father's head. He wanted to know the answers, the secrets. He wanted to know how to harness this knowledge for himself. "And what, pray tell, does the *Tserys* want us to do with these bones?"

"Herald a new generation," Osza murmured softly.

"Herald a new generation?" Amias's tone darkened, anger seeping into his words. "And how do the bones of the dead help us with that?"

"Do you think the bonesss will ssstay dead?"

Seth's father let out an exasperated sigh before bowing his head to the queen. "Queen Osza, with all due respect—"

"You do not think your ssson's legsss were our firssst foray into bringing back the dead, do you?"

"*What?!*" Seth exclaimed, the question bursting forth before he even had a chance to fully register the Asaszi's words and his own emotional response. His stomach clenched so hard that it hurt. Lisanthir's grip on his hand tightened.

Osza turned to Seth, her tongue flickering out, and her lips curling into a sardonic grin. "Though it wasss difficult altering our ssspells to a living sssubject... But we have learned *ssso* much thanksss to *you.*"

Amias forced his way between Osza and Seth, waving the torch in her face. Octavia and Lisanthir took a few steps back to give the older Provira room, jostling Seth between their uncoordinated movements. The grin slipped from Osza's face, and she let out an angry hiss, raising her hand to shield herself from the flame. Amias balked. "You're saying the *Tserys* wants us to bring this dragon back to life? *That* is the answer to opening His tomb?"

Osza lowered her hand a little to meet Amias's gaze. "You heard Hisss command."

Amias shook his head. "But that's not... He *showed* me how to open the tomb. This wasn't *it*."

Silence filled the space between Amias and Osza.

They're trying to raise the dead. Seth continued to stare at the Asaszi queen, stricken with disbelief. *She's lost her mind, they both have. Magic is gone; there's no way they can do this... But Szatisi's potion did work, even if only for a limited time.*

"It'sss not jussst about opening the tomb," Osza continued as if she were explaining something to a small child. "If we are to ressstore Hisss empire, we mussst alssso ressstore the bloodline."

Gooseflesh spread across Seth's arms and neck. He dug his fingertips into Octavia's shoulder, trying to ground himself.

Amias lowered the torch. "The next generation. After you and I die." All anger vanished from his voice as he spoke.

Osza simply flicked her tongue against the cool cavern air. Her gaze drifted to Seth and Octavia. Amias followed, turning to face his children. A low buzz filled Seth's head as he waited with bated breath for someone, *anyone*, to speak. He wanted nothing more than to leave, be gone from the presence of the ancient creature that should be no more than dust and dirt in the earth. He wanted to escape the hum, break free from whatever dangerous spell had fallen over Iszairi and ensnared his father, the other Provira, and the Asaszi.

"Thank you, Queen Osza. I will consider what you have shown us today," Amias murmured, his eyes never leaving his children. He gave the Asaszi queen several moments to respond, and when she didn't, he returned to the stone corridor, leaving the dragon's crypt behind. Octavia and Lisanthir wasted no time in hobbling after the man, leaving Osza to stand alone in the darkness.

CHAPTER XXIII: MUNNE

The two suns were barely peeking above the horizon when Munne, Mayrien, and Araloth departed from the Elviri outpost the next morning. Sleep clung to her body, her eyes straining underneath the torchlight and oncoming dawn, but her mind was clear, and warmth lingered on her arms, back, and head from her dreams the night before. From Ely's touch.

Gone were the dark thoughts that had plagued her mind the past few days. *Judgment from my kin can wait. Ely is right—I'm on the right path to both save myself and my people. Kherizhan holds the answers, and I'll be there soon.* The suns shone down on her and she felt something change in the breeze that blew from the lakes. *I'll carry Ceyo's strength with me. If not for her sacrifices and efforts, the Elviri would never have been freed from Asaszi captivity.*

The southern road out of Trent followed the tree line of the Imalar Woods, the open plains of Promthus to the west. The eastern shore of the Hourglass Lakes could be seen from around the outpost's walls, the sky's blue and purple hues reflecting in the water below. Before they had departed from the outpost, Munne ensured they had loaded their saddlebags with supplies—bedrolls, a tent, food, water, and hunting equipment. It was enough for two weeks for the three of them. She couldn't risk bringing more without raising suspicion at the outpost. Tethe and his companions would have to make do on their own.

The caravanners weren't yet on the road, but that was no matter. Munne set a slow pace on the road south of Trent, nodding her farewells to the sentries on duty. Araloth and Mayrien rode alongside her.

"Any plan to stop and wait?" Araloth asked quietly. There was no hostility in her voice, just a sullen resignation.

"Around the bend up ahead," Munne replied. *Out of sight from the outpost* was the unspoken portion of her response. It didn't need saying; the other two women understood the implication.

As the road curved to the left toward the Imalar Woods, the sound of hoofbeats could be heard from behind them. Munne cast a glance over her shoulder and saw five riders on horseback approaching at a brisk pace. She tugged on Alathyl's reins and navigated her steed to the edge of the road, leaving plenty of room for the others to pass her.

"Hail, good morning!" Tethe called out to the trio and slowed his steed to match their pace.

"Good morning, travelers," Munne responded, raising a hand in greeting. "Share the road with us?"

"Gladly!" Tethe fell in line beside Munne, his companions riding behind Araloth and Mayrien.

She noticed that they were all equipped with weapons today and idly wondered if they had purchased them before leaving the city because they certainly hadn't been armed yesterday. Various weaponry was strapped to their hips and their saddles, including a particularly large halberd secured to Jion's saddle. The sight of the caravanners being so well equipped made Munne uneasy, but she had to trust them. They were taking her to Kherizhan, after all, and their path would come very close to Moonyswyn. It was entirely possible that they'd come across a Provira patrol and would have to defend themselves.

Birds could be heard in the trees to their left. Above them the sky brightened, golds and oranges glowing amidst the blues and purples. "A fine morning, is it not?"

Munne glanced up, then at the man next to her, and her lips curved into a small smile. "That it is," she replied.

Tethe spurred his horse into a faster pace, and Munne and the others did the same. Time was of the essence. Kherizhan awaited.

"How long will the journey be?" Munne asked after several moments of silence.

"Should be no more than ten days as long as we make good progress," Tethe answered.

"And if we have to stop to hunt?"

He let out a thoughtful hum and tilted his head to the side. "Perhaps twelve or thirteen days, then, if we make good progress."

Munne nodded. "We were only able to get enough rations for the three of us, but I do have a bow and arrow."

"Oh, that's quite alright. We have some rations of our own. We'll be okay for a few days yet." Tethe offered her a disarming smile. She felt compelled to smile back, despite the action feeling strange. "We'll have to turn away from the road in about three days' time." Tethe withdrew a scroll from a satchel on his hip. He unraveled it and studied it for a few moments, trusting his horse to guide him true.

"Is that a map?" Munne inquired, stretching her neck to catch a glance of the parchment.

"Aye, with routes drawn through the Woods and the rainforest. We'll have to see what the road looks like ahead. Might be safer to go through the rain-forest."

Munne frowned. *The rainforest. Moonyswyn. He must be insane to think it'll be safer to pass through there than the Woods. Quicker perhaps? Is it worth the risk of running into the Provira?*

Tethe rolled the map back up and tucked it away into his satchel. He caught Munne's gaze, saw the frown, and said, "Might be, might not. We'll see how the road looks."

"We'll see how far north the war has reached, you mean," Munne mut-tered.

"Aye."

She let out a quiet hum and looked forward at the open road, which had turned into a well-trodden dirt path. Stones were sporadically placed along the edge of the road to mark boundaries. Lesser-used paths branched off from the road, leading to farmsteads and homes tucked into the woods and the gentle hills of Promthus. Every so often she could see cows and horses grazing in their pastures. They passed several fields of barley, onions, pumpkins, and even an orchard with pear and apple trees. Munne idly wondered if there was a winery nearby to turn those fruits into a fine vintage.

"Jion, Adalia, go see what you can buy from some of these farms," Tethe told his companions. "My lady, I would recommend we rest up ahead in a nearby grove, so they have time to shop around."

Munne arched an eyebrow and looked over at Tethe again. "They're still dressed like Elviri soldiers. No, they may not go and solicit crops from these farmers. Not dressed like that!" she snapped, her frown deepening. It'd be too suspicious for a couple of Elviri soldiers to ask for rations when the war hadn't reached this far east. Munne didn't want any attention to be drawn to their journey.

Tethe pursed his lips and tugged on his horse's reins to turn around, so he was facing his companions. "We'll stop at the grove, then you two change back to your other clothes. Then head out." He turned back to Munne. "Is that alright, my lady?"

Munne stopped Alathyl, turning to face the others as well. *I don't appreciate how he's making his own decisions on this. But I suppose we will need the food...* She nodded. "Lead us to this grove."

Tethe knocked his heels into his horse's side, driving the beast forward. They continued on the road for a few more minutes before Tethe tugged his horse off to the left toward the edge of the forest. They passed into the forest, sunslight rippling through the leaves and branches. It felt cooler beneath the canopy and Munne was reminded of the oncoming winter.

Ahead there was a break in the trees, leading to an open clearing. Tethe stopped his horse and dismounted, spreading his arms wide as if inviting the others to join him. Yvanna and Ormes were quick to dismount as well while Jion and Adalia lingered near the edge of the clearing. Araloth and Mayrien stayed close to Munne, taking their time with dismounting and turning their backs to the caravanners. Munne was the last to climb off of her horse, eyes warily tracking Jion and Adalia as they removed the Elviri riding jackets and hoods and replaced them with the cloaks and robes they had been wearing the day before back in Auora.

I'll bring those clothes back to Elimere when this is all over. They might not make it back to their rightful owners, but at the very least they'll be back in the proper lands.

When they finished changing clothes, Jion and Adalia left the grove, heading back toward the farmsteads they had passed earlier in the day. Though the suns were hardly visible through the forest boughs, Munne guessed that it was nearly midday. They had been on the road for about five hours, and likely would be for another five to six hours. They would be, anyway, once Tethe's two returned with food.

"Is there a brook or pond nearby for the horses?" Mayrien asked.

Tethe nodded. "Ormes, show them the way."

The three Elviri exchanged glances and silently agreed to go all together, rather than splitting their numbers. *Not that I think these caravanners pose a threat to us, but Mayrien and Araloth would never forgive me if I stayed behind while they left with the horses,* Munne thought.

Ormes led the three of them further into the forest, the grove slipping out of sight. No more than five minutes had passed before they reached a small creek running through the trees. All of the horses immediately took to the cool water, and the Elviri hovered by their mounts protectively. Ormes stood off to the side, trying his best to not make eye contact with any of the women. It brought Munne a small shred of pleasure to know Ormes was uncomfortable in their presence. She was sure that Araloth took even greater pleasure in that knowledge.

"Do we expect there to be much snow this winter?" Araloth said to Mayrien and Munne, perfectly happy to exclude Ormes from the conversation.

"This far south? No, it'll be chilled winds and nothing more," Munne answered, stroking Alathyl's mane.

Mayrien was doting on her horse as well, speaking quietly to it in the Elviri tongue.

"Let's fill our waterskins while we're here." Araloth held her hand out and beckoned for Mayrien and Munne to hand over theirs, which they both gladly did.

Out of the corner of her eye, Munne saw Ormes kneeling down to fill his own waterskin. Beyond the trickle of water over rocks, the only other sounds nearby were the quiet snorts of the horses and the leaves rustling in the wind. Munne inhaled deeply through her nose, savoring the scent of fallen leaves and moss. It reminded her of home, and she took comfort in that thought.

The Elviri took their time refilling their waterskins and tending to their horses. Not long after they returned to the grove, Jion and Adalia returned as well with several pouches and sacks secured to their satchels.

"Looks like a good haul," Yvanna said.

"It's enough for about seven days. We'll need to get more before we turn east," Adalia replied, pulling an apple from one of the bags and tossing it to the Elviri caravanner.

"Are we ready to get back on the road?" Munne asked, though her tone conveyed that it was less of a question and more of an order. The caravanners were quick to mumble their agreements and climb back on their horses.

The rest of the day passed uneventfully. The road twisted through the gentle hills of Promthus, the Imalar Woods always on their left and the Hourglass Lakes out of sight on their right. The farther south they went, the further away from the lakes they got, and soon the sounds of gulls and waves disappeared. They passed two small hamlets, both tucked in between hills.

Few travelers were on the road that day. They passed by a man and his son hauling a cart back to their farm. Tethe exchanged polite waves with them. Munne didn't feel comfortable socializing with the locals; the less attention they drew, the better.

I don't want word getting back to any of the Elviri outposts describing my current company. Or where we're heading.

"Might I suggest we stay the night at a nearby inn? Avoid sleeping in the dirt until we have to?" Tethe asked as the suns began to set. "Up ahead there's a lovely little cottage with enough room for our traveling band."

Munne grinded her teeth, trying to decide the best way to argue against his suggestion.

"That sounds like a good idea. What do you think, Vere'cha?" Araloth's voice cut through Munne's thoughts, and she had to stop her jaw from dropping. She hadn't expected Araloth to support any decision Tethe proposed.

If Araloth thinks it's a good idea, then I'd be wise to go along with the plan and trust she's making a sound decision. Munne unclenched her jaw and nodded her head.

"Excellent. It's just around the bend up ahead. We'll be there in no more than ten minutes."

True to his word, a column of smoke floated through the air and lanterns framed a small path that split off from the main road and led to a large two-story wood-and-stone building nearby. Attached to the building was a small stable with just enough room to accommodate their horses. Only two other horses were hitched underneath the awning, which led Munne to believe that they either belonged to the owners of the inn or a couple of other travelers.

"I'll head inside and speak to the innkeeper. Be right back," Tethe said, quickly dismounting and walking to the front door. Munne didn't even have time to verbally protest his actions.

Her frustration must have been apparent because Mayrien snickered and nudged her shoulder. "It's okay, Vere'cha. He's probably got jitters, traveling with Elviri royalty."

Munne just rolled her eyes in response, but truthfully, she was thankful for Mayrien's jest. They could use all the levity they could get.

A few moments later, Tethe returned to the stables, beckoning to the group to join him inside the cottage. A brightly burning fireplace greeted them with chairs and benches surrounding it to catch its warmth. To their right, a staircase hugged the wall leading up to the second floor. Opposite from the entrance was a threshold leading further into the main floor where a young girl was disappearing around a corner.

"The family is preparing us dinner," Tethe announced, turning to face the group. "We're the only guests here this evening."

Munne stepped beyond Tethe into the room, hovering near the fireplace. Further within the cottage she could hear a woman's voice—the innkeeper's wife she assumed—speaking to the child, instructing her to prepare rooms upstairs.

A moment later the woman stepped out from the threshold. Her blonde hair was piled on top of her head, an apron covered in flour tied around her waist. "Pardon, milords, miladies, how many rooms was it again?" she asked.

A second child peeked out from around the woman's skirts, no older than three or four years. The woman placed a hand on top of the child's head and spun them around back toward the kitchens.

Tethe looked over the group, his gaze lingering on Munne, allowing her a chance to speak first.

"Three or four?" Munne replied, leaving the final response in his hands. Her triple could share a room, depending on the number of beds available.

"Four," Tethe agreed, pivoting back to the woman. "If you're able?"

"Aye, sir, just a moment." The woman turned back to the kitchens, calling after her older child.

"Charming family," Tethe murmured to Adalia who rolled her eyes.

The first child, a girl around thirteen, came out from the threshold holding a keyring and candle dish. She curtseyed to the group, then made her way to the staircase. "If you please, follow me."

Tethe was the first to follow, then his companions with Munne and her triple bringing up the rear. Upstairs the girl used her candle to light a few sconces in the hallway before setting the dish on a small table. She removed four keys from the keyring, speaking quietly, "Mama said the first four rooms." Starting with the left side of the hallway, she unlocked one door, passed the key to Tethe, and continued to the next.

"Thank you, miss," Tethe said with a polite smile. "You'll let us know when food is ready?" She nodded, then curtseyed once more and descended the stairs. Tethe passed one of the keys over to Munne, another to Yvanna, and the last to Jion. "I'll see you all downstairs for dinner." With that, he turned toward the room his key belonged to—the second on the right side of the hallway—and disappeared inside.

"Is there anything in the stables we need to bring inside?" Adalia asked Yvanna as they went into their room—second on the left.

Munne's key unlocked the first door on the left. She led her triple inside, and was pleasantly surprised to see two beds, a dresser, a nightstand, and a table with two chairs. They had certainly slept in worse conditions before, with fewer beds.

"Are we sharing, or are we keeping a watch?" Mayrien asked with an impish grin.

Munne looked at Araloth with a tilted head, allowing the older Elviri to make the decision. "Let's see how dinner goes, and then make the decision," Araloth murmured.

The young girl came back upstairs less than half an hour later to announce that their meal was ready. The three Elviri had taken off their riding coats and larger weapons, enjoying the warmth and walls around them. Munne kept one of her boot daggers sheathed, hoping she wouldn't need to use it, but not feeling entirely comfortable leaving it behind.

The girl led the group through the entry room into the dining hall where the innkeeper and his wife were setting down a few more dishes of food onto one of the tables. Bread, ale, roasted vegetables, and mutton awaited them. Munne felt her stomach rumble in appreciation.

"Thank you for your hospitality," Tethe said, using the same overly pleasant tone and wide smile. His cheery demeanor was starting to grate on her nerves, but Munne supposed he was putting on a show to make the innkeeper feel at ease. Still, she doubted he needed to put *that* much effort into his appearance to calm or befriend those around him.

The three Elviri sat at the table and filled their plates with the bounty before them. Tethe took his time picking which cuts of meat and vegetables to pile onto his own plate. The innkeeper and his wife disappeared back into the kitchens, presumably to enjoy their own dinner with their children.

The table was silent for several minutes as the four of them ate. Tethe's companions were still upstairs, and Munne idly wondered if they were coming down for food or not. Surely they would. She didn't quite understand the delay, considering they hadn't had any substantial meals during their travels that day. And Tethe was right; it would most likely be their last night under a roof for several days to come.

Before Munne could get too wrapped up in unspoken questions, Adalia and Yvanna entered the dining room and claimed two of the seats closest to Tethe.

"Looks lovely," Adalia murmured, tearing off a chunk of bread and biting into it before laying claim to the other dishes. Yvanna was less aggressive with the food and waited patiently for Adalia to finish before filling her own plate.

"Where are the others?" Tethe asked Yvanna before drinking from his mug of ale.

"Heard Ormes trying to wake up Jion through the door. They must've been taking a nap," answered Yvanna. She stabbed her piece of mutton and cut off a small bite to chew on.

Tethe hummed and said no more.

Ormes and Jion entered the dining hall a little while later as Munne was finishing her plate. Araloth had already cleared her own plate and was reclining in her chair, gaze intently focused on the table rather than the other individuals.

"We'll meet you upstairs?" Munne said quietly to her friend.

Araloth raised her eyes to Munne and tilted her chin down ever so slightly. If she hadn't been watching her, Munne wouldn't have even noticed the gesture. The older Elviri stood and bowed to the table and took her leave and ascended the stairs.

As Munne turned her attention back to the table, she noticed Tethe's gaze lingering on the doorway where Araloth disappeared. *Curious.*

"What time will we be departing in the morning?" Mayrien asked, glancing between Munne and Tethe. Tethe's companions also seemed interested in the question, eyes darting all over the table.

"The earlier the better," Tethe started to say, but then he paused and looked to the Warlord. "But it's ultimately your decision, my lady."

Munne felt a curious wave of relief wash over her. "As soon as there's enough light for us to see where we're going."

Tethe nodded and raised his mug in agreement. "At dawn, then."

Munne returned the gesture, finishing the remaining liquid inside her mug before she stood. Her head swam for just a moment, the ale disturbing her balance. Inhaling deeply, she forced her mind to clear, and she climbed the stairs, Mayrien trailing not far behind.

At dawn, then, she repeated in her head.

CHAPTER XXIV: SETH

Iszairi: Day 7, Month 12, Year 13,239

Even after retreating from the dark catacombs beneath the *Tserdanii*, Seth couldn't get the image of the dragon skeleton out of his head, nor Osza's words. *You do not think your ssson's legsss were our firssst foray into bringing back the dead, do you?*

When Seth, Octavia, and Lisanthir returned to their suite, Seth became violently ill. He lost control of his body and could only taste the foulness as it spilled out of him. Both his sister and his lover stayed with him to ensure the worst of it had passed, and they made sure he drank enough water to wash the filth from his mouth. Seth's bed was crowded with their bodies, but he fell asleep knowing he was loved and safe.

Seth and Lisanthir spent much of the next day discussing what had happened the day prior. Octavia had disappeared before the others awoke, much to Seth's disappointment. Lisanthir wasn't entirely sure where she went, but they both had to trust that she would be okay. She and Seth held the favor of the Asaszi queen, which surely meant that no harm would come to them while they were within Iszairi.

"I wish I knew more about the spells and potions the Asaszi have been working on," Seth grumbled to Lisanthir, fidgeting with the hem of his tunic. They sat in the study, sprawled across one of the couches together. Seth's legs were perched on Lisanthir's lap with the Elviri's arm cradling them against his torso.

Lisanthir sat up, snapping his fingers. "You said the Asaszi queen gave you the freedom to go anywhere you like in the city?"

Seth's brow furrowed, but he nodded. Osza had said that to him when she had summoned him to her chambers several days prior. Part of him wanted nothing more than to get lost in another library and spend hours with Lisanthir perusing the literary collection of the Asaszi. Another, much stronger part of him was wary of the open invitation. Osza was dangerous and she knew too much. It bothered Seth that he didn't know how she would use this freedom to *her* advantage.

"Well, the academy library should be open to you now, shouldn't it? Do you think there would be any records of their work there?"

Seth's eyes widened, and he rushed to sit up straight, reaching out to grasp Lisanthir's hands. He gave each a quick kiss before grinning from ear to ear. "Brilliant, you're brilliant! Yes, they must. I don't know where else in the city they would conduct their experiments. Let's go there, right..." He trailed off, turning his gaze to the balcony. The suns were setting, casting a fiery glow across the horizon.

"Tomorrow," Lisanthir murmured. He gave Seth's hands a comforting squeeze before leaning back against the cushions. "Tonight, we rest. I fear we'll need all our strength for whatever is upon us."

The next morning, Seth arose before Octavia. Lisanthir aided him in getting dressed and ready to leave. Before they left the suite, Seth had the Elviri check in on his sister. Walking back to where Seth waited by the entrance to the suite, Lisanthir murmured, "She is still asleep. I don't recall hearing her return last night."

"I don't either," Seth said softly, the corner of his lips tugging downward. *Where did you go yesterday, Tav?*

Seth and Lisanthir descended the *Tserdanii* and emerged onto the streets of Iszairi below. Despite the early morning hours, the city was already alive with noise and action. Provira and Asaszi alike filled the streets, but the sight was much different than the streets of Lithalyon. Several Provira wore armor while most others wore the casual garb of soldiers. The Asaszi, however, were dressed in more lavish and regal clothing denoting their higher status in the city. Seth recognized the black and green robes of the academies, though nearly every student he saw was an Asaszi.

Where are all of the Provira?

The roads within Iszairi were in pristine condition with nary a bump or crater to impede Seth and Lisanthir's progress through the city. His mind returned to the stark difference between Iszairi and Yiradia and couldn't help but wonder why Iszairi was paved with brick roads while Yiradia was left for the forest to spread its roots and reclaim its land once more.

Though they walked down the major roads of the city, there were no distinct signs for any shops, nor were there any merchants peddling their wares. Despite the number of people traveling the roads around them, Seth felt totally alone. It was a stark contrast to his time in Lithalyon where he recognized all sorts of shops despite not being able to read the signage.

They passed several entrances to the coliseum on their route to the academies. Guards stood at each entrance, brandishing polished spears and shields. Seth couldn't recall guards ever being posted at the coliseum on days where there were no performances or speeches, so the sight startled him. Lisanthir tapped on his shoulder and twitched his hand toward the nearest entrance, drawing Seth's attention to the two Asaszi stationed there. Their gold serpentine eyes followed the two men as they continued down the road.

"I don't know why there are so many of them," Seth murmured, keeping his voice low enough so that only Lisanthir could hear him. The Elviri didn't respond, but Seth was sure he had several thoughts racing through his mind.

Does Osza's protection extend down here without her presence? He closed his eyes and shook his head once. *What a foolish thought. None of these Asaszi would dare go against her orders, and they all surely know there's an Elviri in their city.*

The red and gray-stoned pyramids loomed ahead, filling the sky and casting their shadows across the city. The cold winter air seeped through Seth's clothes and into his bones. The suns weren't high enough in the sky to combat the shadows. Even at midday, he doubted the suns would be able to warm the city very much. Clouds lingered on the horizon, threatening to cover the suns completely.

"Greetings, Lord Kharis," a woman called out, drawing his focus back to his surroundings. Seth looked down from the sky toward the red pyramid as a Provira woman approached them. She wore the elaborate black and green robes of the academies, nearly covering her from head to toe. Her tanned face was the only uncovered patch of skin, her green eyes matching the embroidery on her robes.

"Have you come to visit the library?" she asked.

"Yes, um, good morning," Seth mumbled, his cheeks heating with embarrassment as soon the words left his mouth. He knew how to speak to others; he had just been caught off-guard. "Yes, I'm here to visit the library."

The woman had to be only a few years older than him at most. Her eyes were still bright with youth and cheer, unlike many of the other Provira he knew. "Very good! Queen Osza sent word to us letting us know you may stop by. It's an honor to meet you, my name is Tyrarian. Are there any particular texts you'd like to see?"

Seth's skin crawled at the mention of the Asaszi queen. *Of course word has spread. Osza will want to know where we go and what we see, no doubt.* "Thank you, Tyrarian. For now, I'd just like to explore the library. This is my first time here."

"Oh, of course," Tyrarian said, half-bowing to him as they continued toward the ramp to the entrance. "If there's anything you need, please don't hesitate to ask for me, or another one of the scholars within."

Though there was enough room on the ramp for her to walk beside Seth, she stopped and allowed him and Lisanthir to go past her. When Seth cast a glance over his shoulder, he saw her bowing at the base of the ramp.

A much different experience from the Great Library in Lithalyon, Seth thought. Tyrarian reminded him of how Lisanthir had acted when they first met. *But perhaps some things are the same between our people, like our love for knowledge.* Thoughts of Amias came unbidden, and Seth regretted allowing himself to get carried away. His father's hunger for knowledge was nothing like what he had seen in Lithalyon. He was dangerous, and the thoughts and concepts he pursued in his quest for knowledge were even worse.

But perhaps there was someone worse than his father—Osza. Her schemes seemed to pose a greater threat to the Provira than Amias. *And that's just what I'm here to look for, isn't it?*

At the top of the ramp, two beautifully carved stone doors were pushed open from within, revealing two more Provira academy scholars eager to welcome Seth.

"Welcome, Lord Kharis!" they said together as Lisanthir pushed his chair through the threshold.

"If you'll follow me, Lord Kharis," Tyrarian said from behind them. Seth and Lisanthir both turned to see the woman entering the pyramid at a brisk pace. "I'll escort you to the library."

Seth flicked his eyes to Lisanthir and shrugged. The Elviri adjusted his course and followed Tyrarian deeper into the pyramid. The walls and floors were made from the same red stone as the exterior, casting the rooms in a warm glow underneath torchlight. The entry hall was filled with mosaics and banners heralding the Asaszi royal line. There were no traces of Provira ancestry here, which made Seth feel like a stranger entering hostile grounds. He wondered if Tyrarian and the other Provira felt the same.

The library was on the second floor of the red pyramid. While its collection stood no chance at rivalling the Great Library of Lithalyon, the sight of so many books and scrolls took Seth's breath away. It pleased him to be around such fountains of knowledge once more, and his heart ached at the thought of his mother's library back in Yiradia. He silently cursed his father once more for taking and destroying the books he had found in Lithalyon.

Did Grandmother leave anything behind in this library for me to find? Is that even worth pursuing, given what's going on between Father and Osza? But Grandmother had said that Osza was pursuing the wrong thing...What did Grandmother know that Osza doesn't?

Or has Osza unraveled the mysteries since Grandmother's death?

"If there's anything you need, please let me know. I'll be on this floor in one of the studying nooks," Tyrarian said softly.

Seth twisted in his chair to look at the Provira woman and nodded. "Thank you."

Tyrarian turned, her robes swishing around her ankles, and left the two amidst the rows of bookcases.

Seth angled his head so he could gaze up at Lisanthir, wishing he could gaze upon the Elviri's green eyes rather than his black veil. "I don't even know what to look for," he whispered with a self-deprecating smile. "At least last time I had a starting point."

Lisanthir chuckled quietly then leaned down, voice barely audible. "We need to know how they sort the books first."

Seth nodded and pulled his chair toward one of the bookcases, pausing to look back at the Elviri. "Do you need me to help translate?"

Lisanthir shook his head. "I should know enough."

Seth arched an eyebrow but said nothing else. His *ebilin* had studied the Elviri-Asaszi wars, so it only made sense that he would be somewhat familiar with the Asaszi cultures and customs. He wondered how many Asaszi texts the Elviri had seen before... But it didn't matter. Seth needed whatever assistance Lisanthir could give him, so he wasn't about to challenge him on this. A thrill of excitement raced through him. *We're doing this together.*

Focusing on the books in front of him, Seth browsed the various titles to try to find a pattern in the shelves. Most of the titles he was able to read, although some were written in the ancient Asaszi language. He didn't spend too much time trying to translate the titles out of concern for what little time he actually had to conduct his research.

Tinctures from the Forest. Minerals and Ores. Something Seth couldn't translate. "What's the pattern?" he murmured to himself, fingers brushing against the leather spines. After a few more volumes, he developed a theory that the section was related to rituals and ingredients. He considered finding Tyrarian to ask her how the books were sorted, but the fear of Tyrarian asking *him* questions or reporting anything back to Osza kept him from seeking her out.

Instead, he moved to another bookcase and continued to browse. Most of the titles were similar to the ones he had just turned away from, but he persisted. *Perhaps there's something in this "ritual" section about the* Tserys. *Wouldn't it have been written during the Eldest Days, though? Maybe I shouldn't be skipping the books written in the old language after all.* He grimaced and began searching specifically for those books, taking the time to translate the titles as best as he could.

Herbs and Seasons. Our Practices. Hymns.

With a sigh, he plucked *Our Practices* from the shelf and opened it but was dismayed at the lack of descriptions within. Seth set it on his lap and went back to browsing the books. After several more minutes, he had a small stack of books in his lap that he wanted to dig into, and he began searching for a table or nook where he could retreat to. Lisanthir appeared at his side, carrying his own stack of books. The Elviri nodded his head toward the end of the row they were standing in, and the two set off.

Not too far away was an alcove carved into the side of the pyramid, with sunlight pouring in from an opening in the slanted ceiling. Glancing around, it seemed that they were alone in this section of the library, so Seth positioned his chair along the open side of the table in the middle of the walkway. Lisanthir slid into the curved seat behind the table, setting his books down with a quiet thump.

"What did you find?" Seth whispered, leaning forward on his elbows.

"A few tomes on rituals, as well as one about wyrm caretakers," Lisanthir replied, taking the book from the top of his stack and opening it.

Seth nodded thoughtfully. *Decent starting places. Hopefully, we'll find something.* He moved his stack of books from his lap to the table then grabbed the top one—*Holy Nights*—and began reading.

Reading through the ancient script was very time-consuming, and there were several times where Seth had to put the book down and cradle his face in his hands. He felt a headache coming on. With a scowl, he pressed his fingertips into his brow, then returned to the book. Learning the Elviri language had been easier. It bothered him immensely that he was struggling to understand the older version of the Asaszi language, considering he was well versed in its modern equivalent.

"How are you faring with translating?" Seth mumbled unhappily, raising his eyes to Lisanthir.

The Elviri was hunched over his own book, fingers tracing words on the page. Though Seth couldn't see underneath the veil, he was sure Lisanthir's brow was furrowed and that he was frowning. "It's... difficult. And I can't tell if I'm reading about the moon or an egg," Lisanthir replied.

If he weren't so stressed, Seth might have laughed at the absurdity of the Elviri's remark. In the modern tongue, the words for "moon" and "egg" were distinct enough, but perhaps in the older version of the language, the words were more closely related. "What's this talk of eggs?"

Lisanthir pushed his book toward Seth and pointed to a specific passage. "Here. This is referring to an event of some kind, that much I can deduce, but this phrase—does this mean 'last of nights' or 'last of eggs'?"

Seth pulled the book closer, lifting the cover so he could read its title—*The Setting and Rising Suns.* "Where did you find this?"

Footsteps echoed down an aisle nearby. Seth and Lisanthir froze, staring down at the books on their table. Seth's blood raced and throbbed in his ears, nearly drowning out his surroundings. He tried to focus, listening intently for those footsteps to fade away, but they paused somewhere nearby.

Damnit, why can't they go away? He closed his eyes and inhaled through his nose as quietly as he could before opening his eyes again to focus on the book in front of him. He could at least translate the text while he waited.

The book included no mention of dates or names, which made it very difficult for Seth to determine who specifically it was referring to in its passages. He recognized some more common words for "soldiers" and "courtiers", and he could tell that they belonged to someone, a ruler perhaps, but there was no mention of the ruler anywhere that he could find.

Lisanthir reached out and gently pried the book away from Seth, drawing his attention upward. The Elviri had raised his other hand to his face, gesturing for Seth to stay silent. Rather than voice his confusion, Seth arched an eyebrow. Lisanthir pointed to the book and bent over it, presumably trying to find something to show Seth. The footsteps started up again and traveled away from their alcove. It faded away beneath the heartbeat and hum in Seth's ears.

"What are you looking for?" Seth whispered.

Lisanthir turned the book back toward Seth, then grumbled quietly under his breath and slid across the bench so he was sitting closer to Seth, knees bumping under the table. He leaned closer, their arms brushing together as he spoke softly. "There's mention in here of when the Asaszi held the Elviri captive. That was during Tser's lifetime."

"The Golden Emperor," Seth breathed. He gave Lisanthir an apologetic grin. "Sorry. He was also known as the Sun King, so perhaps that's what the title of this book refers to. King Tser's lifetime."

Lisanthir patted his hand and nodded. "Perhaps, then... yes... What do you know about the dragons from the Eldest Days?"

I know many stories and legends—but where did Mother's fables end and the truth begin? Seth's mouth tightened into a frown. "They lived in Moonyswyn before the Asaszi claimed the land, and they coexisted together after that."

"What happened to them?"

Seth was silent for several moments, drawing upon his childhood history lessons. Though not great in numbers, the dragons were mighty and powerful creatures that King Tser had brought under his control before launching his assault on the Elviri people. They were revered and worshipped as gods even after they vanished from Daaria. The dragons had spawned many wyrms who the Asaszi had kept as pets and guards in Iszairi.

"It's believed that the Elviri killed the dragons and their offspring during their revolt, when the Golden Emperor was slain in the coliseum," he told Lisanthir.

"Offspring?"

"Well, of course. The Asaszi had laid with the wyrms in Moonyswyn to keep their bloodline pure. They're descendants from the great dragons, after all." Lisanthir muttered something under his breath in his native tongue, flipping through several more pages in the book. "What is it?" Seth urged, leaning further over the table.

"Why would we not have records of such acts? The wars were so thoroughly documented..."

"You mean back in Lithalyon?"

Lisanthir nodded. His hands stopped moving, so Seth assumed he had found what he was looking for. Seth tried craning his neck to one side to better read the passages he could see for himself.

What's this about slaves and wyrms? Seth frowned. Surely, he was mistranslating what he was reading. *Why would the Golden Emperor have allowed slaves into the wyrm caverns?*

"Seth." Lisanthir's voice was barely audible. Seth strained to hear the Elviri's words over the *thump-thumping* in his ears. "Why do you think Osza wants to revive that dragon?"

We mussst ressstore the bloodline.

Seth's eyes widened. "She means to breed with the creature."

"But if *she* meant to do it, why has it taken her so long to do so? Wouldn't she have already tried?"

"She should have... It *is* her ancestor, so why...?"

"You're sure the Asaszi believe that to be true?"

Seth glanced up at Lisanthir, brows knit together, and lips tugged downward. "They teach it to Asaszi and Provira alike. Why wouldn't it be true? They even physically resemble the dragons."

Lisanthir fidgeted with the sleeve of his robe. "The Elviri have no record of the Asaszi descending from dragons. We didn't even know about the dragons' existence until hundreds of years *after* the Asaszi waged war against us."

"Then who...?" *The slaves.* Seth returned to the book, rereading the passages where he found the words "slave" and "wyrms". It took him several moments, but his fears coalesced into one horrid thought. The Asaszi hadn't laid with the wyrms; they had forced their Elviri slaves to do so. "Oh, *gods.*" *But why would they do that? Were they trying to create a new Asaszi people?*

Seth pushed the book to Lisanthir, allowing him the chance to read the passages. His gaze fixated on the Elviri's veil, wishing he could see his facial expressions as he read the ancient script. It took longer for Lisanthir to finish reading, but to his credit he didn't ask Seth for any assistance with translating. When he leaned back in his chair, he swept the veil from his face, revealing a look of horror.

"What devilry...?" Lisanthir muttered.

"Do you think she means to—" Seth choked on his words. He couldn't stomach asking his question, but he knew he needed to speak it into existence. They were already planning on fleeing Iszairi, but now they needed to *hurry.* "She knows you're an Elviri."

The half-spoken question lingered between them. Seth felt as if his chest were caving in. He knew the Asaszi queen to be ruthless, focused on the war with the Elviri. Perhaps that explained why she was so tolerant of Lisanthir's presence in Moonyswyn despite him being her enemy. She was planning on using him in some twisted breeding ritual with an undead dragon.

To restore the bloodline.

Unspoken, he thought of the other Elviri prisoners within the city. Amias was planning on sacrificing them in a ritual to open the Tomb of the Prince, but would Osza allow that, or would she confiscate them for her own nefarious plans?

"We need to find Octavia," Seth breathed.

Lisanthir inhaled deeply, nodding. He allowed the veil to drop across his face once more and slid out of the alcove. He collected their books to return them to the shelves.

Like we were never here. Seth tried to calm his racing heart, knowing that Lisanthir was doing the right thing. That way Tyrarian, or any other scholar, wouldn't know what they had been researching. But still, it would only be a matter of time before Osza made her move against Lisanthir. *Hopefully Tav's figured out a way for us to get out of this city.*

CHAPTER XXV: RAY

Keitri was the one to wake Ray and Niamnh the following day. He knocked on the door with his tail, the gentle *thud* stirring the girls from their slumber. Ray simultaneously felt like she had slept too long and not long enough. Her eyes didn't burn when she opened them, but she had the strong desire to burrow further into the pile of furs and fall back asleep.

Beside her, Niamnh stirred from her side of the furs. They had pushed their piles together to sleep side by side. With the Doshara no longer inhabiting her body, Niamnh's skin was warm once again, almost burning hot. Ray had pushed a few of the furs away during the night so her own skin could cool down. Less furs were preferable to moving away from the princess.

Niamnh climbed to her feet and let the Enthai into the room, Ray cracking open one of her eyes to observe. Only one candle in the room still burned, although its flame was small. She heard Niamnh and Keitri exchange whispers.

"We leave soon. My tribe has prepared you belongings for the road," Keitri said.

"Thank you." Ray heard the tension in Niamnh's voice. The princess still held a healthy distrust for the Enthai, even after their displays of hospitality. She couldn't really blame her. Even with all of the unbelievable things they'd witnessed the past couple of days, Ray struggled to determine who she could trust, and how much she could trust them.

"I also bring a gift. For you, princess." Keitri reached into one of the pockets on his robe, withdrawing something and handing it to Niamnh. "*Eikkis* of your brother, fashioned into bracelets. We take no pleasure in what we have to do to keep the Dosharas from escaping Na'roc. From my tribe to yours, I hope this gift brings you some semblance of peace."

Niamnh and the Enthai were silent for a few moments as the princess looked over the gifts. Ray wished she could see the look on her face, but she didn't want to intrude on their private discussion. She hadn't known Prince Robyn, beyond knowing he was royalty. It didn't make sense to butt in on something familial. Personal.

"Thank you." When Niamnh spoke the words, her voice cracked, and the message was genuine.

For the first time, Ray looked upon the Enthai with respect. They weren't bloodthirsty creatures bent on killing anyone who stepped foot in their lands. They had honor and humility. If only more Proma could see it, perhaps then the horror stories would cease to spread.

But what would we warn our children away from?

A physical jolt pulled Ray back into consciousness. "Ray, it's time to wake up," Niamnh called out softly,

"I'm gettin'," Ray mumbled. She hadn't realized she fell back asleep while Keitri was in the room. She blinked a few times and looked over Niamnh's shoulder to see that the Enthai had already left.

"Keitri brought us clothes to change into," Niamnh continued. She shifted her weight from her toes to her heels to give Ray some space, which she gladly took to sit up and stretch her arms over her head. "He said someone will be waiting outside to escort us to the sleds."

"Back to the sleds, huh?" Ray rubbed her eyes. "Their wolves are enormous."

"They really are," Niamnh echoed in agreement. She stood and paced around the room, dropping some clothing onto the ground beside their bed. "Here, for the journey."

"Thanks." Ray twisted her torso to pick up the clothing and inspect each piece.

The Enthai had given them new robes, coats, and boots to wear. The coats had hoods sewn onto the backs along with a pair of mittens secured to the wrist cuffs. Everything was extremely soft to the touch, and Ray knew she would be comfortable traveling in them. Looking over at her own coat struck her with a pang of sadness. She didn't want to abandon the blue handprint and lidless eye of the Walkers, but it probably made no sense to bring it with. She wasn't even entirely sure where they were headed.

Rymo-tehp. The word repeated over and over in her head, but it sparked no memories. The place was clearly important, although it remained to be seen as to why. But surely the Enthai would return to the temple after the trip, and Ray could retrieve her belongings before going home to Promthus. Or at least, that's what she hoped for. Still, she decided it would be beneficial to at least take Naro's sunsdial, if for no other reason than to orient herself once she was outside again. As the wooden box slipped into her left coat pocket, she tried to push away the budding resentment and fear growing inside of her. *Naro's kept so many secrets from me, from the Walkers. What can I trust is true?*

"Do you know anything about where we're going?" Ray asked the princess.

Niamnh shrugged. "Not very much, I'm afraid. I know it's a ruin far to the northwest. An Elviri ruin if I remember correctly."

Ray let out a thoughtful hum and said nothing more. She couldn't recall the name from any of Naro's history books. And as far as she knew, the Elviri had always lived in the Telatorr Mountains and to the southwest. She couldn't remember anything about a northern city.

The new clothing fit her quite well, and she enjoyed the slide of fur and hide against her skin. As she finished pulling on her new boots, she looked over to Niamnh, who stood near the door staring at something in her grasp. Ray struggled to decide if she should ask after the bracelets, or if she should clear her throat to draw attention to herself, allowing the princess to slip the bracelets away, out of sight.

Would she want to talk about them? Ray thought. *She hasn't brought up her family at all during our journey.* She opened her mouth before she could consider any other course of action. "What's that?"

Niamnh cast a quick glance over her shoulder before returning to the bracelets, she replied, her voice barely above a whisper, "My brother, Robyn."

Ray crossed the room and peered over Niamnh's shoulder, marveling at the fine craftsmanship of the bracelets. The yellow-white bone had been secured to a thick strap of leather by braided rope. Little blue and white beads were woven into the braid, bringing beauty and color to such a macabre scene.

"It looks lovely."

Niamnh nodded. "He's finally going to come home."

Ray had no response to that. None that wouldn't bring tears to her eyes, anyway. Glancing toward the princess, Ray saw she was biting her lower lip, her eyes downcast. She placed a hand on the girl's shoulder and squeezed gently. "Time to go?"

Niamnh nodded again, inhaling sharply through her nose. "Back onto the ice."

"Back onto the ice," Ray echoed, although as soon as the words left her mouth, she started wondering just how brutal the trip would be, even with their comfortable new clothing.

Outside of their room, another Enthai was waiting for the two girls to depart. Ray was fairly certain she hadn't met that Enthai before. The creature didn't say a word to them as they made their way through the corridors and back to the surface level of the temple. In the main halls, the fire pits burned brightly, their flames dancing off of the ice pillars and walls. She felt an urge to look over her shoulder at the massive mural at the back of the hall but forced herself to keep her gaze forward.

The sky outside was dark, but the snow provided a strange soft glow on their surroundings that made it easy for Ray to see. Waiting at the foot of the steps was Keitri, along with a few other hooded, robed Enthai. Their escort bowed to Keitri, sweeping their bushy gray tail over their feet before taking their leave.

Keitri turned his attention to the girls and flicked his tail away from the temple. "Come, the sleds are just beyond this bluff."

It brought Ray relief to know they wouldn't be journeying through those pitch-black tunnels again. Or at least not yet. It seemed that Rymo-tehp was in a different direction than Promthus, which made some degree of sense. Ray's hand instinctively went to her left coat pocket, feeling for Naro's sunsdial. When her fingers grazed the wooden box, her face twisted into an ugly frown, and she jerked her hand from her pocket.

I can't, was her first thought. But then she tried to rationalize with herself. *It's simply a tool. I can use it to orient myself.*

"*We go northwest.*" Mother Shade's voice filled Ray's head, prompting her to turn toward the entrance to the temple.

Niamnh must have heard the voice as well because she also turned around, and they both saw the ethereal woman standing at the top of the stairs, white light emanating from her robes like a lantern in the night. The Enthai hooted and yipped softly, tails swishing frantically against the snow. Ray's lips parted in a silent gasp as Mother Shade descended the stairs, appearing to float rather than walk.

The woman paused in front of Niamnh. The princess raised her chin, trying to meet the woman's gaze. They stood still for several minutes, drawing Ray's curiosity and concern.

Mother Shade is talking to her, no doubt about it. But what *is she talking about? What's she hiding from the rest of us?* Ray thought.

Gooseflesh littered Ray's skin as a warm tendril wrapped around her mind, soothing her thoughts and shielding her from any sharp questions. Mother Shade's voice echoed in her head once more. "*Be at peace, Ray. All will be known before the end.*"

Ray blinked, pulling herself from her reverie to see that Mother Shade had floated past Niamnh toward the Enthai. Behind the woman trailed a dark shadow, shaped vaguely like...

Daerion.

Ray's heart thudded loudly in her chest. She tore her gaze off of the Doshara and toward Niamnh to see if the girl had noticed him. To her dismay, she had. An ugly scowl covered Niamnh's face, and she turned away from him coldly, moving quickly to catch up to Mother Shade. With one final glance in Daerion's direction, Ray followed the other girl.

Rather bold of him to show his face after everything he's done.

"*And yet there is still more he must do before the end.*" Ray couldn't stop the look of confusion from twisting onto her face. She looked toward Mother Shade and opened her mouth to speak, but the woman cut her off. "*Remember my words. All will be known.*"

Off in the distance, dimly illuminated by the light of the rising suns, Ray saw four sleds each outfitted with a pack of wolves and several sacks and crates stacked on top. Three Enthai were looking over the sleds, ensuring everything was properly secured and that the wolves were ready to run. Keitri let out a series of high-pitched barks, which the others echoed back with slight variation. He jerked his tail forward and picked up the pace, the group now moving in a haste to get to the sleds.

"Princess, you join me. Little Walker, you join Enesse," Keitri said to the girls over his shoulder. He touched the tip of his tail to Niamnh's hand and led her off to the front-most sled while Ray was guided to the third. She remembered Enesse from the previous day, although the Enthai had bundled up and covered her face with scarves and a hood so Ray couldn't easily identify her.

Enesse guided Ray on how to properly sit on the sled so that the leather straps wouldn't pinch or hurt her while they were riding. Enesse took up the rear perch, gathering the reins in her paws. She tapped her left paw against the large sack that sat between her and Ray.

"Better to lean against this than try to sit straight," the Enthai said.

Ray twisted around to see what the Enthai was referring to and then leaned back against the sack. Ahead of them, Niamnh had already settled down on Keitri's sled and the chieftain was standing at the back. The other two sleds were covered with pelts and bags, each with one Enthai standing at the rear. Keitri let out a few barks and was answered with several yips and whines from the other Enthai riders.

The three creatures who had been tending to the sleds took several steps away from the pack, and with the crack of the reins, Keitri's wolves took off, dragging the sled behind as they charged across the tundra. Enesse howled and her wolves responded. She cracked her own reins and the pack took off. The momentum pushed Ray back against the rucksack behind her, and she was very thankful she wasn't leaning forward before they started running.

The air was cold and frigid against her skin as they raced down a gentle slope and out onto the open plain. Through squinted eyes, Ray watched Keitri's sled out in front and realized Mother Shade was floating right beside the Enthai as he steered his pack of wolves. In a panic, she twisted her head from side to side looking for Daerion, but the Doshara was nowhere to be found. She squirmed uncomfortably on the sled, her muscles refusing to relax.

He's here somewhere. But Protector above, I wish he wasn't.

Ray was unsure of how much time passed during the first sprint, or how much distance they covered. After descending the slope and starting away from the temple, the sky turned a lighter gray and snow began to fall, obscuring her vision and making it difficult to see the landscape around her. The ground was flat, and the wolves never swerved, so it seemed safe to assume that they were traveling on a straight—or straight enough—path to Rymo-tehp.

There were a few instances where she wanted to pull Naro's sunsdial from her pocket and see which direction they were moving in, but each time she stopped herself. Mother Shade had told them that they were heading northwest. That should be good enough for Ray.

Ajak wouldn't've let that stop him.

She wanted to curse her treacherous mind for drifting back to Ajak, and her treacherous heart for squeezing and throbbing in pain. Thoughts and feelings surfaced, unbidden, and she could do nothing to stop them from drowning her in bittersweet memories and heartache. It had only been two weeks since the castle heist, but it felt like two years, yet the pain of losing him was still so fresh.

Naro may have hidden his true identity from her, but Ajak never did. She knew all of his flaws, as well as his strengths, and he had offered himself to her, nonetheless. He may not have been able to give her everything she wanted, but at least she would've known exactly *what* she was getting. Memories of their last night in the safehouse bubbled up, and if she closed her eyes, she could see him stretched across one of the beds, wine bottle in hand, tanned skin flushed from the drink. Candlelight flickering across his warm brown eyes. An open invitation.

I should've slept with him in the safehouse. We both needed comfort that night, and I could've given that to him, and he could've told me I was his one and only...

A sob ripped its way through her chest and throat, but the noise was lost to the howling winds. If Enesse heard her, the Enthai did nothing to acknowledge her. Tears spilled from her eyes, going from hot to frigid cold on her eyelashes in a matter of seconds. She raised her hand to rub away the moisture before it could freeze. As she cried, she felt a heavy weight being lifted from her chest, and it felt *good*. She needed to be honest with herself and allow herself the chance to mourn not just Ajak, but the life she could've had with him.

I need to be strong like he would've been.

Taking a deep breath through her mouth, she shoved her hand into her pocket and pulled out Naro's sunsdial. Her thumb idly stroked the outside of the ashen gray box as she mustered the courage to open it and withdraw the compass itself. As she slid her thumb down to pry the box open, Enesse let out a sharp bark over the howling wind, and her wolves responded. They slowed down, as did Ray's courage. Sliding the box back into her pocket, she pressed her lips together in a tight frown.

I will be strong... but not yet.

Snow still fell from the sky but at a much slower rate than earlier in the day. Enesse's wolves came to a stop near Keitri's and the other two sleds. The female Enthai hopped off the back of her sled and trotted over to the wolves, running her paws along their sides and nuzzling against their faces. The wolves surrounded her and nudged her back, licking her fur and letting out happy huffs of air into her face. Keitri's deep howl filled the air, and it was joined by both the other Enthai and all of their wolves. Ray was glad that they were her allies because their combined howls were frightening enough to turn even the bravest knight's blood to ice.

Thank the Protector we never heard that while we were traveling. I would've never slept again. With a grimace, Ray realized that still may be the case. It was a sound she would certainly never forget.

Keitri leaned over his sled, presumably saying something to Niamnh, before approaching Ray. "The wolves rest and eat. We'll continue our journey shortly."

Ray nodded her head and thanked him for the information before unstrapping herself from the sled and climbing to her feet. It felt good to be standing after hours of sitting and being dragged across the tundra. She stretched her arms up, out, then down to her toes. When she straightened herself out again, Enesse was standing beside her, pressing a waterskin into her hands.

"Drink," the Enthai commanded.

Ray took the waterskin, raised it to her lips, and drank. At that stage in her journey, she felt confident enough to trust whatever food or drink the creatures gave her, even when the bitter taste hit the back of her throat. They were feeding it to her for a reason; she just needed to trust in them and finish it off.

"What was that?" Ray asked after swallowing the last drop. She forced it down with a wince, wiping her mouth on her sleeve.

"Muddled herbs from the swamplands to the south," Enesse responded, her tail idly flicking from side to side. "It keeps away the hunger while we travel, so we don't weigh down our *ahkkoros* with unnecessary burdens."

Ray had heard of such herbs before back home. The Barauder of the Black Lakes would trade them with the Imalarii who would bring them to Auora. Because of all the hand-offs and the distance traveled, the herbs fetched several shiny pieces of gold once they hit the marketplaces in Auora. The herbs were considered luxury items for merchants, craftsmen, and soldiers who traveled across Daaria. To be eating—well, drinking—them now left Ray with a mixture of pleasure and confusion. Part of her felt wrong about drinking it, knowing she could never afford to buy it back home. But another part of her was thrilled at the new experience.

These would've helped on the journey to Na'roc. If only Naro—

Her stomach clenched tightly, and a grimace passed across her face.

"The bad taste should pass soon," Enesse said with a softer tone, seeing Ray's distress but not understanding its source.

Ray simply nodded and murmured, "Thanks."

The Enthai's gaze lingered on her for another moment or two before she turned away to speak with the other Enthai in their own language. Ray rubbed her eyes again, taking in her surroundings. The four Enthai were huddled together nearby, tails curling around each other. She wondered if it was just a pleasantry, or if the gesture meant something more. Now that the fear of death had subsided, she found herself wanting to learn more about the beings and their culture.

Opposite from the Enthai, Niamnh was taking sips from her own water-skin. Their eyes met and Ray couldn't help but smile at her. The princess perked up, her lips curling upward as well. Something dark crossed her eyes, and her smile faltered for a moment.

Panic seeped through Ray's bones. *What did I do?* But then she realized Niamnh wasn't looking at her, but *past* her. Twisting her neck to the side, Ray caught a glimpse of what the princess was really looking at—Daerion. His shadow lingered within arm's reach of her, looming overhead.

The sight of the shade startled her, and she jumped forward a bit, trying to put some more space between them. When she glanced back to Niamnh, the girl was closer. She had taken a couple of steps toward them, the waterskin forgotten at her side. Ray saw a sea of emotions swirling across Niamnh's face, ranging from anger to sadness to *fondness*. A dark emotion reared its ugly head from within Ray's mind, and she found herself moving forward to stand in between Niamnh and Daerion, to block him from the princess's sight.

After getting nearly within arm's reach, Niamnh quickly turned and walked back toward Keitri's sled. The girl moved too fast for Ray to read her face, and she was left feeling hurt and confused. She squeezed her eyes shut and inhaled deeply through her nose before spinning around to face the Doshara, but he was gone.

Ray tilted her head to the side, her brow furrowed. *Why does Niamnh still hold some kind of affection for him? And why did she turn away from me?*

Mother Shade's words echoed in her head, but she couldn't tell if it was from memory or if the woman was speaking to her again, *"All will be known."*

Ray spent the remainder of their short rest pacing around Enesse's sled. She didn't know how long they would be riding for, so she wanted to take advantage of the freedom as much as possible. Neither Niamnh nor the Enthai interrupted her, which only provoked her thoughts to spiral out of control. By the time they were climbing back onto their sleds, Ray was in quite the sour mood. She tried closing her eyes and getting some rest, but the wind bit at her exposed cheeks and nose, leaving her feeling uncomfortable and eagerly awaiting the next break in their run. She stubbornly refused to open her eyes because she didn't want to stare at Keitri's sled, nor get startled by Mother Shade or Daerion.

Several more hours later, the pack stopped near a small overhang with enough space to sit underneath. The sky grew dark once more, the snow little more than specks of dust. Nighttime was approaching. Ray marveled at how her stomach still felt full thanks to the herbs from earlier in the day.

Wonder how long that'll last.

As she paced around Enesse's sled, she caught sight of a shadow approaching Keitri's sled where Niamnh was sitting. Ray turned toward the princess, raising a hand to call out to her, but she hesitated when she heard the other girl's voice.

"What do you want, Daerion?" Weariness seeped through Niamnh's voice.

Ray couldn't hear the Doshara's response over the low whistling wind. Part of her wanted to cross over to them and tell Daerion to go away. To leave Niamnh alone. To—

"*Those two have walked a long path together,*" Mother Shade whispered in her ear. "*And they must walk a little further before the end.*"

"The end?" Ray repeated, turning her head to the right. The woman's white robes filled her vision, leaving only a sliver of gray sky on the edge of her peripheral.

She felt a gentle weight settle on her left shoulder as Mother Shade spoke again. "*It is inevitable.*"

Ray lost herself in the woman's glow. The bite of the wind lost its edge, and warmth curled through her body down to her toes. It was like being nestled in a bed full of blankets. After several moments, she turned to face Niamnh and Daerion again and was surprised to see the girl standing in front of him, chin tilted up in defiance as she spoke, but Ray couldn't hear her words. She couldn't hear anything except her own breathing and Mother Shade's comforting whisper.

"She looks unhappy," Ray murmured, watching as Niamnh's face twisted into a scowl. The princess looked back down to the ground, hands tightly clutching something—Robyn's bones?

"*She struggles to decide on how she wants to treat him.*"

Ray frowned, turning back to Mother Shade. She had to tilt her head back to see the hood and the void underneath. The briefest reflection of light indicated that the woman was returning her gaze. "He killed her mother, ruined her whole life so she couldn't eat or be trusted around her father, no doubt killed countless others—"

"*All cruel actions, without a doubt. But Daerion Valha was not always a cruel man, and even when driven to acts of cruelty, he still held room for mercy in his heart.*"

Ray was no stranger to people with dubious morals. Naro, Ajak, Sabyl, and all the other Walkers had stolen, bribed, or killed before. Ray herself was no paragon of virtue. She had kidnapped the princess of Promthus and spirited her away to the frozen northlands, never mind all of the other petty thievery from merchants and churches back home. But Daerion, the Doshara who had possessed the princess for six years, threatened Ray multiple times during their journey, and even attempted to kill her? She struggled with the idea that the fiend had any room in his heart for goodness, or even neutrality.

But Niamnh cares about him.

Ray looked back to the princess and was surprised to see she had turned away from Ray and the others, and Daerion had his hand hovering over her shoulder. Could Niamnh feel his touch? His coldness? An ugly feeling twisted Ray's stomach and seized control of her heart. The sky turned an even darker shade of gray and snow began to fall again in earnest.

"If you seek understanding, perhaps Daerion could provide the answers to you."

Ray physically recoiled at the suggestion, several thoughts racing through her mind. *That monster? He'd probably rather tear me apart than talk to me. Not to mention, is it even safe to be around him—*

"The threat he posed to you and everyone else has diminished. Daerion Valha is little more than a shadow waiting for his sun to set." As Mother Shade's words filled Ray's head, Niamnh stepped away from Daerion and wandered off to the overhang to take shelter from the new snowfall. The Doshara didn't follow.

Ray pulled her hood closer to her face, burrowing her chin into its fur lining. Snowflakes fell *through* Daerion. The wind didn't rustle his hair the same way it did hers. Immaterial. *He can't harm me.* The revelation nudged against her, her head bobbing slightly in response. Still wary, she looked over his form and tried to look upon him from a new perspective. *He has a history with Naro. Maybe he can tell me more about him.*

The air around her grew colder. She tucked her hands into her armpits and hunched over, trying to retain as much warmth as possible. Glancing back toward the overhang, Ray saw that Mother Shade had disappeared. Daerion hadn't, though.

Be strong. Like Ajak.

Inhaling sharply through her nose, Ray approached Daerion. "Um, Daerion, is it?"

The Doshara threw a look at her over his shoulder, giving her a full view of his profile. The bridge of his nose had a distinct curve to it, and he had a strong jawline. Strands of dark hair fell across his face.

The corner of his lip was curled upward in a deprecating smirk. "You can do better than that, little moth," he said.

"I could always go back to simply calling you 'Doshara' or 'demon' if that's better?" Ray's retort was equal parts aggression and fear. There was very little venom in her words, which he would no doubt shrug off.

She caught sight of Daerion's smirk shifting into a genuine grin before he turned his back to her, facing the tundra. "Even with blunted edges, sparring has its joys. But I do prefer hearing my actual name if it's all the same."

"Why didn't you give Niamnh your name?" As soon as the words left her mouth, Ray wished she could've taken them back. Daerion went rigid, his hands twitching and slowly curling into fists. Disregarding concern for her safety, Ray continued, "She told me you never gave her your name. She only found out about it—"

"Is the name 'Daerion Valha' remembered in the cities of Promthus?" Daerion spun around, his voice eerily calm and quiet. "Do the Proma remember their crown prince, wrongfully slain by his Sworn Sword for false accusations?"

Crown prince?

Ray met his stare but stayed silent. She knew very little of the royal family, other than the fact that every firstborn son was named Nelle and had been for generations. She knew no Daerion Valha, other than the ghost standing in front of her now.

"They twisted my image, painting me as a demon and monster. The cursed prince," Daerion hissed. He snapped his head to the side, squeezing his eyes shut. He was silent for a moment before he nodded and opened his eyes again. "Cursed, indeed."

Ray *did* have some recollection of a cursed prince in Auora's history. She must've read about him in one of Naro's history books. Hundreds—maybe thousands—of years ago, one of the Nelles fought valiantly against a challenger to the throne and had slain the man. She opened her mouth to tell Daerion, but something about his stance and facial expression, made her pause. He was hunched over ever so slightly, as if carrying a heavy burden upon his shoulders. In his dark eyes she saw centuries of sadness and anger. Daerion had already lived through those history books; he knew how he was remembered.

Ray shifted her weight uncomfortably between her feet. It was unnerving seeing the Doshara so vulnerable, so she decided to change the subject, asking a question that had been bothering her for the past day. "Do you know where we're going and why?"

"Rymo-tehp, the ancestral home of the Elviri. Why, I couldn't say. Mother Shade must've seen something in either Niamnh's or your memories that scared her to set out so quickly and push the Enthai like this."

What did she see? Was it something in my head, or Niamnh's? Ray looked down at her feet and kicked her heel against the snow, disturbed by the quiet revelation. Mother Shade had said something about Daerion potentially dooming everyone. *Does he know she said that?* She wanted answers, but she wasn't sure if she was going to get them, even if she asked.

After a few moments she looked back up at him from underneath her eyelashes, ready to avert her gaze or close her eyes if needed. She decided she wanted to change the subject again, but before she could consider *what* she wanted to say, she blurted out, "I had to lie to bring you here."

"Not the first time you've had to lie, knowing your allegiance," he replied.

Her stomach lurched and she squeezed her arms around her chest. Tilting her chin up so she could fully look upon him, she asked, "Would he have lied to you, too?"

She already knew the answer. *Yes, Naro would've lied.*

Daerion's eyes flicked to the side, breaking their stare. A silent admission if there ever was one. But that wasn't anything special, nothing indicative of who Naro was beyond a skilled liar—an important trait for a gang lord to have.

"You said you've known him for three thousand years?" she asked, shifting her weight to her toes. Easier to jump away, just in case.

Daerion let out a quiet chuckle that sounded more like a cough. "How quickly time passes in between the bodies and blood." His words made it sound like anything but.

"But... how?" That was the part she couldn't fully understand. If Naro had been around for thousands of years, how come no one had noticed? He had a very distinct appearance with his mismatching eyes, never mind his dyed hair. The man loved to draw attention to himself and could always be picked out from a sea of strangers in a tavern.

"Many-Faced One," Daerion murmured with something akin to respect. With the way he gazed past her head, she wondered if he was even aware of how he spoke. Blinking slowly, his attention returned to her, and he seemed to find himself again. "Not a title given without merit."

Ray struggled to wrap her mind around the concept of changing faces, but she had always known Naro was magic-touched. But she hadn't understood just *how* magical he was. Her eighteen years suddenly felt so small and in-significant next to the idea of Naro being over *three thousand* years old.

How long has he been leading the Walkers? How many of us has he seen come and go and die? Do we mean anything to him? Do I?

A knot formed in her throat, and she found herself reaching for Naro's sunsdial box. As her hand wrapped around it, she froze and looked at Daerion, who had his eyes on her pocket.

His voice was barely above a whisper. "You still carry his sunsdial?" She nodded mutely.

His gaze softened and something she couldn't recognize crossed over his face. It appeared as if he was waiting for her to fish out the box and bring it out in the open. Drawing strength from the Doshara, she pulled the box out and held it in her open palm. Daerion reached out with one hand and placed it gently on top of the box. Ray expected to feel the added weight of his hand on hers, but there was nothing. His skin flickered and glowed with soft light, melding with the ashen gray wood.

"He always had an eye for exotic trinkets."

A small smile crept onto Ray's face. *That he did.* She raised her other hand and slipped it *through* his, opening the box to reveal the sunsdial and paint-ings within. Watching her gloved hand pass through Daerion's was strange, almost frightening. Nothing happened and his hand remained hovering over the box, completely unaffected by her movements.

"It looks just as it did the last time I saw it." Daerion's voice was barely above a whisper.

The words weren't meant for her, she could tell. But Ray decided to prod him further. "When *was* the last time you...?"

The Doshara didn't respond. His gaze was fixed on the painting of the sun. She wondered if he knew of the inscription surrounding the orange-and-red orb, or what it said. With deft fingers she picked up the sunsdial and pocketed it, holding the box up so Daerion could see the painting better.

"Do you know what the inscription says?" she asked, hoping he would respond.

The shade let out a quiet hum. "He told me it was a poem in his native tongue. I never learned what the translation was, though."

A third hand reached out for the box, skin soft and glowing as her fingers brushed against the painting. *Mother Shade.*

Ray looked up at the woman, her sudden appearance sending a small shiver down the girl's spine. "'*One joins another, only to be torn asunder,*'" the woman said, her rumbling voice twisting Ray's small shiver into a full-body convulsion as she translated the inscription. "*One of Nahaesyraellonore's visions, no doubt. And soon the sundering shall begin. We must make haste.*"

CHAPTER XXVI: MUNNE

Eastern Promthus: Day 2, Month 12, Year 13,239

Munne and the others had been traveling south for four days, only turning east toward the Imalar Woods the previous night. Tethe and his companions weren't the worst group to travel the roads with, but Munne did find herself missing the company of Lagazi and the other Barauder. It wasn't that Tethe wasn't pleasant. If anything, he was *too* pleasant, and it grated on her nerves. The rest of his lot were usually silent, only speaking to each other in hushed tones.

Araloth's rage and frustration had faded to a dull annoyance, no longer casting withering stares in Munne's direction. She had resigned herself to the journey and for that, Munne was thankful. If they returned to Elimere, she was sure that Araloth would unleash the full extent of her anger at that time, giving her heartache and bruises that would last for weeks.

If? Munne's brow furrowed as she considered that dark thought.

"The weather should favor us today, I think," Tethe announced to the party.

Munne latched onto the distraction, casting her gaze up to the sky. The two suns beat down on the land with not a cloud in sight. She greatly appreciated their warmth today, as it had gotten colder in a short amount of time. Soon they'd be traveling underneath the boughs of the Imalar Woods, making it colder still. The heat from Ely's imprints was fading; he hadn't visited her since the night in Trent. She wondered when she would see him next.

Perhaps tonight? She held onto that thought, that hope, and let it linger on the edge of her mind. Perhaps he would hear her that way. *Perhaps we can talk about what Kherizhan will be like, now that there are no other distractions keeping me from my journey.*

"I don't think we've asked yet, but what goods does your caravan normally carry?" Mayrien asked, targeting her question at the caravanners.

Munne glanced over her shoulder, noticing Adalia and Ormes looking to Tethe, as if waiting for him to respond.

"It depends on our contracts." Tethe's voice was steady and slow as he spoke, choosing his words carefully. "Sometimes Moon's Wares ferries goods between Imalar and Promthus. Other times we travel to Kherizhan and other faraway places to search for treasures."

Odd way for a caravan leader to speak. Shouldn't he be proud of his work, especially if he's off discovering treasure?

"Where do you bring these treasures to?" Araloth asked.

"Patrons in Auora and Lithalyon," Yvanna replied, drawing all eyes to her person. She hadn't been very forthcoming with information up to that point, so Munne was a little shocked by the woman's voice. The Elviri seemed to recognize that she had suddenly become the center of attention, and quickly dropped her gaze to her horse, pursing her lips tightly.

"Though most of what we bring back are mundane artifacts. Rare is it that we unearth something magical like the disk I showed you," Tethe went on. A grin crossed his lips, more like a predator than a placater. The sight churned Munne's stomach, leaving her feeling very unsettled.

"I beg your pardon, but how many of these 'magical trinkets' have you unearthed?" Araloth asked, most certainly *not* begging Tethe's pardon. "I've never heard of such things, and word would've circulated among the nobility in the Elviri provinces if any of the families had come across one."

"Anyone with a connection to the Daarian Council would have mentioned it, surely," Mayrien added, although her voice was not as firm as Araloth's.

Munne was inclined to agree with her companions. The Elviri weren't so greedy that a noble would keep knowledge of a magical object from their peers. If anything, they'd share the news, so that expeditions could be set up to travel to Kherizhan and try to find more. The Moon's Wares would be a famous caravan, and Tethe's face recognizable upon first glance. But neither was true.

Munne opened her mouth, intent on questioning Tethe about the names of his clients, but he spoke before she had a chance to. "Our clients pay us well to maintain their anonymity. If word got out that magic was, in fact, still in Daaria, it would paint a target on the backs of whoever held it in their hands." His predatory smile disappeared, his expression serious.

She couldn't find any flaws in his logic, but it still disturbed her that there were people in Elimere, Elimaine, or Elifyn who had met with this caravan previously, had *seen* something magical, and hadn't spoken about it to anyone.

Unless the nobility have such great mistrust in me that they wouldn't deem it appropriate to tell me? Have I fallen so far from grace? Munne closed her eyes tight, willing the negative thoughts away. *No, I would have heard about this. Araloth, Mayrien, Elvarin, my father... Even if the nobility have lost faith in me, they haven't lost faith in the others.* "Do we need to hunt today, or can we keep moving until nightfall?" Munne inquired, shifting the topic to something else in an attempt to diffuse the situation.

"Jion?" Tethe called over his shoulder.

"Could do a stew tonight without, if we find a river or some other body of water," Jion responded from the rear of the pack. He had been taking care of the pack mule during their journey, and Munne had to acknowledge that the man had a natural affinity for animals, and he knew how to put together several delicious meals. He tended to all five of the caravanners' mounts. "We may want to stop sooner, though. Looks like a couple of our horses're getting tired for the day."

"Yve, ride ahead and find us somewhere to make camp." The order came smoothly from Tethe's lips, and his Elviri companion urged her horse to a gallop. He was clearly no stranger to issuing orders and expecting others to follow his every whim.

Why take up caravanning and not some other profession? Or even an aspiration to knighthood? Munne wondered if it was even worth taking the time to ask the man those kinds of questions. She couldn't easily tell his age, but she was familiar enough with Proma customs that he was too old to follow the traditional path to knighthood. Perhaps he had been a wayward youth, and didn't actually decide on his future until he was much older and therefore cut off from certain paths. She was surprised at just how much she wanted to learn more about the Proma, but she kept her thoughts to herself. She didn't need to know any of that information. She just needed to get to Kherizhan.

Yvanna came galloping back to the group thirty minutes later. "If we dip into the forest, there's a clearing with a small creek running through it. We'd be stopping early, but we could leave earlier in the morning."

"Alright, lead us there," Tethe replied, gesturing for the Elviri to ride in front of the others.

Munne fell into step with Tethe and asked, "Do you not set camp in the same locations with each trip?"

He shook his head. "No trip follows the same path. Weather and war often change our routes."

She let out a quiet hum. Weather was a constant threat to travelers but not so great of a threat that it would force the Elviri to abandon their roads and paths in Elmaine or Elifyn. The Proma had established their own web of roads in Promthus as well. So, she struggled to understand why the caravan wouldn't follow a specific path of their own making. The thought didn't sit well with her. *Is it because they don't want to be followed?*

No more than thirty minutes had passed before Yvanna was raising her hand as a signal that they had arrived at the campsite. The clearing was large enough to accommodate all eight of them, and they would have enough space to spread out, so they weren't sleeping on top of one another. Mayrien and Araloth were already gravitating toward the far end of the clearing closest to the creek. Tethe's group gave the Elviri a wide berth, and soon they were settled in for the night with tents, cooking pots, and plenty of water to go around.

Sleep came easy enough for Munne that night, and when she opened her eyes, Ely was waiting for her, standing just out of arm's reach. If she put aside the fact that there was no creek running through it, she could almost pretend that they were in the same clearing she was sleeping in—that he was with her in both the dreaming and waking world.

Ely turned to face her almost immediately, no doubt sensing her presence. His voice was quiet as he spoke. "How are you feeling?"

Munne looked around the clearing then settled her gaze on Ely's face. He wore his emotions plainly tonight—no masks or aloofness. She saw that he was concerned about her by the way his brow furrowed ever so slightly. Although he had no pupils, she felt his eyes on her, following her movements.

"I'm feeling alright. Cold, mostly," she said, rolling her shoulders back to stretch them out. "It's early winter out there."

"How does it compare to your valley?"

Munne tilted her head to the side and considered his question. The valley was no doubt colder than Promthus. Her journey across the Telatorr Mountains just weeks ago was colder than Promthus was now. And yet, despite that, the cold had started to seep through her clothes and into her bones.

"I think your... marks... make the cold more manageable," was the response Munne chose, watching his face carefully.

Ely's shoulders dropped ever so slightly as he exhaled, a faint smile crossing his face. "I'm glad they're helping you beyond their intended purpose."

Munne turned her chin upward to the sky, taking in the sight of the stars. Here in this dreamscape, it was the night of the new moon, the stars shining brightly, and no clouds to be seen. Quite different from the waking world where the full moon was quickly approaching, no more than three or four days away. She walked around the clearing, studying and memorizing the stars.

"Do you wish for me to let you rest tonight?" Ely called out to her, having not moved from where he stood in the center of the clearing.

Munne turned to look at the man, noticing he wasn't wearing his black gloves tonight. When she opened her mouth to speak, she felt her cheeks heat up. "Actually, I was wondering if you'd sit with me for a while. If it's not too taxing?"

His smile grew a little wider as he came to her side. "I think I can manage that, yes."

The corner of her mouth tugged upward into a small grin, and she immediately cast her gaze to the ground, strands of black hair falling across her cheek to hide how it flushed with color. She took a seat right where they stood, crossing her legs and placing her hands on her ankles.

"I could bring some chairs, or a bench—"

"That's alright, I'd rather feel the earth underneath me."

Ely chuckled, the noise pleasing to her ears. He knelt down beside her and adjusted his posture, so he sat with his legs extended in front of him. He threw his arms out behind him and leaned against them, crossing his ankles. He was barefoot, she realized, his feet the same pale green as his face and hands. It felt intimate seeing so much of his skin. The thought brought another wave of heat splashing across her face and ears, which mingled with the heat radiating from the man. With a glance in Ely's direction, she saw their arms and thighs were almost touching, the warmth feeling like a lesser version of when he had touched her arms, her head, her back...

"What do the stars look like from your home?" Munne asked and tilted her head again to look at the sky, seeking to distract herself from how close they sat together—how that stirred something deep inside of her.

"We share the same stars as your valley, actually," Ely responded with a low rumble. "Though I'd imagine the stars look much different with what happened to the land..." He trailed off, chin tilted to his left so that his horns were angled in her direction, and all she had to do was lean ever so slightly to the right to be pressed up against them.

"What do you mean?" Munne murmured, the weight of his last words pulling her out of her stupor.

Ely straightened and shook his head as if shooing the thought. "Forgive me, I misspoke."

Munne threw an arm out to her left, twisting her torso so she was facing him. "You won't tell me of your home? What happened to it?"

"I want to do more than that; I want to *show* it to you. But not yet, not while..." Ely turned his head, locking eyes with her. "I don't have the strength, but you'll be there soon enough and at least see what it has become."

Munne could see a swirl of emotions in his pale green eyes—apprehension, pain, *hope*. Her mind reeled as she digested what he said, understood his meaning. "Kherizhan." Ely nodded. "I didn't realize others made Kherizhan their home, beside the ancient Olaava," Munne said, reflecting on the various history books she had read at home.

"They haven't." Ely turned his gaze to the sky, leaving Munne to stare incredulously at him.

He can't be one of them. The Olaava vanished before the rising of the Second Sun. He'd be thousands of years old. But with all of the magic he can do, is there really any other explanation? Who else, besides the gods, could keep the Ardashi'ik *at bay?*

Ely's soft voice cut through her thoughts. "I hope to one day share what it used to look like with you."

Despite all of the questions and suspicions in her mind, Munne's stomach curled pleasantly at Ely's words. She found herself reaching out and placing her hand on top of his left, curling her fingers around his palm. Heat flooded her body, and she felt an overwhelming sense of calm and peace. She squeezed his hand, hoping to convey the same feeling to him. Ely snapped his head to look at her, an expression of shock quickly dissolving into something else that she couldn't quite read. Awe?

"I'd like that," she murmured as her lips curled into a warm smile, her gaze softening.

CHAPTER XXVII: SETH

Later that evening, when Seth told Octavia of what he found in the library, she had thrown up.

"Have you found out anything that we can use in our escape?" Seth asked while Lisanthir rubbed Tav's back, guiding her to one of the lounge chairs in the room. After she was seated, the Elviri left for another room, presumably to get something to clean up the cooling pool of vomit.

Octavia groaned quietly, rubbing her mouth with the back of her hand. Her face was flushed and sweat beaded along her hairline. "We have to find Szatisi's chambers, or wherever she brews her elixirs. The only way we can get out of here is if we make a run for it."

Seth's stomach squeezed, and he felt as if he might throw up, too. "There's no other way?"

"None that I can find," Octavia mumbled. "Astohi is keeping every soldier on alert. For what, I don't know, but all of the exits are guarded. The only way we can slip out is during a rotation, preferably at night. This isn't going to be like it was in Yiradia."

Seth gripped onto the armrests of his wheelchair, allowing the wooden frame to ground him.

"Seth," Octavia said quietly. Seth's gaze snapped to his twin. She shifted uncomfortably in her seat. "It might be best if Lisanthir leaves the city before us."

Seth's face twisted, mouth opening to argue and retort, but Tav raised her hand, and he stopped himself.

"If you truly think Osza plans on using him in her schemes, he's not safe here."

"None of us are safe," Seth countered, keeping his voice low.

Lisanthir entered the room again, and Octavia's eyes fell to the floor.

She doesn't want him to know. Seth considered pressing her anyway, letting his *ebilin* know what she was thinking, but he held his tongue and considered what her reasoning was. *Lis wouldn't leave me behind, even if it means putting his life in danger—more danger than its already in. Can I let him do that? Could I live with myself if he stayed, and Osza dragged him away from me tomorrow? The next day?* His throat closed up, the protests dying before they reached his lips.

"So, we need to find the priestess?" Lisanthir asked after a few moments, looking between the twins.

Octavia nodded, adjusting her posture so she could sit up straight. "She lives within the *Tserdanii*, but I don't know if her laboratory is within these walls as well."

"How can I help?" Lisanthir replied.

"Do you think you could slip away from here for a little while?" Tav asked, cocking her head to the side. Seth lurched forward in his chair to stop her, but she continued on without a moment's hesitation. "Explore the pyramid? I can try to get you some soldiers' clothes if that would help."

The Elviri hummed and carried the dirty linens from the room. When he returned, he nodded. "I think I can figure something out. I've gone down to the kitchens on a few occasions but not many other places. I'll see what the other stewards will let me do."

"Lis," Seth blurted out. *What am I thinking?* "Be careful, okay?"

"Of course, *ebilin*." Lisanthir knelt down beside Seth's chair and raised his hand to his lips, pressing a gentle kiss across his knuckles. He cast a glance over his shoulder toward Octavia. "And what of my kin?"

"I'll find a way to get them out. I know where they're being kept, I just need to find a way out." Seth couldn't tell if she was telling the truth, or if she was just offering reassurances to keep Lisanthir calm.

"Thank you, Octavia," Lisanthir said with a small smile. "We should get our rest if we're going to plot a prison break."

"A-actually, you go ahead. I'd like to talk to Tav some more before I go to sleep." Seth met his twin's gaze, conveying with his eyes that their earlier discussion was not yet finished.

Lisanthir stood and kissed the top of Seth's head before heading to their bedroom. "Don't stay up too late."

"We won't," Seth called over his shoulder. After watching the Elviri disappear behind the stone door, he tugged the wheels on his chair and led his sister into their dining room. They sat at the table in silence for a few moments, both trying to muster the courage to speak.

"Your Elviri knows how to take care of himself," Octavia said softly, breaking the silence.

Seth inhaled deeply. He wanted nothing more than to leap from his chair and spirit his sister and lover away from Iszairi, but he was bound to the chair. If they fled, they would have to help *him*. His stomach churned. Tears pricked at his eyes. "I know, it's just—"

"I know," Tav murmured. "Let me get him out of here, so he's safe, and so we can focus on getting *you* out of here."

"Us." Seth blinked, wet droplets smearing across his eyelashes.

Octavia nodded, her lips pressing together in a tight line. "Us, and the other prisoners."

Us. He looked down at the table, his vision blurring. *If Szatisi delivers the new potion to me before Tav finds a way to free the prisoners, will that force her hand, or will she leave without them?* They didn't know the prisoners, they had no connection to them beyond pity. Seth didn't know if that would be enough to jeopardize their escape to Kherizhan. Guilt poked and prodded at his stomach. *I'd save them if I could,* he tried to reassure himself, but even that was cast in a shadow of doubt. *Wouldn't I? Will Lisanthir even allow us the option to leave without them?*

"Lisanthir's right, though. We should get some sleep," Octavia said, pulling Seth from his thoughts. "Tomorrow he and I will explore the pyramid and try to get some answers."

Seth nodded, knowing his sister was making a justifiable decision, one that would get them closer to escaping. Still his stomach churned and clenched at the thought of Lisanthir roaming the pyramid on his own, surrounded by Asaszi. It didn't matter than Lisanthir knew how to fight—any battle fought in Iszairi would be met with death. As Seth returned to his bedroom, he couldn't help but feel guilty for bringing Lisanthir to Iszairi and not insisting that the Elviri flee when they were still in Yiradia.

As Lisanthir helped him move from his chair into the bed, Seth vocalized that guilt. "Do you regret coming with us to Iszairi?"

Lisanthir gently set Seth down on the bed, then knelt in front of him, entwining their hands. "No, of course not."

"But it's so dangerous here, and if we're not careful you could be killed." Seth's throat seized at the words.

"*Ebilin*, you've inspired me to bravery," Lisanthir's green eyes glowed in the dim candlelight. "Let me be brave with you here."

Seth relented, no longer wishing to challenge his loved ones on their resolve to stay put and find answers. He had to stay with them and share their strength, otherwise all would be for naught. He shuffled backward on the bed and then slid underneath the silks.

Lisanthir fell asleep almost immediately, but it took Seth longer to relax enough to feel at ease. Despite Lisanthir's arm wrapped around his waist and warm breath against his neck, Seth felt cold. He conjured an image in his mind of the ancient Asaszi book they had discovered in the library, mulling over the words he had read earlier.

Why would the Asaszi have forced the Elviri to mate with the wyrms? If the Asaszi descended from the dragons, why would they not lay with the wyrms themselves? Father said the Tserys *gave him a specific date for when to open the tomb... How much longer do we have before that day comes to pass?*

A shiver coursed through his body, pooling at the base of his spine. He intertwined his fingers with Lisanthir's, and the Elviri squeezed his hand gently in his sleep. The gesture brought a smile to Seth's face, and he was overwhelmed with grief and fear. Tears threatened to spill down his cheeks.

Tav is right. We need to find a way to get Lisanthir out of here. He'll be safer that way. And perhaps that will buy us time to find Szatisi, or for the priestess to even deliver the elixir to me herself. Osza did say that she wants to restore my legs...But why? What purpose do I serve for the Asaszi queen's machinations?

He thought back to his meeting with Osza and tried recalling what she had said to him. *Craving my "other half"... Calling me* py'tsera... *She spoke of us having a bright future together... What are you plotting, Osza?*

Lisanthir and Octavia left the suite the next day, Tav promising to return soon with information about the Elviri captives, and Lis promising to find out what he could from the servants' quarters. Octavia wouldn't be able to get Lisanthir out of the city just yet, but if she could hide him amongst the Provira soldiers or stewards, then hopefully Osza would be thrown off his trail long enough to give the twins time to find Szatisi's chambers.

Seth was left alone with his thoughts for company, which didn't bode well for the evening. He moved from the dining chamber to the study, trying his best to lose himself in the pages of his books. He lit several candles in the room, intending to stay there until either Tav or Lisanthir returned.

Flipping through the pages of the Moonyswyn flora book, he tried piecing together what kind of herbs and plants Szatisi might have been using to create the elixir that restored his legs. If he could figure it out for himself, then they may not need to steal anything from her. They could create it themselves, even if it only lasted a few days at a time.

With the high priestess on his mind, Seth's thoughts eventually slipped into hostile territory. Osza wanted Szatisi to brew him another elixir. Perhaps he and his sister could just wait until Szatisi was finished and then escape soon after. *But what if she's planning on doing it during a special ceremony or somewhere public? What if that's tied to the ceremony of devotion Father wants me to go through?*

He turned the book over and set it down on his lap, rubbing his hands against his face. Screaming out into the night air was a tempting thought, except that it would draw attention to him. Servants and stewards would come to investigate. He couldn't risk that, couldn't deal with the unwanted attention. He considered throwing the book across the room, but that compulsion didn't feel right. Ultimately, he chose to put the book away and retire to his room.

Octavia eventually returned to their suite, heading straight for Seth's room. The heavy thud of her hand against the door woke him, and he pulled himself into a sitting position as she approached the bed. Tav fell to her knees on his side of the bed, and he could hear her panting quietly.

Did she run up the ramps to get here? "Tav, what's wrong?" he mumbled, his voice heavy with sleep.

"Nothing's wrong. Not yet. But I wanted to talk to you before I went to sleep, so you knew what's going on." She spoke quickly, almost too fast for Seth to keep up with.

"What *is* going on?" A small lump formed in his stomach, a messy tangle of frustration and fear. He wished he could get out of the suite and help Octavia and Lisanthir track down Szatisi and find ways to break the Elviri prisoners out. He hated being bound to his wheelchair.

"Lisanthir's going to be staying down in the stewards' quarters for the time being." He saw her fidgeting with the hem of her sleeve. "So, he can listen out for any important news, and so he can spend more time in the pyramid looking around."

Seth's mouth formed a tight line, but he swallowed down his protests. Osza wouldn't expect Lisanthir to leave Seth's side, so perhaps that would buy them some time with their investigation. "What about you? How are you going to free the prisoners?"

"Those tunnels Osza showed us. They're clearly near where the tomb's located. Perhaps they connect to the caverns underneath the coliseum, and we can spirit the prisoners away through there—"

"How would we get back down there?" Seth interrupted her. "Osza had to use a key to access those tunnels."

"Well, perhaps there's another key. Maybe the stewards know about it," Tav responded stubbornly. "Lisanthir can investigate that, too."

"Did you even tell him about that?" Seth sighed. "There's got to be a better way, something more dependable—"

"Is there?" Octavia spat. "I'm listening! I'd love to know what it is!" The twins glared at each other, fury brewing within them.

Seth was the first to break the silence, averting his gaze to his blankets. "I just mean, there's got to be some other way that isn't as reliant on luck."

"I'm trying, Seth." He heard the fear and frustration as Octavia's voice rose in pitch. "We're all alone here with no one to help us. Even if we were in Yiradia, I don't know that I could get us out of this. At least in Yiradia, the Provira have some kind of control over the city, and I could try sneaking us all out disguised as soldiers. But here? The Asaszi don't see us as equals; they see us as pawns to use in *their* war against the Elviri."

Octavia sucked in a deep breath, but when she tried to speak again, she broke down crying instead. She buried her head in the blankets of the bed, clutching the silks tightly. Seth didn't know how to respond to his sister. He tried conjuring words of comfort, words of affirmation, *something* to make her feel better. But every time he tried opening his mouth, his voice failed him. He listened to her sob, her breathing muffled against the blankets. He focused on the noises, focused on his fingertips where he could *feel* her body shaking against the stone bed and the uneven buzz of her breath. His vision unfocused, blurred, and his ears rang as her sobs blended together into one distinct thrum.

Hum.

Seth's entire body jolted as the hum overwhelmed his senses. As quickly as it curled around him, it was gone, and he was left panting.

Octavia raised her head, fixing Seth with a curious glare. Her lips were parted, shallow breaths coming and going. "What—?"

"It's Him. *Him.*" Seth ran his hands through his hair, pressing his fingertips against his scalp. "The *Tserys*. That damned *hum* is His doing. I don't know *what* it's doing to us, but it's not good."

"You sound like Father," Octavia whispered. The twins' eyes met.

"Don't say that," Seth muttered, lowering his hands from his head. Tav looked away, though he couldn't tell if it was from guilt or pity. "Don't you hear it?"

Octavia replied with great reluctance. "I do, but—"

"But what else could it be?" She didn't reply, and he didn't push her for a response. *But surely, she gets it now? The* Tserys *is manipulating us, getting into our heads. But why?* His face fell and he shrunk back into his bed. *Perhaps I do sound like Father, rambling about a dead man.* "How can I help you, Tav?"

His sister looked back at him, her hazel eyes filled with sadness. "Just... stay safe. Stay here. If Lisanthir comes back, make sure he knows to look for a key into the caverns. And if Szatisi brings you a new elixir, then we'll just... We'll get out. We'll find a way."

Seth spent the next few days sitting around the suite, feeling restless and tense. Lisanthir hadn't returned, and Octavia spent most of her time elsewhere in the city. He only saw her in the evenings late at night when she returned from wherever she had been. She reassured him that Lisanthir was still alive and doing okay, but neither of them had made much progress with Szatisi or the Elviri prisoners.

At the thought of his lover, Seth's throat tightened. He wished he could see him and hold him, but the Elviri was still down in the stewards' quarters. For how long, he wasn't sure. He had to trust that Octavia knew what she was doing, and that if there was an opportunity for escape, she'd make sure Lisanthir came with.

Did Mother ever think to flee Yiradia? Tears came unbidden and spilled down Seth's cheeks. His lips were forcibly parted in a sharp inhale, and he found himself yearning for his mother's embrace. How he wished she were there to hug him, comfort him, protect him from the Asaszi. From his father. *She stayed for me and Tav*, he realized. *She had no way to get us out, and so she couldn't get out either.*

The silence in Seth's room was shattered as his door swung open with a slow creak. His gaze immediately shifted to the door, forcing himself to stop his crying and figure out who was there. Octavia had already stopped by to see him and reassure him of Lisanthir's safety for the day. *Did she forget to tell me something?*

He couldn't make out who it was in the darkness of his room, but Seth thought the shadow was taller than Octavia. His heart thudded painfully in his chest. *Did Lisanthir sneak away from the other stewards to come see me?*

"Seth…" a hoarse whisper called out to him, followed by heavy footsteps as the shadow approached his bed. "Seth, are you awake?"

That voice… it can't be. "Father?" Seth breathed, hoping he was wrong, that Amias *wasn't* the person sneaking into his bedroom. Fear gnawed at his stomach, twisting and tangling it into knots.

"Praise be, I was hoping you'd be awake!" Amias spoke a little louder now, his words slurring together. Seth felt a heavy weight slump down on the bed beside his midsection; his father must have sat down, none too gracefully. The stench of wine wafted off of Amias, filling Seth's nostrils with the putrid smell.

He's drunk. "Wh-what are you doing here?" Seth asked, sliding his legs and hips toward the center of the bed.

To his dismay, Amias also shuffled closer, swinging his legs up on the bed so he could lay beside his son. "I wanted to tell you about our plan." Amias let out a quiet chuckle and hiccup.

Seth froze, remaining silent. Perhaps his father was so drunk that if Seth ignored him and pretended to be asleep, maybe Amias would leave.

"Seth. *Sssseth.* I need to tell you." Another hiccup. "I need to tell you about the assassination."

A jolt of fear ran through Seth's limbs, forcing him into a sitting position. "Assassination?"

"Yes." Amias chuckled. "We're going to assassinate Osza now that she's outlived her usefulness. Clever, isn't it? The snake won't suspect a thing."

"Father, I-I…" Seth's mind raced. He fidgeted with his silk blanket to keep the fear from creeping into his voice. "Can you explain…?"

"Oh, yes, I suppose you should know… Since you weren't there when I figured it out." His words were accusatory, as if Seth *should* have been there.

Should've been where? Did I miss a summon from him? Or is he so drunk that he's forgetting…?

"I know the snake's plans, and I know how those plans fold into my plans, and I know how to take it all over." Amias hiccupped again and fell silent. Rather than disturb him, Seth waited to see if he would start speaking again, which he did a few moments later. "Admittedly, it took longer than I would've liked to figure out her bizarre mating ritual, but now… Now I don't need her anymore. With the *Tserys* giving me the orders, and with you children and your children, we'll rule Daaria."

So many thoughts flew around Seth's mind. *The mating ritual. "Our children". But no mention of Lisanthir or the other Elviri.* "What mating ritual?" Seth dared to ask.

Amias let out another chuckle that deteriorated into a coughing fit. For a moment, Seth feared—and hoped—that his father would choke on his own spit.

What would happen if the stewards found Amias dead here? Or would Tav find us first? What would she think? Would we be forced to run away before finding Szatisi's elixir?

Amias cleared his throat and took a deep breath, easing Seth's pounding heart ever so slightly. "The snake thinks she can create a new kind of Asaszi using that dragon, you, and your sister. She believes the Asaszi are descendants of the Elviri and Isyth, rather than Isyth alone. Seems blasphemous, but who am I to challenge her?"

Several different feelings flooded Seth. Relief that Lisanthir wasn't the target of Osza's twisted intentions. Panic that he and Octavia were instead her targets, and that they had done nothing to keep her from using them in her schemes. Confusion over the Asaszi's origins. Osza's beliefs went against everything he had been taught, but the indirect confession painted her earlier words to him in a clearer image. When she had spoken of their "other halves", she had been referring to the Elviri, how they both shared that heritage.

"But why us? Why not—" Seth had to stop himself from mentioning his lover. "Why not an Elviri?"

"Royalty," Amias muttered, his jovial tone melting into something more sinister. "You and your sister are the future of the Provira. If one of you sires the reincarnation of the *Tserys*, you will be, beyond a shadow of a doubt, the father or mother of our peoples."

Seth's mouth went dry. *This is why Osza wants my legs working again. Why she and the other Asaszi have been referring to Tav and I as* py'tseras, *princes and princesses of Pyredessi.* His head spun and his stomach lurched.

"But I can't have Osza controlling everything. Not when I've worked so hard to master what I have, when the *Tserys* speaks to *me*," Amias continued, shoving his fists into the blankets. "We must kill her, Seth. She's a threat to all we've done and all we can be. She thinks it's the era of the serpent, but it's not. It's the era of the Provira."

Seth wanted to vomit. Instead, he forced himself to speak, daring himself to challenge Amias—something he would never do when his father was sober. "If it's the era of the Provira, why must we breed with the dragon? If you already hear the voice of the *Tserys*... why must we reincarnate Him?"

Amias merely hummed in response. Seth felt him moving around on the bed and then an arm slung around his shoulders that pulled him against his father's chest. He didn't dare breathe, paralyzed with fear and unsure of what his father was doing.

Is he embracing me? After all of these years? Seth's heart ached. He wanted to relish the touch, especially with his mother dead and gone—killed by this man, this *monster*—but he knew Amias wasn't embracing him out of love.

"My son," Amias murmured, his rank breath hot against Seth's ear. "Do you not want to sire a god?"

Amias wouldn't consider what Seth and Octavia *really* wanted, so Seth had to play into his father's paranoia. "That... That's what Osza would want us to do." Amias hummed again, seeming to consider Seth's words. Seth felt emboldened, so he continued. "If this was what the *Tserys* wanted, wouldn't He have told you? Instead of Osza?"

"You... Perhaps you're right," Amias whispered. He leaned away from Seth but kept his arm tight around his son. "I should... I should speak with Him. Tomorrow."

Amias sat still for a moment. Seth's heart pounded in chest, blood racing through his veins and blocking out all other sounds. Even the hum was gone beneath his fear.

"I will let you rest," Amias said, climbing to his feet. "Tomorrow is a very important day." He made his way to Seth's door, his footsteps uneven as he stumbled forward.

"Why's that?" Seth asked.

Amias paused as he opened the door. "Tomorrow, we open the tomb, of course."

As his father shut the door behind him, Seth was left in complete darkness, too afraid to lay back down. He considered his options, wondering if he should climb into his wheelchair and make for Octavia's room or not. Even if he convinced her to leave that night, there was no guarantee they could get Lisanthir to slip away unnoticed from the sleeping chambers he shared with the other stewards. The Elviri prisoners would surely be abandoned. But if he waited until morning, what would that do for him and his loved ones?

Maybe Father won't remember what happened tonight, and he'll wake up feeling too ill to do anything. If he was truly planning on opening the Tomb of the Prince tomorrow, Octavia or Lisanthir would have heard about it by now. No, he must have just gotten too drunk to speak any sense. But he knows about Osza's mating ritual. How? No, he's just a madman pretending to hear the voice of a dead man. Isn't he?

CHAPTER XXVIII: MUNNE

The full moon shone brightly on the land even before the suns had set that night. Munne and her company had taken advantage of the light the moon provided and continued their journey a little farther. They skirted along the edges of the Imalar Woods and crossed the plains between it and Moonyswyn. The open ground made Munne nervous, even though there were no traces of war in the area. No settlements, no battlements, nothing but open grass and air.

Their campsite was nothing special. It was almost as if Tethe just decided to stop his horse and throw down his bedroll. To his credit, there was a small pond nearby which they were able to gather water from. They boiled it and prepared a fine vegetable stew. Jion tended to the horses as usual and secured them to a couple of hitching posts he drove into the ground. Before they had left the Imalar Woods, Tethe had his men chop down a few smaller trees to ensure they'd have wood for any of their needs in the plains.

Banter had bloomed between the caravanners and Elviri over the past few days. Mayrien exchanged jokes and pleasantries with Ormes and Adalia nearly every night, regaling them with mischievous tales of her antics back home. Araloth would occasionally stand and chat with Jion as he brushed the horses' manes. Munne and Tethe discussed trade between the members of the Daarian Council and the other routes he took when he wasn't journeying to Kherizhan. It proved an enlightening discussion, learning more about the goods ferried between the Imalar Woods and Trent, a favorite route of Tethe's. Though there was a large overlap in goods, the Imalarii preferred the wine from Trent, and in turn the Trentians coveted Imalarii lutes and flutes above all others.

As the fire died down, Munne retired to her bedroll and got comfortable, falling asleep to the quiet murmur of Adalia, Yvanna, and Araloth discussing watch shifts.

"Hello again," Ely murmured with a smile on his lips as she appeared in the dreamscape clearing.

Munne smiled back, ready to tell him about her day when he raised a hand to stop her, the smile falling from his face. "What is it?" she asked.

Ely cocked his head to the side, eyes flickering around the clearing. Looking at the trees behind her and to either side. All she could hear was her breathing. The silence normally didn't bother her, but she was growing uncomfortable in its staggering presence.

Ely opened his mouth. "Munne, I—"

The clearing vanished. Darkness covered her vision, her lungs filling with damp, earthen air. She blinked rapidly, as if closing and opening her eyes again would make the clearing reappear.

"Ely?" Munne called. His name echoed all around her. She threw her hands out in front of her, trying to feel something, *anything* around—

Her hands collided with solid rock, bolts of pain leaping through her fingers, hands, wrists, up her arms. She cursed loudly, pressing her fingers into the palms of her hands to curb the agonizing feeling from spreading further.

She was back in the tunnels.

Munne swore again, louder, the curse echoing down the corridors off the dank walls. Darkness pressed in on her from all sides. She closed her eyes, squeezing them tight until she saw hundreds of tiny, fuzzy stars.

"Ely, if you're here," she said with as much calmness as she could muster. "If you can hear me, I'm asking you... *please* get me out of here."

Far ahead, coming from one of the twisting tunnels, a faint echo came bouncing toward her. Munne opened her eyes, for as much good as that would do her, and she strained to make out the echo.

"*Out... of here...*"

At first Munne thought it was just an echo of her words, but as she stayed silent and listened, she could hear other things stirring within the caverns far away from her. She felt herself being pulled into the earth, her jaw and stomach both dropping and her blood running cold.

The echo grew louder, the voice moving through the corridors. *"Help... us..."*

She shook her head, closing her eyes once more. "This isn't real."

"Warlord, help!" another voice cried out, closer and louder than the first.

Munne let out a scream, pressing both hands against her ears, desperate to silence the onslaught of voices, wails, screams.

The screams.

"This isn't real!" Munne repeated, shouting the words as if that would banish the nightmare.

The earth under her feet trembled, and another wave of terror toppled over her, threatening to drown her.

The creature.

From behind her came the sound of wings flapping, something breathing heavily, and a menacing growl. Her heart leapt into her throat, and she took off running further into the tunnels. She threw a hand out in front of her as an afterthought, as if the skin of her palm would prevent her from colliding with a stone wall if–*when?*–she was unfortunate enough to run face-first into one.

Ahead of her the screams and wails got louder. The creature's growls turned into shrieks, and she could hear it both in front of and behind her. It had somehow passed her and made its way to the people ahead, tearing into them, hurting them, making them scream so loudly, cry out for her help.

Munne's fingers brushed against a curve in the wall, and she followed it around a corner, leading her to—

The clearing?

She emerged into Ceyo's clearing once again, her sight restored to her. The grass, night sky, and trees had never looked so welcoming as they did in that moment. In the middle of the clearing stood Ely, panic in his form, his gaze snapping from one side to the other. When his eyes fell upon Munne, he ran to her, and she to him.

"Munne!"

"I-I was back there, in the tunnels," she stammered, hot tears welling in her eyes.

They met each other halfway to the clearing's edge, and Ely reached out to grab her arms. Warmth flooded her body, but it wasn't nearly enough to drive away the panic eating at her senses, the fear of returning to those nightmarish caverns. The tears spilled down her cheeks with renewed fervor and she had to choke back a sob.

"Something's wrong. In the waking world," Ely's grip on her arms tightened. "You have to wake up."

The panic in his voice grabbed Munne's attention and she met his eyes, anxiety replacing panic. "What? What's happening?"

"I don't know, but you have to wake up. Be careful."

Before she could ask any other questions, Ely and the clearing were gone, and she was looking into Tethe's green and white eyes, illuminated by the light of the full moon. Munne let out a startled gasp, feeling Tethe's hands on either side of her head, holding her in place. His weight pressed down on her midsection; he was straddling her. He gritted his teeth, muttering something under his breath—gibberish? With each inane word that passed his lips, Munne felt something heavy and dark tugging at her heart from within, reminiscent of the tunnels she had just escaped from.

What kind of betrayal is this?

"She's awake," Adalia hissed. Munne's eyes darted to the side, seeing the Proma woman hovering over Tethe's left shoulder like a shadow.

"Draw your blades," Yvanna whispered darkly over Tethe's other shoulder. Steel hissed against leather as daggers and swords were withdrawn from sheaths. "Jion, off the others."

Does she mean Araloth and Mayrien?

Munne locked eyes with Tethe again, and he only offered her a wolfish grin. She forced her body into motion, desperately needing to get out of this situation and into one more favorable for her. Her skull cracked against his, interrupting his chanting and knocking him off of her torso. Yvanna and Adalia both shuffled forward, blades angled toward Munne.

"*Aza'rae Elvintar!*" Munne shouted, pulling out one of the daggers sheathed in her boot and lunging forward. Aiming for Tethe. Missing because he was pulled away by Ormes.

Her battle cry worked as intended though because Araloth and Mayrien were stirring. The caravanners failed to pivot in time, which gave the three Elviri time to spring into action. Munne leapt to her feet, twisting her grip on the dagger so she could stab at Ormes. The blade nicked his arm as he turned away from her. She quickly pulled back, twisting her torso to pull the short sword on her right hip free with her left hand.

Now standing, Munne took quick stock of the moonlit battlefield before making her next move. Tethe had been pushed out of her range and was now protected by Ormes who had a longsword leveled in her direction. To her right were the other three, attempting to take down Araloth and Mayrien as quickly as they could.

Yvanna let out a screech and threw herself at Mayrien, trying to hold the Elviri down to allow her companions to strike with their weapons. The two grappled at each other, Mayrien rolling them out of reach from Jion's halberd. Adalia brought a dagger down on Araloth, who caught the woman's wrist and pushed her back, leaving Ormes and Tethe to Munne. Then she could help her triple.

She led with her sword, slashing across Ormes's chest once with the longer blade, then thrusting forward with her dagger. He leapt back, dodging the larger blade with ease. He raised his sword to block the dagger's stab, driving Munne back a step. She adjusted and reversed her actions immediately, now leading with the dagger.

Ormes pressed forward, trying to reduce the space Munne had to stab and swipe in, which she had been prepared for. The dagger swiped high, which he ducked under and led with his shoulder, no doubt to bull rush forward and send her sprawling to the ground or at least stagger her back several steps. She twisted her torso to slide her sword into his stomach, pushing up into his chest.

A choked gasp escaped Ormes's lips as he froze in place, realizing his error, knowing that a blade had pierced his skin. With no hesitation, Munne pulled the blade free, hot blood spilling onto her hand and wrist. She raised her right foot, kicking him in the gut and sending him falling onto his back.

Her head snapped up, hunting for Tethe, but she didn't immediately see the cretin. Movement to her right demanded her attention, and when she looked, she saw Adalia sprawled in the grass, wailing loudly, a dagger protruding from her eye. The woman was clutching the hilt, her hands shaking badly.

Serves the traitor right. But why have they turned against us?

Araloth dragged Yvanna off of Mayrien and grappled with the Elviri traitor. Munne's eyes widened when she caught sight of Mayrien clutching her side, the gleam of dark blood standing out against her linen shirt. She had a sword in her other hand, pacing unevenly in a circle against Jion who brandished a menacing halberd. The range of the weapon was its most intimidating aspect. He could keep the Elviri swords away from him and deal damage from a distance. One swing of that weapon would certainly slice through any bones it collided with. In Mayrien's weakened state, any blow he dealt would be devastating. Jion needed to die next.

Munne swapped her dagger into her left hand and her short sword into her right, stalking toward the man. She would have to prioritize getting inside his reach, preventing him from using the polearm effectively. If she could just—

Yvanna must have seen her move. She shrieked, "Jion! Behind you!"

The man twisted around, bringing the halberd blade with him. Munne had to jump backward to avoid the attack. Mayrien tried to take advantage of the opening, rushing forward with her sword to drive the blade through his back, but he snapped his torso back again, halberd following, and his blade bit into her sword arm. Mayrien screamed and staggered to the side, sword falling from her grasp.

The blood roared in Munne's ears as she ran in and raised her dagger, driving it into the back of Jion's neck before he could follow through with his swing. He crumpled to the ground in an instant. Munne's eyes flashed to Mayrien, who lay in the grass clutching her injured arm, gritting her teeth with a pain-filled grimace on her face. Part of Munne wanted to run to her friend's side and tend to her injuries, but first she had to ensure all of their foes were defeated, one way or another.

She flicked her eyes to Araloth and Yvanna. Araloth had ended up on top of Yvanna, her hands wrapped tightly around the woman's throat. Yvanna pummeled into Araloth's sides with her fists, scratching at her arms with her nails. She snarled, thrashing about, but her movements got slower and weaker as Araloth pressed down, cutting off her source of air.

The horses snorted and one whinnied. Munne snapped her head toward the beasts, seeing Tethe cutting loose their reins and trying to mount his own. She broke out into a sprint, tossing her blades to either side and throwing her body at his as he was mid-climb. They landed on the grass in a tangle of limbs. The collision slammed all of the air out of his lungs, and he breathed in deeply, heavily, trying to pull any of it back inside of him. He grabbed Munne's arms, kicked her legs, doing whatever he could to force her away from him.

I'm not letting you get away, traitor. With all the strength she could muster, she fought back. Tethe managed to pull one of his arms out from her grasp, sliding it down toward their legs. As she angled herself to grab his arm again, a scorching heat pressed against her cheek. She could smell burning flesh, and she let out an agonizing scream as Tethe pressed his hand against her face.

The fiery coin.

Munne slapped away his arm then slammed her elbow down into his shoulder. He cried out in pain, the coin falling from his hand. A tendril of blue flame curled through the air, connecting his fingertip to the coin on the ground. She knew she needed to extinguish the flame somehow, but she now had the upper hand and was easily able to pin Tethe down and restrain his arms. Their positions had been reversed, but she wouldn't let her guard down for him to dislodge her.

"Vere'cha!" Araloth shouted, her voice scratchy and raw.

"I'm here," Munne responded through gritted teeth. "Mayrien is hurt."

She heard Araloth walking over to the younger Elviri, could hear Mayrien groaning as Araloth helped her sit up as she assessed her injuries. She wanted to be by her friend's side, but she had to deal with Tethe first. He continued to struggle underneath her, but his attempts were much weaker than before. Whether he had worn himself out or whether he knew the futility of his efforts, she didn't know. She didn't care.

"Are they all dead?" Munne shouted, her eyes never leaving Tethe's. Where in the previous days and nights she had seen mirth and light in his green and white eyes, now there was only malice. She hoped he saw the same in hers.

"Looks like. Wouldn't hurt to slit their throats, just in case," Araloth responded, and something inside of Munne twisted pleasantly at hearing those words.

They had been our allies, and they betrayed us. All that these people deserve are cut throats and to have their bodies left behind for the crows.

The pleasant rage gave way to dread as she considered Mayrien's state. She silently sent a prayer to Aeona and Azrael to protect Mayrien, and to hope against hope that the injury wasn't life-threatening. "Mayrien?"

"Alive. It hurts. By the *gods* does it hurt, but I'm alive," came Mayrien's response.

"Now," Munne dropped her voice to a low murmur, addressing Tethe, "would you care to explain *why* you chose to attack us? What were you doing to me before I woke up?" The man didn't respond. Even in the face of defeat, he stubbornly clung to some semblance of control over the situation.

I will not *have that.* "Bring me my dagger," Munne barked to her companions, shifting more of her weight into her hands, cutting off the blood flow in his arms.

From behind, Mayrien hissed in pain as Araloth slipped away from her friend's side and approached Munne. She raised her left hand and found the discarded coin, tapping its surface with one finger. The blue tendril dissipated into nothing. She held out her open hand, waiting for the weight of her dagger to be pressed into her skin. To his credit, Tethe stayed put. Munne felt none of his muscles tensing up in anticipation for action. If he thought of escaping, his body didn't react.

After passing the dagger to Munne, Araloth knelt down beside her, placing a hand on Tethe's right shoulder to hold him down. The movement was slow, deliberate. The older Elviri was issuing a silent threat to the man.

If you move, you die.

Munne allowed a few moments to pass before she lowered the blade to his throat. He tried to push his head away from her further into the grass, but he couldn't escape the cold steel. She held it against his skin, close enough for the blade to bite at his flesh and draw a thin red line. For the first time, fear flashed across his mismatching eyes. His muscles tensed underneath her.

Good. She leaned down over him and whispered, "Explain yourself."

Tethe blinked rapidly a few times, parting his lips and drawing in a shaky breath. The red line darkened where his throat bobbed against her dagger. He let out a pained hiss and blinked once more. And then the fear and panic were gone. His eyes darkened and he closed his mouth, exhaling through his nose. Munne felt his body relax under her. Her brow dipped slightly for a moment as her resolve broke and confusion overtook her.

This isn't right.

Tethe spoke, but it wasn't his voice. It was something colder, darker, and she could hear it through her ears and inside of her head. *"I've been waiting for you."*

Munne thought she recognized the voice, the tendrils twisting in her mind. Her grip on the dagger faltered, her muscles twitching in fear. The waver in her resolve cost her. Before she had a chance to blink away the fear and press the dagger firmly against his flesh again, Tethe moved underneath her.

Araloth let out a startled cry as Tethe pushed her away from him with alarming strength, sending the older Elviri stumbling backward. Munne snapped her head to the side and moved to slam her left elbow into his shoulder, but he was too quick for her. Tethe grabbed Munne's wrist, the one holding the dagger. She thrashed against him, trying to pry his hand off of hers, but for all of her effort and adrenaline coursing through her veins, he wouldn't budge.

"The Asaszi could never have offered me a finer gift," came the dark voice from Tethe's lips.

Munne couldn't stop her jaw from dropping, nor the freezing grip of panic from seizing her stomach. She wanted to throw herself away from the man, needed to get away from him, run away, where he couldn't see her, couldn't see *in* her—

"Come, Elviri, let us bring beautiful death to the world." Tethe's grip on her tightened, and he pulled her hand down at the same time as he raised his head off of the ground.

The dagger bit into his skin, then bit further, tearing through muscle, then bone. He let out a gurgled laugh, one that sent Munne into a full-blown panic. She couldn't tear her eyes from his as her hands were covered in his blood, and he fell back against the ground, all strength and life seeping from his body. The darkness in his eyes diminished and he became nothing more than a corpse bleeding into the dirt.

Munne threw herself backward off of the body, leaving the dagger in its flesh. Her bloodied hands slipped on the grass, and she fell onto her back.

Above the full moon and stars looked down on her, and the chill of the night swept through her. A quiet sob wrenched itself from her chest.

"Munne. Munne!" Araloth said to her, her voice dripping with desperation.

Munne tried to turn her head to her companion, but her body wouldn't obey. A new wave of dread washed over her, and her muscles tensed as she tried to move.

Another voice whispered to her. She heard it not in the open plain of Promthus but deep within her mind, its tendrils burrowing deep. *"Munne."*

Darkness flooded her vision, and she could see nothing. Feel nothing. She was floating through endless darkness, and then she was falling. She tried to scream, but her mouth wouldn't open. She tried to twist about and orient herself, but her arms and legs wouldn't move.

And then Munne was standing upright, but she still couldn't see. She tried to move, and then she felt her hands touching her arms. She moved her hands to her face, pressing her fingers into her skin just to relish being able to touch and feel. But she still couldn't see. Then she knew where she was.

The tunnels.

Behind her came the telltale sound of wings flapping and low growling, and she knew she needed to run. Munne sprinted into the darkness. The beat of its wings grew louder, and she felt its growls vibrate through her limbs. If she could just find a source of light, even if it was just a tunnel with less oppressive darkness, she could find her way out.

"Malion tried to run, too," the beast snarled, its vile voice gravelly and wet. Munne could feel its hot breath on the back of her neck, and she had to stop herself from screaming.

Ely, Ceyo, gods, ANYONE! Tears fell down her cheeks and her chest heaved, her lungs burning. She couldn't stop running. She had to find a way out.

And then she heard the screams, and she couldn't stop her own from ripping out of her throat. Munne's foot collided with something protruding the ground, and she went sprawling on the ground before her. She threw her hands out to catch herself, expecting her skin to break on hard rock and gravel but instead felt leaves and grass underneath. The unexpected feeling was enough to distract her from her landing, and she hit her head on the ground before pushing herself to her knees. She was in the clearing again, and

Ely stood in front of her, her hands almost touching his feet and the hem of his black robes. He stood with two hands extended above her, as if to hold something back.

"Ely," she breathed.

His gaze drifted down to her, and she watched as fury and frustration gave way to relief. One of his hands lowered and he beckoned to her, wordlessly asking her to place her hand in his. Munne grabbed onto his hand without a second thought. His skin felt like fire, and she craved every bit of it that she could touch. She could feel the darkness burning off her as Ely helped her to her feet and pulled her behind him. When she turned to see where she had come from and what he was facing, her jaw dropped.

The forest surrounding the clearing was no longer there. Shadows had replaced the trees, and towering above them was the winged beast from her nightmares. Its form was dark, darker than the shadows surrounding it, and she could barely make out any distinguishing features. She heard the beating of its wings and felt the air being pushed all throughout the clearing as Ely faced down the beast. Two golden orbs stared down at them, filled with malice. Munne withered under its gaze, squeezing Ely's hand as she held onto him like her life depended on it. She felt like she was looking upon an avatar of ultimate dread.

The *Ardashi'ik*.

"I deny you entry here," Ely snarled to the beast, tightening his grip on Munne's hand.

The beast belted out a roar that would've turned Munne's blood to ice had it not been for Ely's touch. Its wings beat louder, faster, wind gusting through the clearing.

"You *will not* have this one!" Ely shouted. Although they were standing beside each other, holding onto one another, Munne struggled to hear Ely over the wind.

In all her years, Munne had never seen or experienced anything like what she was before her. She was no stranger to fear or dread, but she'd been trained to suppress those emotions to keep a steady hand as she joined the battlefield. But now...

"Aeona, Allmother, protect your child until it's their time," Munne whispered under her breath. She couldn't hear the words pass her lips but fell into the routine prayers to the gods, nonetheless. "Azrael, Moon in the Dark, shield me from the shadows."

Ely's voice rose above her prayers, above the wind, above even the beast. He spoke in the same foreign tongue she had heard only a handful of times prior. She couldn't make out one word from another, but she felt the power in his words.

"Belleol, Farseer, grant me the knowledge I require." Energy hummed all around them and Munne thought Ely started to *glow*. Light emanated from his body, a pale green to match his skin. "Ceyo, Mother-god, be with me in all."

The beast shrieked, and Munne knew that whatever Ely was doing, it was working. She squeezed his hand even tighter, his glowing aura spreading all across his body and hers. She was surrounded by an inferno, Ely's voice crescendoing into a deafening roar. The beast could no longer be heard over his chanting. The clearing filled with bright light and suddenly it vanished.

Munne and Ely stood in an empty place, devoid of any trees, leaves, or sky. She closed her eyes, senses overwhelmed by the brightness and nothingness.

"Munne. Munne." Ely's voice was quiet again, a soft breeze compared to the earlier maelstrom.

Ely's hand touched her cheek, and her eyes flew open, meeting his pale green gaze. Glancing at the brightness behind him, then back to him, she murmured, "Where did the clearing go?"

"Listen to me," Ely insisted. His touch hardened, drawing her attention back to his face. "I can't both keep us here and keep *him* away, so I need you to listen."

Munne blinked. Her mind went blank as the weight of his words pressed down on her. Ely spoke of *him*. The one who had come for Malion. The one from the Eldest Days. She nodded, willing him to speak.

"I'm a fool for not discovering this sooner, and I can only pray that I have enough strength to protect you, so you're not punished for my mistakes," Ely began, lowering his hand to hers and squeezing tightly. "Those people you were traveling with were Provira. Spies from Moonyswyn. And their leader, that man, was touched by Ardulphyx. I should've been able to sense him; I've always been able to, until now. *K'nyk yth'tras!*"

Ely's sudden outburst startled Munne, and she staggered back. "What can I do?" she asked, her voice barely more than a whisper.

He took a deep breath before continuing, steadying himself. "You must make all haste to Kherizhan and find a way to stop him. I'll do what I can to keep him at bay, but it will require all of my strength. Do you understand?"

Munne nodded, despite the fear gnawing at her stomach. Ely tried to offer her a small smile, the corners of his lips curling upward ever so slightly. Her chest ached at the sight. She felt as if she was losing something she didn't even know she had.

"I'll do what I can, but you must wake up. *Now.*"

Munne blinked and she was staring up at the night sky, basking in the light of the full moon. Hands cradled her cheek, tucked underneath her back, placed on her chest. Looking down from the sky, she saw Araloth on her left and Mayrien on her right. Both women had tear streaks on their cheeks and blood on their hands. They let out sighs of relief when they saw her blue eyes flickering wildly between them.

"Munne!" Mayrien cried out, the name scratching her throat. Munne saw pain flash across Mayrien's eyes, her teeth clenched, but she was too focused on pressing her hands against Munne's chest, moved up to her face to touch and stroke her hair—touching to believe she was alive.

Munne knew these touches, had felt and given them before. As her friends held her close, she felt her own labored breathing underneath their limbs. "Wh-what...?"

"We thought you dead, s-stabbed by some hidden blade, or-or killed by some kind of *magic*," Araloth spat the word out.

"You just kept thrashing and shaking," Mayrien said softly, fresh tears welling in her eyes. "I was afraid it was poison."

Munne let out a shaky breath and forgot to breathe in again. *It certainly was a poison of some kind. My mind has been poisoned. And they need to know.*

"But you're back with us now. Yes?" The words sounded more like a plea than an inquiry as they fell from Araloth's mouth.

"I'm here," Munne breathed. She gripped one hand each of Araloth and Mayrien's and held onto her friends tightly. "I'm here. But you need to know what happened."

"Mayrien first." Araloth squeezed her hand back, nearly to the point of pain. She scrambled out from behind Munne, moving to Mayrien's side. "Mayrien needs bandages and herbs. Can you fetch some? Can you stand?"

"Yes, I-I think so." Munne leaned forward, trying to gather her bearings.

Mayrien hissed as she tried to straighten, nearly doubling over as she pressed her hand against her side. Munne climbed to her feet and looked around the area, trying to make out where everything was. Their campfire had burned out, leaving a small trail of smoke wafting into the sky. Most of the horses were still tethered up, neighing and stamping their hooves angrily. The fight had clearly agitated them, and it would take a while to soothe them and get them to calm down again. The corpses of the caravanners were spread throughout their camp. Tethe's body lay close to her, his throat split open. He died with a chilling grin pulling his lips tightly apart. Munne grimaced at the sight. She was no stranger to the horrors of battle, but the sight unnerved her. His death was no ordinary death.

The Ardashi'ik *did this.*

Taking a deep breath, she retraced her steps back to her bedroll and grabbed one of her packs, digging for bandages. Behind her, Mayrien hissed and gritted her teeth as Araloth helped her out of her shirt to get a better look at her wounds.

"How's your arm?" Munne called over her shoulder as she gathered up the bandages, her waterskin, and a few other things.

"Bleeding. Badly," Mayrien growled.

As she returned to her friends, Munne threw a glance at the deadly halberd that Jion had used to hurt Mayrien. Both of them were very lucky that Jion hadn't landed a more solid blow against them, although Munne figured that Mayrien wouldn't necessarily agree.

She's still alive. That's got to count for something.

Munne knelt down beside Mayrien as Araloth leaned back to give her space. The moonlight was bright enough to reveal the deep wound on Mayrien's upper arm. White flickers of bone could be seen beneath the pools of red. The

Elviri's skin had paled from so much blood loss. It was truly a blessing from Aeona that she was still alive.

"It needs to be closed up before we can wrap it," Araloth murmured to the two younger Elviri. "Munne, can you rekindle the campfire and get some water boiling? I'll put together a tourniquet."

Munne nodded and shuffled back to the center of the campsite. A part of her knew that Araloth was issuing orders to keep her mind occupied, so that she would focus on helping Mayrien and ensuring their safety. Standard procedure following any battle. Munne was thankful for her guidance and pushed herself to fall into a familiar routine.

It was easy enough to gather the necessary firewood and encourage the dying embers to lap it up. Soon the fire was raging in earnest, and she had a small pot of water simmering. Rather than sit and wait, Munne removed the dead bodies from their campsite, laying them on top of one another. The effort sapped at her strength, but it was good to move, to feel blood pumping in her veins. Pain was life, and she relished the feeling.

After moving the five bodies, Munne inspected their corpses more closely. Yvanna, who she thought to be an Elviri, had shorter ears than she originally realized. They were nowhere near as long or pointed as her own. Looking over the other four bodies, she noticed that all of their ear tips were slightly longer and more pointed than typical Proma. Ely had told her the caravanners were Provira. Seeing the evidence before her, a shiver of disgust ran through her body. How easily she'd been fooled by their honeyed words and pleasant mannerisms.

Cesa trained me better than this. I've seen more than enough Provira in my life. How did they keep their identities hidden from me? I can't afford to lose my senses now, not with Kherizhan so close and the Ardashi'ik *in my mind.*

"I can hear the water bubbling. We're ready for it," Araloth told her, disrupting Munne's thoughts.

Munne turned away from the corpses and returned to her friends. It took some time to clean and close the wounds on Mayrien's arm and side. Although she was no stranger to getting hurt on the battlefield, it didn't make the pain any more bearable. After they finished, they untied the tourniquet from around her arm and laid her down to rest.

"Wait," Mayrien said after Araloth and Munne had moved over to the campfire to their wounds. She pushed herself up into a sitting position, grinding her teeth and biting back a groan of discomfort. "Munne, what happened to you? You said you needed to explain something."

Munne held Mayrien's gaze, but she was miles away from the plains of Promthus. The weight of Araloth's hand on her shoulder brought her back and she cleared her throat. "I don't think there's any way I can explain this without sounding like I've lost my mind." *But I have, haven't I?*

"You can trust us, *etilith*. We'll follow you wherever you go." She caught a glimpse of Araloth frowning, but the older Elviri's words were comforting.

Munne let those words resonate within her, and she drew strength from them. With a nod she breathed in deeply and said, "Those people were Provira, and Tethe was something worse. Some kind of host to the same madness as Malion. When I met him in Elimere, I thought he suffered the same affliction as me, and that's why he offered to take us to Kherizhan. But now I know how wrong I was to make that assumption. My nightmares were of a faraway land, but Tethe and Malion..." She paused to take another breath. Araloth's grip on her shoulder never wavered, and Mayrien's eyes stayed locked with hers. "It's the *Ardashi'ik*. He had possessed them and driven them to madness. Their bodies were hosts to his spirit, and he used them to... to..." *To find me and take over my mind.*

Munne cleared her throat, trying to dislodge the lump that had formed unexpectedly. "When he forced Tethe onto my blade, he jumped into me. Into my mind."

"It cannot be!" Mayrien exclaimed, her body jolting forward. She tried rising to her feet, but her wounds knocked her back onto her bedroll, and she seethed with pain.

Araloth's other hand flew up, and she gripped Munne's shoulders tightly, spinning her to look her in the eye. The older Elviri was searching her expression for any kind of malice, any hint of deception. "Vere'cha, if what you say is true, then you're a danger to us, to anyone you come across."

Munne nodded again. Her hands trembled, so she balled them up into fists and pressed them into her thighs.

"But you're not finished with your tale, are you?" Araloth asked, her head tilting to the side as she continued to study Munne's face. "You wouldn't be able to speak of the *Ardashi'ik* if he dominated your mind."

The corner of Munne's mouth curled into a small lopsided grin. "The gods couldn't have given me a finer pair of friends. No, there's another presence in my mind. He's protecting me from the *Ardashi'ik*. Giving me time to get to Kherizhan to find a way to stop this before I'm completely lost."

"Some agent from the gods?" Mayrien asked.

"No, he's..." Munne paused, still unsettled by the potential revelation that Ely was an Olaava. "I'm not sure what he is. But tonight, after Tethe infected me, Ely saved me. And he told me that the only way to save myself is to go to Kherizhan."

"Ely," Mayrien echoed, then let out a quiet hum. Araloth's hands fell away from Munne's shoulders, but she stayed close. The two looked at Mayrien who held her chin high. "Then nothing's changed, has it? We must make haste to Kherizhan."

Araloth sighed and shook her head, but Munne saw a slight smile on her face. "You're in no condition to travel, Mayrien."

"We're not letting her travel alone."

"And what's to stop me from binding your wrists and ankles to a saddle and sending the horse off to the nearest village?" Araloth snapped.

Munne stepped between them, hands raised. "Until today, I wanted nothing more than to have both of you by my side as I made this journey. But after tonight, I can't in good faith ask either of you to follow me any further. I'll go on my own."

"You're a fool if you think we'll let you," Araloth said fiercely.

"Maybe *she's* the one you should be strapping to a horse!" Mayrien shot back.

The three Elviri exchanged stares. It became a silent struggle of wills as Munne toiled over whether or not she could allow her friends to travel with her.

I want nothing more than to have them by my side. And I trust Ely to keep me safe from that beast, but Mayrien's in no condition to be traveling. I would go faster if

I left them behind. But what other troubles await me in Kherizhan? What if I have need of their blades before the end?

Munne let out a loud sigh and hung her head. "We leave at first light. As quickly as we can, and I can only hope my guardian can protect me long enough for us to find what we need to put an end to this."

CHAPTER XXIX: RAY

The pack traveled northwest for seven more days, only stopping long enough to let the wolves rest, and for the girls and Enthai to drink their herbal concoctions that kept the hunger at bay. During their breaks, the Enthai often ignored the two Proma girls, which was fine by Ray. She preferred Niamnh's company anyway, and so she tried spending as much time with her as the princess would allow. Oftentimes, the princess wouldn't even stir from her seat on the sled, which led Ray to worry for her wellbeing. After translating the "poem" inside of Naro's sunsdial box, Mother Shade had disappeared again, leaving both Ray and Daerion with more questions than answers. The ethereal woman said that soon the sundering would begin, but Ray didn't understand what that meant.

Is that why we're making haste to Rymo-tehp? Is that where this supposed sundering is supposed to start? Ray thought.

The day began with very little light from the two suns. Dark clouds filled the sky, and shortly after the pack started their next leg of the journey, snow began to fall. The snowfall was so thick that Ray could barely see Keitri's sled in front of hers. Niamnh hadn't spoken to her that morning, so between the silence and the weather, Ray couldn't keep her stomach from twisting as they traversed through the storm.

"I'm worried about her," Ray said to Daerion, who had kept her company in Niamnh's absence.

The Doshara's presence wasn't entirely unwanted at this point. Over the course of their journey northwest, Ray and Daerion had exchanged stories about Niamnh, Naro, and the Syrael Walkers of old. When the Doshara spoke of the princess, Ray could hear the fondness in his voice for her. He had gone to great lengths to protect her from the uglier, nastier side of his nature, blacking out her vision and dulling her senses so she wouldn't have to taste the blood and flesh of animals during her nightly feedings.

"At least she still looks upon you fondly," Daerion replied, his voice tinged with resignation. An odd emotion to hear from the shade. There was truth to his words, though. As the days progressed, Niamnh spent less and less time with the Doshara to the point where she hadn't spoken or looked at him in multiple days. While she kept Ray at a distance as well, she at least still managed to make eye contact and offer a few sheepish smiles every so often.

Niamnh's coldness was bitter to them both. Ray couldn't help but wonder if Niamnh had decided that Daerion wasn't worthy of kindness, and that the sins of his past weighed too heavily against him.

But what about me? We talk less and less with each passing day. I know *she hates the quiet. So why is she choosing the quiet over me? Even after everything, I thought we had become close...*

Ray rubbed her eyes and saw Mother Shade floating alongside Keitri's sled once more. With a lurch she realized that the ethereal woman must have been keeping Niamnh company during the journey, filling her head with a soothing voice that neither Ray nor Daerion could provide. Her heart ached at the thought. Someone else was filling the silence for her.

"We're almost upon the Elviri ruin," Daerion announced a little louder.

From behind Ray's seat on the sled, Enesse let out a shrill bark. The Enthai's wolves responded in kind, as did the other Enthai on the other sleds.

"Just how old is this place?" Ray asked the Doshara.

"Ancient. Older than the second sun," Enesse responded before Daerion had the chance to, her voice carrying over the wind.

That'd explain the lack of information in Naro's history books, Ray thought. *But would he have known about this place?* Lowering her voice so only Daerion could hear, Ray asked, "Has he been here before?"

Though she hadn't said his name, the shade knew she was referring to Naro. "Not since I've known him," Daerion murmured.

The more she talked about Naro to the Doshara, the easier it was to think about him. She could ask questions without a lump rising in her throat or acid filling her stomach. And with the way Daerion answered her questions, she thought he was also getting some kind of closure in regard to his relationship with Naro, which she still wasn't entirely clear on. In his tales, she caught glimpses of fondness, but more often his words were dripping with malice. He never talked about the events that led to such animosity, or even what kind of a relationship they had, but she was thankful for the opportunity to learn more about her mentor.

Enesse's sled slowed, and Ray leaned forward, twisting her head around to try to spot their destination, but the snowfall obscured her vision. Daerion floated past her and was enveloped in the storm. She placed her hands on the wooden sled and dug her fingertips into her gloves, trying to ground herself. Being inside of a blizzard as it raged around them and turned everything a pale gray felt very much like walking blindly through the Enthai tunnels. The storm would only be a temporary hindrance. It would soon pass, and she'd be able to see her surroundings again.

I'm not blind. Or alone. I just need to wait.

Ray closed her eyes and tried to locate Enesse and her wolves just by sound. Their noises were muffled underneath the snow, but they had adjusted their barks and yips so they could be heard. Around the sled, she heard other Enthai and wolves responding to Enesse. Ray wondered if they were discussing waiting the storm out, or if they were going to keep moving.

"They nearly drove off into the bay," Daerion said, suddenly right beside Ray. He spoke into her left ear, voice easily heard over the storm. "It's impressive they stopped their sleds in time."

"What bay? How far northwest have we traveled?" Ray asked, nearly shouting the words.

"When the storm passes, you'll be able to see the Telatorr Mountains to the south," Daerion replied. He straightened and floated away from the sled, beckoning for her to follow. "You need to get inside. Come."

She frowned. "What about the Enthai?"

Daerion held her gaze for a few moments, and in that time, she realized she could no longer hear Enesse, or the other Enthai, or even the wolves. There was only a faint, incessant hum underneath her breathing and wind howling.

Where'd the others go? They must've left me behind to get inside.

The Doshara stayed silent as Ray fiddled with the leather straps of the sled and climbed to her feet. Daerion stayed just out of arm's reach, receding every time she took a step forward.

They continued this for a short distance until he stopped in place, pointing downward. "Stairs here. Be careful."

Tilting her chin down, Ray could barely make out a flight of snow-covered steps. She put one foot in front of the other, climbing to the top of the stairs. Daerion stayed three steps in front of her and was now leading her to what appeared to be a pair of massive doors carved out of ice. She raised her hand as if to caution him from backing into them, but he simply melted into the surface and disappeared. Brow furrowed, she continued forward and placed her hand against the door, giving it a shove. It didn't immediately budge, so she had to lean into it with more of her weight before it slid inward.

Looking up, the structure she entered was eerily reminiscent of Mother Shade's temple. Everything was carved out of ice. The ceiling soared overhead, easily four to five times her height. Daerion stood in the center of the room with his back to her, staring at the archway leading further into the building. The entry hall was cold and dark, but she could see more than two arms' lengths in front of her thanks to the dim light that surrounded him.

"What is this place?" Ray asked after stepping inside and pushed the door closed behind her. "And where are the others?"

"The Enthai won't step foot in here," he murmured. "They believe this place is cursed. By what, I cannot say."

"Wait, then where are they?" Ray wrapped her arms around herself and suppressed a shiver that nestled into her lower back. "And why did Mother Shade have them come out all this way?" Daerion didn't respond.

Inside, away from the snowfall and howling winds, the low hum was louder and easier to hear. As she walked around the room, the sound of her footsteps filled the chamber, echoing against the ice walls. Ice crunched underfoot in some areas where the floor had chipped away. Her eyes struggled to adjust to the darkness, instead being drawn to Daerion's soft glowing light. She stopped a few steps behind him, letting his figure fill her sight.

"What do you know about this place?" she asked again, raising her voice so he couldn't pretend to not hear her. Her words echoed throughout the room.

"Very little," he responded tersely. "But *She* will reveal the answer when She feels like it." Venom dripped from his words, no doubt referring to Mother Shade.

Turning away from Daerion, Ray inspected the room. Though she couldn't see much, she thought she saw similarities between the room and the entry hall of Castle Auora. There were no furnishings present, but she could easily imagine suits of armor standing against the walls with shields and banners hanging above them. She wished there was a chandelier or candelabra so she could bring forth more light, but she couldn't find any. Not that she would've been able to light a fire anyway; all of her supplies were either on Enesse' sled or back at Mother Shade's temple.

The door was opened once more, groaning as it slid across the ice floor. Ray turned to see who it was and was surprised to see Niamnh running across the floor towards her. "Ray!"

"Niamnh?" Ray whispered. She was nearly tackled to the ground as the princess wrapped her arms around her and squeezed tightly, burying her head in her shoulder.

"The Enthai and I have been looking for you for hours," Niamnh responded breathlessly. She pulled back just far enough so they could look at each other. Her gray eyes were lit up with such excitement and relief, Ray couldn't help but feel guilty for—

"*Hours?*" she muttered in disbelief. "Daerion and I just walked inside a few moments ago..." Ray trailed off, looking past Niamnh to see Mother Shade floating in the doorway. *Did she tell Daerion to bring me here, or did he bring me to escape her? No, she must've done something, just like back at the temple. How else could time have passed so quickly?*

"Well, I'm glad you're not hurt." Niamnh smiled, drawing Ray's attention back to the princess. She couldn't help but smile in return. "Have you explored much of the place yet?" The two glanced around the empty entry hall together.

Is she ignoring my mention of Daerion on purpose? Where did he go, anyway? "No, just... just this room, so far," Ray responded. She felt extremely disoriented, as if she were just a plaything to powers too great to understand, and she loathed that feeling. The smile fell from her face as she looked back to Mother

Shade. "Why are we here? What was so important that you had to drag us all the way across the tundra to get here as quickly as possible?"

Mother Shade simply stared at them, offering nothing in response. Anger flared inside of Ray, and she took a step toward the woman to do... *something*.

Niamnh placed a hand on Ray's chest, holding her in place. When their eyes met, Ray thought she saw something resembling sorrow in Niamnh's gray eyes, and that extinguished the budding rage inside of her.

"I think... we'll find those answers soon. Let's go see the rest of the ruin?" Niamnh said softly, the plea in her voice tugging at Ray's heart.

Ray's feet itched to move, and she was overwhelmed with the desire to put as much space between them and Mother Shade as possible. She nodded fervently, pulling Niamnh's hand off of her chest and holding it tightly at her side. She cast another glance over the princess's shoulder to see that Mother Shade had vanished, but the room was bathed in very dim light left over from the ethereal woman's presence. Tilting her head back, she saw a chandelier glowing with blue flames that looked very much like the blue flames she had seen in the hidden stairwell in Auora. Her stomach clenched, the urge to flee only heightening.

We're here for a reason. Might as well move forward and see what lies at the end of this path. Just like back in Auora.

The blue flames led the girls through another archway into a long hallway decorated only with wall sconces lit with more blue flames. Their hands unclasped as they continued down the hallway, passing several closed doors. Ray's mind idly wondered what secrets lay hidden behind them. The only answer she received was the hum, growing louder the further they journeyed into the ruin.

Will we come across any signs of life? How long has this place been abandoned?

"I've never seen candles like these," Niamnh said softly, her voice barely louder than their crunching footsteps.

"I have," Ray muttered reluctantly. The princess tilted her chin in confusion, but Ray decidedly did not elaborate. "Let's see where they go."

In the back of her mind, she dared to hope that the flames would lead to a door that opened into a garden in the Sky District, and that they could be done with the journey. Niamnh was free from Daerion just like Naro said she'd be, so now it was time to return home. As much as she wished for the impossible, she knew it wouldn't happen. They had business to finish in Rymo-tehp first, whatever it was.

As they continued through the twisting hallways and up the winding staircases with only the crackling flames for company, Ray felt her heart beating faster and faster. The walls surrounding them were in pristine condition, but everything felt cold and forgotten. No furnishings, no decorations, no signs of anyone having set foot inside since...

Before the second sun, Enesse had said. Although they were out of the snowstorm, Ray felt coldness seeping deep into her bones.

Desperate for some kind of warmth, she turned to look at Niamnh. "How are you holding up?" She wanted to curse herself for asking such a stupid question, but she wanted to fill the silence. Breathe life into the forgotten place.

Niamnh let out a startled laugh. "I've been trying to figure out how to answer that." The princess drifted closer to Ray, and their shoulders bumped against one another as they walked. The touch sent a shock through her body, one that she found herself craving to feel again.

"You've been so distant lately," Ray murmured.

Niamnh hummed in agreement. "Mother Shade showed me so many things before we left. Back when we were standing on the steps of Her temple."

Of course it's Mother Shade's doing. Something ugly stirred in Ray's heart, making it beat too hard against her chest.

"Just when I got my thoughts back to myself, someone stepped in and started talking again." Niamnh shook her head and laughed again, but it was a quiet self-deprecating sound. "I've been trying to make sense of what She showed me, talk to Her about it, but She told me that I'd have to do this myself."

"You don't have to do this, or anything, on your own," Ray blurted, her hand darting to Niamnh's shoulder and squeezing it gently.

Niamnh's lips curled upward, casting a warm glance at Ray. "But I do. At least, I did at first. I had to discover my place in all of... *this.*" She waved her hand in the air. When it fell to her side, it brushed against Ray's. "Some events are fated to happen, but it's my choice—*our choices*—to decide what role we play in them."

"You're not making any sense." Ray frowned.

"Sorry," Niamnh said softly. "And I'm sorry for being so distant these past few days."

"*Several* days," Ray mumbled under her breath.

"Several days," Niamnh agreed. "I didn't want to hurt you, but I needed to find my place, or at least my footing, and I think I finally have."

The princess stopped in place, and Ray had to backtrack a few steps to stand beside her. They were standing in front of a plain, nondescript door. It was carved from ice like the rest of their surroundings. Niamnh gazed upon it as if it were something special, and Ray pored over every detail to see what could've drawn her in. Two sconces framed the door, bathing the ice in a soft blue light. Glancing around them, she realized they had just finished climbing a spiral staircase and were standing at the end of a short hallway.

Niamnh reached out and took Ray's hand in hers, squeezing tightly. "I didn't think we'd get here so quickly." Ray looked back at the princess and arched an eyebrow in a wordless question. "This was one of the places She showed me, but I didn't fully understand until now."

Ray's head spun, and she shifted her feet further apart to steady herself. *Niamnh knows why we're here.*

She opened her mouth to ask even more questions, demand answers, but Niamnh squeezed her hand again to stop her. The other girl said quietly, "There's, um... something I need to do before you and I can go any further." The princess pulled her hand away from Ray's and walked back down the hallway a few steps, tugging off her gloves. "Daerion, can you hear me? Are you there?"

The stairway filled with a soft white glow, and the Doshara appeared just below the landing, craning his neck up to look at the girl. "Princess?"

Niamnh inhaled deeply through her nose, straightening her back to her full height. "Daerion Valha, I forgive you for the past six years, for causing my mother's death, and for taking the suns' warmth from me. I hope that one day you'll find true peace." When she spoke, her voice was firm and resolute, like that of a queen.

Daerion stared at her with a mixture of awe and fear, his eyes flickering with blue light, his lips parted in a silent breath. His voice wavered as he said, "Princess Niamnh, what are you...?"

Niamnh raised her arm, her bare hand reaching for him. Wide-eyed, Ray watched as the princess placed her hand on the Doshara's shoulder, and she thought she saw his shoulder sag under the weight of her touch. With aching slowness, Daerion lifted his hand to touch hers. For a moment, jealousy seized Ray's heart at the tenderness of the moment, mind in disbelief that Niamnh could forgive this man for all of the horrors and heartache he had caused. But she was also in awe of how the other girl could be strong enough to forgive him.

Ray blinked and Daerion faded away, the staircase returning to darkness. *Is he... gone? For good?*

Niamnh turned back to Ray, a soft smile spread across her lips and a few tears rolling down her cheeks. Ray wanted nothing more than to wipe away those tears, but she held herself back as the princess returned to her side in front of the door. Niamnh fidgeted with something on her wrist and Ray realized she was taking off one of her bracelets—her brother's bone bracelet.

Niamnh reached out for Ray's wrist, wrapping the leather around her skin with delicate care. "I want you to have this."

"But... this is your brother's...?"

Niamnh's eyes dropped to the leather wrapping, her fingers tying off and securing the bracelet around Ray's wrist. "Please make sure he gets home safely. He's been gone for too long."

Ray's brow furrowed and the corners of her eyes pricked with hot tears. "Please tell me what's going on."

After she finished with the bracelet, Niamnh took Ray's hand in between hers and looked back up, gray eyes appearing blue in the candlelight. "I know you'll get home fine. You took care of me during our journey."

Her stomach dropped, her blood turning to ice. *She's not coming with,* Ray thought. *She's not coming with?* She lifted her other hand and squeezed Niamnh's hand between hers. "Niamnh, whatever's going on, whatever Mother Shade said you've got to do, you don't have to do it alone. And I'm not going to leave you. You're coming back—"

Niamnh shook her head. "I have to stay."

Ray's voice turned desperate. "What does she even want? What did she tell you to do?"

"*We are here, at the beginning of the first end.*" Ray felt the floor vibrate underneath the weight of Mother Shade's voice. The woman materialized beside the two girls, towering over them both in her white robes. Ray's eyes flicked over to her ethereal form but quickly looked back to Niamnh, wanting to keep the other girl's attention. Didn't want her looking away to Mother Shade. "*We the guardians did not intervene soon enough the first time, but we are here to change that this time.*"

"The second end," Niamnh whispered, eyes never leaving Ray's.

"Why must it be the end?" Ray asked breathlessly.

"'*One joins another, only to be torn asunder.' So it was spoken under the first sun, and so it must come to pass underneath the second sun.*" Mother Shade reached out and placed a hand on each girl's shoulder. Ray looked at the woman, searching underneath the hood, within the void, to find two bright white orbs staring back. "*Our Nahaesyraellonore said it was so, and now he must pay his penance, right his wrongs, when the sundered sun comes. This you must tell him, Ray Finnegan.*"

Ray's mouth went dry, and her grip on Niamnh's hands weakened. "I can't leave Niamnh here alone, not after everything."

"*She won't be alone,*" Mother Shade replied warmly.

Looking back to Niamnh, Ray saw the same warmth reflected in her eyes, a serene smile on her face. "I'm glad to have met you," the princess said softly.

Ray's heart twisted in her chest. She had so many more questions, so many more protests, but all of the words died on her lips. She wanted to demand Niamnh to reconsider, to leave this place with her, or at least allow her to stay. She didn't want to leave, not when Niamnh had finally been freed from the curse of the Doshara and had her own life to live.

"*Daerion,*" Mother Shade called out to the staircase. "*You must make haste to Ekerrin's Guard. My children have heard my call and will carry you both there swiftly. Ray Finnegan must return to Auora.*"

Daerion? He's still here? Ray's eyes darted to the staircase, searching for the shape of the ghostly man.

"Yes, Lady," Daerion's voice came from around the bend. Mother Shade burned brighter than the candles and the Doshara, drowning everything out in her white light.

"This can't be goodbye," Ray protested, squeezing the princess's hands once more.

"Not forever," Niamnh murmured in agreement.

Ray wanted to howl back that *no, not forever, because this isn't goodbye, I can't leave you.*

She committed the sight of Niamnh's face to memory. The dimples that formed when she smiled. The hint of teeth through her lips. The corners of her eyes crinkled upward. The loose strands of white hair falling across her cheeks. Gray eyes bright against warm brown skin. She was beautiful.

And then she was gone.

Ray stood in front of the large ice doors of Rymo-tehp, back outside in the cold. With as much strength as she could muster, she tried to pull the doors open, but they wouldn't budge. She slammed her fists against the door and let out a primal cry, tears spilling down her face. Out of the corner of her eye she saw Daerion standing beside her, his face a visage of pain and sadness.

"What was that?!" Ray screamed at the Doshara, turning her fury upon him. "What's She doing with Niamnh?"

"I-I don't know," he responded, staring ahead with unfocused eyes.

She wanted to hit him. Beat her fists against him until her knuckles were bloody or he stopped her. But she knew she couldn't do that; she'd just fall through him as soon as she swung. *How come Niamnh could touch him?*

Ray let out another anguished scream at the thought of the other girl. That last smile flashed across her vision when she blinked. She wanted nothing more than to close her eyes and lose herself in that smile. But she wouldn't be able to—she was gone, trapped inside the frozen castle.

Did Naro know this would happen to Niamnh? Did he see this in one of his visions? Her face heated as rage boiled her blood.

A shrill bark cut through her inner discourse. Spinning around, Ray saw the four Enthai standing at the bottom of the stairs. Keitri beckoned to her, his tail brushing against the ground in agitation. "Come, *rhiekka*, we must leave this place."

As the Enthai's words sunk in, Ray felt the fight leave her body. Her hands throbbed from where she beat against the door. Weariness tugged at her eyelids, and she desired nothing more than to curl up in a ball and go to sleep. Her feet were so heavy, and she didn't know if she could move from where she stood.

"We need to go, little moth," Daerion murmured in her ear.

The closeness of his voice startled her and cleared the haze from her eyes. With great reluctance, she took her first step. She wanted to look back at the ice doors, the frozen ruin, but she knew it would only make her chest hurt worse than it already did.

Another step. *The Enthai will make sure I make it back to Promthus.* Another step down the stairs. *Daerion will follow along, no doubt. All to deliver some message back to Naro.*

Another step, and another. Daerion's form glowed beside her, and she took some small comfort in that. At the bottom of the stairs, she finally looked beyond the Enthai and at her surroundings. The snowstorm from earlier was gone, and now the tundra was silent underneath a dark nighttime sky. A full moon hung high above them, providing enough light to see the great bay behind the Enthai. Large chunks of ice floated idly in the black waters. Far in the distance she could see the outline of mountains stretching upward into the sky.

Again, Ray felt the urge to turn and look upon the frozen ruin, but she kept her chin held high and followed Keitri and the others back to the sleds where the wolves paced restlessly. Keitri signaled her over to join him on his sled. He helped her secure the leather straps around her legs and soon they were running off into the night away from Rymo-tehp.

Daerion floated alongside the sled in silence. Ray's eyes kept shifting between him and the wolves, but eventually she slipped into a dreamless sleep, the cold of the wind not bothering her as much anymore.

When Ray awoke, the pack had stopped for a break. The sky was lighter, more of a dark blue than a black, but the suns were still below the horizon. Keitri and the other Enthai were standing together off in the distance, talking in their own language, no doubt about what had happened at Rymo-tehp. She rubbed the sleep from her eyes and rolled her neck from side to side, finding it stiff and uncomfortable.

She undid the straps around her legs and climbed to her feet to continue stretching. Keitri and Enesse noticed her, and flicked their tails in greeting, but they kept their distance from her. Turning her head, she saw Daerion beside her. He looked exhausted, which brought an inappropriate grin to her face.

What do ghosts have to be exhausted over? An image of Niamnh's face came unbidden to her mind and she flinched, her stomach twisting sharply. His appearance was suddenly understandable, uncomfortably so.

"You slept," Daerion said, more of a comment than a question.

"That obvious?" Ray grumbled, pulling an arm across her body to get the blood flowing. "How long have we been on the move?"

"A couple of hours at most," Daerion responded. "Look to the west."

Ray frowned, not entirely sure which direction to turn without the suns. She couldn't gather her bearings from the moon's position, so she plucked Naro's sunsdial out of her pocket and opened it up. Following it to the west, she raised her eyes, and her breath was taken away by the sight before her.

She had been impressed by Mother Shade's temple, but that paled in comparison to the sprawling frozen ruin in the distance. Underneath the moonlight, she saw Rymo-tehp in all of its ancient glory. At its prime, it would've been an awe-inspiring castle. Even in ruin it was a sight to behold. Frozen spires stretched upward, their sharp points piercing the sky. Towers of all shapes and sizes stood above the bulk of the building. The castle had to be larger than even the city-island of Auora, with different wings connected by spanning bridges and covered walkways. Though the ruin was completely still and silent, Ray found herself unable to tear her gaze away.

Niamnh is in there somewhere.

The silence became unbearable, but she didn't know what to say. She ached. And perhaps the only person in the world who could understand that pain was standing beside her.

"I miss her," Ray mumbled, voice weak underneath the weight of... *everything*.

"She'd want you to be strong," Daerion replied, his voice barely above a whisper.

Ray shook her head, throat squeezing tightly around her next words. "I can't. Not like her."

Daerion let out a huff of air, something akin to a chuckle. "In all my years, I've met very few people with strength like hers."

Ray nodded, unable to do much more beyond that. Her vision became blurry behind fresh tears. She rubbed her arm against her face and sniffled. "She put up with you for six years."

That elicited a loud cackle from the Doshara, sounding more than a real man's laugh than any other she had heard from him. "You've no idea. Most are so frightened or cowed by my presence that they break within months, if not days. To last a year, or multiple years, takes such strength and resolve... Very few can do that."

"She was never afraid," Ray whispered, thinking back on their journey north and east. "Never let anything get to her."

Daerion scoffed. "Of course she was afraid, but she didn't let her fears hold her back."

Ray finally turned her gaze to the Doshara. "What happens next?" she asked quietly.

His eyes met hers and he shrugged, grimacing. "You return to Auora, to your lord. Then comes 'the second end', whatever that may be," he murmured.

Can I even face Naro after all of this? Was this plan from the very beginning?

The girl and the ghost looked back to Rymo-tehp. The sky had grown lighter as the suns rose in the east. The light danced and flickered off the icy ruin. Ray swore she saw a light appear in one of the towers, but it must have been one of the suns' rays catching on the ice. She heard Daerion mutter something under his breath, but her mind didn't process it. She was transfixed on the beauty of Rymo-tehp.

As the suns climbed higher into the sky, the light in the tower grew until she was certain it was its own creation, not that of the suns. White light emanated from the castle, burning brighter and brighter—

The ground shook and Ray fell to her knees. From behind her, she heard the Enthai wailing and howling. Another tremor struck. Daerion's hand crossed over her face, barely distinguishable from the brightness in the west.

Finally, his words pierced through the haze in her mind. "Look away!" the Doshara cried.

Ray tucked her chin to her chest, screwing her eyes shut. An outline of the ruin, jagged spires and tall towers seared across her eyelids, burning white against black. Hands gripping ice, a violent shiver shook the earth and coursed through her body as the outline morphed into a figure reminiscent of Mother Shade from her visions back at the temple. She had just caught sight of something historical, catastrophic, something that hadn't been seen for thousands of years.

Magic was returning to Daaria.

CHAPTER XXX: SETH

Seth awoke well before sunrise. As he rubbed at his eyes and rolled onto his back, he pondered what had disturbed him. His room was still dark, and he didn't hear anyone talking out in the common area. He was about to roll over and try falling back asleep, when he heard—no, *felt* it.

The pyramid rumbled and shuddered.

What's going on?! Seth curled inward on himself, throwing his arms over his head. The stones and bricks groaned, sending vibrations through his bones. *Is the pyramid going to come crashing down?*

"Seth!?" Octavia shrieked from somewhere else in their suite. "Seth!"

"Tav!" he shouted back, pulling his head off the bed so he could look at the door. His twin shoved it open and ran to the bed, throwing herself over him. "What's going on? Are we under attack?"

"*Earthquake,*" she hissed, her warm breath tickling his ear.

Their father's words surfaced in his mind: "*on the day the ground trembles.*" As the world around them grew silent and still, a new rush of fear surged through his veins. His father's drunk words had plagued his nightmares in what little sleep he had managed, and now—

"*Tomorrow, we open the tomb, of course.*"

"He's going to open the tomb today," Seth blurted. "We're out of time, Tav."

He was gripped with panic, his body paralyzed. Octavia pulled back, her eyes searching Seth's as a look of horror passed across her face. Lisanthir wasn't with them, the prisoners would be escorted to the tomb entrance today, and *they were out of time.* Seth tried to force words from his mouth, but they died in his throat. He didn't know what to do, and he knew his sister was just as lost and afraid as he was.

"How do you know?" Tav managed to ask, her voice hoarse.

"He told me," Seth whispered. Before his sister could ask any questions, he continued. "Father was here last night... He was drunk, a-and he was telling me about his plans, he..." Seth inhaled deeply, his breath hitching. Then he told her everything, hoping Octavia was keeping up. "He told me that Osza *is* planning some kind of mating ritual with that dragon after bringing it back to life, to try reincarnating the *Tserys*, and she plans on using *us*, not Lisanthir or any other Elviri, probably because she thinks she can control us better than Father. Father seemed to think it was a good idea, but I tried talking him out of it, tried telling him to talk to the damn voice in his head, and he said he'd ask it today, after opening the tomb."

"So, we still have a little bit of time. It doesn't end today," Octavia said as hope crept into her voice. "When's the last time any of Father's experiments worked? *Actually* worked? They might not even get the tomb open today, and even *if* they did, we still have time to find the elixir and get out of here."

"But what about the Elviri prisoners?"

Octavia's face fell, and it pained Seth to see, but he had to be realistic. Those poor souls were doomed to die today if Amias was truly going to try opening the tomb.

Or will he only kill one or two of them today, and save the rest in case his plan fails?

"If we escape, maybe we can bring word back to the Elviri. Give them closure. Maybe even revenge." His sister's expression morphed into something he hadn't seen from her in a long time—determination. Genuine strength and drive to see this through to the end.

Seth nodded. "Revenge. We can do that."

Octavia climbed back to her feet, straightening her tunic. "I'm sure the servants will be up with food sometime soon."

Seth sat up and pushed his blankets aside. "And then either Father or Osza will send for us not long after that. With the earthquake, Father will no doubt convince her to move forward as soon as possible. Can you bring me my chair?"

Their father must have moved it last night when he came to Seth's room. Tav pushed it back over to Seth's side of the bed, holding onto the handles as he shuffled over and pulled himself into the seat.

"Do you need help getting dressed?" Octavia asked, stepping away from the chair.

"Not yet. I'm sure Father will expect us to dress up, but I don't want to yet." Until the servants came with a summons, Seth could pretend that today was like any other day. He wanted to cling to that for as long as possible, though he wished Lisanthir was with him. "Do you want to sit on the balcony with me?"

Octavia nodded, and the two spent their morning in the cold winter air, watching the suns rise above the canopy of the forest and bathe the city of Iszairi in golden light. That's where Taszo and three other Asaszi servants found them when they came a few hours later to prepare the twins for the ritual.

"Good morning, *py'tseras*. It isss a gloriousss day today," Taszo said jovially. "Come, we have brought the clothesss you will wear."

Seth and Octavia returned inside, each being led off into their respective bedrooms. Two stewards went with Seth, lifting him from his chair and dressing him in a luxurious black and gold robe that reminded him of his father. Amias would surely be wearing something similar today, and Osza most likely would be too. When the stewards were pleased with how he looked, they returned him to his wheelchair, then returned to the lounge, one steward pushing his chair while the other led the way.

Taszo was standing with Octavia and the other steward. When he saw Seth, he clapped his hands together and hissed in delight. "*Sssplendid.* Now, we mussst be on our way. Follow me, *py'tseras*."

The steward pushed Seth after the Asaszi courtier, with Octavia following behind them. The journey through the *Tserdanii* felt ominous, the shadows from the skylights hanging heavy over the halls and ramps. As they descended to the bottom floor, Seth felt his stomach getting progressively heavier and tighter. He was thankful he hadn't eaten anything that morning, though he wished he had some water to parch his throat. Not that he would speak during the bloody ceremony, but it would give him some small relief.

Taszo led the small procession down another ramp below the surface into a series of hallways that had been constructed underground. They were the formal tunnels connecting the *Tserdanii* to the coliseum and other pyramids, separate from the natural tunnels and caverns that Osza had shown them several days ago. Torches lined the halls, the scent of burning wood and oil filling the air.

Though the hallways were spacious and tall, Seth felt cramped in the underground space. He craved the light of the two suns. He wanted to get out. *In time*, he told himself.

Cracks ran along the walls—*perhaps from the earthquake that morning?*—adding to Seth's fears. He had never experienced such a strong earthquake before in his life. There had been some smaller quakes and trembles, resulting from his father's experiments, but nothing that had caused structural damage like this one had.

Will it be safe to be underground for this ceremony, or will we get swallowed up by the earth in another quake? Will there even be another earthquake? Part of him hoped there would be, if for no other reason than to put an end to both Amias and Osza. What disturbed him was that the thought didn't give him any pause or fear. He would *welcome* it.

They passed through the network of caverns and tunnels beneath the coliseum. Several other Asaszi and Provira traveled to and fro, a mix of soldiers, servants, and courtiers. Seth wondered if Osza wanted the whole city present for the ceremony and if there was even enough space to accommodate so many bodies in front of the tomb.

Maybe she plans on addressing the city in the coliseum once the entrance of the tomb is opened.

Taszo led them further underground under what Seth assumed was the center of the coliseum. Very few other people were traveling in the same direction as them, lending credence to his theory. The distance between torches grew longer, the shadows growing deeper and darker. Seth felt like he might vomit or faint.

What would they do if I did faint? Would they wake me, or send me back to my suite? Would the entire ceremony be delayed? He considered taking the risk and finding out, but he knew his father wouldn't let anything detract from today's events. Blood would be spilled today, all in the name of the *Tserys*.

After another twist in the corridor, they emerged into a large cavern where a modest gathering of Asaszi and Provira assembled. On the wall opposite

Seth and the others was the entrance to the Tomb of the Prince. The entrance had been carved out of the surrounding stone, depicting a mural of the Eldest Days. In the center was a man with a serpentine helmet, scaled armor, and flaming sword. Behind him were the pyramids of Iszairi with two dragons flying overhead. Above his head was a single orb, which must have been a sun. The mural was in near perfect condition, showing no signs of age nor any damage from the earthquake. Seth had never seen a depiction of the *Tserys* before, but he knew right away that it was Him.

Underneath the murmurs of the crowd, he heard the familiar low hum. If Seth focused on it, it seemed to be coming from the mural, sounding more like someone quietly muttering. Dread filled his stomach as he realized his father had been right—the *Tserys* was trying to speak to them. His skin prickled, gooseflesh raising all along his arms and neck.

Taszo led Seth and Octavia to the front of the crowd where Amias and Osza stood together in similar black and gold robes. Looking around, he saw that Astohi and Szatisi weren't too far away from their queen, hovering near three forms dressed in scrap clothing and chains.

The Elviri prisoners.

Seth looked over them closely, taking in every detail. The three had been beaten many times, their clothes torn and dirty. Manacles connected their hands and feet together with chains. All three were on their knees, heads bowed. If they spoke, cried, or made any other noises, Seth couldn't hear them. Astohi held a whip in his hand, eyes fixed on the Elviri. Szatisi stood a little farther away, stoic in her black priestess robes.

Lisanthir isn't among them, though. Thank the gods for that. The thought brought Seth little relief. Even though his *ebilin* was not among the captives, he would still be forced to sit and watch those three lose their lives.

He forced himself to look at his father and the Asaszi queen. A dagger hung on his father's hip. Today he didn't wear any gloves to cover his hands. Today he wasn't above getting blood on his skin. The thought made Seth's skin crawl. Both of their attentions turned to the twins.

Amias approached them with open arms, a smile plastered on his face. "My children! Praise be," he said.

He embraced Octavia first, then clasped his hand on Seth's shoulder. All signs of his drunken stupor were gone, and he had been cleaned up. It was as if the previous night hadn't happened. His grip on Seth's shoulder tightened just for a moment, then he let go.

"Good morning, Father," Octavia said, her voice soft enough that it was easy to believe she was pleased to see him.

"We'll begin the ceremony shortly. I can't wait for you to hear His voice." Amias smiled at them once again, then turned and took his place beside Osza once more.

"Thisss way, *py'tseras*," Taszo murmured, gesturing to a spot near some other Asaszi standing at the front of the crowd.

Octavia met Seth's gaze, but her expression was unreadable. It had to be. They were deep in the snake's nest and couldn't risk breaking the façade that they wanted to be here. It took all of Seth's effort to keep his emotions in check and not show any pity or empathy toward the Elviri captives. The twins took their place among the crowd, eyes fixed on the Asaszi queen and their father.

After a few moments, Osza raised her hands and clapped twice. Silence fell over the crowd like a wave, starting first in the front then spreading to the back of the cavern. Once their murmuring came to an end, Osza lowered her hands and addressed the crowd.

"Welcome all to our new beginning!" she said. "Today we break the ssseal on thisss tomb and breathe in the air that hasss been kept from usss for thousssands of yearsss."

Though the cavern was silent, a feeling of awe settled over the Asaszi and Provira. Seth watched the faces of those around him twist with delight, eyes wide and bright. Osza turned to Astohi and beckoned with a finger. Her consort bent over and grabbed the hair of the nearest Elviri, yanking their head back so they could look upon the dreadful Asaszi queen. With his whip, Astohi pointed at Osza's feet. The prisoners slowly pushed themselves to their feet then approached Osza, the rattling of the chains echoing off the stone walls of the cavern.

All three Elviri stood taller than the Asaszi queen. One was so bold as to look down his nose at her. He muttered something to Osza, but Seth was too far away to hear the words. Osza's eyes widened for a moment, her mouth curving into a hungry smile. She held the gaze of the Elviri as she spoke to the crowd again.

"Today we ssspill the blood of our foesss, feeding the Suneater."

A few Asaszi in the crowd couldn't contain their eager hisses and murmurs of support. They craved the violence, wanted Elviri blood to be spilled. Osza allowed the crowd to work themselves into a frenzy before she turned to Amias and beckoned him forward.

Seth focused on his father, watching as he drew the dagger from its sheath. The blade was white and opaque, unlike anything he had ever seen before. Then it dawned on him. *It's made from bone.*

Amias and Osza had planned on using some form of the dragon's skeleton in the ritual. Seth had assumed the skeleton would be present for it, maybe its skull or a tooth. A dagger made much more sense, and of course it would be used to spill Elviri blood. That's why Seth hadn't considered it. His stomach lurched and he swallowed down bile.

His father approached the first of the Elviri prisoners. Astohi came up behind the Elviri and kicked at the back of their knees, forcing them into a kneeling position. Their chains clanged together loudly, nearly drowning out the sound of the Elviri grunting in pain. Amias's brown eyes were bright as he raised the dagger into the air. The Asaszi and Provira responded with delighted hisses and cheers. They were no better than the circle of soldiers egging on their brethren to fight and spill blood. Seth was disgusted with his people, but his father was the most disgusting of them all.

Amias grabbed onto the Elviri's hair and slid the sharpened bone along their throat. A gurgling noise came from the Elviri prisoner as they slumped forward, held aloft only by Amias's hand. The bone dagger dripped crimson red. Osza approached Amias to his right, dragging her fingertips through the neck wound, coating her hands in Elviri blood. She cupped her hands underneath their head to catch more of the red liquid as it spilled forth.

Seth gagged, his hand flying to his throat to choke everything back down. Octavia found his other hand, squeezing painfully. They were both powerless in that moment, doomed to watch these innocents die because it was the will of their monstrous father. *I hope Lisanthir is far away from here right now. Gods, I hope he isn't watching this.*

The crowd broke into a cacophonous roar as Amias and Osza moved to the second prisoner and repeated the gruesome actions. Soon Osza's cupped hands overflowed with the blood of the three Elviri. Amias's hand was coated in red as well with specks of blood spattered across his face. More was surely spread across his robes, but the black hid its color.

Vengeance. We must find a way to avenge them. Seth grimaced.

Osza turned to the mural and raised her hands in the air, blood running down her jade scales. She let out a loud wail then spoke in the ancient Asaszi tongue. Amias's voice joined hers, then Astohi's and Szatisi's. As they continued to chant, the three Elviri bodies slumped together, their blood pooling on the ground.

With a final word, Osza let out a terrible shriek and flung her hands forward, drenching the stone in dark red blood. She took a step to her left, allowing Amias to approach and stab the dagger into the center of the splatter. Seth expected the bone to shatter, but it slid into the stone with no resistance. Szatisi stood on the other side of Amias, and together with Osza called out to the stone, "*Tserys! Tserys!*"

The crowd joined in, the chant becoming a deafening roar that filled the cavern and shook the ground. The vibrations rattled Seth's chair as the force grew stronger. His eyes darted between his father, the two Asaszi women, and the stone wall. Where his father had struck his dagger, a solid line formed, severing the mural in two. It grew larger, deeper, and the dagger fell away. Amias pulled it back to his side, stumbling back a few steps as more of the wall parted and opened. A blast of cold air blew from the stone doors as they parted. Seth flinched, squinting against the force of it. The voices in the crowd wavered for a moment, then continued their chant with renewed vigor.

Though the cavern was filled with torches, the light couldn't penetrate the depths of the tomb's shadow. Osza and Amias both took a few steps forward, no doubt in awe that their ritual worked and eager to see what lay beyond the stone that had separated them from their dead savior for so long.

The hairs on the back of Seth's neck stood on end. *Something is coming.*

Over the roar of the crowd, another voice could be heard, though Seth couldn't tell if it was out loud or inside of his head. The voice of the *Tserys.*

"My prison doors have been cast open, and I am finally free. FREE. My voice will be heard, and My will be obeyed by all. Soon I shall be made flesh once more, and I will devour the suns!"

CHAPTER XXXI: MUNNE

Each of the next six days was torture for Munne as she traveled southeast with Araloth and Mayrien. The morning after their battle with Tethe and his caravanners, the three broke down their camp as quickly as they could. They kept the three horses from the Elviri outpost, along with one of the horses given to them by Ethelmar back in Auora. The other five horses were turned loose. As she watched them snort and trot away, she wondered where Tethe's company had acquired theirs.

Did they steal these horses from someone in Auora? Or did they buy them with honest coin? She found herself doubting that they had ever done an honest thing in their lives. Provira were known for their treacherous actions and behavior.

Munne and Araloth chose to leave the bodies for the crows rather than honoring them with any kind of burial or funeral pyre. Before they departed the campsite, Munne pocketed the small fiery coin as well as Tethe's map. She wasn't entirely sure why she retrieved the coin, but she found herself periodically reaching into her pocket to touch it over the next several days. Its flames had burned her cheek, leaving behind a small patch of pink that Araloth had helped her treat.

Mayrien's movements were sluggish, and she struggled to keep up with Araloth and Munne even after they slowed their pace for her. Munne wondered if she was making a mistake by letting Mayrien accompany her south, but she knew that her friend would hear nothing of it if she tried to convince her to turn back toward Trent.

If our roles were swapped, I'd fight tooth and nail to stand beside her. Munne grimaced. *But we have to be careful of the wound in her side. It could get infected if we don't tend to it properly.*

Against her better judgment she said nothing to Mayrien, instead putting her friend in charge of the easier tasks around the campsite. She tended to her own wounds well enough, and she wasn't that bad of a cook, although normally that task fell to Araloth. The group had gathered enough firewood and kindling before they left the Imalar Woods that they didn't need any more during their trip, allowing Munne and Araloth to focus on other tasks.

Their days were filled with quiet conversation and easy banter, which eased the guilt lingering in her mind. Munne hadn't realized just how closed off she had become, and she was thankful to have Araloth and Mayrien by her side. Though they all cast glances to the southeast where Kherizhan awaited, they were more at peace than they had been since departing Elimere.

Munne had never traveled the stretch of lands between the Imalar Woods and Moonyswyn before. She always stuck to the northern roads that crossed through the Imalar Woods. These southern lands were entirely uninhabited. Off to the south, ever present during their journey, were the edges of the Moonyswyn border. The trees weren't as tall as those in the Elviri lands, but the threat looming behind them cast a large shadow.

That's why these lands are so empty. The Proma know better than to get close to that cursed rainforest. What secrets have the Provira unearthed there? Had Tethe been aware of those secrets?

Further to the southeast were the peaks of Kherizhan, distant at first, but as they drew closer, they darkened the horizon, standing even taller than the rainforest before them. The peaks matched the height of the Telatorr Mountains and were perhaps even taller than the major peaks of Mounts Belyn, Karrus, and Lianyn. Somewhere within those mountain ranges and valleys was the key to stopping the *Ardashi'ik*, but Munne had no idea what to look for.

During the day, Munne didn't allow her thoughts to drift toward Tethe, the Provira, or the *Ardashi'ik*. She willed herself to be grounded in the company of her friends and draw comfort and strength from their presence. After the first night, Araloth and Mayrien asked very few questions. They understood that they knew as much as Munne did, or almost as much, and that would have to suffice. Questions and speculation wouldn't help them get to Kherizhan any faster, so it wasn't brought up.

However, one afternoon Mayrien did raise one valuable question. "How will we gain entry into Kherizhan? Aren't the mountains impassable?"

"Those bastards got in somehow," Munne muttered. "We'll follow their map as best we can."

"And what if there's other bastards there waiting for us?" Araloth asked.

Munne met Araloth's gaze. "Then we'll kill them."

Her hand drifted to her pocket again to touch the dark coin. She felt a small spark resonate from the stone and immediately tapped it, severing the connection and pulling her hand out of her pocket. Both Araloth and Mayrien caught the movement, but neither commented on it. They had more pressing matters to be concerned about than some stone that could create small tendrils of blue flame.

Maybe they think we can use it once we get to Kherizhan. I can't deny the thought has crossed my mind more than once.

After the suns fell, Munne's thoughts would drift to Ely and his ongoing battle with the *Ardashi'ik*. She hadn't seen him since the night the *Ardashi'ik* leapt into her mind and began his assault on her conscience. It had only been a matter of days, but she found herself desperately missing the sight of Ely's bright red hair and soft green eyes, craving the feeling of his hand holding hers. She wondered what other madness ailed her and drove her to those thoughts and feelings.

Surely, it's just because of what he's doing for me. That's why I want to see him, to know that he's doing well and that he's not being overpowered by the Ardashi'ik. But even as she projected those thoughts to herself, she knew that wasn't it. Before she could dig deeper, she drifted off into an uneasy slumber, where she was blessed with no dreams or nightmares.

Eventually the rainforest of Moonyswyn collided with the mountains of Kherizhan. One night the Elviri triple made camp along the fringes of the mountains where their peaks were smallest. The next morning, as the two suns climbed above the horizon and spilled light onto the earth, Munne sat up from her bedroll. Her eyes burned and her stomach rumbled. She hadn't gotten much sleep the night before, tossing and turning with fear. Across the dim campfire, Mayrien reached out with her longbow to poke Araloth. She had kept the last shift the night before and was already preparing their breakfast. It probably wouldn't amount to much. They had started rationing their food two days ago when they realized there was about five days' worth left. Araloth and Munne spent more time hunting before winding down each night, but prey was scarce.

Araloth stirred almost immediately. She must not have gotten much sleep either. With the jagged brown peaks of Kherizhan looming over them, it would be a miracle to feel at ease long enough to sleep.

Munne climbed to her feet and fell into a stretching routine to awaken her body. It would be several more minutes before Mayrien had their food ready, and they needed to break down their camp. Today they would enter the lands of Kherizhan.

"Do you think it snows here?" Mayrien asked, looking up from the pot of stewed berries. "I didn't see any snow on the peaks as we approached, but..."

"There's a lot that we're going to learn from being here," Araloth replied as she rolled up her bedroll and secured it to her horse.

Breaking down camp took little time, and Mayrien was ready with their food when they finished. The three ate in silence. After, Araloth helped Mayrien onto her horse then climbed onto her own. Munne mounted Alathyl, and they departed for the mountains.

The ground sloped up gently at first, green grass turning brown beneath the horses' hooves. Clouds drifted through the sky, covering the suns and shielding the land from their light. Trees were scarce, and the ones that did grow were the height of the Elviri. There was more shrubbery than anything else. As they climbed further, their surroundings turned to gray rock and brown stone. It seemed as if the land was starved for water and air, a stark contrast between Promthus and where they were now. Munne could appreciate the natural beauty of rock and stone, but this felt wrong. The land wasn't supposed to be so dry and deserted. She wasn't sure where that feeling came from, but it dug its claws into her and lingered in the back of her mind.

An hour into their day, the horses slowed their pace and began snorting angrily. They stamped their hooves on the ground and refused to move, even with the Elviri women murmuring words of encouragement to the beasts.

"Predators nearby?" Araloth asked the others.

Munne frowned. "It's possible, but—"

She was interrupted by a tremor that shook the earth. Pebbles and gravel rained down around them from higher up the mountains. Clutching onto Alathyl's reins, Munne called out to her companions with a wordless shout. All four of the horses whinnied and stumbled along the ground. Munne braced herself in her saddle, her legs locking onto Alathyl tightly. Araloth lurched and secured the reins of their fourth horse.

After a moment, the tremor ebbed and faded away. "By the gods, what was that?!" Mayrien hissed.

Did the tremor reopen her wounds? "Mayrien, are you alright?" Munne called, twisting around in her saddle.

"I think so." The other Elviri was leaning heavily against her horse's neck, but seemed otherwise alright.

"I've never felt a tremor like that before," Araloth muttered, barely containing her fear. "What kind of place is this?"

Munne forced her body to relax, straightening her posture. She raised her eyes toward the plains of Promthus and grimaced. The green grass had turned dark underneath the clouds. Turning back to Kherizhan, she eyed the passageway they were traveling and let out a resigned sigh. The path was still relatively open, but the farther in they traveled, the taller the mountains became, surrounding the path on both sides. If another tremor like that occurred while they were walking between the cliffs, it could trigger an avalanche and bury them beneath a shower of rocks and boulders. But she needed to travel along that path because it would take her to where she needed to go.

Where do I need to go?

Something inside of her churned and lurched forward, and she felt herself pulled onward, deeper into the mountains.

"Munne?" Araloth's voice cut through her thoughts like a clean blade.

Munne blinked and realized she was farther into the mountain pass than she had been previously. Looking over her shoulder again, she saw Araloth and Mayrien lingering far behind, where the tremor had first struck. She had moved without realizing it.

"We need to keep going. I can feel... *something* beckoning me on." As Munne spoke, her voice cracked a little.

She could see Araloth's frown, and even Mayrien managed a worrying expression in between bouts of pain. Araloth asked quietly, "Are you sure you can trust that feeling?"

Munne considered her words. *It's a valid question. Is this Ely or the Ardashi'ik's doing? Should I be blindly following this instinct? Do I have a choice?*

"Let's just try to avoid being trapped between cliffs?" Mayrien offered. "And before we really start, we probably should check my wounds."

Araloth muttered a curse under her breath and dismounted before Munne could return to her friends. "Vere'cha, the horses."

Munne dismounted from Alathyl and led her horse back to the others. She picked up the reins to both Araloth's horse and their fourth, watching as Araloth gently poked and prodded at Mayrien's bandages.

"Doesn't look like any of the stitching was pulled out," Araloth murmured. "But your side is weeping again. I'll go ahead and replace the wrapping."

"Do we have anything for the pain?" Mayrien asked.

"Here. Only have one more bundle of Aeona's Tears left," Araloth responded, referring to some herbs they had brought with them from Elimere. A standard remedy for pain. "Chew the leaves sparingly."

"Well, thank the Allmother for one more bundle!"

Munne's gaze wandered away from her friends and back to the mountain pass. Blurred landscapes crossed her mind as she considered their course for the day. Once they crested this ridge, the path would take a sharp left and hug the cliffside and descend into a narrow valley. They would follow that valley for a few hours before climbing again to...

How do I know this? And where are we going?

Araloth brushed by Munne, startling her from her focus. "Are you okay, Vere'cha?"

"I have to be," Munne answered, not giving herself the option to be anything else. "I was just thinking and... listening."

"To whatever's telling you where to go?" Munne nodded. Then came the familiar sight of Araloth frowning. "I don't like this."

"I don't see any other option at this point," Munne said stiffly. She climbed onto Alathyl once more and they went back to climbing the mountain path.

The view from the top of the ridge took Munne's breath away. Before them stretched a vast, desolate land of browns and grays. Tall, jagged peaks framed the horizon with softer rolling hills and valleys filling the foreground. Judging from the sheer cliff faces and varying layers of rock and minerals, rivers once ran through Kherizhan.

Is this what Elimere would look like if the rivers dried up and everything died?

The path they walked on curved to the left, hugging the cliffside of the eastern mountain as it descended down into a narrow valley. Just as it had appeared in Munne's head.

Ely, are you the one pulling me forward? She closed her eyes, finding it suddenly difficult to swallow. Out of instinct she raised a hand to her forearm, seeking warmth. Only a lingering trace could be found, bringing little relief from the fear that threatened to overwhelm her. *Don't falter now. I'm coming. I'll find a way to end this.*

Another tremor shook the ground, but it was much quieter than the first. The horses shuffled uneasily on the path but otherwise were unbothered. Araloth cursed under her breath. From their view over the land, Munne saw rocks tumble down the side of mountains into the valleys below—where they needed to be traveling to.

Without a word, Munne gently tugged on Alathyl's reins and steered the horse toward the downward path. It was wide enough for three horses to stand side by side, but they instead chose to form a single-file line to be prepared for when the next tremor struck.

"Do you know yet where we're traveling to?" Mayrien asked quietly. Her voice carried along the stone easily enough without needing to raise her voice. No doubt her friends were concerned about what lived in those lands, and whether or not their voices would draw any attention.

"Not yet," Munne replied. "Just that we need to cross that valley down there, and then climb up again... somewhere..."

"I wonder if the tremors are a normal occurrence here," Araloth whispered.

No. The denial was overwhelming, to the point that Munne had to clutch her face to keep her skull from rattling about. She forced herself to speak. "I don't think they are."

"Right, well... Keep your eyes open for any signs of movement," Araloth responded. "Though anyone traveling through here would have to be *mad* to do so..."

The corner of Munne's lips curled into a sardonic smile. Mad, indeed.

They made it to the valley without any injury, even with two additional tremors coursing through the ground. Their fears reverted back to avalanches descending upon them, or other falling hazards, rather than the fear of them falling off the path. The valley was wider than the initial pass into Kherizhan, so if rubble did fall, they had a better chance of avoiding it.

Clouds still filled the sky, preventing the Elviri from gauging the exact time. The journey felt like it had taken the majority of the day when in reality it couldn't have been more than an hour or two at most since they entered the mountains.

"How are we supposed to make camp in this place?" Mayrien's voice floated up from behind Munne.

"I'm sure there'll be a plateau somewhere," Araloth murmured.

We're not meant to stay here. Munne wasn't sure how to interpret the latest thought that passed through her mind, but she knew without a doubt that it was correct. The three Elviri weren't meant to sleep in Kherizhan. Whatever they were searching for, they would find before sunset.

"This must have been the bed of an ancient river at one point," Munne said softly.

She noticed the cracks in the ground spread all around them like a massive spider web. The sloping walls on either side of the valley climbed well above her head. An uneasy feeling swept over her, and she searched for pathways leading up out of the riverbed.

What if the river returns, and we get swept up in its waves? "Look for any way to climb out of here," Munne said over her shoulder. "We need to get to higher ground." Araloth grunted in agreement.

Several tense minutes—or was it hours?—passed without any word spoken between the Elviri. Kherizhan was silent as well. No birds flew overhead, and no creatures crawled or skittered over the land. Munne felt as if she were cut off from the rest of the world.

And no one knows we're here. We could die here and never be found.

As if in response to her fears, another tremor shook the earth, one more violent than the others. Munne pulled tightly on Alathyl's reins and led the horse into the middle of the riverbed, trying to stay away from the edges. She barked out to her friends, "Form up!"

"Watch for boulders!" Araloth called out.

The three Elviri formed a small circle, eyes glued to the mountains surrounding them as they rode out the tremor. Rocks tumbled down into the riverbed, but mercifully none came close to them. Dust clouds filled the ravine, limiting their view of their surroundings. Munne allowed her vision to unfocus and blur in order to concentrate on her hearing, listening for any other falling debris.

The earth stopped shuddering, leaving the Elviri with their irritated nickering horses and an unstable rocky region. Munne stroked Alathyl's mane, trying to calm the horse down. Mayrien did the same, whispering to her horse through clenched teeth. She heard Araloth curse and shout but could hardly see her friend through the dust.

"Our fourth got loose."

Munne forced her muscles to stay relaxed. She needed Alathyl calm. After the dust settled, they would look for the fourth horse. It was too dangerous to try that now. It took several long minutes but Kherizhan eventually settled down and returned to a silent slumber. There were longer gaps of silence in between rockslides, and it became easier to see through the dust.

Mayrien let out an excited cry. "What's that? To the east?"

Munne tried to orient herself and turn toward whatever her friend was looking at. She could make out the shape of Mayrien on horseback and tugged on Alathyl's reins to face the same direction. Squinting, she could make out some odd shapes on the slope of the riverbed. Statues of some kind, but she couldn't yet make out their forms.

Beacons.

She followed the tug forward, knowing this was the path they needed to take. "Good observation. Let's go."

"What about the pack horse?" Araloth asked.

"We can look for it when we climb out of here!" Munne snapped over her shoulder, not slowing her pace. She didn't care if Araloth or Mayrien were following. She was being beckoned onward, and onward she would go.

As she neared the edge of the riverbed, she could better make out what Mayrien had spotted. Two statues lined a path up from the riverbed, carved to resemble some kind of winged serpentine beasts wrapped around two columns. Their coloration matched the stone surrounding them. It was as if the columns had sprouted from the ground itself. Their jagged wings were outstretched and their mouths open revealing sharp fangs. It was as if they were calling to Munne to continue forward. Or perhaps warning her to stay away.

Climb.

The path turned into a staircase, leading out of the riverbed and twisting against the cliffside. More winged beasts had been carved into the stone walls, leading her further up away from the riverbed. The steps were steep and unfit for a horse. She would have to leave Alathyl behind.

"We won't be able to take the horses with us," Munne announced, climbing off of her mount. "We should secure them to one of these statues."

"What if there's another tremor? Vere'cha, you need to stop and think!" Araloth demanded, quickly catching up and grabbing Munne's wrist. "This place is dangerous."

"What's inside of my mind is more dangerous than this place," Munne hissed. "And the cure is within reach. It's wherever these stairs take us. We *have* to go."

Mayrien's voice was soft, cutting through the tension. "And are you willing to carry me there?"

Munne looked at her injured friend and felt her hostility melting away. Dear Mayrien, who had come so far with her, despite everything. "Of course, *etilith*."

It took several minutes to help Mayrien down from her horse and find a suitable means of tying off the horses' reins to one of the statues, but the three Elviri were climbing the stairs before too long. Munne had Mayrien's uninjured arm thrown over her shoulder, her own arm wrapped around her side to help distribute her weight better. Araloth followed behind, a couple of their packs slung across her back. They brought food and medical supplies but left everything else with the horses.

Almost there.

The stairs twisted along the cliffside, hugging it as it curved away from the riverbed. As they reached the top of the stairs, Munne saw they were following another dried-out riverbed, although it was much shallower than the one they had just left, and it led to the face of a mountain. It had once been a waterfall, she realized. Ely had told her there used to be waterfalls here. Her heart squeezed uncomfortably. With the riverbed to their right and a line of winged statues to their left, they continued to the mountainside where a cave awaited them.

"You don't mean to take us in there, do you?" Mayrien rasped. The climb had sapped her of all her strength, and she was sweating profusely. Her wounds might have even reopened, Munne realized.

Munne's voice was barely above a whisper. "Yes."

Mayrien grunted and hissed. "Then I need to rest for a few minutes before we go on. And the rest of the 'tears'." Munne nodded, slowing her pace. "And you're carrying me back down when this is finished."

"Of course."

The three Elviri stopped outside of the cave entrance. Munne helped ease Mayrien into a sitting position, leaning against the rocky cliffside, and then took a seat beside her. They distributed some of their rations and water, and Mayrien chewed on the last of their supply of Aeona's Tears. Araloth stretched and paced around.

As she ate a handful of berries, Munne studied the cave entrance. It was sunken into the stone, and no doubt would have been hidden from sight when the river flowed, and water fell from above. The entrance was taller than the gates of Elimere, leading straight into the heart of the mountain. The darkness of the cave was deeper than any other darkness she had seen before. They would need torches to traverse its depths.

This leads to the tunnels, Munne thought, letting out an involuntary gasp. *I've been here before. In my nightmares.*

Mayrien shook Munne's shoulder gently. "What is it, Munne?"

Before she had a chance to respond, another tremor tore through Kherizhan. Araloth threw herself over Munne and Mayrien, covering them with her body as she braced herself against the cliffside. Mayrien clung to Munne tightly, burying her head against her friend's chest. Munne threw an arm over Mayrien's head and tucked her chin down. The ground cracked and rumbled. Dirt and rocks rained down on them from above. It was louder than any storm she had ever witnessed. It sounded as if the earth was being split apart and would swallow them whole.

I can't die here, Munne voicelessly pleaded with whoever would listen. *Ceyo, don't let me die here.*

Several harrowing minutes later, Kherizhan settled once more into an uneasy slumber. Munne looked out from around Araloth's body to see if anything had fallen to prevent their entry into the cave. The way was clear.

Munne let out a shaky breath, pleased at the sight. No matter what was causing the violent tremors, they wouldn't keep her from moving forward. *I'm coming, Ely.*

"Are you two okay?" Araloth asked, pushing away from the other Elviri.

"I think so," Mayrien answered. "You?"

"I'm alright, thank the gods."

Munne climbed to her feet and then offered her hand to Mayrien. "We need to keep moving."

Araloth spun to face her, eyes blazing with fury. "You're mad! What if a tremor like that strikes again while we're in there?!"

"It doesn't matter," Munne said through gritted teeth. She mustered every bit of courage she had as she pressed on. "We have to stop the *Ardashi'ik,* and the only way to do so is in those caves. The fate of the world is in our hands, Araloth. This is the only path forward."

The two faced off in silence for a few moments before Araloth relented and dug through one of her bags. "Let me figure out a godsdamned torch, then, and let's be off."

Munne helped Mayrien to her feet and inspected her side, content to see the wrappings still holding. They waited until Araloth had a torch lit, and they moved together toward the cave entrance. Munne felt the terror rising inside of her, the darkness of the tunnels pressing in on all sides, and she forced down a scream. She had a torch. She had her friends. She had Ely. She would be able to face whatever they found in these tunnels and would find a way to stop the *Ardashi'ik*.

EPILOGUE

For the first time in her life, the cold didn't bother Princess Niamnh. She felt like a small child again, basking in the glow of the summer suns. The warmth returned the color to her sun-kissed skin, and she felt whole and wholly herself.

Mother would be so proud.

"*Your father would be proud, too.*" Mother Shade's voice slipped into her mind, like a cloud sliding across the sky to shield her from the suns. "*And your brothers, and your little sister.*"

"I know," Niamnh breathed, a smile tugging at her lips. She was still staring at the space where Ray Finnegan had been standing several moments ago before she vanished with the blink of an eye. Mother Shade had sent her and Daerion away, back to Auora.

Ray was carrying one of the bracelets that bore a bone belonging to her brother Robyn. The matching bracelet was tied around Niamnh's left wrist, which she idly rubbed her thumb against. The bone was cool to the touch, and though she was enamored with her newfound warmth, she found the contrasting temperature incredibly soothing on her skin. She missed Robyn so dearly.

Tearing her gaze away from the empty corridor, Niamnh looked to the glow of Mother Shade and asked, "What comes next?"

"*For Daaria, the second end, and another rebirth. But for you, little princess?*" Mother Shade was still for a moment, and then raised her hand, gesturing to the door they stood in front of. The ethereal woman's voice filled her head. "*Your path leads beyond this door.*"

Niamnh nodded. She knew that. The image of what lay beyond the door had been seared into her mind ever since she had first met Mother Shade in her temple. When she blinked, she could see it still, like staring at the two suns for too long. She had carried the burden of knowledge for several days now, making her heart ache. Niamnh wanted nothing more than to confide in Ray and Daerion about what was to come. But how would the others feel, hearing tales of her death and their own? The thought of her own death still troubled her greatly, despite knowing what would come after and seeing how lovely that image was, *hearing* it as it sang a beautiful wordless melody that reached her ears alone. It had started as a low hum when they arrived at Rymo-tehp, but as she and Ray had traversed through the ruins, it crescendoed into a symphony of sounds she had never heard before.

Magic.

She also knew that her death lay beyond that door. Just days after she had turned eighteen. She should have been back in Auora, preparing for the tournament celebrating her birthday and being fitted for gowns to wear to all the balls her father and the city would be throwing in her honor. She should've been home with Trys, preparing for the rest of her life.

Her smile faltered at the thought of her fair-haired knight, her first love. The boy who had always looked past her crown and her ailment to see the girl who wanted nothing more than to paint and eat sweets. As memories of their shared childhood resurfaced, memories of stolen kisses and secret touches raised gooseflesh on her skin, the princess realized that she didn't want to think about Trys being here with her. She knew that he wouldn't turn away from her; no, her knight would raise his sword and shield to protect her from her fate. But it was her path to follow, her threshold to cross, and she had to do it. And she found that it was Ray that she wished to have cross it with her.

Ray, the street urchin from Auora that had kidnapped her from her bedchamber all those nights ago. Spirited her away across the Hourglass Lakes, across Northern Promthus, and into Na'roc of North. It had been less than a month, and for many of those days Niamnh felt disdain and almost hatred for the girl, but she couldn't imagine crossing this threshold with anyone else. Ray had taken care of her, treated her with such kindness. Even when she had lied, she'd done it as gently and mercifully as possible. Ray was just a pawn in this whole matter, just as Niamnh herself was. Niamnh knew this now, and she forgave Ray for everything. It was Ray's hand she wanted to hold, Ray's smile she wanted to take comfort in as the light washed over them both.

"Ray Finnegan still has a part to play in this final act," Mother Shade murmured, her voice reverberating down Niamnh's spine. The princess shivered. *"But you won't have to do this alone. I will stand beside you."* The woman lowered her hand and entwined her fingers with Niamnh's.

Niamnh raised her other hand to the wooden door, and she felt the thrum of magic reaching out to her from the other side. It resonated within her body, sending vibrations from her fingertips to her toes to her eyelashes. As she extended her arm forward, those sensations grew stronger, the hum escalating into a dull roar in her ears. Within that noise she heard voices singing to her, telling her stories of Ray Finnegan, Daerion Valha, the mysterious creature known as *Nahaesyraellonore*, and many others she didn't know. Names of Elviri, Proma, and Provira filled her head, along with whispers of the war to the south. One name stood out amongst all the others, their song clashing with the beautiful music of the others. *Ardulphyx.* She didn't know that name, but she knew the weight it carried and the horrible things that had been done in service to it. All of those names and stories were now connected to her, and to what lay beyond the door.

With the weight of the world bearing down on her, Niamnh froze. *Will they all be okay, or will my sacrifice be for naught?*

Mother Shade squeezed her hand. The voices cried out a name, *Doshanaroelyan,* singing a song of the dead that entwined with her own melody.

"That's your true name," Niamnh murmured, more to herself than the woman.

Mother Shade didn't move, but a gentle sensation of acceptance swam from her fingertips to her face. The voices inside Niamnh's mind quieted as the woman spoke. *"Take heart, princess. Heroes will follow in your footsteps."*

Heroes. Does that make me a hero?

"One of the bravest."

Niamnh shook her head and said, "But I hesitate to do what I must. I... I'm scared of what happens after." *When I die.*

"Heroes are not heroic because they're unafraid. They are heroic because they do what they must, even when they are afraid."

Niamnh inhaled sharply and nodded. She would be a hero for Daaria. For her family. For Ray. She took a step forward, her hand touching the wooden door. It was warm and rattled gently under her fingertips.

Remember me fondly, Niamnh silently wished as the door opened.

LIST OF CHARACTERS

Munne Vere'cha

- <u>Munne Vere'cha</u> [*Myoon Ver-ek-aw*]: Warlord of the Elviri and daughter of Huntaran. Warring with the *Ardashi'ik* who has infiltrated her mind. 253 years old. Dark brown hair, blue eyes, and pale skin.

- <u>Araloth</u> [*Air-aw-lohth*]: Member of Munne's triple and one of her closest friends. 412 years old. Blonde hair, green eyes, and pale skin.

- <u>Mayrien</u> [*Mey-ree-ehn*]: Member of the Warlord's triple and one of her closest friends. 256 years old. Brown hair, hazel eyes, and pale skin.

- <u>Huntaran</u> [*Huhnt-ahr-ahn*]: *Se'vi*, ruler of all Elviri, and Munne's father. 499 years old. Light brown hair, green eyes, and pale skin.

- <u>Elyxphyrthalyondrall (Ely)</u>: A mysterious shapeshifter who inhabits Munne's dreams.

- <u>Malion</u> [*Mal-ee-uhn*]: Munne's ancestor who was plagued with nightmares from the *Ardashi'ik*. Killed his wife and himself.

- <u>Rhorek Gondamire</u> [*Rohr-ek Gawn-dah-mah-yuhr*]: Knight-general of the Proma army and one of the high lords in Auora. Proma, male, 42 years old; golden blond hair, brown eyes.

- <u>Eldo Talltree</u> [*Eld-oh Tawl-tree*]: Emissary from the Imalar Woods. Leader of the woodworking caste, and famed bowyer. Imalarii, male, 46 years old; brown hair, brown eyes.

- <u>S'raak, One of Three</u> [*Sur-awk*]: One of three emissaries from the Black Lakes. Barauder of the Itorh tribe, female, 35 years old; dark green hair, black eyes.

- <u>Druuk, One of Three</u> [*Drook*: One of three emissaries from the Black Lakes. Barauder of the Sirh'ah tribe, male, 29 years old; black hair, dark blue eyes.

- <u>Lagazi, One of Three</u> [*Lah-gawz-ee*]: One of three emissaries from the Black Lakes. Barauder of the Y'lah tribe, female, 39 years old; dark blue hair, dark green eyes.

- <u>The *Ardashi'ik*</u> [*Ahr-dah-sheek*]: A demon of legend from the Eldest Days.

- <u>Captain Nathen Munhart</u> [*Nath-in Muhn-hahrt*]: Captain of the guard in Auora. Proma, male, 45 years old; brown hair, brown eyes, pale skin.

- <u>Ethelmar</u> [*Eth-ihl-mahr*]: One of the rotating commanders at the Fer-ilin outpost. Elviri, male; black hair, green eyes.

The Moon's Wares:
- <u>Tethe</u> [*Teth*]: Caravan leader of the Moon's Wares. Dark hair, olive skin with jagged scar across his face; green and white eyes.

- <u>Adalia</u> [*Ad-al-ee-uh*]: Middle-aged Proma woman with black hair, olive skin, dark eyes.

- <u>Yvanna</u> [*Ih-von-ah*]: Young Elviri woman with blond hair, pale skin, green eyes.

- <u>Jion</u> [*Jee-on*]: Young Proma man with black hair, brown skin, dark eyes.

- <u>Ormes</u> [*Ohr-meyz*]: Middle-aged Proma man with brown hair, tan skin, brown eyes.

Ray Finnegan

- <u>Ray Finnegan</u> [*Rey Fin-i-guhn*]: 18-year-old Proma girl with brown hair, hazel eyes, and peach-colored skin. Member of the Syrael Walkers and protege of Naro.

- <u>Princess Niamnh</u> [*Nee-ahm*]: 18-year-old Proma girl with silver-blonde hair, gray eyes, brown sunkissed skin. Heir to the throne of Promthus. Shares her mind with the Doshara named Daerion.

- <u>Naro</u> [*Nah-roh*]: A man whose age and origins are unknown. Dark blue hair, bronze skin, and mismatching blue and green eyes. Leader of the Syrael Walkers.

- <u>Daerion</u> [*Dair-ee-uhn*]: Doshara spirit occupying Niamnh's body. His original identity is unknown.

- <u>Ajak</u> [*Ey-jak*]: Another of Naro's proteges and a charming young rogue. Proma, male, 23 years old; brown hair, brown eyes, bronze skin. Deceased.

- <u>Mother Shade</u> [*Sheyd*]: A mysterious and powerful woman living in Na'roc of North.

- <u>Enesse</u> [*Ehn-ess*]: Enthai female with white fur.

- <u>Kohda</u> [*Koh-dah*]: Enthai male with pale gray fur.

- <u>Keitri</u> [*Kay-tree*]: Enthai chieftain; male with white fur.

Seth Kharis

- <u>Seth Kharis</u> [*Seth Kahr-ihs*]: Son of the Provira rebellion leader; crippled during one of his father's experiments. Provira, 19 years old, dirty blond hair, brown eyes, tan skin.

- <u>Octavia Kharis</u> [*Awk-tehy-vee-uh Kahr-ihs*]: Seth's twin sister and youngest *pyredan* in the Provira army. Provira, 19 years old, dirty blonde hair, brown eyes, tan skin.

- <u>Amias Kharis</u> [*Ah-my-uhs Kahr-ihs*]: Seth and Octavia's father, and leader of the Provira rebellion. Close allies with the Asaszi. Provira, 167 years old, dark blond hair, dark brown eyes, tan skin.

- <u>Lisanthir</u> [*Lees-an-theer*]: Elviri who Seth meets at the Great Library of Lithalyon. Elviri, 62 years old, black hair, green eyes, pale skin.

- <u>Osza</u> [*Oh-zha*]: Queen of the Asaszi with jade scales, black hair, and golden eyes. Unknown age.

- <u>Astohi</u> [*As-toh-hahy*]: Asaszi. Osza's consort. Dark green and golden scales and golden eyes. Unknown age.

- <u>Szatisi</u> [*Zha-tee-see*]: High Priestess of the Asaszi. Black scales and golden eyes. Unknown age.

- <u>Arcyr'ys Wynn</u> [*Ahrk-eer-ihs Win*]: A *pyredan* in the Provira army who Octavia is very close with. Provira, 45 years old, brown hair, brown eyes, tan skin.

- <u>Taszo</u> [*Tah-zho*]: Asaszi. One of Osza's courtiers. Dark blue scales and golden eyes. Unknown age.

- <u>Tyrarian</u> [*Tye-rahr-ee-ahn*]: Student at the academies in Iszairi. Provira, 25 years old, blonde hair, green eyes, pale skin.

Appendix

History of Daaria

The history of Daaria can be broken up into two eras, the Eldest Days and the Second Sun. A sizable portion of the Eldest Days was not recorded on paper, due to the races not developing their own alphabet or record of time until much later. The first calendar was created by the Elviri, and is what's used by most of the races of Daaria.

The Eldest Days began with the emergence of the First Ones and the creation of Daaria. The First Ones would go on to create the different races of Daaria and be known as gods. Each of the races developed their civilizations in peace, their gods intermingling with the people in different ways.

The Eldest Days were dominated by the Elviri-Asaszi wars. The other races kept to themselves, avoided the lands of Central Daaria, and developed their cultures. The Asaszi were a bloodthirsty people, and quickly grew bored of their peaceful lifestyles. They began raiding the Elviri lands, taking slaves and destroying settlements. The Elviri were slower to develop their civilization, and it only took the Asaszi a handful of months to enslave the large majority of the Elviri race and lock away their gods in caverns deep underground. Those that weren't enslaved fled to the forests of Elimaine, where they rebuilt their settlements and began preparing for war.

For years, the Elviri and Asaszi clashed and fought. The Asaszi controlled much of central Daaria, naming the land Pyredessi. Those who were taken as slaves staged their own revolts throughout the years, but never found any success. It wasn't until nearly two hundred years after the initial strike that the slaves managed to overthrow their oppressors and escape.

Following the revolt, the Elviri-Asaszi war only got worse. Many of both races were slain. Their warring kept on for many centuries. The Asaszi attempted to ally with the Barauder from the Black Lakes, but they were met with hostility. The Asaszi were eventually pushed out of Pyredessi, and took refuge in the massive rainforests to the south, which they named Moonyswyn. Between the rainforests and the shore of the ocean, the Asaszi created their new home.

Soon after the Asaszi abandoned the fertile lands of Central Daaria, the Proma were spun into existence. They allied with the Elviri to help fight against the Asaszi. With the aid of the Proma, the Elviri were able to drive the Asaszi to near-extinction. Afterwards, Daaria saw a time of peace and prosperity. Art, music, and science were made and pursued. The Hunting Throne was officially founded in Elviri lands.

The Asaszi still pursued war with the Elviri and Proma, and eventually did manage to harness powerful magic that could turn the tide and grant them victory over their foes. This magic threatened the gods, and their life essences began to drain away. Fearing death, they left Daaria through various means, such as boarding ships and sailing into the unknown. Before she left, Ceyo, the god-queen of the Elviri, sent forth one of her trusted soldiers, a mortal Elviri whose name has been lost to time, to confront the Asaszi in Moonyswyn.

There are no recorded details of what happened in Moonyswyn, but the effects were seen and felt throughout Daaria. Magic vanished from the world, and the land was torn asunder. In Central Daaria, the ground crumbled and waters from the north rushed down to form the Hourglass Lakes. To the southeast, massive mountains rose from the land, separating Kherizhan from the rest of Daaria. A second sun rose in the sky, thus beginning a new era of Daarian history known as the Second Sun.

Regions of Daaria

Daaria is home to several diverse biomes and lands.

The western coast is home to the Elviri and their three provinces - Elimere, Elimaine, and Elifyn. The city-province of Elimere is nestled in a large valley in the Telatorr Mountains. To the south are the expansive woods and forests of Elimere. Elifyn controls a smaller portion of the woods along the southern edge of Daaria.

The Hourglass Lakes dominate Promthus, the center of Daaria, where the Proma make their homes in the farmlands surrounding the lakes. In the middle of the lake is the city-island of Auora, along with Castle Auora where the Proma royal family reside. On the mainland, the Proma have built three major cities near their largest farms to promote trade in the area.

The northern stretch of Daaria is Na'roc of North, a vast desolate tundra that no one dares traverse. A wall spans the only natural access point into

Na'roc of North, which the Proma patrol day and night. Proma tell their children scary stories of a group of strange cat-like creatures who live beyond the wall, who will kill and devour anyone who dares encroach on their lands.

To the east of Promthus is the Imalar Woods, a vast forest home to the Imalarii. The shortfolk make their homes in the treetops and facilitate trade between the Elviri and Proma to the west and the swamplands to the east.

The eastern swamplands are home to the Barauder, who call their lands Balach Yor. They've built their villages around the shores of the three lakes, and are predominantly a water-based culture.

The southeastern lands of Daaria are dangerous and few travel here. The jungles of Moonyswyn are where the Provira have retreated to in recent years, and from here wage their war against the Proma and Elviri to the north. They've made their homes in the ruined pyramids from the Eldest Days.

Far to the southeast are the barren mountainous lands of Kherizhan. Not much is known about this place, for few travel here, and even fewer return to tell the tale. Rumors persist of treasure being buried underneath the mountains, which has drawn several adventuring groups to the lands in recent years...

People of Daaria

Asaszi

The Asaszi are vicious snake-like people who warred with the Elviri and Proma in the Eldest Days. It's believed that the Asaszi were driven to extinction in the early years of the Second Sun.

Barauder

The Barauder live in Balach Yor, the Black Lakes in eastern Daaria. They call themselves the children of the lakes, because rather than being born from the coupling of a male and female, they emerge from the lakes as small children. They worship the lakes, and personify them as their three mothers, and the sea as their father. They are tall, sinewy creatures with dark, mottled skin. They have a pronounced underbite, large fangs, gills, and webbed feet. There are three tribes of Barauder that surround the Black Lakes: *Sirh'ah, Y'lah,* and *Itorh.* Every Barauder takes the surname of the lake that they live beside.

Elviri

The Elviri are the most well-known and well-versed race in Daaria. The common language originates from the Elviri language melded with the Proma language. The Elviri calendars are used throughout the lands, and even some of the Elviri festivals are celebrated by other races. The Elviri are definitely the most influential of the races, and their gods have had the biggest presence in this world.

The Elviri are tall, slender, and graceful. They have long pointed ears and live to be hundreds of years old. They are not immortal, and can easily be killed in battle, die from old age, or waste away from disease.

Enthai

The Enthai are a mysterious race living in Na'roc of North. Proma parents tell their children scary stories of bloodthirsty fox-like creatures who wait beyond the Wall to kill any Proma who dares stray into their lands. Men stationed at the Wall will occasionally ride north to hunt the Enthai and bring back their pelts to warm their beds. Not much else is known about these creatures.

Imalarii

The Imalarii are short folk who live in the trees of the Imalarii Wood. When standing beside a Proma or Elviri, an Imalarii will only come up to their waist.

They are master woodworkers and leatherworkers. They also love the arts, and have dedicated guilds created for music, poetry, and storytelling.

Proma

The Proma are very proud, decisive, and sometimes rash. Most will act first, and think later. Proma are the most human-like race in Daaria, and have the shortest lifespan, often only living to 60 or 70. They live around the Hourglass Lakes in Promthus.

Provira

The Provira are the offspring of unions between the Elviri and Proma. These unions are not common occurrences, but have happened often enough during the Second Sun that the race was given its own identity.

Provira can live to be 200 years of age, although with the recent wars and border skirmishes, that number has dropped drastically. Unlike their ancestors, the Provira are not overtly religious and feel no strong ties to the Elviri pantheon or the Proma's Protector. Instead they lust for knowledge and seek to unravel the mysteries of Daaria, which clashes with the ideals of the Elviri and Proma, and was part of the reason the mixed-bloods were driven out of their lands.

Acknowledgements

So many thank-yous to distribute! Thank you to Andrea for the amazing cover art. Thank you to Katie for the edits and feedback. Thank you to all the readers of the first book, "The Whispering Pass" for supporting a debut indie author. Thank you to my spouse Tyler for having my back and keeping me going with my writing. I appreciate each person who picks up one of my books and I'm so thankful I get to share Munne, Ray, and Seth's journeys with you all.

About the Author

Jay Olsen-Thrift holds many titles: Project Manager, Raid Leader, Business Wizard, and Content Creator.

I have been building worlds and telling stories since I was a child. I write across many mediums: novels, short stories, tabletop roleplaying campaigns, screenplays, and stage plays. I have a bachelor's degree in software engineering with a minor in professional writing. I earned my master's degree in business administration in May 2024. When I'm not working or writing, I can be found online leading raids in Lord of the Rings Online or tending to my farm in Stardew Valley.

You can connect with me on my socials by going to www.jayolsenthrift.com or scanning the QR code below: